HALF TRUTHS

CLAIRE

CONTRERAS

Half-Truths
Claire Contreras
© 2019 Claire Contreras
Cover design By Hang Le
Edited by Christine Estevez
Proofread by Janice Owen
Formatted by Champagne Book Design

ISBN: 978-0-9983455-7-4

"Come closer, baby. I want to see what you're made of."

-Lydia

PROLOGUE

"I WISH YOU'D STAY OUT OF IT."

"I wish you'd stay out of it." He glared at Lana, sitting in his passenger seat. "You don't even know what you're getting involved in."

"I know more than you think."

He shook his head. They'd been arguing about this for a month. So often that people thought they were a couple. It was a thought that wouldn't have disturbed him had it not been for what he knew about her and what she was doing. It was stupid of him to think he'd manage to change her mind, but he couldn't bear the thought of letting her continue on this self-destructive path.

"I'm trying to help you." It would be his last attempt at convincing her.

"I want you to stop helping, period," she yelled, then lowered her voice. "You should slow down."

He eased his foot off the pedal as he took the first curb. He hadn't ever known Lana to be loud, and chalked it up to the situation she'd put herself in.

"I'm just saying, he's no good for you and you're going to regret—"

"Pull over."

He exhaled. "Will you calm down? I'm not going—"

vi | CLAIRE CONTRERAS

"Pull over," she said, cutting him off again.

He was getting furious, but tried not to let it show. Once again, trying to be the bigger person in the situation. Before he knew what was happening, her hands were on the steering wheel. She pulled hard to the right. On instinct, he pulled the other way, slamming on the brakes. She pulled once more to the right and between the water on the winding road, the steering wheel battle, and the braking, he lost control of the car. The last thing he saw was the tree right before he slammed into it. His seatbelt caught the impact of his body propelling forward, and the airbag slammed him back into his seat.

It took him a moment to recover and look over at where Lana had been sitting. He expected to find her sitting there, but her door was ajar and there was no sign of her. His heart pounded in his chest. Had she flown out of the car with the impact of the accident? He scrambled with his seatbelt, but managed to get it off. His door opened with a creak as he stepped out. His entire body seemed to shake as he walked around the car in search of Lana. He could hear water running nearby. A waterfall was near.

"Lana?" he called out. His breath caught when he spotted her near the edge of the waterfall. His pace picked up slightly, as fast as his injured leg let him. The gorge was miles high and he didn't need the crashing sound of the water as it cascaded to tell him the only thing that would cushion her fall if she fell . . . if she jumped were rocks.

"Lana?" He called out her name again, his voice desperate. Could she not hear him above the sound of the running water?

She glanced back at him, a haunted look in her eyes, and then she jumped.

CHAPTER ONE

THE AIR WAS THICK WITH FOG AND A COLD CHILL THAT SEEMED TO flow through the turning leaves and straight into my chest. I reached for my inhaler out of the pocket of my jacket, shaking it a few times before pushing three times to inhale—two to open up my chest and one for good measure. Asthma was an affliction I'd recently been diagnosed with. Mild asthma, but asthma nonetheless. I guess that's what I got for trading the concrete jungle for some nature. Now, even after moving back to my home state, I couldn't seem to get rid of it. I stopped walking at the end of the sidewalk and waited for the group of people in front of me to finish looking at the campus map before stepping up to it.

The only thing worse than transferring to a new university was transferring to a new university your senior year. I didn't know where anything was and this campus was so big it had its own zip code—literally. Even in my thoughts, I shouldn't have been complaining. It was an Ivy League university people would kill to have the opportunity to attend, and technically it was the one I was supposed to attend before I decided to follow my boyfriend to Duke instead. Now I was boyfriend-less and following my father's and brothers' footsteps instead. My mother joked that I'd swapped herds, trading one boy for another, as if I was a sheep. I found it difficult to argue her point, even if hearing it upset me.

One thing I couldn't argue with was the fact that my father had been right about a lot of things. Like when he told me I would regret following a boyfriend to college and that the minute we broke up I'd run home crying and begging to enroll here instead. The breakup wasn't exactly what made me run home crying and begging to transfer, though I couldn't deny it playing a part. It was my brother's accident that had done it for me. My brother, who'd been my best friend my entire life and the most vibrant person I knew, suffered an accident that made him miss graduation, give up being captain of the hockey team, and run home with his tail between his legs. Since his return home, he'd been put on anti-depressants and was going to the therapist three times a week. A therapist, who was my mother's colleague, and was constantly giving the news that my brother still wasn't speaking to him. That made it worse. He'd only discuss certain things with us, but nothing of substance, and definitely nothing with relation to the accident. It was as if he'd blocked the memory out completely, or was trying to. My parents broached the subject carefully at first, but had now moved on to not saying anything at all, out of fear that they'd trigger him. Behind closed doors, when I knew he wasn't listening, I asked my parents questions about that went unanswered and ignored and further perpetuated my curiosity and the turmoil I felt over it.

Nevertheless, my journey to this school had taken a long essay, countless letters of recommendation and my father calling the dean incessantly whilst telling me he told me so every single time he hung up the phone with him, but I'd managed to make it here. Now, I was determined to do quite a few things. Graduating was high on that list, but finding out what happened to my brother—*what really happened to him*—was my priority, as well as finding out what happened to Lana Ly, the student that seemed to vanish without a trace. The media coverage on her was at a minimum these days, and maybe it was because she'd gone to our high school and it felt like her disappearance hit close to home, but I wanted to at least gain that attention back.

After all, people didn't just vanish. Especially not people like Lana Ly. Shaking my head, I picked up the pace. I needed to get to the headquarters of the school paper sooner rather than later. I was already running behind on everything else—meeting my new, albeit temporary roommate, getting the rest of my textbooks, coordinating with the movers my mother hired to bring the rest of my belongings. I was a substantial mess and I needed to get my life in order. Looking down at my phone, I made sure that the little blue dot was still headed in the right direction. That was when I bumped into something, or rather, someone. My phone tumbled out of my hand and I grasped at air as I tried to catch it while stumbling backward. I was preparing myself for the blow, but wasn't prepared for a shattered phone. I finally caught the phone in mid-air, and the blow never came.

Just as I thought my ass was about to meet the ground, hands reached out and caught me, straightening me upright. I held on to muscled forearms, blinking up at a cutting jaw and sharp green eyes that looked like they were slicing through me. He had the kind of skin people who liked to sunbathe lusted over, the perfect shade of golden brown, but he didn't strike me as someone who would lay out in the sun. He didn't strike me as someone who liked much at all, with the way he was scowling at me and holding my shoulders as if I was contagious.

"I am so—"

"Maybe you should reconsider those heels." He looked pointedly at my shoes.

"Maybe you should reconsider your manners." I frowned,

stepping back, out of his grasp. "I didn't bump into you on purpose, you know?"

"But you bumped into me nonetheless and I'm running late."

"So am I." I threw a hand up and started walking past him. I needed to get there before they shut down for the day and this conversation was going nowhere quick.

"You're welcome, by the way," he shouted.

I had half a mind to stick my middle finger up, but I just kept walking, refusing to acknowledge him any further. If he was in such a hurry, he shouldn't be bothered with what I was doing or what kind of shoes I was wearing, though I had to say, my feet were killing me. I'd swapped out my flats for the heels when I was on my way over here, not realizing how much I'd have to walk to get here.

When I finally arrived at the building that housed the newspaper office, I paused up front. The campus in its entirety felt like a mixture of progress and history. Even though a portion of the campus had been built in the 1800s, most of the buildings I'd been to today were sleek and modern. I'd envisioned the newspaper to be in one of those. This building was quaint, made of brown bricks and white doors, with green ivy that clung to the face of it like a wet toga.

Because it looked more like a house than a place of business, I paused at the door, wondering if I should knock or just make my way inside. I decided on the latter. A few people were walking by from left to right and right to left, none bothering to take their eyes off the pages in their hands to acknowledge their new intruder. I walked around, hoping to catch someone's attention. Finally, a woman in a navy pantsuit walked from the back of the building and greeted me.

"May I help you?"

"I... yes... hi. I just transferred here and was wondering if there were any openings in the paper. I was going to apply online, but I was in the area so I figured I'd just drop by. I'm a double major, Business and English and worked for the Duke paper for the last three years, so I have experience." I paused, aware that I was speaking too fast for most people to follow. "So, yeah. That's why I'm here. My name is Amelia by the way. Amelia Bastón."

"Any association to Felipe Bastón?"

"Um." I hesitated. "Maybe."

"Maybe." The woman smiled wryly. "That's definitely a Bastón answer. Felipe was my boyfriend for a short time while we were here. Great human being, lousy boyfriend. He left me for his current wife and they're still married, so I guess maybe he was just a lousy boyfriend to me."

"Yep. That's my dad. Sorry. The Bastón men can be real bastards." A weak laugh escaped me.

"So you're Amelia." She assessed me a little longer, tilting her head as she looked at me, as if trying to decide what to do with me. "You do resemble your mother when she was young. I only met her briefly when we were here. As much as it killed me to admit back then, she was stunning. The kind of beauty that made you stop and stare."

"Uh. Thanks?"

"You're here for a job," she said. "We should get to that."

"Yes, ma'am."

"Ella Valentine." She waved me off. "Call me Ella or Elle. Definitely not ma'am."

"Ella then."

"Follow me to my office. I'll see what we can do."

I let out a breath, walking down the corridor and past the students walking in and out of cubicles. There was a constant chatter here that I was used to. In my old university's newsroom, it was the kind of thing that made chasing a story worthwhile. It was the buzz that made my palms sweat and blood pump a little faster. When we reached her office, Ella shut the door behind us. I looked around and took in the plaques on the wall hanging beside her degrees. When she sat behind her desk, I helped myself to the seat across from her.

"What year are you?"

"Senior."

Her brows rose. "And you just transferred in?"

"Yes, I know how that looks," I said. "My goal was to start last spring, but I had to wait until this fall. I was accepted and was supposed to attend here originally, but decided to follow my boyfriend to Duke instead."

"Your father must have been thrilled."

"That's an understatement." I bit back a smile. "He was definitely a lot happier when I told him I would come here."

"And you're closer to home."

"Yeah."

"How's he doing? I hope you don't mind me asking. I can't remember the last time I saw him." She pursed her lips as she thought it over. "I did see your mother while I was out to dinner with my daughter a few months ago. She was with one of your brothers, who looked like he was in bad shape, I'm assuming from the accident."

"He's doing well. They're all doing well," I said quickly.

If I liked the idea of being a reporter, it was because I didn't want to be reported on. Years of my older brothers appearing on *Page Six* headlines and getting reprimanded for it ruined that for me.

"Please send them my regards." She put her elbows on the desk and clasped her hands together. "I take it there's no longer a boyfriend in the picture?"

"No. We broke up."

"And you said you were working in the paper down in Carolina? What kind of stories were you working on?"

"Mostly events and student life. We had a lot of marches and organizations getting together for protests, so I covered those. I would really love to get into more investigative stuff, but to be honest, I'm not sure what's allowed."

"Investigative like what?"

"Like for instance, Lana Ly. I searched and noticed the paper hasn't written much on her disappearance."

"That's because we tried and were quickly shut down." She raised an eyebrow. "There's money, and then there's money. Le's parents have the latter. They don't want us spewing untrue things, even though we were doing thorough investigations on everything."

"Oh." I sat back slightly.

"Did you know her?"

"We went to high school together. We weren't friends, per se, but friendly."

"I'm sorry. The whole town is shaken up about it, but alas, I can't print anything about it."

"That's understandable, I guess." I felt myself frown. What was the point of freedom of speech if we couldn't even keep a student's memory alive?

"What about sports?"

"What about them?"

"We need someone in sports right now. Our guy graduated and the one who was supposed to take his place runs a full-time college sports blog now. He's still working with us part-time as a favor to me, but he needs to be replaced."

"I . . . " I paused, trying to figure out how to verbalize this. "I don't really know much about sports. I mean, I know basketball since my boyfriend played and I know soccer, since I played in high school, but that's the extent of my sports knowledge."

"Do you know hockey?"

"Not really."

"Football?"

"I can learn."

"Wow. Three older brothers and none of them bothered to teach you the rules of football or hockey?"

"The older ones are too far apart in age and the closest to me tried and failed." I paused, smiling sheepishly. "Like I said, I know basketball."

"Well, it's something." She frowned. "The one closest to you in age was the one who played here, right?"

"Yeah. Lincoln."

"My daughter had such a crush on him." She smiled, shaking her head. "Like mother like daughter, I guess. Thankfully, he never found out she existed and she moved on and was spared the Bastón heartache."

I pressed my lips together in what I hoped was a smile. What was I supposed to say to a woman who thirty-plus years later, clearly wasn't over the fact that my father dumped her? Especially one I was hoping to get a job from? Silence really was the best answer to most things. I broke after it stretched for a moment too long.

She cleared her throat before she spoke. "Do you take good photographs?"

"I've been told I do."

"Would you be willing to photograph sports and write about other things? Maybe student relations or dating life as a college student? Something we've been lacking is a column on things to do outside of campus, though I'm not sure this is the right timing for that after what happened to Lana." She sighed heavily.

"Did you find anything? I mean, when you were allowed to investigate?" I sat up straighter.

"We got as far as finding out that she was trailing some secret societies, but they won't talk. Hell, we don't even know who's in all of these little secret cults." She sat back in her chair. It squeaked and bounced back with the force of the movement. "One of the organizations has agreed to let us list them by name every year so that people know who the members are, but the rest are still hiding beneath their red and black cloaks."

"Oh."

"Well, it's settled. I'll provide you with a camera and paperwork. There's a sports event happening on Friday night. Some sort of mixer. Your assignment starts then."

"Thank you so much." I stood up and shook her hand. "I'll take the best pictures I can."

"And please, if you have anything you'd like to write about, shoot me an email and we'll talk. I don't want to discourage you from doing something more." She gave me another sweep. "Maybe you can write about fashion around campus."

"Um . . . maybe. Yeah."

I let go of her hand and walked back to the main campus, where the human resources department for the paper was and spent the next hour filling out paperwork and thinking about the kind of secrets people must have in order to be involved in a secret group. Then, I called my brother and filled him in on the last few days of my life.

"Why would she put you in charge of sports? You don't even like sports."

Lincoln sounded tired. He always sounded tired, whether it was from the lack of sleep or the meds he was on, I wasn't sure, but his voice was always drowsy.

"I'm just taking pictures of the sports things."

"You're a senior. Shouldn't you be in charge of that paper?"

"I just got here, remember?"

"So? Tell them who your father is."

"Seriously?" I rolled my eyes. "I refuse to fall into that bullshit."

"Which is why you're going to be taking pictures of sports instead of writing actual content."

I paused in front of my door, with my key midway to the lock. Under any other circumstance, using my family name might work in my favor. Even in this case, it may have worked in my favor, but who knows. She was letting me get in on the action despite not having applied for a position there. Still, my brother's tone, as bored and matter-of-fact as he sounded, bothered me.

"I did tell her who my father is, but guess who she dated in college? Dad. And guess who screwed her over? Dad," I said, pushing the key into the lock and turning it. "She was dating Dad when he met Mom."

"So she's punishing you for Dad's actions." Lincoln snorted. "Just when I think I can't hate him any more than I already do."

"Lincoln." My eyes widened. That was the only thing he actually did talk about these days—his hatred toward our father. "You're living under his roof again."

"Not by choice. Besides, he's never home anyway. I wouldn't be surprised if he doesn't know I'm here."

"Stop saying things like that."

"Whatever, Mae. He's an asshole and that lady tried to put you in charge of fashion," he said. "So, fuck her too."

"Well, I'm not going to argue that sentiment." I bit back a laugh, because it was the most Lincoln-thing he'd said since the accident. He responded with a laugh of his own, which made me smile wider.

"What do you think dad will say now that you got another job with another paper after he specifically told you to forget about that dream?"

"I don't know." I set my bags down on the counter and cradled the phone on my shoulder as I undid the straps of my wedges. "He's the one paying for school and you know he wants all of us to work in one of his businesses, so he'll probably scream at me, but what's he going to do? March over here and make me quit the school newspaper?"

"Are you asking? Because I wouldn't put it past him."

"Lincoln." I sighed. "I'm trying to think of what else has happened since I've been here. Oh. I bumped into some guy today. He was really mean about it."

"Want me to go beat him up?"

"Would you come back here to do that for me?"

"I wouldn't go back there for anything."

His words stung even though I tried not to let them. I stayed quiet for a moment, hoping he'd add to that statement, wishing I hadn't been so stubborn and followed a boyfriend to another state instead of attending here with my brother. He would've finished a year ahead of me, but that would have been okay. At least I would know what happened to him and maybe help him somehow.

"How was your day at the psychologist's office?"

"Same."

"You need to talk about it, Linc," I said, finally. "If you won't speak to a professional, at least tell me. I'm supposed to be your best friend."

"If I could talk to anyone about it, it would be you. Just stay out of trouble. I have to go."

"Okay, I—"

He hung up before I could tell him I loved him. My shoulder slumped. Whatever happened to him here had turned him into a different person and I refused to let it go until I found out what it was.

CHAPTER TWO

"**S**O YOU MADE A FOOL OF YOURSELF IN FRONT OF A HOT GUY ON day one of your arrival?" my new roommate Celia asked, looking at me like I was some kind of alien she wasn't sure she wanted to associate with.

"I don't think I made a fool of myself," I muttered. "I tripped. Big freaking deal. And I didn't say he was hot."

"You didn't have to." She laughed. "I can tell that from the way you flushed while you were telling the story."

"I didn't flush." I frowned. "I don't flush."

"If you say so." She looked around. "So, your parent's own this place?"

"They do. All my brothers have lived here. Two in this apartment."

"That's cool. So you have family ties to this place." Celia rummaged through the box she'd brought into the kitchen, pausing to look at me. "Thank you for letting me rent the room on such short notice and for such a short amount of time. I didn't think I'd ever find someone who would lease on a month-to-month basis."

"It's not a problem." I waved her off. "I've never had a roommate before, to be honest, but it'll be fun."

"You've never lived with a roommate?" She stopped fiddling with the kitchen. "Like ever?"

"No."

"Why?"

"I never needed or wanted one." I shrugged. "But this is a two-bedroom and my mother insisted, and I agreed because you know, with the whole Lana Ly situation still ongoing I figured it wouldn't hurt."

"You know about that and you still came?"

"Yep."

"Hm." She eyed me suspiciously, as if there was a chance I had anything to do with her disappearance. "Where are your things?"

"They're being sent here." I looked at my phone. "They should be here in the morning."

"You had all of your things shipped?"

"Most of them."

I didn't really want to explain the fact that my mother insisted on having everything white-glove packed and delivered for me for the same reason I didn't want to explain that my father owned the entire building, not just the one apartment. Dating Travis for the last couple of years of my life opened me up to new experiences and made me realize that my life was anything but ordinary, and because I'd been walking on eggshells for so long, I wasn't sure what was boastful and what was just a statement I could make and shrug off without looking like a spoiled brat, which ultimately meant that I was a spoiled brat nonetheless. It was something I knew and accepted, but not something I wanted people to think I was proud of.

I turned away from her and walked toward one of the two bay windows the apartment had. The other was in the bedroom I'd already claimed as mine. When my parents showed me the place last week, my father told me to take that room because of the view. The bay window in there had a reading nook, complete with bookshelves surrounding it. It was a lot like the one in my childhood bedroom, and one of my favorite parts of the otherwise sterile, luxurious apartment.

"When I was looking for a temp place, I definitely did not envision myself living in Millionaire's Row, I'll tell you that."

I let out a laugh. I'd heard that was what locals called this block. After my father announced to his friends that he was having this building designed and built, they all decided to do the same, contributing to one of the most expensive zip codes in the area.

"I guess I shouldn't make fun of you about the roommate thing," Celia said. "Before this, I had the same roommate since freshman year, but she transferred out after what happened last year. Lana lived in the building right next to ours."

"I expected vigils and posters everywhere, but so far you're the second person to talk to me about it. Where's the outrage? The concern? The nightly searches?" I asked. "I looked online and the last one I found happened like two months ago."

"Yeah." Celia walked over to the living room and sat down on the couch. I sat across from her, knee bouncing as I waited for her to give me the inside scoop. Normally students talked more than staff, so I was sure she had her own take on what happened. "Honestly, people are still looking, but it's more on the downlow now. I think we're all scared, you know? Like, maybe if we don't talk about it, it never actually happened?"

"But it did happen. And a missing student isn't really something people should forget."

A missing rich, beautiful, female student that the news talked about on loop was even less likely to forget, so why try? Why not look for her?

"The media is saying she ran away. It's happened before, from this very campus. Girls have run off with bad-boy boyfriends, some pregnant, some not. Guys have run off with boyfriends because they knew they wouldn't be accepted by their families. It's not uncommon."

"That's not Lana though." I shook my head.

Celia frowned. "Did you know her?"

"Sort of. She and I went to the same high school. She was a year ahead, but we had shared interests, worked for the paper together before she graduated."

She stared at me for a beat. "Will you be okay when I move out? Do you want me to help you find another roommate?"

"I'll be fine. Why wouldn't I be?"

"I don't know. I'm terrified of living alone after what happened."

"Do you think it would happen again?"

"It could. If you listen to the conspiracy theories around here." She gave me a grave look. "Personally, I think she was being followed and targeted."

"What conspiracy theories? And why? I heard they didn't even ask for ransom."

"I heard they never even called after they took her."

"Did the building have a camera?" My stomach twisted. "Don't they have video surveillance somewhere?"

"Nope. Not according to the police anyway. The entire thing is very sad and worrying," she said. "Anyway, this entire thing is creeping me out and I already know I'm going to have nightmares, so let's change the subject. What are you majoring in?"

"Business and English. Double major."

"What are you going to do with that?"

"Hopefully work for an online journal or newspaper."

"That sounds cool. I'm a psych major, but I think I want to work in career services."

"For a university?"

"Yup. Hopefully this one. Right now, I work at the career services office shuffling papers. My boyfriend got me the position to help pay for my books, so being there has made me realize that I want to help college graduates find jobs."

"It'll look good on your resume," I pointed out. "Maybe they'll hire you once you graduate."

"Maybe. That's the goal." She smiled.

We talked for a little while longer about our schedules during weekdays and weekends. I liked to sleep in. Celia liked to get up at the crack of dawn, no matter what day of the week it was. As far as first days went, we seemed to be a good fit. When we went our separate ways, she went to call her boyfriend, whom she'd been dating for three years and also attended school here. According to what she told me, when they weren't together, they always called each other at seven thirty. I went to my bedroom to unpack the few things I had on hand, showered, and changed into my silk pajamas.

I was putting my hair into a braid as I walked past the bay window in my bedroom when I saw four figures walking to the other side of the street.

Two had lit cigarettes dangling from their hands. The other two were looking straight ahead. They were all dressed in dark clothes and had stopped just at the edge of the park, near one of the oak trees that had surely seen and heard a lot more than we ever would. I watched as they stood there talking. It seemed like an odd place for four men to be at this time of night. I sat on the bench beside the window and tried to get a closer look. I was on the fourth floor, and they were far enough away from the street light that I couldn't make out their faces. My curiosity got the best of me, and I squinted, pressing as close as I could to the window, until my forehead touched it. One head glanced up toward me, as if sensing me sitting there. *Him.* The rude guy I'd bumped into earlier. I was only four stories up, and the light of my nightstand was on, but I was sure he couldn't see me, not really anyway, but it felt like he was looking right at me, into me. The sound of the front door of my apartment slamming made my heart thump into my chest, pulling me from my trance. I looked away for a second to listen for Celia, and when I looked back outside, they were all gone. I blinked. I wasn't crazy, but was it possible I'd imagined them there?

CHAPTER THREE

WHEN I STEPPED OUTSIDE MY APARTMENT AND TURNED TO LOCK the door, I saw a flyer for a nearby coffee shop attached to the knob. I pulled it off and looked at it as I locked up. It had a couple of pictures showcasing the homey environment and a coupon for fifty-percent off a drink. I looked at the other doors. Everyone else must have risen way earlier than I had because there were no flyers on their doors. I had to walk a good three blocks away from Millionaire's Row in order to get the small-town vibe the idyllic town promised. When I reached the area that, according to my doorman, Gary, people around here called College Town, I got that vibe. With mom and pop shops lined along the streets and a plethora of bars and coffee shops, it was exactly what I'd been hoping for. Yet, as the winds picked up, blowing my hair in my face, I wondered what the hell I was doing here. Between my talk with Celia about Lana and thinking about Lincoln all morning, I couldn't help that nagging thought. I shut it off and kept moving forward until I reached the coffee shop from my flyer.

As I pulled the door open, the smell of old books and coffee beans hit me. There were bookshelves all along the walls, big blue couches with wood coffee tables in front of them, and a couple of two-seater tables with chairs. It was the perfect place to sit and read, write, or endlessly scroll social media whilst drinking a latte. I walked over to the line and ordered my skinny latte, handing over my flyer as I paid, before sliding over to the other side of the counter where I waited for my drink. I continued to look around. It was pretty empty, despite it being a Sunday afternoon.

"They say the temperature should stick a few more weeks."

"That would be nice." I turned my attention to the barista making my latte. We had perfect weather right now—mid-sixties and sunny forecast.

"Gives people a chance to go out on their boats a few more times."

I nodded, smiling as I looked around. Maybe while they were out on their boats, I could camp out in here and do some research—*more* research. Truth be told, I'd stopped Googling things about Lana a month ago, after getting nowhere and not seeing any new information anywhere. Aside from the random Reddit blogs and conspiracy theorists, which I absolutely refused to read, there was nothing to go on. She'd been kidnapped, they said. Taken from her building. But the staff at the building themselves said they'd seen her leave on her own. If that was the case, *what was the deal?*

"Are you new here?" She slid my latte over to me, tucked her lavender locks behind her ears and set her elbows on the counter, the movement making her dainty necklace dangle forward. My eyes focused on the tiny *B* before bringing my gaze to her light brown eyes. "I haven't seen you in here before."

"I am. I decided to transfer over for my last year."

"Oh, where'd you go before?"

"Duke."

"Not bad." Her eyebrows hiked up. "What brings you here?"

"It's kind of a family tradition." I sipped my latte. "Seemed like I'd be letting down a line of men if I didn't attend."

"Wouldn't want to let down the patriarchy." Her smile held a slight grimace when she said the words. "I'm Hailey, by the way."

"Amelia. You can call me Mae." I set down my mug. "How long have you been working here?"

"A while. My mom owns the place. We're one of the few original townies. I also work at the bar across the street at night." She stood up straight and pointed in that direction, my gaze followed and fell upon a place named *The Bar*. "If you ever want to hear some of these people's deepest, darkest secrets, I'm your girl."

"I'll be sure to keep that in mind."

"I get off in about two minutes. If you want, I can sit with you while you finish your coffee and then I'll show you around."

"Actually, I'd like that. I'm afraid I've ventured way out of my comfort zone and my phone died." I wiggled it. "I forgot to charge it last night and I don't think I can retrace my steps back to my apartment."

"I'll take you. I know every single street and alleyway." She reached behind her waist and pulled her apron off, hanging it up on the wall behind her, walking over to where I was.

"I don't know why I thought it would be easier to get around here." I closed the distance to the nearest couch and settled in with my coffee.

"Becca, I'm off the clock," Hailey shouted.

"Got it," someone, Becca, I assumed, shouted back. "Deacon is supposed to be here in five minutes."

"That's an easy way to get off the clock." I smiled over my coffee.

"Family business, remember?" Hailey said. "Owned and operated. Deacon is our uncle, but he's only like five years older than me, so he's more like an older brother and Becca's my sister. Half-sister. Same mom, different dads."

"That's pretty cool. That's my dad's dream, to have all his kids working together in one place."

Of course, a multi-million-dollar media industry, which included various television networks all over Latin America and the US hardly compared to a coffee shop and bar. In all honesty, I'd take this life over the one my father wanted us to be a part of any day.

"What does he do?" Hailey asked.

"He owns businesses."

"Hm. You don't seem thrilled about that." She looked at me for a long, silent moment.

"I'm not." I looked at my coffee and focused on that.

"Maybe you'll end up loving working for your dad. Mine was never around, so I guess you can say I have daddy issues, or abandonment issues, or really any kind of issue therapists try to pin me with."

"I'm sorry." I lowered my mug. "I didn't mean to be insensitive. I should've asked."

"Yeah, because that's a totally normal question—hey, did your father abandon you as a kid? Just checking so I don't bring up my own, loving, doting father." Hailey let out a forced laugh. "Trust me, it's totally cool."

"I never said mine was loving or doting." I raised an eyebrow. "Anyway, maybe you should start telling me all of those deep, dark secrets now before I put my foot in my mouth again."

"What do you want to hear about first? The supposed serial killer? The secret societies?"

"Wow." I didn't know if I should be hearing about either of those things right now, but I shrugged anyway. "Both, I guess. Is the serial killer related to . . . Lana Ly?"

"No. I don't think so anyway." She glanced at me wide-eyed. "I'm surprised you know about her and came anyway."

"Oh my God." I laughed despite myself. "If I had a dollar for everyone who said that to me."

"You'd be the youngest person on the Forbes list this year?"

"Not quite, but on my way there. Let's talk the secret societies. I'm guessing they're less dangerous than the serial killers."

"Depends who you ask." She laughed at the look on my face. "I've been pretty obsessed with them since I was a kid. I know someone in them, well, allegedly, and the idea of them fascinates me."

"Are you a journalism major?" I perked up in my seat.

"More like, nosey as hell. I'm a psych major, but I want to be a private detective."

"As a job?"

"Yeah. As a job." She laughed. "What's wrong with that?"

"Nothing at all. I'd just never really heard of a young person say they wanted to do that."

"What do you want to do?"

"I'm a journalism major, so I'd love to report on world causes, investigative news, things like that."

"I would've pegged you as a fashion blogger."

That gave me pause. I looked at her again, *really* looked at her. "Do you know an Ella Valentine by any chance?"

"Yeah." Her eyes widened. "She's my mom."

"You're kidding."

"Not kidding, pretty sure she's my mom." She let out a nervous laugh.

"Well, this makes sense."

"What does?"

"You both said similar things to me. About Lana and about the fashion blog thing."

"Really? Mom said that to you?" She smiled, as if she was trying not to laugh.

"She sure did."

"When did you meet her?"

"When I went to the paper to try to land an internship there and she interviewed me and then assigned that I be the photographer instead of a writer."

I tried to keep my voice light, but wondered if I sounded bitchy now. I felt bitchy. Two people had reduced me to a fashion blogger in less than ten minutes of having met me. What the hell? I mean, I loved fashion, loved, and would love blogging about it, sure, but I was trying to be a journalist, for fuck's sake.

"Well, I'm sorry I said that. I didn't think it would offend you. I mean." Hailey waved a hand over me as if she was presenting me for sale.

"I know what I'm wearing," I said. "And I know what I look like. I get it."

"You're just really pretty is all. Sorry."

She didn't sound sorry and she was still obviously trying not to laugh, but I let it go. I was used to dealing with girls like Hailey, though I had to say, normally it was because they were jealous over a boy I was dating. In this case, it appeared, she was jealous of the fact that I was pretty, dressed designer, and had a father. I guess there's a first time for everything.

"How'd your mom end up with a coffee shop, a bar, and a job at the school newspaper anyway?"

"It was part of her and dad's agreement when they separated."

"Oh. That doesn't sound like a terrible outcome to a bad situation."

"Yeah, I guess." Her expression told me she didn't agree, but she shrugged it off.

"It seems like she's done well for herself."

"She has." She smiled. "Anyway, back to my interest in the

societies. I've heard that one of the groups meets in The Tower. Smack in the middle of campus. Hidden in plain sight."

"That's an odd place to meet if you want to be secretive." I frowned. "What kind of tower is it? What do they talk about in the meetings?"

"Um, hello." Hailey laughed. "It's secret."

"I guess if they're not bothering anyone, what does it matter?" I shrugged, but in the back of my mind, I remembered Ella Valentine talking about how Lana had been investigating them too.

Was that what happened to her? Had she gotten caught up in something with them? Something so sinister that they had to kidnap her? All the crime fiction I'd been reading wasn't doing me any favors. If I said this to Lincoln, he'd laugh at me and tell me to snap back to reality. If I said this to my ex-boyfriend Travis, he'd roll his eyes and tell me I needed to put my books down and rejoin the real world, as if the real world ever had anything fun and exciting to offer.

"I just think it's crazy that you have to be invited, and not everyone is. Even royalty has been turned down. It's that exclusive," Hailey said. "Organizations like that should be allowed, don't you think?"

"I guess. What are they called? Does anyone know?"

"Well, we have Quill & Dagger, but they've agreed to let the paper publish their names now. I guess the whole secretive thing wasn't working out for them anymore."

I remembered hearing my brother George talk about Quill & Dagger. Of course, even if he had been in a society, he wouldn't have told me. George was thirteen years my senior and the only things we ever spoke about when we saw each other were my grades and babysitting duties when I watched my nieces. My second oldest brother, Edward, didn't really talk about much at all, and now that he was living in Spain, we rarely communicated outside of Instagram. Lincoln was the only one who would talk to me about these things, and being that he didn't want to talk about anything pertaining to the school, I knew that was a longshot.

"I'm not sure which one meets in The Tower, but there are two or three on campus and I think I know a few members of the ones with no names." She slapped her hands on her knees, leaning in to look into my now empty mug. "So, you ready to go?"

"Yup." I stood up and thanked her as she took my mug and set it over by the counter. We walked outside and headed in the general direction of my apartment. It was difficult to navigate with no phone or GPS to go on.

"Speak of the devil," Hailey said under her breath.

I glanced forward in time to catch four guys walking in our direction. They were all wearing different variations of dark clothing, black, grey, dark green. All tall with handsome features and *don't fuck with me* attitudes. One, in particular, caught my eye—the guy I'd bumped into the other day, the one I was nine-ty-nine-percent sure had been standing outside my apartment building smoking and probably talking to these three guys. My heart beat faster as we walked past them. I focused on not look-ing at them, at him specifically, despite being hyper-aware of his presence. A shoulder bumped me, hard, and my gaze snapped up to his.

"Oops. My bad," he said in a tone that was nothing if not patronizing.

"You should reconsider your shoulders," I snapped.

"You should reconsider what sidewalks you walk on."

My eyes narrowed, but I kept walking. I wanted to punch him. Each step I took away from him, with my blood pumping in my ears and my hands shaking in rage, I focused on my breath—in and out, in and out, and tried not to react to him again.

"That guy is *such* an asshole," I said loudly to Hailey, hoping he'd hear me.

"Trust me, I know." She looked over her shoulder. I didn't bother giving him the satisfaction. "That's Fitz and he's an asshole with a capital A. He's also captain of the hockey team, which two of them play in. The other two play some other sport . . . lacrosse I think? And I think they're also part of one of the secret societies. They're very particular about who they socialize with, but I guess that could mean anything. I mean, you know jocks."

Yeah, I knew jocks, but the ones I knew, like my brother and ex-boyfriend, weren't self-centered pricks who got off on being mean to the new girl. Finally, despite myself, I looked back and caught him looking right at me. He seemed upset, his jaw clenched tightly as he watched me. It took all of my control not to roll my eyes as I tore my gaze away from his. I guessed in a way he did look like someone who could be hiding some deep, dark secret, but who wasn't?

On the way to my apartment, Hailey made it a point to tell me all about the buildings we walked in front of.

"This is the beginning of Millionaire's Row," she stated as we crossed the street.

"Oh. This is where I live." I turned around in a full circle. "Let's just walk the whole thing. Once I see my building, I'll know. I think I made a left at this light when I left earlier."

"How'd you come to live here?" She eyed me sideways.

"My dad owns one of these buildings." I paused, feeling like a privileged asshole again and added, "He bought the land forever ago and built it during the recession."

"Interesting. So he lets you live here for free? No rent owed or anything?"

"No rent owed. I mean, unless you consider getting a degree in a major I don't want rent owed."

"I guess. Still, you're a lucky girl." She shrugged a shoulder. "A lot of the hockey players live here too."

"Do you make it a habit of going to their apartments?" I shot her a wry look.

"No." She blushed deeply. "I just . . . I've seen them around here." She bit her lip and paused briefly. "I hooked up with one of them. It was a long time ago and honestly, I wanted to hook up with his roommate, not him, but whatever. In hindsight, I'm glad I didn't hook up with the roommate." She glanced away quickly. "Anyway, the cloaked people meet around here sometimes too."

"Cloaked people?"

"Yeah, some of the societies walk around wearing cloaks. Some red cloaks, some black cloaks, depending on which you belong to."

"Isn't that . . . attention calling?" I frowned. "Another thing that doesn't seem secretive at all."

"You don't get it," she said. "The fact is, they're part of this world that nobody is allowed to unless they're invited. No one is going to look and try to see who's behind it."

"I guess." I slowed down when we got to my apartment building. "You seem to know a lot of information about these secret groups."

"Like I said, I'm nosey."

"You want to come up?" I nodded toward my building.

"Um." She glanced up and down the sidewalk. "Not today."

"You sure?"

"Yeah, raincheck. I should probably make sure all my things are ready for class tomorrow."

"Okay. Thanks for walking me."

"Sure." She smiled. "And be careful out there. Especially around here. You never know who's watching you."

My heart seemed to stop beating as she walked away. Why would she say that? Who would be watching me? The cloaked figures? I thought of Lana and where her investigating may or may not have landed her. A shiver rolled through me. I'd tread carefully in search of truth.

CHAPTER FOUR

I WAS AT THE LIBRARY, TRYING TO SEE WHAT ELSE I COULD FIND ABOUT Lana, when I decided to search the newspaper archives for my brother's accident. It took a lot of scrolling, but when I finally found it, it wasn't front and center, the way I'd expected. It was an article on page two. Page two. The story front and center was of the new hospital that was affiliated with the university and was on the other side of town. On the right of that, there was a small picture you could barely make out, with the words "Mexican Business Man's Son Involved in Car Wreck"—page 2. They'd reduced both my father's accomplishments and my brother's life-altering accident into a short, boring headline and a page two article.

"This is bullshit."

"Shh."

My attention whipped to the person beside me. I was full-on ready to tell her to go to hell when I remembered where I was. I cringed and mouthed an *I'm sorry* instead before going back to the archives. Reading the article with the lack of facts and details made me even more frustrated than I was when I started, so I decided to quit while I was ahead. I'd come back to this tomorrow. For now, I'd promised Hailey I would swing by The Bar tonight, so I packed my things up and headed there instead.

"What's your poison?" Hailey asked from across the bar.

"Honestly? I don't really have one."

"Come on, Mae." She cocked her head, giving me a look. "Even girls that look like Cher from *Clueless* have a weakness."

"First of all, I'm brown." I raised an eyebrow. "So if I had to look like anyone from *Clueless*, it would be her friend with the braids."

With a naturally olive complexion and dark features, I was closer to that than Cher. Despite the fact that most of my life I kind of wished I was a blonde girl from the valley, I'd grown to accept my natural tan and almond-shaped eyes and more importantly, be proud of my Mexican roots. My mother was French, but the only thing I seemed to get from her was her height and haughty attitude. Everything else, I got from my handsome father. Most of the Bastón kids did, except for Lincoln, who had my mother's green eyes and fine features. Features he often broke on the ice playing hockey and off the ice getting into fights.

"I'll just take something with vodka." I looked up at Hailey again. "Vodka tonic. Dirty Martini. Whatever."

"Vodka coming right up." She winked. "For the record, I wasn't calling you a bimbo, I just meant that you dress like you belong on the cover of every single fashion magazine out there. That's what mom and I meant when we said the fashion blogger thing, too, you know." She smiled. "I'm not trying to box you into being something you don't want to be."

I felt myself frown as I looked down at myself. Normally, that statement was warranted, but today I was wearing ripped jeans, a ripped white crop top covered by a black leather jacket, and my Givenchy slides. A far cry from any fashion magazine cover. I glanced back up at her.

"Trust me, you look like a friggin' model."

"Thanks. I guess." I tore my attention away from her to look around the bar. "Is it always this empty?"

"Give it a minute. It's ladies night, so all the guys show up soon enough."

"Funny how that happens." I snorted as she slid me my drink. "Thank you."

"Let me know if you like it. I can make you something else," she said, nodding her head at something behind me. "The band sets up there on Thursday nights. That's another reason it's poppin' in here."

"Poppin'," I repeated. Such a funny word. It was one of those words I felt like I could never really get away with saying. Not with the whole *Clueless* vibe I obviously had going. I sipped on my drink. It was definitely strong, yet fruity. "I like it."

"What did your boyfriend think about you transferring over here?"

"I told you about Travis?"

Hailey's eyes widened slightly. "Yeah."

"Oh." I frowned. *Had I become that person?* The one who spoke about her ex-boyfriend so much she couldn't even remember what she'd said to whom. "He wasn't thrilled, but we'd been more off than on for a while anyway."

"How long were you together?"

"Two and a half years, but a lot of that was off. It was weird. We got together our senior year, right around the time we were deciding where to go and it felt perfect." I sipped the drink. "Probably because I knew my parents hated him and I'd always been such a rule follower, so Travis felt like the only thing that was mine, you know?"

"So you followed him to school," she supplied.

"Right." I set down my drink with a laugh. "I seriously don't remember talking to you about this."

She shrugged and started working on another customer's drink, so I continued my story.

"So, I followed him to college thinking we were going to be together forever, and then . . . we weren't."

"What happened?" She leaned over the bar after depositing the drink in front of the person a few seats down from me.

"Life. I guess. Nothing crazy." I circled the rim of my glass with the tip of my finger. "Other girls started paying attention to him. It's a basketball school, so all of the attention he hadn't received back home, he was now getting in droves. He's a good guy, but I just couldn't be with him. Besides, he doesn't believe in long-distance relationships."

"And you don't miss him," she said, rather than asked.

"Not really."

Missing him was something even my brother hadn't asked me about, probably because he knew the turmoil that came with being with him. Even Travis himself hadn't asked me that question when we'd texted back and forth. Maybe he knew deep down that I would say no and he didn't want to accept that. Travis was the kind of guy who thought he was everyone's type, so I knew he wasn't sitting in his apartment crying to his roommates about me leaving him. He played basketball in a college built around the sport and it was the first season he'd be truly single and not dodging all of the girl's trying to throw themselves at him. Not that he'd been a saint even when I was down there. So, *did I miss him?* I wasn't sure. I'd been too busy coming up with reasons for why he didn't miss me to dwell on whether or not I missed him.

"Well, I've always heard the college life is better when you're single."

"Who have you heard that from?"

"Usually college students who have just been dumped and come in here to drown their sorrows."

That made me laugh. I clicked on my phone to see if anything had come in, but when it lit up, it only showed a picture of Lincoln and me.

"Is that him?"

"No." My eyes snapped up at Hailey. "My brother."

"*This* is your brother?" She plucked the phone from the bar and looked at it, eyes wide. "Lincoln, right?"

"Yeah," I said slowly, waiting to see if she told me about her crush.

"I had a crush on him for a hot second, but then I realized . . . " her voice trailed off. She shook her head. "He wasn't my type. That's crazy that he's your brother." She stared at me for a long moment as I sipped the drink. The way she looked between the picture of Lincoln and me sitting right across from her started to make me feel uncomfortable.

"Do you think he was part of the secret society?" she asked.

"My brother?" I snorted. "I doubt it."

"Are you sure? He was always with the guys we saw yesterday," she said, brows pulling in.

"I'm pretty sure I'd know if my brother was in some secret society." I took my phone back, scowling. "He's my best friend."

"Even best friends keep secrets," Hailey said softly.

"Not us. Besides, he was the captain of the hockey team, so he definitely hung out with them. That's probably why you think that."

"That's possible." She moved down the bar with a small shrug, but I could tell she wasn't convinced.

As she started talking to the couple sitting in the far corner of the bar, I decided to text Lincoln.

Me: What do you know about these secret societies?

Me: Were you in one?

I watched my screen, hoping the little dots with an impending answer would come. When it didn't, I put it away again. I'd call him tomorrow and ask again. For some crazy reason, even though it made no sense, Hailey saying that planted a seed in my head and I knew myself well enough to know it wasn't going anywhere. I'd either have to nourish it or kill it altogether.

"Have you started working on your assignments for the paper?"

"Nope. I start tomorrow, actually."

"That's cool. Are you into sports?"

"Not even a little."

"Not even looking at hot guys in uniforms?"

"My ex is a basketball player. My ex before him was a baseball player." I shrugged. "I've had enough jocks for a lifetime."

"Well, la di da. Not all of us can be as cool as you, Mae." The twinkle in her eye would have made me laugh if it didn't look so . . . *off.* Again with the jealousy. "I'm into jocks myself, but I'm also a biker kinda girl."

"I don't think I've ever met one," I said. "A biker, I mean."

"My uncle's in a club. He's actually touring the US with them right now. They lost one of their members and went to spread his ashes."

"Someone you knew?"

"Yeah, Uncle Pete."

"I'm sorry."

"It's a big family." She smiled sadly. "Uncle Pete wasn't really my uncle. Not by blood anyway."

"I can relate to that."

My father had a long line of cousins that weren't related by blood, but by association. People his parents had known since they were born, and by default, I had a long line of cousins as well. Most of whom I hadn't seen in years, but they were still family.

"Anyway, my dad was never around and my mom was always working, so I was mostly raised by my grandmother and uncles. Riding on the back of the bike feels like home to me."

"That must be hard without your dad." I offered a small smile. "But your uncles sound fun."

We kept talking about family and comparing notes. By the end of the conversation, we couldn't deny the fact that we were from entirely different worlds. Suddenly, when all of the little things I'd taken for granted growing up were made blatantly obvious. I felt beyond spoiled. Not that Hailey's family wasn't doing well for themselves, they owned a handful of businesses, but it was the complete opposite of my family. Sure, we'd all been working summer jobs in Dad's television networks since we were old enough to, but it was only on his insistence. He didn't want us to grow up and act like spoiled brats. Our jobs were always an illusion though, a distraction, something to keep us busy and remind us where we were headed in the future. It wasn't like any of the money we made went to actual bills. Most of the time that money couldn't even afford us anything in our closets. And ultimately, that was what it taught the four of us—we'd never be as comfortable as we were outside of the family business, because at least if we took a job there, we'd always have a credit card that paid for all of the high-ticket items we were accustomed to. Branching off on our own would mean no credit card and no free spending.

But here was Hailey, working her way through college, and there I was, complaining about my role in the stupid school newspaper because of course, I thought I deserved better.

Maybe I did, but Hailey wasn't the person I needed to vent to. Celia, maybe. Lincoln, maybe. Hailey? No.

"Well." Hailey's gaze followed the movement behind me. "Your friends are here."

I frowned as I pivoted around on the stool. My gaze landed on the same four guys from the other day. I gave each of them a once-over. When my eyes met his, I froze, wishing I could turn around and pretend I'd never looked over in the first place, but I wasn't going to be the first to break contact. The alpha in me wouldn't let me. Besides, the way he was looking at me, like he could tear through me without permission, made me want to prove him wrong. He broke first, because his friend slapped his arm, pointing toward a booth they'd found. My eyes followed their movement and I watched him pick the side to sit in, the one that gave him full vantage of my seat. I turned around, drained my drink and stood up.

"You're not leaving, are you?"

"No, but I want to switch seats. I don't like that my back is facing the door."

"Hm." Her lips pressed together as she nodded. "I can't turn my back to anything anymore with all the mass shootings, though from this angle, I'd probably be shot straight in the chest."

Her comment gave me pause. I stared at her, horrified for a moment as I picked up my bag. It wasn't an odd conversation to have. Unfortunately, things like mass shootings happened and since we'd reached the point that the average person knew someone or of someone who'd been personally involved in one, conversations about them were at a peak. The casual way in which we spoke about it didn't make it any less weird though, as if it was just one more obstacle we had to hurdle over. As if it was the norm. By the time I was sitting down on the other side of the bar, away from wandering eyes, my mood had soured entirely. Lana had disappeared from this campus and that hadn't been a shooting. Someone had taken her without consent. Someone kidnapped her and in turn, she'd vanished without a trace.

"Are you afraid of anything?" Hailey asked, spinning around to where I was.

"Definitely shootings," I said. "And confined spaces. I hate confined spaces."

"Yeah, those suck." She looked up and walked over to a new customer.

I looked at my phone and saw a text from my brother.

Linc: Stay away from all of those people. This is not a drill.

My eyes stayed on the words as if they were going to re-arrange and change into something else. *This is not a drill* is something we started saying to each other as kids—when our parents were walking to our rooms and we knew we were going to get caught on a late-night phone call, when our brothers were closing in on us playing spies with our walkie-talkies, when we had a boyfriend or girlfriend over and were in our rooms while our parents were out and they were getting home. *This is not a drill* was serious.

The hairs on the back of my neck began to prickle as I felt a presence looming behind me, so I clicked the side button on my phone and glanced over my shoulder. It was the rude guy I'd bumped into—Fitz was what Hailey had referred to him as. He took a seat beside me. I tore my gaze from his and noticed his left hand was covered in a white wrap, blood seeping through the bandage where his knuckles were. My eyes snapped back to his.

"Let me guess, someone bumped into you and made you angry."

"Are you stalking me now?" His lips curved.

"Don't you wish."

"It wouldn't be the first time a beautiful girl followed me around."

"Rest assured. This beautiful girl will never follow you around." I stared at him. "Why did you come over here? Did you get tired of your agreeable minions?"

"I don't have minions, I have friends, and they're not as agreeable as you think."

I leaned forward, setting my elbow on the bar and resting my chin on my hand. "Did you come over to apologize to me for being rude?"

"I wasn't the one who bumped into someone without looking."

"What a crime." I cocked my head, my hair cascading over my left shoulder with the movement. "You did bump into me on purpose the other day though."

"Well, I'm sorry about that." He raised an eyebrow.

"What? You expect me to clap for you? You shouldn't have bumped into me in the first place."

"Neither should you."

"That was completely different. I was—"I stopped talking and took a deep breath. "You know what? It doesn't matter. I apologized, you apologized. Let's move on."

"Okay." He looked even more amused now. "What's your name?"

"I'm not sure I want to tell you." I pulled back, sitting up straight.

"I'm just asking out of courtesy."

"Out of courtesy?" I swiveled my seat to face him, my knees tapping his as I turned. "Meaning, you already know."

"Amelia Bastón," he said. "Daughter of Felipe Bastón. Lincoln Bastón's sister."

"Wow. Do you keep a file of family trees for all the girls you're interested in?"

"Who says I'm interested?" Again, the ghost of a smile appeared and disappeared just like that.

"I'm deducing, you know, based on the fact that you left that to come over here and sit by me."

I nodded to the table where his friends were sitting. They were flanked by girls on all sides, no longer just a group of guys having drinks at a bar. It had become a spectacle.

"Maybe I'm not interested in that." He nodded over there.

"Which means you're interested in this."

"I am interested in you, yes. I'm trying to figure out how we've never met," he said, "My older brother is friends with your brother George. Obviously, I know Lincoln, and yet, I've only heard of you in passing." He paused, his gaze searching mine. "Why is that?"

"Maybe there's nothing to tell. Maybe what you see is what you get, and as you can see, I'm not worth talking about."

I didn't mean to sound as self-deprecating as I did, but it was the truth. Yes, I was pretty, beautiful even. Yes, my family was wealthy, but I wasn't any more spectacular than the guy sitting beside me. We were just spoiled kids with good genes. To some people that would be the epitaph of their life, I never wanted it to be mine.

"I think that's a very unfair and false assessment of yourself," he said, watching me a lot longer than was the norm for two strangers at a bar who were not going home together. Because I wasn't—going home with him. He licked his lips before speaking again and I felt myself flush despite myself. "Do you play sports? Are you in any clubs?"

"I thought you knew everything about me." I raised an eyebrow.

"If I knew everything about you, I wouldn't have walked over here."

"No, I don't play sports and I'm not in any clubs. I am part of the newspaper as of a few days ago so I'll be taking pictures of those who play sports and are in clubs." I shot him a pointed look.

"Good to know." He nodded, still watching me closely, so closely that I had to look away. My heart was beating too fast, too hard with his proximity. I kept my eyes on the bar even as he spoke again. "Are you planning on joining any other clubs?"

"If you're asking me if I'll join a sorority, the answer is no. I'm limited on friendship capacity at the moment."

"You have too many friends?"

"I have two at the moment and that's enough for me."

At that, he chuckled. Our gazes caught again. The sound and the way his eyes twinkled made my heart skip. I seriously needed to get away from this guy.

"That's an interesting take on friends."

"It's what I know." I shrugged.

To be fair, I couldn't really count Celia as a friend. So far, she'd proven to be a great roommate, with her absence and all, but friend? I guess technically Hailey was my only one here. I searched for her and found her standing on the other side of the bar, enthralled in conversation with someone. I guess as a bartender and barista, she was everyone's friend.

"Why'd you transfer over here senior year?"

"You know, you ask a lot of questions and you haven't even given me your name."

"You haven't asked." His gaze flicked over mine. "You haven't asked me anything."

"So tell me. I already know you play hockey, obviously you go to school here so I'm assuming you're smart, unless your hockey abilities are the only thing keeping you here, but this isn't that kind of school." I searched his eyes, God, it was so hard to search his eyes without seeming interested, or *more* interested. "What's your name?

"Logan."

"Logan." I nodded, looking at him. "I can see that."

"What? I look like a Logan?" His lips spread into a slow, wide smile, and I swear my heart stopped beating altogether.

"Yeah, you do." I nodded slowly, mouth slightly ajar. His friends started shouting, being loud. We both turned our attention in that direction. One of them seemed to be getting in some kind of confrontation with another guy.

"Well, I have to go, Amelia." He stood up, moving closer to me, close enough to touch me, without actually doing so. The hint of cologne he had on smelled really good as he turned toward me. My gaze slid up his obviously toned torso and thick neck as I aimed to look into his deep green eyes as he spoke. "I'll see you around."

He tapped the bar with his uninjured knuckles and walked away. I felt myself staring after him as he went over to where the guys were. There was more screaming, and now shoving. Logan got in the middle of it and started trying to break them up, but one of the guys shoved him hard, and it was all it took for him to pivot his body and punch him square in the jaw. The guy landed on the floor with a thump. It wasn't until Hailey walked over to me that I realized I was gripping the edge of the bar.

"Holy shit," I whispered.

"This is a regular Thursday at The Bar. Welcome to town." She smiled brightly, but it looked more like a grimace. "If you want to go out back, there's a door right there you can use. It'll lead you to the alley, but if you make a quick right, you'll be out in the street."

"Will you have to call the cops?"

"On them?" She looked at me like I'd lost my mind.

"I don't know, on the entire group involved in the fight."

Hailey scoffed. "They'll probably arrest me before they arrest them."

"That doesn't make any sense." I looked back at the brawl, which was still going, but now it was a screaming match between Logan's friend that looked like Thor and some other guy.

"Their money talks. Mine makes me a mute."

"Oh." I blinked. I definitely understood that even if I hadn't been on the mute side of things. "Well, yeah, I think I'll go out the back way then."

I set some money down for the drink I had as I stood and gathered my things. Once I'd made my way to the back door, I glanced over my shoulder one last time. As I did, Logan's gaze lifted and met mine. He looked absolutely furious, but at least this time I knew it wasn't with me. As I opened the door to the back, brittle air shot straight to me. I shut the door behind me and zipped my jacket all the way up, looking up and down the alley. There were two brightly lit streetlamps, so it wasn't dark out here, but it was still much darker than I felt comfortable with. I idled by the door a little longer, looking up and down the alley once more. Finally, I heard a group of people, girls laughing, guys talking, and I sprinted in that direction. When I got to the populated sidewalk, I caught my breath and joined the herd of people walking in the direction of my apartment building.

The guy walking directly in front of me was swaying on his feet, obviously drunk, between two girls who looked like they were sharing the same fate as him. As I absently listened to their conversation, I pulled out my phone and re-read my brother's text messages. *This is not a drill* jumped out at me.

"Yo, what is that?" the guy in front of me said loudly. "Is that a person?"

"I don't see anything," one of the girls responded.

"Brent is drunk," the other said.

"I'm drunk but I'm not crazy," he said. "You don't see that?"

"No, Brent," one of them whined.

"Shut up already," the other added, also whining.

I put my phone back in the pocket of my bag and looked around, searching for whatever it was drunk Brent was seeing that nobody else was. The streets were crowded. Students were pouring out of bars and onto the pavement, joining the herd. Brent jerked to a stop suddenly. I was staring at the back of his head and still bumped into him. The person behind me bumped into me. I opened my mouth to complain, when Brent lifted his arm up and pointed.

"There," he shouted. "Does nobody see that?"

My gaze followed in the direction of his pointer. I stood on the tips of my toes, placing a hand against Brent's back to steady myself. I didn't know the guy, but I was sure he wouldn't remember this tomorrow and I needed to see what he saw. In the midst of the crowd that had overflowed onto the street, there were two people walking in blood-red cloaks. People shouldered past them, without hesitation, as if it was the most normal thing in the world.

"What are they doing?" I asked, forgetting my face was so close to Brent's ear. He whipped around so quickly, I had to step back to keep from falling over.

"You see them?"

"Of course I see them."

"Does nobody else think this is weird?" he yelled.

"Dude shut up," some random guy said.

"They're in a society. They're hunting for new members," another added.

Anticipation coiled deep in my belly. *How would they choose? What society was it? Was it the one Lana had been investigating? And why did they call it hunting?* It was just as Hailey had said, they did things in broad view of everyone and nobody seemed to care. They were used to it. The rest of the way home, I was all up in my thoughts, wondering what would happen if I went up to one of those people and asked questions. Maybe I'd wait until it was daylight. The crowd thinned out as we walked, everyone going their separate way toward their buildings. I could see the navy blue awning that hung over the main door of my building as I stood on the side of the street, waiting to cross, and knew I was almost home free. I wondered if Celia was there or if she was staying at her boyfriend's again tonight.

Loud female laughter rang out on the otherwise silent street as I reached my building, and I noticed there was a group of people standing beneath the street light on the other side, at the entrance to the park. My hand reached into my purse in search of my keys as I kept my gaze on them. I could make out four guys and three women. One of the guys was letting out a cloud of smoke while passing something to the next, a joint, I presumed. The fourth guy was standing a few steps away from the rest of them, leaning against the black fence. All of the guys were wearing black and had similar builds, but I knew from the way my stomach clenched, and his height, and the way his hair was slicked back like that, I knew it was Logan, and even though I couldn't make out his face entirely from where I was, I knew that he was staring right at me.

How had they gotten here before me? Last I saw them, they were all in the middle of a brawl at the bar. One of the women broke away from the rest of the group with the joint in her hand and walked over to him, lifting it as an offer. He shook his head. She stood closer, wrapping an arm around his neck and pressing against him. He didn't take his eyes off mine as she did this and my heart pounded furiously at the sight. Why was he looking at me? Why was I still standing there, looking at him? My feet couldn't seem to move for a full minute. When her hand snaked its way down his chest and onto his southern region, I forced myself to break away and practically ran into my building.

I rushed to the elevator and hit the button quickly, as if being chased, and made my way to my apartment with the same enthusiasm. Why were they hanging out across the street? Didn't they have somewhere more . . . private they could go to? When I got to my apartment, I called out for Celia but got no response. Of course, she wasn't home. After making sure all of the windows were closed and switching off some lights that had been left on, I went to my room and walked over to the window. My hands shook as I lifted them to the blackout curtains and began to pull them shut. I looked outside one last time, but they were all gone.

CHAPTER FIVE

I AWOKE TO THE NEWS THAT MY BROTHER HAD BEEN RUSHED TO THE hospital. Instead of waiting around to hear any details, I shoved some things into a bag and ran out of my apartment. Fuck my classes and the orientation I was hoping to sneak into. The thought of Lincoln, alone, in a hospital room, was making me sick. I was rushing out of the building when I nearly bumped into Logan. Again. This time, I had the mind to look up just as he pushed away from the revolving door and walked inside. He took one look at me and frowned. God knows what the hell I must have looked like, makeup-less and riddled with worry.

"What the hell happened to you?"

"Nothing." I shoved myself into the revolving door and picked up the pace toward the black SUV that awaited me on the corner. *Why didn't they park directly in front of the building?*

"Hey," he called out.

I halted in my steps and turned around to see Logan jogging up to me. It was then that I noticed how sweaty he was, his dark hair sticking to the sides of his face before he pushed it back. He was wearing basketball shorts and a Toronto Raptors t-shirt that looked like he'd cut the sleeves off himself to make it a muscle tee. He'd probably just gotten in from a run. Under any other circumstances, I might've considered that he looked really hot right now, but my mind was overloaded with the flight I needed to catch and my brother's state. I hadn't even bothered to ask my mother what happened. I heard—Lincoln, hospital, in her grief-stricken voice, and I ran. I'd bypassed dad and called his favorite pilot and driver myself, not wanting to waste any time. Surely, Dad had told them picking me up was okay though, otherwise they wouldn't have shown up.

"Yeah?" I asked impatiently, because Logan was just standing there staring at me.

"Where are you running off to?"

"I can't talk right now."

The door to the building swung and a woman stepped out. I watched as she walked toward us.

"I was wondering where you ran off to this morning," she said, her voice a coo.

"I told you I don't stay over," he said, his voice gruff. "What the fuck are you doing out here anyway? I'm trying to have a conversation with someone."

"Oh." She blinked and looked over at me. "I hadn't seen your little friend there."

"I have to go," I said, turning around.

I didn't have time for this bullshit. I ran to the SUV, climbing inside and shut the door. I said hello to the driver and turned in my seat as I pulled the seatbelt across my chest. Logan and the woman were still standing on the sidewalk. He was now typing into his phone, completely ignoring her as she held onto his arm. She seemed to be begging him for attention, but he wasn't having it. I turned and faced forward as we drove off. Whatever was happening back there was none of my concern.

"What happened?" I ran straight to my mother when I got to the sixth floor of the hospital.

One of the nurses had personally escorted me there. Apparently, the sixth floor was one nobody spoke of, where celebrities often were treated but never talked about. Mom stood from her chair and met me halfway, opening her arms for me as I reached her. That alone scared the fuck out of me. Mom wasn't the most affectionate person. To her, limited affection was key to a successful being. It was one of the many outcomes she'd come up with during the extensive studies she'd done on human interactions. It was an idea my father always frowned upon, being that he came from a family of huggers and over-affectionate people and had obviously turned out just fine.

"What happened?" I pulled away. "Where's Lincoln?"

"Oh, Amelia." Her voice cracked, tears filling her green eyes as she looked at me briefly before pulling me into her again. "He's gone. Lincoln is gone."

If there was ever a time when I would have fainted, it would have been then, in my mother's arms, in the middle of a sterile, quiet hospital. A fat tear rolled down my face, then another, and another, but my mind still couldn't process those words or what they meant.

"What do you mean gone?" I croaked. "What does gone mean? Where did he go?"

Suddenly, her arms felt like cages that I needed to rip away from. I pulled away and stepped back, swaying on my feet.

"Where's dad?" I asked. "What do you mean gone?"

"He's dead." She wiped her face.

I took a good look at her then. I'd never seen my mother without makeup. I'd never seen her wear anything outside of the house that wasn't tailored to perfection and pressed. She was wearing green and blue checkered Polo pajamas. Pajamas.

Out of the house. I'd never seen wrinkles or hair in disarray. I'd never seen grief so blatantly etched on her face. I stumbled back, this time, landing on my ass, and I sat there, on the hard, cold floor. Who was dead? My father? Lincoln was gone, had he killed him? No. He may have had issues with dad, but he wouldn't resort to murder. Would he? I looked back up at mom, my pent-up confusion and pain rolled together as I wailed.

"Who's dead? Who died?"

She took a shuttering breath as she walked over and crouched in front of me. I could see that she was doing everything in her power to calm down, to pull the perfect psychiatrist mask over her face in order to help me deal with this, but she couldn't. Not when she obviously didn't know how to process it herself.

"Your brother is dead," she said slowly, taking a breath. "He killed himself last night."

"No." I shook my head, tears filling my eyes again.

"Yes."

"No." I continued shaking my head. "No."

"Amelia," she said softly. "Do you think I want to accept this? That my own son—" Her voice broke. "My own son . . ."

"No." I slapped the floor on either side of me. "He wouldn't do that!"

"He did. He overdosed. He did."

"He wouldn't." My brother was the ultimate health nut. He hated the mere idea of drugs. I stood quickly, pacing, walking down the corridor as I yelled. "Where is he? Where is he?"

"Amelia please," Mom sobbed. I'd never seen mom sob. I'd never seen her cry—period.

"How?" My chin wobbled. My arms shook. "How could this happen? Weren't you watching him? Aren't you a fucking expert in this?"

It was unfair. I knew it even as I blamed her, but I couldn't help it. My brother. My best friend. My . . . I started to sob, my shoulders shaking as I held myself together. He was a light in this world. Why would he want to extinguish it? How could he? It wasn't possible. A door opened and shut loudly, and my head snapped up, fully expecting Lincoln to walk out of there. Lincoln, with a presence so massive, he'd take up an entire arena. Instead, it was my father.

"He's not dead," he said.

Mom and I both gasped loudly.

"How can that be? Felipe. He was dead. We saw him," she said rapidly. "How? Did he—"

"They revived him. They revived him," Dad said, and then he stumbled into the nearest chair, buried his face in his hands and started to cry. "Oh my God, that was so scary. Oh my God. I thought I lost him."

Mom rushed over to him, taking the seat beside him and wrapping an arm around him. They cried together as I stood there. My brother wasn't dead. They didn't let me see him until the next day. When I walked into the room, he was attached to tubes, and needles were protruding from his skin. He looked frail and uncomfortable. It was just the two of us in the room when his eyes snapped open. I stood right beside him, holding his hand. His eyeballs moved to look at me. He looked scared, as if he was trying to tell me something, but couldn't with the tube that was in his mouth.

"I'm going to call for the nurse," I said.

His hand squeezed mine slightly. He shook his head no.

"But, Linc, I can't do anything." My hand shook over his. "I need to tell them to come—"

His hand squeezed again. He shook his head no.

"Why'd you try to kill yourself?" I asked, unable to keep

from crying. I brought a hand up to wipe the tears from my face, but they kept coming.

He squeezed my hand again. Shook his head no, but his own eyes filled with tears.

I stared at him. "You didn't try to kill yourself?"

He shook his head slightly.

"Why would . . . " I frowned. "I don't understand."

He started tapping on my hand. At first, I thought that was all it was, but then he tapped harder, squeezed harder, opened his eyes wider as if he needed me to pay attention. Morse code.

"Morse code?" I asked, my voice barely audible over the knot in my throat.

He nodded.

I took out my phone and opened my notepad, writing down all of the dots and dashes. I couldn't remember the alphabet.

"I'll have to translate this," I said. He shot me an exasperated look. "I can't remember the alphabet."

His eyes twinkled and he made a noise from his throat, as if he wanted to laugh, and then fell into a fit. I hit the button for the nurse and stepped away when they rushed in. His entire body shook the bed and his eyes rolled back.

"What is happening?" I shouted. "What is happening?"

More nurses rushed inside. "Step back, he's having a seizure."

"Get her outside," another shouted. Arms wrapped around me as they ushered me towards the door.

"Lincoln," I yelled, fighting against the nurse. "Lincoln. I love you."

Lincoln was forced into a coma that day. In twenty-four hours, I went from having a brother, to losing him, to having him again, but not quite.

CHAPTER SIX

T WASN'T FAIR.

I walked around my parent's house in a haze, with that thought in mind. It just wasn't fucking fair. Travis wrapped his arm around my shoulder and kissed the top of my head.

"You okay?"

I didn't speak. I couldn't. No, I wasn't okay. My brother was in a coma. A medically induced coma, my father reminded me constantly. He was going to be okay. Mom had all of the scientific facts to back it all up, too. They'd flown in a doctor from Cleveland to treat him and nurses who worked strictly with coma-induced patients, to monitor him. Still. A coma meant I couldn't speak to him, and he was my go-to person. Now, I was in my parent's backyard, sitting on a chaise lounge, as the house filled with people from everywhere who had just attended the mass mom set up for him. Prayers for Lincoln's full recovery, was what she'd asked for. Of course, I prayed too, but seriously? My brother was in a coma. They needed to get him out of it and let him heal while he was awake.

"Your parents said you may not go back to classes this semester," he continued. Travis said I talked a lot, but he never seemed to mind voicing his opinions about my life. "Maybe you should come back to Duke. Finish school there."

I didn't respond.

"Mae. You need to talk to someone," he said.

I continued to stare at the pool, where Lincoln and I took swimming lessons when we were kids. Where we hosted pool parties every year for his birthday, since it was at the end of May. Where he jumped in from the second-floor balcony of the house during a party we had while our parents were out of town and broke his nose. I felt myself smile at that memory. Idiot Lincoln. And then just as quickly, I was crying again. God, I was so tired of crying. I wiped my face quickly and looked around at everyone here. Most were our neighbors, parent's friends, Lincoln's friends from high school. I spotted Lana's parents, talking to dad. They all looked somber.

"Who are those guys?" Travis asked.

I still didn't talk, but I did glance at him and then followed his line of vision. I hadn't seen them before, but Logan and the three guys he was always with were standing on the other side of the lawn. They were all wearing black suits, white shirts, and black ties. I must have missed them earlier. I knew I definitely hadn't greeted them. I'd remember them. I'd definitely remember Logan. As if reading my thoughts, he looked over at me. I couldn't be sure what he was thinking, but I could swear I saw sympathy in his eyes. It was something I normally didn't want from anyone, but for some reason, he made his look genuine. Maybe because Logan didn't strike me as the kind of person who gave handouts. He seemed like the kind of person who said what he meant and meant what he said. I could appreciate that.

"Are you hungry?" Travis asked.

I shrugged. I was starving, I just wasn't sure I could keep any food down.

"I'm hungry." He stood up. "I'll go get us food. Stay right here."

He walked away. I stayed there, staring out at the pool again. It wasn't hot enough to go in there, but the only thing I could manage to think about was jumping in there, dress, heels, and all. Maybe I'd get hypothermia and end up in the hospital next to my brother. Maybe I could wait there until he woke up. My phone buzzed in my lap.

Unknown Caller: She's out there. She's still out there.

Dread crept into my belly as I stared at the ominous text.

Me: Who? Who is this?

No response.

I dialed the number and got a loud dial tone. "The number you are calling has been disconnected."

I pulled the phone away from my ear slowly and pressed the red button to end the call. They'd just texted me. *She's out there. She's still out there.* Who? Who was still out there? Lana? I glanced over at her parents. Her mother was now crying in my father's arms as he patted her back softly. They'd known each other a long time, her father being dad's accountant and all, but I never knew they were this close. Maybe it was the grief. Grief knew how to bring people together.

CHAPTER SEVEN

"**Y**OU'RE SURE YOU'RE GOING TO BE OKAY?" CELIA ASKED FOR the fifth time.

"Positive. It's not like you were much of a room-mate when you lived here anyway."

"I paid rent though." She stuck her tongue out. "Seriously, if you need anything, please call me. It doesn't matter the time. I can't imagine what you're going through."

"I'm okay. I promise."

Word traveled fast, even here. Then again, mom had re-quested a prayer chain in the school paper for Lincoln, which was also tweeted out and put on the online portal, so every time you logged on to look at school related things, you had the prayer chain for Lincoln's recovery and Lana's appearance. It must have been one of the many things our parents discussed that day at the house.

"We're having a party tonight at the house," Celia said. "I know you probably don't feel like partying at all, but if you want to forget about everything for a night, you should come."

"Maybe."

"I left those two boxes in the closet," she said as she walked out of the apartment. "I figured you didn't want them in the middle of the living room."

"What boxes?"

"The ones you had sent here. The ones with your brother's name on them."

"Oh. Yeah. Cool. Thanks for putting them away." I held the door for her and watched as she walked toward the elevator. "Maybe I'll see you later."

"Please come. It'll be fun. I promise."

I smiled and walked back into the apartment, shutting the door and locking it before heading to the guest bedroom closet. I pulled out the two boxes. They had my brother's name on the top and sides. A part of me wondered if I should just leave them alone. They were private. I wouldn't want someone rummaging through my stuff. But he was in a coma. He said he hadn't tried to kill himself. With that thought, I tore the tape off the first box and started going through it. Hockey equipment, a jersey, two jerseys, jockey straps. I cringed. Gross. I'd brought his computer with me from his room, but I hadn't found anything in there worthwhile. So far, there was nothing in this box that was worthwhile either. Who'd brought it though? Celia said it had been in the living room. I'd been gone a week, and I wasn't sure how often she'd come around, but for the boxes to be inside the apartment when only the two of us had a key? That was odd. I looked at the time. I was going to be late for my first assignment, since I'd missed last week's. I stood from the floor, grabbed my bag, camera, and left.

On my walk to campus, I started scrolling Lincoln's Instagram. He wasn't much of a poster to begin with, but in recent months, he hadn't posted anything at all. My memories kept flashing back to the hospital, to seeing him with that tube down his throat, not letting him speak, and then the seizure. I shivered. Then I remembered the Morse code. I exited Instagram and opened my notepad. There were a lot of dots and a lot of lines. Shit. How could I have forgotten about this? I needed to decipher it immediately.

When I got to campus, I looked everywhere for Ella Valentine, but never found her. I did find a guy holding a recorder to a girl's face and assumed he must work for the paper as well. I just hoped it was the same paper I was with. I waited for him to finish talking to the girl he was interviewing.

"Hey," I said. "I'm here to take pictures for The Gazette."

"Hey. Ella told me to expect you." He smiled, holding a hand out. "I'm Max."

"Amelia."

"Nice name."

"Thanks. You can call me Mae."

"Cool." He waved his recorder. "So, you want to do this together? I interview, you snap photos? Or are you going to take some candid photos?"

"I can do both. I'll take some after you interview first so I don't look so lost."

"I heard about your brother," he said, starting to walk over to another group of girls in uniforms. I kept up his pace. "I'm sorry. If there's anything you need. I mean, we don't know each other, but I figured I'd . . . I don't know. If you need anything, I'm here." He chuckled nervously.

"Thanks." I offered a small smile.

"Is he going to be okay?"

"The doctors say so. I think so. He's the strongest person I know."

Even as I said the words, I felt like a liar, and then like a traitor because of it.

"That's good. He was always one of my favorite people to interview." Max smiled. "He was always nice."

"Is."

"Uh, yeah, but I meant when he was here," he said, voice lowered as if to not offend.

"Oh. Yeah. Of course." I shook my head. "Have you interviewed a lot of people so far?"

"The basketball team, volleyball team, soccer team, and lacrosse. I still need hockey and swim."

"And you're going to cover every single sport in one edition?"

"No." He chuckled. "I'm going to do a page of quotes, so whatever stands out, I'll put on that page."

"Oh. Like a high school yearbook?"

"Like that but not corny."

"If you say so."

He laughed. "How 'bout I show it to you and if it's corny you let me know?"

"Okay." I wanted to ask him about Lana, but hesitated. Was that a weird thing to bring up when you first met someone? Deciding I didn't care, I brought it up anyway. "Did you know Lana Ly?"

"Yeah." He eyed me strangely. "She worked at the paper."

"Don't you think it's weird that nobody is looking for her?" I asked. "The media is saying she ran away. Isn't that weird?"

"The media is doing more for her than they've done for the girls who have disappeared in the past."

"What girls?"

"Are you sure you want to hear about this? I mean, with your brother being . . . you know," he said, "The last thing you need is something else to worry about."

"I want to hear about it." If nothing else, it would help take my mind off my brother.

"One girl has disappeared each year since the beginning of the founding of this university. They stopped reporting on it because, well, a lot of them have been found. Some of them have managed to get out of the woods, and others have been found in states across the country." He lowered his voice as we passed a group of people. "Those are the ones who have been found alive. The ones presumed dead haven't been found."

"One girl a year?" I whisper-shouted. "That's impossible."

"It's not. Look it up. Go to the archive newspapers in the library. The local paper usually hides them in page two or three. Never page one."

"But these girls, wouldn't their families be looking? Wouldn't there be press conferences or something?"

"Most of them are foreign students. Those are the ones targeted. People from out of the country."

"Lana wasn't a foreign student."

He shrugged. "Well, the media is reporting about her. They have a knack for pretty blonde girls."

"Lana is Vietnamese."

"A pretty Vietnamese girl, then," he said. "They switched it up for once."

"One a year doesn't make any sense. Even a serial killer acts with more frequency than that."

"In the last thirty years, we've had a total of sixty missing girls. That's two a year."

"So, more than one."

"Right. And not all of them have been foreign."

"Yet nobody has an idea who's behind it?"

"A lot of us have an idea. I mean, you go on Reddit and it's full of ideas."

"Well, who do they think is responsible?" I pressed. "You can't give me all of this information and then withhold the important parts."

"Thing is, it's just an idea. We could be way off base."

"Tell me anyway." I got closer. We stopped walking.

"I think the secret societies are using them as sacrifices."

My jaw dropped. I let out a laugh. "Yeah right."

"There's a secret society that formed after the first girl went missing, back in 1910. It is said that every year they conduct their own investigation and try to look for the missing."

"How do you know this, if it's a secret?"

"The girls who are found talk. They say it was a group of people in cloaks who helped them to safety, but they won't say anything beyond that. Gratitude buys their silence."

"So they're not sacrificing them."

"Not all of them return." He shot me a look.

"That doesn't prove anything."

"Like I said, it's a theory." He shrugs.

"So what's your theory on Lana?"

"I don't have a theory on her. I just hope she doesn't end up being one of the disappeared girls." He shot me a grave look. "The ones that are gone longer than a year, never come back."

Jesus. I let out a breath. In an effort to calm down, I unclipped the camera cover and brought it up to my face, taking photos of the trees and flowers around us to test it out and make sure I'd be ready to shoot whoever Max was interviewing next. When I lowered it and looked around again, I caught sight of Logan and his friends. They seriously looked like greasers from *Grease*, not because of the way they were dressed, but because it was the vibe they gave out. I nudged Max.

"Do you think those guys are part of a secret society?"

"There's no telling."

"A friend of mine told me they were in a secret society."

"I don't think they'd have the time for everything that goes into it." He glanced over at the group again. "They're definitely popular though. Big men on campus. Fitz especially. He has this cult following that started in high school. All of his fans show up at the games, do a big racket. It's kind of fun to witness."

"Fitz meaning Logan?"

"Well, yeah." He chuckled. "Not sure he'd answer to anything other than Fitz though."

"Interesting." I looked at Max.

"You must have experienced the Fitz craze firsthand when your brother played here."

"I can't say that I have." I smiled. "I only went to a game when he was a freshman and I was still living at home. Logan wouldn't have been here then."

"Well, I guess you'll be experiencing it soon enough. Season starts soon."

I looked over again and found Logan staring at me.

"What's his deal anyway?" I asked Max. "If he's so coveted, why does he look so lonely?"

"You're probably the first person to ever say that," he said. "Fitz is never alone and is definitely far from lonely."

I looked back at Logan with that thought in mind. He was still staring at me. I didn't care how many people he had around him, he definitely looked lonely. I knew the look because it was the same one I'd walked around wearing for as long as I could remember and I was definitely never alone. Max walked in their direction.

"Hey, guys, mind doing a quick interview for the paper?"

"Sure, but only if your pretty friend asks the questions." One of them broke away from the group and walked over to us.

It was the one who looked like Thor, but with dark hair. He had defined features that made him looked like a rugged Viking, even without a beard. Another followed with a chuckle. He also had hair down to his shoulders, but he was dirty blond. They both looked like perfect California surfers. I remembered seeing them in my parent's backyard, both wearing dark suits, looking like they were guarding secrets as they stood in the shadows. I should have gone up to them then, but Travis made it impossible.

"I wouldn't know what to ask." I waved the camera. "But I'll take your picture."

"That's a start." He grinned, putting a hand out for me to shake. "I'm Nolan."

"Amelia, but you can call me Mae."

"Beautiful name for a beautiful girl."

"Thanks." I dropped my hand.

"Sure you don't want to get one question in?"

"About hockey?"

His gaze darkened. "About anything."

"Dude." Logan stepped forward, putting a hand on Nolan's shoulder. "Let them do their job so we can go."

My eyes jumped between the two of them. There were a lot of questions I wanted to ask them, starting with my brother's accident, but that wouldn't have been appropriate for this setting.

"About hockey," Nolan said, shrugging Logan's hand off his shoulder.

"Well, I don't know a lick about hockey and whatever question I ask would sound ridiculous."

"Maybe you should check out our games."

"Apparently, it's part of my job."

Someone in their group of friends scoffed behind him. I didn't even bother to see whom but I wouldn't have been surprised if it was Logan himself.

"Are you excited to get back on the ice?" Max asked, clicking the recorder.

"Sure. I'm always excited. We have a good squad again this year. It'll be fun to bring the championship back."

"Do you think losing last year will make you work ten times harder to get it back?"

"Fuck yeah," he said. "But it doesn't matter. We're ready to bring that trophy home this year."

The rest of the guys cheered behind him, throwing their fists in the air. I snapped some pictures and looked at the little window where it appeared. It looked more like we were at a frat house than a sports mixer, but it would have to do. Even Logan had his fist up and was smiling in the photo.

"Thanks for your time," Max said, clicking the stop button.

"There's a party tonight, if you want to come by. Eleven o'clock, Senior Hall."

"Maybe," Max said.

"I was talking to Mae," Nolan said, "But you can come too, Max."

"I already have a party I'm going to, but thanks."

"This one will be better." He winked as he walked away. "Take good pictures of my ass. It'll sell more papers."

"Hey, Mae. You wanna grab dinner tomorrow night?" Max was putting his recorder in his backpack. "I mean an early dinner. Around seven?"

"Um, I guess so." I smiled.

I wasn't in the mood to party or have dinner with anyone, but if doing those things was going to get me answers about this society and Lana, I'd do them. I dressed for the party in the most casual thing I could find—black skinny jeans, black vans, and a white crop top. No designer anything. Well, except for my jeans and the crop top, but nobody would know that. I was going to blend in with the crowd tonight. After I applied my make-up and finished brushing my hair, I opened up my brother's computer and searched Google for Morse code. I plugged in the dots and dashes, just as I wrote them down.

The Lab

What? That didn't even make any sense. What lab? I opened up a separate tab and searched "the lab". A ton of things came up, from children schools to makeup schools. None of it made any sense. The lab. Why would he waste precious seconds on that? Was he trying to make me laugh? I shook the thought away and Googled *Logan Fitz*. My screen instantly filled with Logan. *Logan Fitzgerald turns down NHL contract, stays in school.* I clicked on the article, where Stephen A. Smith called him nothing short of an idiot for turning down millions in order to go to school and risk getting hurt and not being able to get paid millions. I kept clicking.

His social media profiles were all set to private, but I was able to find a ton of pictures of him from a Toronto newspaper. Apparently, he was the Lebron James of hockey, his career followed all through high school and being scouted by NHL teams ever since his blades hit the ice freshman year. I wondered if Stephen A. Smith was right. Why had Logan bothered with college at all? What was the point of a degree if you were guaranteed to make millions?

According to his profile on the school website, his full name was *Logan Moriarty Fitzgerald*. I laughed, assuming one of his parents must have been a Sherlock Holmes fan. Why would they name their kid after the villain? It definitely fit though. He had a mysterious aura about him that matched his namesake. Even in his official photograph, he didn't smile.

He was six foot four, two hundred and twenty pounds. I always found it fascinating that athletes gave away their weights and heights so openly. I zoomed in on his picture. His dark hair was longer than he wore it now, his green eyes deep, even there, like they encompassed an entire forest. There was nothing else to see, but on a whim, I decided to go to my brother's Instagram account and look around. There was a picture of him and Logan that I'd apparently liked last December. I vaguely re-membered seeing the picture but hadn't really paid attention to it. I liked anything Lincoln posted out of solidarity. I kept star-ing at the picture. They were both smiling as they joked around about something. It was obvious there was a friendship there. I wondered why he'd never mentioned him in the past. Unless their friendship had turned awry.

I went down a rabbit hole until I landed on an old head-line: *Patrick Fitzgerald accused of raping woman. Former hockey star turned businessman accused of statutory rape. Businessman, Patrick Fitzgerald, acquitted of rape charges.* There was a knot in the pit of my stomach as I clicked on his picture. Evidentially, Patrick was Logan's older brother, older by ten years, according to the news report. I wondered if this was the guy who was friends with my older brother George. He was handsome. The kind of handsome that made women in juries not convict because they didn't believe a person who looked that good had to take some-thing without permission. It was a slippery slope, of course, because anybody with that kind of money and power would be able to take something without permission and get away with it. I wondered what Logan's take on it was, and why I even cared to hear it. It was that thought that made me shut down the com-puter and head to the party.

CHAPTER EIGHT

I WAS HOLDING A RED PLASTIC CUP IN MY HAND AS I STOOD IN THE corner of the party watching everyone else get piss drunk. Maybe Nolan had been right. Maybe I should have gone to their party instead of this one. At least there, I would've gotten answers.

"You need to turn that frown upside down," Celia said as she walked over and stood beside me. "Come on, Quentin's friend keeps asking about you. He's hot, he thinks you're hot, it'll be a match made in double date heaven."

"No thanks." I laughed, sipping my lukewarm beer. "I'm just not in the mood. Besides, I just got out of a relationship with a basketball player. The last thing I need is to get in another."

The door opened wide and a shirtless guy walked through with his hands thrown in the air as he screamed, "Party's here."

It was one of the hockey guys who was always with Logan. My heart skipped. I stood a little taller. Was he here too?

"Oh. I see. You want to rebound with a hockey player." Celia laughed at the warning look I shot her. "Hey, I'm not judging. They're definitely wild."

"I need another drink."

She held up a black flask. "On it."

I took a swig and coughed. "This tastes like something a pirate would drink."

"That's because it's whiskey."

"Why is it hot?" I took another swig.

"Take three more and you won't care what temperature it is."

I took one more and handed it back. "I think I'm good."

She took one. "Well, I have to go check on Q. You gonna be okay here?"

"Yep." I shook the red plastic cup and leaned back against the wall.

When she walked away, the door opened again, and Nolan walked in, also shirtless, also throwing his hands up screaming about partying. What in the world were they on? I didn't know but I couldn't help but laugh. Three girls trailed behind him, a blonde, a brunette, and a redhead. He seemed to have all bases covered. They were all laughing at him as they walked toward the kitchen. The third guy they were always with walked in, this one with a t-shirt on that pressed against his muscles, and no screaming. He kind of looked around quickly and headed in the same direction as the others. Lastly, Logan walked in. My heart jumped into my ears. He was wearing a loose black t-shirt and jeans. His gaze did a sweep of the room, landing on me momentarily. Two girls walked in right behind him, both with long brown hair, like mine. Both with tanned skin, like mine. He tore his gaze away as one of the girls jumped on his back with a laugh. He didn't smile, not even as he walked over to the kitchen and set her down on the counter before walking away, without further acknowledging her.

Any idea of asking questions about my brother went out the window as I watched Nolan make out with two of the girls he arrived with, at the same time. It was something I'd only ever seen in illicit videos, but I guess it was a thing. I couldn't imagine him handling three girls at once. My gaze shifted to Logan,

who was talking to the other guy in their group with a shi̇.
on, by the keg. The two girls he'd come here with went over
to them. Something akin to jealousy bloomed inside me and I
forced myself to look away. Pushing off the wall, I decided to
leave. I walked outside and emptied the beer on the lawn before
tossing the cup into the trashcan on the side of the house.

"Just when I thought I couldn't like you less, you go and
waste alcohol."

I jumped at the voice beside me and turned to see Logan
standing beside me. My brain struggled to come up with a
comeback for what he said, but I kept tripping on it. *He couldn't
like me less?* I hadn't even given him a reason not to like me. I
turned and kept walking. At the sound of footsteps behind me,
my heart began to race. I looked over my shoulder.

"If you dislike me so much, why are you following me?"

"I'm not." He scowled. "I'm walking home."

"Okay, well, walk beside me and not behind me like a
creep."

He looked amused as he shrugged. "Okay."

We started walking side by side. He was much taller than
me, even in the three-inch wedges I wore. We walked in complete silence for two desolate blocks. When we reached the
stoplight, there was a group of drunk people who instantly lit
up and started shouting and yelping when they saw Logan.

"We're just on our way to Q's party, why'd you leave?" one
of the guys asked.

Logan shrugged. "Got bored."

"Bored?" One of the girls stepped forward, placing a hand
against his chest. "I'll make sure you're not bored if you go back
with us."

"Or we can meet you at the pool in your apartment building again," the other girl suggested.

I glanced away, focusing on the streetlight, which was still not changing to give us the walking signal.

"Seriously, Fitz," the first girl said.

The scene was making me restless. Worse, it was making me jealous and even worse, it was making me wonder if this was what Travis was up to in North Carolina. Late nights with an unattainable jock will do that, I guess. The second the light flashed for us to walk, I took off, not bothering to tell him I was going ahead without him. It wasn't like this was a thing, or he was walking me home or anything. I heard the voices behind me grow louder but didn't turn to see what the commotion was about. I had one goal in mind, and that was to get back to my place, shut the door, and go to bed. At the sound of fast-paced footsteps behind me, I glanced over my shoulder and caught Logan jogging toward me. By this point, I was far enough from where I'd left him, but he looked completely at ease and not out of breath at all with his slow jog.

"You call me rude, but you walked away without so much as a goodbye."

"I was bored of the whole *let's see who can convince Logan to party with us or fuck us* bit." I stopped walking and faced him. "Where's your harem of groupies anyway?"

"Why does it matter?"

"I don't know. You're over here lecturing me on being rude, but you got to the party with two girls and left with none."

"They'll survive."

"Why'd you leave?"

"I got bored."

"Bored," I repeated. "Because I'm curious, what part were you bored of? The harem or the rambunctious friends you were hanging out with?"

"Both." His eyes were still twinkling, still amused.

"Interesting," I said. "I find it interesting that you left all of that boredom behind to come after me, especially after you said you don't like me."

"Does that bother you?"

"Does what bother me? That you said it or that you meant it?"

"Both."

"No." I grit my teeth together. "I could care less."

"Really?" He raised an eyebrow. "Because you look a little upset to me."

"You obviously don't know anything about me. I always look upset."

He threw his head back in laughter, and it caught me so off guard that all I could do was stare at his thick neck and the way his Adam's apple bobbed with his amusement. When he was done laughing, he pointed those piercing green eyes at me and grinned.

"You're funny."

"Thanks, I guess. Though I'm not exactly signing up for a position as your personal comedian and you already made it very clear that you don't like me, so I don't know why it matters."

"Maybe I was wrong about you."

"You probably weren't." I started walking again.

"Why are you so serious all the time?" At his question, I lifted my gaze to his briefly. "Your brothers are all so—"

"Outgoing? Fun? Athletic?"

"Yeah."

"I guess we were raised differently."

"How's that?"

"I don't know you well enough to talk to you about that."

"I guess you're not so different after all." He squinted at me momentarily before looking straight ahead.

"What do you mean?"

"You all act like you have more skeletons in your closet than anyone else."

"Excuse me, but I have exactly zero skeletons in my closet. In case you've forgotten, I'm kind of going through a lot right now." I raised an eyebrow at him. "Besides, I don't like talking to people I don't know about my life."

"Why?"

"Do you tell everyone you know about your life?"

"If they ask nicely." He winked.

My face heated. "Stop winking at me."

He chuckled again. I bit my lip and looked away. Why did he have to be so damn handsome?

"Why are you suddenly so interested in me anyway?"

"Suddenly?" His eyes twinkled. "I was talking to you at the bar the other night."

"Right. Before you went and got into that fight." I looked down at his hands. His knuckles were no longer wrapped in anything, but they still looked chaffed. "This is me." I pointed at the front door and froze, panicking when Logan walked to the door and held it open for me. "I'm not inviting you in."

"You're not?"

"No. Did you walk me home because you thought I was going to sleep with you?"

"I already told you, I'm not walking you home." He shot me a look. "Did you think I would think you were going to sleep with me? Even after declaring to yourself and the world a hundred times that I don't like you?"

"Well, you were the one who said you didn't like me."

"And you were the one who repeated it the entire walk over."

"Whatever." I crossed my arms against the cool air of the lobby and hoped the bellman wouldn't be alerted by our argument. The last thing I needed was my parents getting a full report on what was happening in their building. "I'm not inviting you in."

"Can't you just thank me for opening the door for you?"

"Oh." I stepped forward, brushing past him, blushing furiously again because *what the heck was wrong with me when I was around this guy?* "Thanks for opening the door for me."

"And for walking you home."

"You just said you weren't walking me home."

"Thank me anyway."

I huffed out a breath, rolling my eyes. "You're seriously confusing me with your boring harem."

"Boring harem." He was clearly trying not to smile. "I definitely don't think you can be part of that harem."

"You know, if you're just going to insult me all night, I think this conversation needs to be over." I lifted my chin up to him. He walked inside and let the door close behind him. "What are you doing? Why aren't you leaving?"

"I've decided to walk you home after all."

"Well, I'm home." I waved a hand around the lobby.

He exhaled. "To your door, Amelia."

My heart skipped. Stupid, idiotic instrument. Nobody ever called me Amelia. As soon as they heard my name, everyone tried to shorten it, which was why I made it easy for them by introducing myself as *Amelia, but you can call me Mae,* most of the time. I thought about it for a moment. What could really go wrong if he walked me to my door? I reminded myself: black belt, some self-defense, my father owned the building, and Gary the security guard would most certainly be watching the cameras. Fuck it.

"Fine." I turned toward the elevator. Logan followed.

We rode up to my floor in silence. Awkward silence.

"You're not much of a talker," he said.

"Depends on who you ask. My ex said I never shut the fuck up."

His face darkened. "Why would he say that?"

"Because I never shut the fuck up." I cracked a smile.

"You should smile more often."

"Why? You'd like me if I smiled?"

His mouth twitched. "You're really stuck on that."

"Want me to be honest? I think I feel a little offended by it."

"Because normally men throw themselves all over you."

"Not all of them." I held his gaze. "Obviously."

Neither of us spoke, but the amusement in his eyes was gone, replaced by something darker, something that tugged me and spread heat inside me. He was looking at me like someone who wanted to kiss me, and against my better judgment, I would totally let him. When the elevator doors opened and chimed, neither one of us moved. I felt like he was rooting me in place with some spell cast from his eyes. The elevator doors started to close, and Logan put out his arm to stop it. He was still looking at me, having this never-ending staring contest that only had one ending, an animalistic make-out session followed by hours of fucking.

My core clenched at the possibility of the second option. I hadn't kissed a guy that wasn't Travis in well over two years. I wouldn't even know how to do it, but I wanted to so badly right now. The elevator started alarming us to either get out or stay in, I broke away from his gaze and walked out. He followed.

"Where do you live anyway?" I asked, licking my lips as I searched for my keys in my crossbody.

"Down the hall."

"Down this hall?" I stopped walking. My gaze followed as he pointed to the apartment opposite of mine, way down the hall. I looked at him. "I haven't seen you here before."

"That just means that you don't pay attention to your surroundings nearly as much as you should."

"Have you seen me?"

"It feels like I see you everywhere."

"I'm not sure what to make of that statement," I said absent-mindedly as something caught my eye. "What is that?"

There was something on the floor in front of my door. It looked like a flower. I swung the key ring around my finger as we walked in that direction, my eyes on the white flower—a gardenia? My mother was obsessed with them and always had them planted in our house. Beneath it, a white envelope with my name written in script on it. Before I could bend down to pick it up, Logan did it for me.

"Secret admirer?"

Nobody knew I lived here, only Celia. Logan handed me the flower and envelope. It was really thin, so thin that it could very well be empty. I stared at my name on it a moment longer and looked up at Logan.

"It's probably from my parents." I frowned. "Nobody knows I live here."

He cleared his throat. "How's Lincoln?"

My shoulders slumped. "Still in a coma. I don't know how long they plan to keep him like that."

Logan idled a little. "Well, if you need me I'm in 408."

"I am not going to 408." I looked up at him from the envelope. "Not one of your groupies, remember?"

"How can I forget?" He sort of smiled.

"How come everyone calls you Fitz?" I asked.

"That's my name." He tilted his head slightly. "Logan Fitzgerald."

"Logan Moriarty Fitzgerald." I raised an eyebrow. "I did my research."

"You did, huh? What else did you find out?"

"A lot of random facts, like your weight and height." And things about his brother that I didn't want to bring up right now. I licked my lips. "You tell everyone to call you Fitz."

"You tell everyone to call you Mae."

"You can call me Mae if you want to."

"I don't want to."

"Why not?"

"I don't know." He shrugged. "I don't like to follow the herd."

"Hm." I put the key in the hole and turned it, unlocking it before facing him once more. It was so stupid, but I couldn't let this go. "But I introduce myself to everyone as Amelia and give them the option. You introduce yourself as Fitz—period."

"Everyone except for you." His eyes danced as he said that. He knew where I was going with this. It wasn't like I wasn't being obvious.

"Why is that?"

"I don't know yet."

He looked at me for what felt like an eternity. I was sure he was going to lean in and kiss me. His large hand reached out. I held my breath as it neared my face, but instead of touching me, he tugged on a strand of hair that had loosened from the ponytail I'd tied up during our walk home.

"Good night, Amelia." He dropped his hand and walked away, leaving my heart in my throat as I watched his broad shoulders retreat to the other end of the hall.

When he got to his door, he unlocked it and glanced over his shoulder. I swear he smiled at me before he went inside and I felt a wave of disappointment at the fact that he hadn't run back over here. At the fact that he hadn't kissed me. I shook all of my crazy emotions away and opened the envelope as I walked inside and shut the door. I peeked inside to see a thick, black card inside. Plucking it out, I saw that one side was plain black and said YOU'VE BEEN SUMMONED. The other had a gold octopus with an address, 900 Stewart Avenue. 12am.

I looked at the time. It was well past twelve-am. Something told me this was extremely secretive. Could it be one of the societies? Which one? The one that kidnapped girls and potentially sacrificed them? A shiver rolled through me at the thought. I set the card down on the counter, showered and changed into my pajamas and went back to the guest room to open the other box.

Once I took the tape off, I frowned at the sight of a pink blanket, Gucci slides that were probably my size, definitely not Lincoln's. I kept taking things out until I reached the bottom, where there were credit cards. No, a license and school ID. I pulled them both out of the box and sat there, stunned, as I held Lana's identification in my hands. Why the hell did Lincoln have any of this stuff? And how'd it get here?

CHAPTER NINE

I TOSSED AND TURNED ALL NIGHT BEFORE GIVING UP, PUSHING MY sheets off, and rushing downstairs. If nothing else, I needed to know who brought those boxes. There were cameras everywhere in this building and I knew my father saved footage. Well, at least according to the conversation I overheard him having with Lana's parents that night. He could've been lying. Dad wasn't beyond that. When I reached the lobby, Gary's head snapped up from behind the desk.

"You're up early."

"Or late."

"Miss Bastón, you need your rest," he said, frowning. "Your father—"

"Yes, I know, wouldn't approve. I need something important. Do you have footage of last week?"

"Um . . . "

"I just want to see something. Please, Gary. It's important. I only need to see footage of my floor, nothing else."

"I can do that." He stood up and disappeared into the office behind him. I walked around the desk and sat down in one of the chairs. He set a USB drive on the table when he came back. "This is last week. I've been dividing them by week and saving them individually as per Mr. Bastón's orders. After the whole thing happened with Ms. Ly, we figured it was best to have it all on file."

"Lana didn't live here," I said, frowning up at him.

"She might as well have, with how often she was here."

"Doing what?"

"Visiting someone would be my guess. A lot of students live here, in case you haven't noticed."

"I've noticed."

I thought of Logan down the hall from me. I hadn't even seen him or known he lived here until last night. Maybe I should be paying closer attention to people. I inserted the USB into the drive and set it on speed. If I saw something I needed, I'd pause and rewind. I yawned on day two of footage. Rubbed my eyes on day three. Day four and five were nonconsequential. Then, I saw Logan walking out of the elevator. I stopped it there and played it on regular speed. He was with a girl. I rolled my eyes. What else was new? I hadn't seen her before. She had short curly hair and fair skin and they looked like they were arguing. I waited on bated breath, fully expecting this to turn into yet another make-out session. Instead, she walked back into the elevator and he stomped toward his apartment. Odd.

I kept fast-forwarding. Shortly after, the door to the emergency exit by my apartment opened and two people wearing black cloaks walked out. I gasped, holding my hand over my rapidly beating heart. They were both carrying one box each. Boxes that clearly said Lincoln on them. Boxes that I was positive they were about to drop off by the door. One of them took a key out and unlocked my door. They both walked back out not even five seconds later, still cloaked, but with no boxes.

"Can I get footage for this same day and time in the lobby?" I asked Gary.

"Sure, let me check."

He disappeared and reappeared again quickly, with another USB drive. He set that one beside me. I fast forwarded through the entire thing until I got to that date and time and waited. People were in and out, in and out, none wearing cloaks. What the hell? I searched for someone I would recognize, but that didn't work either. I saw the girl with the short curly hair that had been arguing with Logan upstairs, but she was dressed normally, in jeans and a sweater. No cloak. I sighed, leaning back in the seat and rubbing my face.

"I need a locksmith to come and change the locks to my apartment," I told Gary.

"Of course. I'm on it," he said. "Anything else?"

"No."

"Will you be up there? You need to get some rest, Miss. Bastón. You have bags under your eyes."

"I know. I know." I shut my eyes.

I was so incredibly tired. I thought of Logan, who had offered if I needed anything and said I could go to his apartment. Would it be weird if I went there and just slept? Maybe. I was doing it anyway. I stood, thanked Gary, and headed back up. When I got to my floor, I knocked on Logan's door, softly at first, and then louder. He opened, shirtless, with a toothbrush sticking out of his mouth. He frowned.

"Amelia?" he said around the toothbrush.

It was the first time he'd ever sounded ridiculous. He looked ridiculous, albeit hot as fuck, with his hair sticking up everywhere and those grey sweatpants that clung low on his hips.

"I'm tired. I need a bed. Or a couch. Or the floor. I don't care," I said. He jogged over to the kitchen sink and spit, turning on the water. I made a face as I walked in. "That is disgusting."

"What's wrong with your bed, or couch, or floor?"

"It's been compromised. I'm having a locksmith change the locks but I can't keep my eyes open. I feel like I'm going to—"

"My bed is empty," he said, walking over to his bedroom.

We had a similar layout, but my view was better, and I had two bedrooms, where he only had one. Same kitchen and living room though. His walls were dark gray, where mine were white. He had posters on the walls of different movies. His bedroom walls were bare, except for a shelf that seemed to go across the entire room and was filled with trophies and medals. He must have brought every single momentum they'd given him since birth. I must have said that aloud, because he chuckled.

"It keeps me working harder."

"Oh. Wow." I blinked hard, yawning. "It would make me want to quit."

He chuckled again. "There's the bed. Obviously. Don't worry, I don't do dirty things on it, so you're safe."

"What?" I frowned, then blinked fast. "Oh. Oh. I hadn't even considered that."

"It's a germ-free zone. Well, my germs are on it, but you'll have to live with that."

"Sure." I waved him off as I kicked off my slides and climbed into bed. "Holy crap this is comfortable."

"Thanks."

"Really comfortable." I snuggled into the pillow, pulling the sheets tighter to my chin. "It smells like you."

"I'm going to the gym," he said. "I'll be back in an hour and a half. You'll be fine?"

"I'll be sleeping." I yawned again. "Thanks, Logan."

"Any time, Amelia."

With that, I shut my eyes and fell asleep.

CHAPTER TEN

LOGAN

"I CAN'T JUST KEEP HER IN THE DARK ABOUT HER OWN BROTHER." I lift the bar up and set it on the stand.

"So don't." Nolan wipes the sweat off his face, standing over me as he spots me. "Just tell her."

"That's against the rules, asshole. I'm not forfeiting my money or future for her. I'm just saying, I feel kind of bad."

"Since when do you feel bad? You treat girls like they're disposable."

I sat up quickly, glaring at him. "I don't treat anyone like they're disposable."

"Mandy was crying the other night because you didn't invite her back to your place."

"Please." I rolled my eyes. "Not fucking someone hardly constitutes as treating them like they're disposable."

"Do you like her?" He started working on biceps with the free weights. "Mae, I mean."

"I think she's interesting."

"Since when do you think girls you aren't fucking are interesting?"

"I've never thought any of the ones I fucked were interesting, otherwise, I would be doing more than just fucking them."

"You're an asshole." He chuckled.

I shrugged, going back to the bench press.

"So you think she's interesting," he said, setting down his weights and coming back over to where I was to spot me again. "You know she has a boyfriend, right?"

"When have I ever let that stop me?"

"You're crazy, bro." He shook his head. "He's a big guy."

"And I'm not?"

"I don't know. I see you going slow on these weights today. Two-thirty? You can do better than that."

"You're an asshole." I chuckled, shaking my head as he adjusted the plates. "You need to work on your motivational speeches."

"We'll have a meeting about it. Maybe it's time," he said once I started lifting again.

"Right." I set the bar on the stand again. "I'm leaving after this rep."

"What the hell? You just got here."

"I have things to do today."

"Like not train to kick Mae's boyfriend's ass?"

I flashed him the finger. The mention of her boyfriend was annoying me. I had seen her with him though, sitting by the pool of her parent's house. I couldn't just ignore his existence. Or maybe I could. I guess it all came down to just how interesting I found her and how much I was willing to put up with.

CHAPTER ELEVEN

AMELIA

I AWOKE TO THE SOUND OF MY PHONE VIBRATING WITH TEXT MESSAGES coming in, and sat up in a strange bed. Then I remembered. I was in Logan's bed. In Logan's apartment. I'd been seriously delirious when I decided to walk over here and make myself at home like we were buddies. Maybe I should leave before he got back. Yeah. I should. I stretched as I made my way out of bed and inhaled. The entire room smelled like him—clean soap and pine tree. I shut my eyes. Like Christmas. I picked up my phone and looked at it. Five text messages—one from my mother, one from Hailey, one from Celia, and two from an unknown number.

Mom: Everything is fine. The same. Love you.

Hailey: Hey, come by the coffee shop! Free coffee and gossip!

Celia: I didn't see you leave last night. You okay?

Unknown number: Don't you want to know what happened to Lana?

Unknown number: To your brother? She's out there.

My heart was in my throat as I called the number back. Again, it said the number was disconnected. What the hell? I stood up, slid my feet back into my sandals, and walked out of the room, heading to the front door. I pulled it open just as Logan was pushing it.

"Hey," he said, then frowned. "What happened?"

"I . . . I need to go. I have to go." I brushed past him, but he grabbed my arm.

"What's wrong? Did something happen?" He looked back into his apartment. "Is someone here? Fuck, Mae, you're shaking."

"I've had a long night. A long day. A long week. A long month," I said quickly. My phone rang in my hand and I jumped, clutching it, but it was Travis's face kissing my cheek that popped up as he called. I seriously needed to change that picture. "I ummm, I should go. Thank you."

"Yeah. You should." Logan's scowl deepened.

I picked up the phone as I walked back to my own apartment.

"Hey, just calling to see how you're doing. I know we said no calls and no texts after the breakup, but I feel like we need to make an exception," Travis said. "How's Lincoln?"

"The same." I sighed as I unlocked and walked into my apartment.

"I'm sorry. What are the doctors saying? Have the seizures stopped?"

"They're waiting one more week before taking him out of the coma just in case, but they've stopped for now." I bit my lip. I could barely stand talking about it, but I was glad for Travis.

"You sound tired, Mae."

"I am tired."

There was a loud knock on my door. I gasped and jumped. "What was that?"

"Someone's at my door. Probably the locksmith."

"Locksmith?" he asked loudly. "Why? Did something happen?"

"No. I just don't know who had this key before. You know Lincoln gets a little crazy when it comes to girls."

"Oh." He chuckled. "Yeah, good point. You don't want any unwanted stalkers."

"Exactly." I walked over and unlocked the door. Gary and

the locksmith were on the other side. "I have to go, Trav. Thanks for calling."

"Of course. I'm here if you need me."

"Thanks." I hung up.

"This will only take a second," the locksmith said.

"Go on with your business, Ms. Bastón," Gary said. "I'll watch him."

"Thanks." I smiled and walked to the guest bedroom, back to the second box with all of Lana's belongings. There was another student ID—Lincoln's, and a black card with his full name on it—Lincoln Bastón. On the back, the words, *You've Been Summoned.* My hand shook as I held it. Those were the same words on the card on my kitchen counter. There was also a black flip phone that had been torn in half, a computer, that I took out. It said, "Property of The Gazette" on it. I sat on the floor and opened it up.

"We're done here, Ms. Bastón," Gary called out.

I stood up and walked over, taking the new keys and thanking them for their help. Gary assured me that Dad had already paid the man as they headed toward the elevator. When I closed my door and locked it, I felt safer than I did last night. Heading back to the computer, I looked at the screen. It needed a passcode. I wondered if she set it or if the newspaper did. I thought about what Gary said, about Lana frequenting the building. Between that and the black card with Lincoln's name on it, I was convinced this had to do with the secret society. I called Max. He answered on the second ring.

"You said Lana was investigating secret societies," I started without preamble.

"Yeah."

There was rustling on the phone line and it took me a second to realize he sounded like he'd just woken up. An apology was at the tip of my tongue, but the anxiety gripping me was louder.

"How often did she hang out with my brother?" I asked. "Do you know?"

"It seemed like she was friends with a lot of athletes. She was taking pictures at the sporting events."

I sat back. "So basically, the same job I currently have?"

"Yep and Ella had told her she could write about student life and she chose to write about the secret societies we'd all heard about."

My grip tightened around my cell phone. So what if we had the same task assigned to us? It didn't mean anything. Not really, anyway.

"Mae?"

"Yeah." I blinked out of my thoughts and cleared my throat. "I'm here."

"Why are you asking all of these questions at this ungodly hour?"

"It's like noon, Max." I pulled the phone from my ear briefly and looked at the time. "It's twelve twenty."

He sighed. "It feels earlier."

"I'll let you get back to sleep. Sorry I woke you up."

"No biggie." He was quiet for a beat. "You know, normally when people wake you up, it's because they're going to invite you to brunch or something."

"I would, but I have a ton of things I need to do," I said. "I'll see you tonight though."

"Yeah."

"Oh. Before I forget," I said. "Does the paper usually provide a laptop?"

"Usually yeah. I mean, unless you have great picture editing programs on yours. Why?"

"I didn't quite catch the password for the one they gave me." I opened the laptop in front of me again. I doubted

Max would find out I never got one from the paper, to begin with.

"Oh. It's *fuck you pay me*. All together and all caps," he snorted a laugh. "The interns in IT thought that would be funny."

I tried the password FUCKYOUPAYME and clicked return. Sure enough, the laptop started up quickly. I held my breath and told Max I had to go as I hung up on him. The laptop had a few folders on it, one which was labeled: SS photos. The other: Hockey. I clicked on SS first. There was a photo of the little black card I'd received and the white gardenia. The next one I clicked was taken outside in a wooded area. The next one was of a waterfall, and lastly, a building on top of the waterfall. Five photos in total. I looked at each of them one more time, making a mental note before pulling out my phone and taking pictures with it as well.

I didn't want to email them to myself and create a paper trail. As it was, I wasn't sure why I had this in my possession, to begin with. I knew I'd have to confront Lincoln about it. The last thing I wanted was to bring my brother down, but there was no way around this. I looked at the hockey photos she'd taken. There were over two hundred pictures, mostly games, practices, and group shots. Some were individual shots—my brother holding his hockey stick, Logan looking straight at the camera with a serious look on his face that showed off his high cheekbones and defined chin, Nolan grinning, and some other guys I didn't know.

There was another folder within this one that was labeled: MY PICS, with two pictures of Lana by herself. One was a selfie in which she wasn't fully smiling at the camera. The other was with a waterfall behind her. She was wearing a pretty white dress with spaghetti straps and a huge smile, her long black hair hanging straight over one shoulder, one hand on her hip and the other flashing a peace sign. She looked gorgeous. She'd always been one of the prettiest girls in high school, and popular—head cheerleader, captain of the debate club, involved in the community, super smart. I wondered how she'd faired here. Was she still just as popular or did she just blend in as one does when the pool stretches as big as it did in college?

After sleuthing for another hour or so, I closed the laptop. I needed to find whatever articles she'd written about the secret societies. I needed to find out what the police had and why this wasn't in their possession, but that would mean that I'd have to come forward and potentially throw my brother under the bus. As far as I knew, he'd never been questioned by the police because he'd gone home so quickly and they didn't find reason to ask him anything, but something was off about all of this. Why would he have so many of her things? Had someone sent this stuff to implicate him? Who was sending me those texts and how had they gotten my number? And if Lana was still out there like they were suggesting, why was nobody searching?

I sat across from Hailey, knee bouncing, as we sipped on our lattes. I hadn't told her everything, but I did tell her about the red cloaked people I saw on the street the other night and the ones wearing black cloaks near my apartment. I left out the part about the card, figuring it probably wasn't a good idea to say anything about it since I was pretty sure I'd show up the next time I got one, especially after seeing my brother's.

"So there *are* two different societies," she mused. "I've only seen the black cloaks."

"They weren't doing anything interesting, just walking, but even that was weird."

"What? The way they were walking?" She inched closer, setting her elbows on her legs.

"No. The fact that no one said anything about it at all." I sipped. "Well, one guy did, but everyone told him he was ridiculous." I set my mug down. "I also heard something else that was interesting."

"What?"

"Someone told me that there's a rumor that these girls disappear because one of the societies sacrifices them."

"Hm. I'm not sure I believe that. Why do so many of them come back? It seems like most of them do, actually. And they all live normal lives." She sipped her latte as she looked at me. Hailey did that a lot, she just looked at people. Or maybe it was me she was busy staring at. I tried not to focus on it, but I found myself constantly looking away to avoid awkwardness. She set the mug down. "Do you think you'd live a normal life if you were kidnapped?"

"If I was kidnapped?" I said rather loudly.

"It's a hypothetical question, Mae. You don't have to freak out about it." She let out a laugh.

"It's not hypothetical when people are actually being kidnapped," I whisper-shouted. "And I'm not sure. Would you live a normal life if you were kidnapped and let go a year later after they did who knows what to you?"

"I think so." She shrugged.

I felt myself make a face, but didn't comment. What was I supposed to say to that?

"How's your brother?" she asked after a beat. "My mom told me she went to a mass for him. I hope he's okay."

"He'll be fine. He's just . . . well, he's in a medically induced coma now. He was having a lot of seizures."

"Oof. Because of drugs?"

"No." I frowned. "My brother doesn't do drugs."

"What were the seizures caused by?"

Drugs. *Shit.* An insane amount of drugs had been found in his system when he died. My chest squeezed when I thought about that. Lincoln had actually died and been brought back. And it had been drugs. But he'd said he hadn't meant to overdose. He hadn't meant to kill himself. Well, he shook his head no. Still. *Drugs.*

"I'm not sure." I set my mug down and looked at my phone. "I have to go. I'm going to dinner with someone and I don't want to be late."

"Oh, a date?" She stood up as I did.

"Not a date, no. I'm going to dinner with a friend."

"A friend?" She wagged her eyebrows. "A hockey player friend?"

"What? No." I frowned. Did she know about Logan? Not that there was anything to know about Logan, but still. "Why would it be a hockey player?"

"I'm just asking." She shrugged. "Anyway, let's do this again soon."

"Sure."

"And stay away from the cloaks!"

CHAPTER TWELVE

I WAS STANDING OUTSIDE, WAITING FOR MAX, AND FREEZING MY ASS off. I had the idea of leaving my jacket open, but there was no use. I should've grabbed a scarf before walking out of my room. I looked up to see Max walking over to me, wearing a suit.

"You look amazing." He whistled.

"Thanks." I made a show of checking him out. "You don't look half bad yourself." He chuckled, cheeks reddening. I could tell Max wasn't used to attention, and as much as I didn't mind paying him a compliment, I didn't want him to take it the wrong way, so I was quick to add, "Just so we're clear, this isn't a date."

"Trust me, I never thought it was." He smiled.

"So, where are we going?"

"This way." He nodded as he started walking. I followed, grateful I'd opted for wedges and not stilettos. "I was able to score a reservation at a new restaurant that opened a couple of weeks ago."

"I hope you didn't go through the trouble on my account. I would've been fine at any pub."

"Trust me, this is me selfishly using this outing as a reason to go. They only take reservations for two people at a time and I can't really pick one friend over another."

"Ah, so you're using me. Got it." I winked.

"Not using, just . . . " He blushed again. "I mean, the place looks amazing and—"

"Max." I shot him a look. He clamped his mouth shut. "I'm cool with it. Thanks for picking me up, by the way. Do you live nearby?"

"A few blocks. I can't afford your block. I think Nolan lives in your building. Or maybe it's the building next to yours."

"Hm. I haven't seen him around."

"Some of the junior and senior players live on your block."

"Yeah, I heard about that." I looked over my shoulder as if they were all going to magically appear behind us. We were at a streetlight, waiting for the crosswalk signal to change, when I spotted a busy restaurant across the street.

"Is that the place?"

"Yeah. It looks nice, right?"

"It looks crowded," I said. "But yeah, nice. I don't think I noticed it when I walked by it before."

"Rumor has it, Fitz's brother owns it."

"Patrick? That's his only brother, right?"

"Yup."

"Why's it a rumor? About his brother owning the place? Either he owns it, or he doesn't."

"I guess he was worried about how opening this place would go over after the legal issues he had."

"So, who do people think owns it?"

"Private investors."

"Hm. Do you think he did what they said he did? Patrick Fitzgerald, I mean."

"I mean, I don't discredit anything like that. When you have the entire world in the palm of your hands, it's difficult to say what you wouldn't be able to get away with."

"That's disturbing but true." I nodded at that. "Still, I'm surprised he'd keep his name out of this restaurant entirely."

"I can't imagine he'd care whether his name was on it or not." He raised an eyebrow as he pulled the door open for me. I thanked him as I walked through. It was just as crowded in here as it was outside. "I'd venture to say it's going pretty damn well for him."

I took my coat off and checked it in the coatroom while Max walked up to the hostess and gave her his name. I busied myself looking around as I walked back to the front. On a table in the waiting area was a bowl of black matches with the restaurant name on it, and on the back, a tiny gold octopus with the numbers 8888. I picked one up and dropped it back down, letting it bounce off the other boxes.

"You're too beautiful to be kept waiting." The voice, low and near my ear, stinking of whiskey, startled me.

I jumped and turned around to face him, his scent flooding my senses, his close proximity causing me to inhale sharply. I braced myself, but it was no use. No point in denying that he affected me, whether I wanted him to or not. The icy look in his eyes made me take a step back, then another, until my back was pressed up against the wall and I was reminded of the saying *between a rock and a hard place.*

"That's the first nice thing you've ever said to me."

"Glad you're keeping track."

"I'm really not."

"Would you like to join me?" He grinned, one side of his mouth curling slyly.

"Are you here by yourself?"

His grin widened. He took a step back and I got a clear view of our surroundings—the three women standing behind him, all watching me curiously. They looked exotic, long dark hair that looked a lot like mine, and near-perfect bodies, as showcased by the tight, revealing clothes they wore. Under any other circumstance, I would see them at the gym or walking in the street and think nothing of them, but knowing they were here with Logan annoyed me.

I met his eyes, tilting my chin up. "I have no desire to be part of your harem."

He was silent for a beat. "Suit yourself, if you want to live like a peasant."

"Have fun pretending you're royalty," I said as he turned around. "Let me know if it makes you any less lonely."

He didn't face me so I couldn't see his reaction, but I knew I'd hit a sore spot. Max approached me as I watched Logan and his women walk to their table—right up front by the entrance, where everyone would surely see him.

"That looked intense," Max said.

I shrugged, noncommittal. By the time we were shown to our table, I was starving. We followed behind the perky hostess and were seated right beside Logan. *Of course.* That would be my luck. The tables in this place were set in a way that it was as if you were having dinner with the entire restaurant—tiny tables with such a small separation between them that they seemed more like a giant table that sat forty people at once. Max stood back as if he preferred the lone seat on the other side. I stood beside him because I did *not* want to share the booth with Logan. Logan was oblivious because he was too busy leaning into the girl beside him to look up and realize I was standing there. I swore under my breath, blood simmering, as I stepped forward and sat in the booth. I bumped him with my purse as I sat down. At least I had a shield between us, albeit a small one.

"You were finally seated," he said.

Ignoring him, I picked up my oversized menu and focused on it. He was being a jerk tonight. He'd been so nice this morning, letting me sleep in his bed, where he supposedly had no germs. Looking at the three girls he was with I assumed that was highly doubtful. I shook that thought away and focused on the words in front of me—ham croquettes sounded good. *Sangria!* I could totally go for a sangria right now.

"I know two things I want." I set down the menu and looked at Max, across from me. "Do you know what you want?"

"I know what I want," Logan said beside me. I turned my head toward him. It was a mistake. Hazy, lustful eyes met mine, making my stomach flip flop.

"I didn't ask you."

"You might be interested in hearing it though." He scooted over a little. My hand shot to my purse, keeping it upright. My shield.

"Why are you talking to me?" I gripped my purse. "You have three beautiful women at your table."

"But you're in this one."

"Logan." I gaped at him. "I'm here with someone."

"On a date?" His arm moved and suddenly I felt his fingers caressing my knuckles. I tightened them more, hating the way my entire body seemed to come alive to his touch, hating the way I swayed a little toward him. "Don't you have a boyfriend?"

"Huh?" I yanked my hand from beneath his reach and confined myself to the small area I was allotted.

"Hey, Paper Boy," he said, looking at Max, whose face was hidden behind his menu.

He glanced over it. "What?"

"You do know Amelia has a boyfriend, right?"

"I do not have a boyfriend." I frowned. "Where'd you get that idea?"

"Yeah, you do." Logan's eyebrows furrowed. "Tall, black guy."

"You mean Travis," I said.

"I didn't catch his name."

"Well, his name is Travis."

"And what exactly is Travis to you, if not your boyfriend? Friend with benefits?"

"What he is to me is exactly none of your fucking business," I snapped, picking my menu back up. *What the hell was taking this waitress so long?* "Mind your harem and leave Max and I alone."

"My harem," he repeated, his eyes alight with amusement. "You really are stuck on that."

"And you're drunk and obnoxious. Please let us eat our dinner in peace."

His eyes searched mine for a beat, then two, seconds that flew by, but felt like an eternity when he was looking at me like that from this close. Finally, without another word, he backed up and started eating whatever was in front of him. I exhaled. Max raised an eyebrow. I shook my head in response, hoping he could sense that I was just as annoyed as he was.

As I scanned the menu, trying really hard not to focus on his presence, one of the girls started laughing loudly, making a show out of whatever he was saying. My hands gripped the paper menu. Finally, the waitress came by and took our orders. When she left, I felt myself ease up a little. Logan stayed on his side of the booth, and I stayed on the other side of my purse.

Max started talking to me about the job he had lined up in Philadelphia, a newspaper where his older brother worked and he'd managed to interview with. It was pretty much in the bag for him. He hoped to work his way up in sports journalism specifically. I told him about how I really wanted to work for an esteemed journal, writing significant stories, but how my father expected me to join in on the family business and I wasn't sure how things would ultimately play out.

"Maybe your dad can buy a newspaper and you can write for the paper."

"Oh my God." I laughed.

"What? I'm sure he can buy one."

"He can, but he wouldn't."

"So you do it."

"Me?" I laughed harder, then stopped. "You're serious."

"Of course I'm serious. Why not? You can start your own digital paper. It'll be small for a while, but then you'd expand. I'd write for you." He smiled. "Gratis."

"That's very kind of you." I smiled back. "But even if I wanted to do that, I couldn't. That would take marketing and effort to push out there for people to actually read it and I don't have money to start one."

"You . . . you don't have the money?" he cocked his head. "Really?"

"I'm not rich, Max. My parents are."

"Spoken like a true rich girl."

"But it's true." I lifted the Sangria in front of me and took a big sip. People always assumed because my parents had all this money that it meant I did as well. Sure, I got to reap the bene-fits of it all—I had all of the designer clothes, took trips at the drop of a hat, but it was all measured by how much they felt I deserved at the moment. Right now, with no Travis and at-tending dad's school of choice, I could probably buy myself a Porsche and he wouldn't bat an eye. Last year around this time, when I wasn't calling home and they didn't approve of any of my choices? Well, my credit card was locked after my fifth Uber ride.

"Anyway, I'm going to finish my double major and see what happens. Maybe I can land a job close to home for a newspaper or something that I do *not* own and he'll be less upset about the entire thing." I sighed. "Or I can win the lottery and not depend on him anymore, but that's looking unlikely."

"How often do you play the lotto?"

"Never." I laughed, breaking a tiny piece of bread and throwing it at him as he laughed. Our food came quickly and we both dug in. It was tapas style, so everything we got was shareable and in the center of the tiny table.

"How's your brother doing?" he asked after a long moment of silence.

"He's . . . the same."

"I'm sorry. I'm sure it's hard on you."

"It is." I lifted my napkin to dab the side of my mouth. "Honestly? I'm trying not to think about it because when I do, I feel like I'm going to break down."

"Well, I'm here." He slid a hand to my side of the table and set it on mine. "As a friend."

"Hands to yourself, Paper Boy."

I jumped. Max's hand disappeared quickly, but he frowned at Logan. "I thought she told you to let us eat in peace."

Logan slid closer to me, so close that not even the small shield between us stood a chance. My heart jumped to my throat. I wasn't sure if he meant to start a fight or not, but I knew that even though he'd been quietly eating his food, he was obviously still drunk. I put my hand on his, pressing down hard. It was futile, my hand was tiny over his, but his gaze snapped to mine nonetheless.

"Please stop," I whispered, a plea. I didn't make it a habit to beg people to do things, but Max didn't deserve Logan's wrath, not when he was so nice and he'd gone out of his way to bring me here. I pinched Logan's hand. I kept my voice low, "Logan. Seriously. Please."

"Yeah." He shook his head, taking his hand from under mine. "I have to go."

Without preamble, the three girls he was with stood, readjusting their clothing and tossing their hair before they started walking. Logan moved his table slightly, squeezed out between the two tables and followed. He didn't say another word, didn't look at us again, and didn't bother to look back. I watched as he put his arms around two of the girls and strolled out. I wasn't sure what was worse—having him sitting beside me, being rude to Max or watching him leave with those girls while my heart felt like it was cracking a little. It was stupid, of course. So, so stupid. I obviously had a crush on him, but I shouldn't care what he did or who he did it with.

"Well, that was eventful," Max said, breaking into my thoughts.

"Yeah." I blinked at him. "I'm sorry. He's obviously a mean drunk."

"I don't think it's that." He chuckled. "He obviously likes you."

"He was on some sort of orgy date. He left with them and I'm pretty sure they're not going to go home and talk about the food." I glanced over at their table. "I don't even think the girls had food."

"Orgy date or not, Fitz likes you." Max shrugged. "And all I can say is, be careful."

"Because he's a player?"

"Eh, I mean, yeah, that too."

"Uh oh, are you going to bring up a Reddit form you read?"

He laughed. "I should've never told you I go on there."

"Hey, it's nothing to be ashamed of. I've ended up there once or twice." I shrugged, still smiling.

"I can't even tell you the things discussed about him on Reddit because it wouldn't be appropriate."

"Women have wild imaginations."

"Actually, I think a lot of them are men." His eyes crinkled as I laughed. "Either way, I'm staying mum about that. If he finds out that I'm the reason you're not giving him a chance, he's going to beat me up and not answer any of my questions for the paper," he said. "You know what is on Reddit though? New Lana Ly stuff."

"What kind of stuff?" I sat forward in my chair.

"More conspiracies. There's a rumor one of the secret societies is using girls as sacrificial lambs."

"That's far-fetched." I scoffed. "I'm sure the cops would've caught them by now."

"True." He shot me a look. "Like I said, conspiracy."

"Who did the cops question, anyway?" I asked. "They'd said they had a suspect."

"If you ask me, the suspect thing was all bullshit. They arrested some guy from around here, Deacon somebody, and let him go after twenty-four hours." He shook his head. "They should've been questioning other people."

"Like who?" I finished my sangria.

Max stayed silent for a long moment before finally meeting my gaze. "Definitely Fitz. Logan Fitzgerald."

CHAPTER THIRTEEN

THERE WAS ANOTHER ENVELOPE IN FRONT OF MY DOOR WHEN I got home. I picked it up quickly, looking from side to side, as if someone was going to run out here and snatch it, or worse, snatch me. I walked inside quickly, locking the door behind me and tearing the side of the envelope. This time, the card had a post-it on it that read: TOMORROW. THIS IS NOT A REQUEST. The instructions were the same otherwise. A drawing of an octopus tentacle on the front with the words: YOU'VE BEEN SUMMONED. On the other side: 900 Stewart Avenue. 12 am. It was ten o'clock now. *Tomorrow.* It wasn't that I was inclined to go to random places by myself at that time of night, but I wanted answers. Why'd they keep sending this to me, and why did my brother have one that looked like a credit card, with a series of numbers in the back and his name etched in the front? I looked at the one in my hand again and decided I'd go. The only thing I had planned tomorrow was the orientation I'd missed when I was back home visiting Lincoln.

The wind picked up as I walked, and I wrapped my coat tighter around myself. It was way too early to be walking to campus. Too dark, too early, and too cold, especially without the cup of coffee that I had to forfeit because I didn't want to be late. Now, I had a killer headache, my chest was tight, even after four pumps of the inhaler, and I was grouchy. I pushed the button at the crosswalk and shifted from foot to foot, waiting for little walker to appear on the other side, alerting me that I could cross. Loud cawing got my attention. I glanced at the park across the street, my eyes on the perfectly dark shapes of the sycamore trees. The cawing got louder. I kept staring, wondering where the birds were. I couldn't see them from here. A church bell rang in the far-off distance, and suddenly the birds flapped their wings. A murder of crows lifted from the tree branches, leaving them bereft of shapes, and began to fly in my direction all at once. There seemed to be hundreds of them, thousands. I held my breath, held my coat tighter, as if it would somehow shield me from their attack. I crouched, on instinct, holding both arms over my head and shutting my eyes tightly. When the cawing quieted, not much, but a little, I peeked over my arm. Some of them were still flying around, but most seemed to be perched on the electric wire that hung from one street light to the next. The crosswalk gave me right of way. I stood quickly and jogged to the other side, heart pounding in my ears.

By the time I reached campus, I was grouchy, scared of birds, and reaching for my inhaler once again. There were about twenty people standing around, definitely freshmen—I could spot their overzealous yet self-conscious stances from a mile away.

"Is this the tour?" I asked.

"I hope so," the guy said, "We've been standing out here for fifteen minutes and it's cold as fuck and early as fuck."

A girl wearing a gray sweater vest over a black long sleeve T-shirt walked over and waved her hands up.

"I'm Sandra, your tour guide." She smiled brightly. "Follow

me as we begin our walking tour through campus. Needless to say, campus is huge so I'm only showing you this portion today."

I'd anticipated an orientation with her pointing around at different buildings and showing us things on a map. I didn't think it would be a walking tour, a thorough one at that, but I followed along anyway. This was my last chance at a group orientation and I wanted to take it. Even if I learned something like, how to get from the Plant Science building we were walking into to the library in under twenty-minutes and without an Uber, I'd call this a victory. Sandra spoke about the architecture of the school, and how the original building, Old Stone Row, with arches and limestone trimmed arches, was built in a style called Second Empire. She moved on to talking about the library, and The Tower attached.

"Is it true people have meetings in that tower?" someone asked, interrupting her. My eyes nearly popped out of my head. That was what Hailey had told me.

"I don't know," Sandra replied. "That's a rumor."

We walked down a flight of stairs in the Plant Science building, and she announced she was showing us an underground tunnel.

"This was originally built to help science students transport things from point A to point B without losing parts or spilling things along the way. We now use it to walk between buildings without having to go outside when it's freezing out," she said, smiling. "One point if you can name another university with underground tunnels."

"Northwestern," I said quickly.

"Concordia," someone chimed.

"University of Minnesota," another added.

"Okay, geez." The tour guide laughed. "My last tour was impressed because they thought we were the only ones."

"Your last tour was full of idiots," one guy muttered.

A few people chuckled. I felt my lips tug into a smile as I tried to contain my own laughter. As we moved through the tunnel, the guide added, "I bet you didn't know that some of our secret societies have their own tunnels."

My ears perked up at that.

"Where are those?" someone asked.

"It wouldn't be a secret if I went around telling everyone."

"But you know where they are?" someone else piped up.

"I have an idea, but I haven't gone to search for it," she said.

"Why not?" a few asked, again in unison.

"I guess I'm not the exploring type." She stopped walking, her expression serious as she turned to us. "Besides, I've heard stories of people who have gone looking and . . . well, they haven't returned."

Her statement echoed through the tunnels, vibrating off of the walls and boomeranging back into us. There was nothing but silence after that. We finally reached an exit. The cold wind smacked into us as we walked outside. Sandra headed the flock and stood in the center.

"Did you know we have our own zip code?" she asked.

"Yes," everyone replied.

The campus was huge. So huge that I probably wouldn't be able to explore it all in one year. Lincoln had once told me he hadn't seen half of it and he'd been here four years.

"Tell us more about the secret societies," someone said.

"No. I don't think I'm getting any sleep tonight after the disappearing thing," a girl added. "That's not a joke, you know? Lana Ly is still missing."

"I know as much as everyone else knows about the societies. Most of them are prestigious, as is to be expected coming here." The tour guide smiled, clearly unwilling to go down the rabbit hole where the disappeared girls were concerned. "They do a lot of work in the community, donating money and goods anonymously during Thanksgiving and Christmas to those in need. Beyond that, I don't know much."

"Do you know anything about The Sphinx?"

"Only that they're no longer around," she said, "But, did you know Carl Sagan bought the building they used to meet in? He turned it into his writing cave slash house. I believe it's privately owned now."

"Probably by another secret society," Nightmare Girl muttered, shuddering. Some people laughed.

"Or maybe by family members," Sandra responded.

I decided to break off from the tour at that point. I'd had enough with the disappearance talk, secret tunnels, and the house that Sagan bought. I was walking home when I got a text message.

Unknown number: I know what happened to your brother

Me: WHO IS THIS?!

No response

With shaky hands, I pressed to call, and again, it said the number was no longer in service. Anger swept through me and the urge to throw my phone in the middle of the street rose. Instead, I breathed in and out and dialed my mother. She answered on the first ring.

"You're up early." Her voice was flat.

"I was in orientation," I said. "How's Linc?"

"The same. They're studying the wavelengths in his brain right now. He has things attached everywhere." She sniffed. "I would've sent you a picture otherwise."

"But he's going to be fine, right? He's going to get out of this and be fine," I said, trying to sound cheerful.

"That's what the doctor is saying."

"Then that's all that matters."

She sighed into the phone line. "How are you holding up?"

"Fine." I shrugged, even though she couldn't see me.

"Are you eating?"

"Yeah."

I was. Probably not as much as I normally ate. My clothes were beginning to fit a little loose around my hips. It wasn't something I'd tell her. Normally, it would've been something mom would've celebrated, but under the circumstances, I couldn't imagine she'd care.

"You need to do college things, Amelia. Meet friends, go to parties. Live. Please don't let this ruin your experience."

I scoffed. "My brother died, mom. It's not like this was a minor thing that happened."

"I know, honey, but promise you'll try."

I thought about the weird texts and the cards I'd received and promised her I'd try. What was I going to try to do? I wasn't sure. Hopefully, find out answers and not get myself killed in the process.

CHAPTER FOURTEEN

M Y KNEE WAS BOUNCING INCESSANTLY AS THE UBER PULLED UP to the address I punched into the GPS. When I looked at the map on her phone, I only saw the water that surrounded us. We were literally at the top of a huge waterfall. On one of the gorges. Outside the window, I could see a structure. It was Carl Sagan's former place—evidently the freshmen on the tour were as smart as they said they were. The secret society definitely owned this place or at least had access to it, assuming it was a secret society that had invited me, which, it had to be.

"This the place?" she asked after a moment of me just sitting in the back of her black Altima.

I nodded. "Can you give me a second, please?"

"Sure, sis." She eyed me in the rearview. "I don't know what you're doing here and it's none of my business, but I wouldn't feel right with myself if I didn't tell you this is creepy."

I nodded and offered her a small smile as I scrolled through my contacts and clicked on Travis's profile. Was it weird to send my ex-boyfriend, whom I hadn't spoken to at all in well over a month, my location? Yes. Was it weird that I was being dropped off in the middle of nowhere at a structure that sat on top of a waterfall in the absolute dead of night? Hell yes. Therefore, texting my ex-boyfriend my location was the least weird thing about all of this. I took a few deep breaths and gave myself a little pep talk: *I can do this. I'm doing this. I'm doing this.*

"Thanks." I opened the door and looked at my driver. "And thanks for waiting for me to get my act together."

"No problem. Remember to five-star me. If you make it out alive."

As soon as I stepped out of the car and shut the door, she drove off. My heart jumped to my throat. *If I made it out alive?* Who said things like that? I stared at the rear lights of her car, wondering if I would've just driven off after dropping off a woman alone here in the wilderness. Probably not. My phone buzzed with a phone call and I looked down to see Travis's face staring back at me. I answered it, grateful to have one moment of comfort.

"Why are you sending me your location?"

"Because I'm in a creepy place and I didn't know who else to send it to."

"You can't do this, Mae." He sighed into the phone. "You agreed that once you broke up with me and left, you wouldn't play games."

"Games? I'm not playing any games. I just need a friend right now, okay?"

"Okay," he said slowly. "Why is it so loud there?"

"I'm by a waterfall."

"Waterfall?" He seemed on alert now. "Where the hell are you?"

"Ithaca Falls." My lip wouldn't stop quivering.

"Why are you there? Are you alone? Is that why you sent me your location?"

"Yes."

"Goddammit, Amelia. Why are you there?"

"I don't know."

"Jesus Christ," he muttered. I could picture him pacing up and down his bedroom. "Does this have something to do with Lincoln? Promise you're not going to hurt yourself, Mae."

"What? No. Oh my God. No," I said sternly. Did he think I called him because I was contemplating suicide? It was rather cocky of him to believe I'd make him my final call.

"What happened? Is everything okay?" The question came from a woman in the background.

Suddenly, his cell phone was muffled, probably by his shirt, as he said something. It was then that I realized how stupid I was being. I wanted comfort and the first person I thought to turn to was my ex-boyfriend, who had clearly moved on, not that I could blame him or cared. I'd chosen to come here by myself at this time of the night and I needed to grow the hell up and accept that nobody was going to come to save me.

"I shouldn't have sent you my location." I wiped my face. "I'm sorry."

"No, don't—"

"Just ignore it. I have to go." I hung up before he could say another word.

I walked slowly toward the wooden door. With the Uber gone and no street lights, it was pitch black out here. I brought a hand up and held it in the air, taking a couple of deep breaths in hopes to gather the courage to knock. I was already here. And it was dark, which I didn't like. And I wanted answers about Lincoln. Maybe they were the ones behind the creepy texts too. It was that thought that made me tighten my fist and pound the door with the side of it three times.

Thump.

Thump.

Thump.

The door creaked open slowly. It smelled like incents, the

kind I'd only smelled at Sunday church, or when my crazy
Mexican grandmother decided she needed to cleanse a new
property my parents acquired. I had a clear view of candles
scattered all over the floor, the only thing giving light to the
otherwise dark house.

"Hello?" I stepped inside, looking for someone behind the
door, but it was empty. I walked toward the center of the room.
"Hello?"

The door shut loudly behind me. I jumped, heart pounding wildly as I whipped around, looking for whoever shut it.
There was no one there, or more likely, I couldn't see them in
the dark.

"This isn't funny," I yelled out, wrapping my arms around
myself as I walked forward, looking up at a big circular window that covered the entirety of the center of the ceiling.

It had the perfect view of the stars. I was almost at the center of it, surrounded by candles on either side of where I stood,
when four tall figures cloaked in black gowns from head to toe
stepped into view. I rocked back, my feet nearly stumbling over
themselves as I tried to give myself distance from the people
before me.

"We didn't intend for it to be funny," one of them said.

"What do you want?" My hands shook. I clasped them in
front of myself.

"What do we want?" He chuckled. "It's more a question
of what do *you* want?"

"What does that even mean? You're the ones summoning
me, which by the way is absolutely ridiculous. I'm not a freaking witch or vampire or whatever."

"Does anyone know you're here?"

"Yes. I'm not an idiot."

The two in the middle looked at each other, though I

couldn't imagine they could see much out of the things covering most of their faces. They turned to me again.

"Rule number one: you speak to no one about this."

"Maybe you should've written that in the invitation," I said, sounding much more confident than I felt. "Why am I here?"

"We'd like you to be a part of our club."

"What kind of club?"

"The secret kind."

"I gathered that much." I signaled at their wardrobe. "You look like satanic monks."

"Is that a yes?"

"What do I gain from joining?"

"Loyalty for life. The keys to any city, in any country you may want."

"I don't need your loyalty."

"Don't you?" They all seemed to cock their heads in the same direction at the same time. It was as if they were all puppets being controlled by an invisible string. My insides quivered.

"You also get $50,000. In increments. Until the end of the year."

"Was this the offer you made my brother?" I pulled out the card with Lincoln's name on it.

"Yes." They cocked their heads in the other direction. I felt a chill wash over me. "And he took it. Do you know why? Think about it for a second. Do you know why?"

I bit my bottom lip. My phone vibrated in my pocket, but I didn't dare touch it out of fear that I'd lose sight of one of them. If one of them came at me, I could try to defend myself. If all of them came at me, I was done for. No amount of Tae kwon do could've prepared me for this moment—not the four years of classes, not the black belt, not the sparring or the older brother who flung me around any chance he could. This was real life and it was absolutely terrifying.

Did I know why my brother didn't turn down the money? No. Before the accident, my brother wanted to go pro in the NHL, despite my father's plans for him in the family business. Lincoln could've been free to live out his dream. Why would he have been willing to sell his soul for money? Why was I considering it? Was this how much we were worth? *$50,000?* Maybe. Maybe for me, anyway. My older brothers didn't escape Dad's control. I didn't—*couldn't*—until I had money of my own.

"Do you know why?" he asked again.

"No."

"Don't you want to find out?" he asked. "Don't you want to find out what happened?"

"Yes." My voice shook.

"Is that a yes, you want to find out? Yes, you'll start taking steps to join our group?"

"I said yes." My hands balled into fists. I was standing my ground dammit.

"Good."

A rush of air fell over us and all of the candles went out suddenly, all at once, and we were all covered in darkness. Not even the stars on the other side of the window above us were helpful to light the room.

"What is happening?" I asked. I looked around, relying on my senses as I blinked in the darkness and prayed my pupils got used to it quickly. I was shaking as I asked, "What are you doing?"

If I'd walked into this room and it had been dark, I could've relied on my senses. I could've listened for footsteps, but I was completely lost right now, unsure of whether to move forward or back or trip over candles if I tried going side to side. I didn't hear their approach, but suddenly, there was something over my head and my arms were being held behind me. My first instinct was to scream and kick, trashing against the grasp of the person who held me and lifted me off the ground, but it was useless. It was definitely a man, a strong one who was probably used to taking hits and stood despite them. My mind went to my brother first. Lincoln could take a hit like nobody's business. Then instantly my thoughts turned to Hailey's words when we first met. She said she suspected that the four hockey players we'd seen, Logan included, were in a society. All of those thoughts jumbled together as I gasped, took in air to scream again, but the oxygen was limited and with him walking as I tried to scream, the cloth kept going into my mouth, making me feel more out of breath. I felt like a fish out of water, quite literally.

His grip tightened around me, but I continued to kick, to move, in hopes that he'd drop me. I shut my eyes tightly in hopes that it would help the feeling of confinement, but all it did was intensify it—the silence, the boots thumping on the floor as he walked with me in his arms, the darkness, my shallow breathing. He stopped walking suddenly and I was set down like a bale of hay. His hands were gone. His footsteps retreated. And then a door shut, leaving me in the complete darkness. I yanked the cloth from my head and tossed it aside, trying to catch my breath in heaping gasps as I sat there.

CHAPTER FIFTEEN

My eyes adjusted to the dimly lit room. There were more candles in here—six of them on the other side of the room. It was like a cave, a dungeon of sorts. Clean though. It smelled clean, as if someone had taken the time to mop the floors and dust off the cobwebs. I launched for the door, trying the knob but found it locked from the outside.

"You can't keep me in here!" I banged. "Someone knows I'm here. I sent the location. He'll call the cops!"

No response.

"My father will end you for this." I tried again, pounding with both fists.

Again, no response.

I searched for my phone, my purse, and found they'd confiscated both. That enraged me further, so I tried again.

"I'll sue you for this. You won't ever get a decent job in your lives!"

Typical rich girl shit, I knew, but it normally worked. Not on them. I was met with more silence. I screamed until my throat felt dry. Finally, I stopped and looked around. There was a water bottle with a little card that read: Drink Me. I rolled my eyes. I wasn't Alice and I sure as shit wasn't going to drink it. I picked it up. It was sealed. I set it down and screamed again, and again, until my throat hurt. Then, I stopped. I walked over to the candles and noticed there was a small box. I sat in front of it, hesitating. What if this was a sick joke and they'd put a rat in it? I put my hand over it cautiously and shook it before picking it up. It was definitely something light. Papers? I opened the lid slowly and saw pictures. They'd taken the time to have them printed. I took out the stack and saw Lincoln. Then, Lincoln and Lana. All of the photographs were taken by someone who seemed to be trailing them without their knowledge. In one, they were standing close to each other, Lincoln was at least a foot taller than Lana, who was short and petite. Something about the picture was weird. I knew my brother better than I knew myself, and I knew how he looked when he was dating someone or interested in them. This wasn't it. They were looking around in some of the pictures, as if trying to make sure they weren't spotted together or overheard. An unsettling feeling settled in the pit of my stomach. For some strange reason, I felt like I was going to throw up. Maybe because my brother looked like himself in all of these photographs and Lana was still here and alive. Were they trying to get me to believe Lincoln had something to do with her disappearance? I hoped not. He couldn't have something to do with that. He wouldn't . . . my stomach lurched again. I glanced up at the water bottle on the table and stood to grab it. It was sealed. It was safe. I intended to take a small sip, but downed half the contents instead.

I twisted the cap back on it and set it down. A slow, tingling feeling traveled through my body. I swayed on my feet, stumbling backward, my sight crossing as the room began to spin. And then I fell. I couldn't say how long I was just lying there before I heard footsteps. The door opened slowly, and I opened my eyes a little, just enough to see two cloaked figures walk inside. They didn't even bother to close it behind them. They knew I wouldn't be able to move. I opened my mouth to speak, to tell them to go fuck themselves, but my voice wouldn't co-operate. They crouched in front of me, and I tried to make out their faces beyond the large hood on their heads, but couldn't. My head lulled to one side and my eyes shut despite my trying to keep them open.

"What do you want?" I asked. Or tried to ask.

"Your brother was one of our best. And then he broke the code," one of them said, a male voice.

"He paid the price for it," the other added.

I reached out. If I could grab one of them by the neck, I would choke him. They laughed, seemingly understanding my motive. My arm dropped with a thump beside me. There was a crash. A pound. Both of their heads turned toward it at the same time. I lifted my arm again and tried to swing, but my arm fell before I could hit either of them.

"What the fuck did you do to her?" the voice shouted. Logan. *Logan?*

"Aw, are you already getting attached to your new pet?" one responded.

"Get the fuck away from her," Logan roared. "Now."

The two figures in front of me skittered back quickly. It must have been my state of intoxication, but they looked like ants scurrying off. I tried to get up, to ask if it was Logan, but in my attempt, I passed out.

CHAPTER SIXTEEN

MY BROTHER BROKE THE CODE. WHAT CODE? MY MIND WAS spiraling as I thought about everything—the darkness, the code, the money, the agreement, the cold concrete beneath my hands, the clean smell, the pounding. What the hell was the pounding?

I awoke with a start, and I was in my bed.

My bed.

In my apartment. Miles away from the Gorges. I sat up in bed and leaned back on my headboard and patted myself down to make sure I was intact. *What the fuck? How* the fuck? The last thing I remembered was screaming at the top of my lungs in that dungeon-looking basement. I closed my eyes to think. Had they opened the door? Had they . . . I whimpered at the thought, my hand cupping between my legs, but no. I didn't feel anything there. My neck was sore though, as if I'd slept in an awkward position. How had they carried me out of there without me knowing? How had they gotten into my apartment? A shiver spread through me. Was it the same ones who brought the boxes in here previously? Were they still here? I brought a hand to my mouth to keep from whimpering aloud, and when my phone vibrated on my nightstand, I jolted. They'd even placed my phone there and plugged into the charger. Who were these people? I stared at Travis's picture kissing my cheek on the screen of the phone for a beat, then two, before deciding to answer it.

"Hello?" My voice was hoarse.

"What the fuck, Mae? I've been calling. Did you make it back home?"

"Um . . . yes. Yeah, I'm home."

"What happened? Why were you in the middle of nowhere last night?"

"I got an invitation to a party," I said, licking my lips.

My lips were so dry. My voice was so hoarse and I felt so groggy. They drugged me. They were spouting about loyalty, yet they'd drugged me. I glanced down at myself again. I was still wearing the same clothes I had on last night and aside from looking disheveled, nothing was torn. I knew they hadn't raped me. I just knew. But still. What if they'd *touched* me? What if they felt me up while I was unconscious, or looked at me naked, or taken pictures? My lip quivered, my eyes instantly pooling with the thought of that.

"Mae?" Travis sounded impatient.

"I'm sorry." I licked my lips again. "Yeah, I'm fine. I should've been more clear last night."

"What the fuck is going on?"

"Nothing." I climbed out of bed and started walking toward the living room. I had to stay on the phone with him while I searched the apartment and made sure I was alone. "What's going on with you?"

"I'm worried about you," he said. "I was worried sick last night. I almost called the cops and sent them your location but I wanted to wait until this morning just in case."

"I'm sorry I worried you." I went into the bathroom and looked around. There was nothing there. The kitchen was next. Nothing. The guest room and bathroom. Nothing.

"Thanks for not calling the cops though. That would have been overkill."

The word kill made me queasy. I put a hand over my mouth to keep from gagging.

"Do you still have a roommate?" he asked.

"No, she moved in with her boyfriend."

"Kind of how I asked you to move in with me?"

"Right. Except we were more off than on in our relationship, and they seem to have something solid going on." I licked my lips again. "I heard a girl with you last night. Obviously, my moving out or moving away hasn't stopped you from exploring other people on campus."

"Don't be like that, Mae." He exhaled. "What do you want me to do? I'm not gonna be a monk. You want me to give up fucking around? Fine, but that means you have to commit to being with me again."

"Travis," I warned. "You could barely commit to me when we were together."

"So don't ask me about my life then. I'm not asking you why you sound like you were sucking dick all night."

"Excuse me?"

"I'm sorry." Another exhale. "It's just, you sent me your location and ghosted my calls. What do you expect me to think?"

"Not that." My eyes felt wide as I went back to the kitchen and got myself a glass of water. "Jesus."

"I'm sorry. I'm sorry. It's just, I miss you, and I know we said no calls or texts but fuck, it's hard, Mae. I'm worried about you."

"Look, I'm sorry I sent you my location with no explanation. That wasn't fair." I closed my eyes as I leaned against the counter. "I won't do it again."

"I'll be there next week, you know?"

"Here?" My eyes snapped open. "Why?"

"We're playing a game there. Scrimmage, nothing official, and the guys and I are going to the football game Saturday. Maybe we can hang out, you know, for old time's sake?"

"Ummm . . . maybe. I guess. Let me know when you're here," I said. "Thanks for calling and checking up on me."

We hung up with that last olive branch. One I wasn't sure I'd give or take, especially after he'd just said he missed me. That was Travis though. That was the way he usually got me back after our break ups. My attention turned back to my apartment. The lock was in place and didn't look like it had been tampered with, not that I would know what a tampered lock would look like. The door was fine. My keys were on top of the counter, in the exact spot I usually set them. What the fuck happened last night and who brought me back? There was no way, absolutely no way that I was going back there again. Not for $50,000 and freedom and not for knowledge. My sanity was worth more than whatever they had to offer.

CHAPTER SEVENTEEN

AFTER A LONG SHOWER, I GATHERED MY THINGS AND HEADED TO my first class. As I stepped out of my apartment, I noticed a sheet of white paper folded in two on the floor outside my door. I looked around and picked it up quickly, my back pressed up against the door as I read it: *We're watching you.* Another shiver rolled through me. I hadn't been able to stop shaking since I woke up. I still didn't know who was watching me. I didn't know what anyone looked like under the black cloaks they wore or why they were so secretive about it all. On my way to campus, I called Max. I'd packed my brother's laptop in my bag and was planning on going to the library with it to do some digging, but I needed to know more about what Lana had found when she was working for the paper. I thought about the pictures I'd seen last night of her and Lincoln and how they'd said he betrayed them. What had he done? What part did my brother play in all of it?

"What did Lana tell you about what she was investigating?" I asked Max once he picked up the phone.

"Not much," he said. "Did you find something? Were you invited to join a society?"

"No." I stopped walking, heart pounding. *What if Max was involved somehow?* He could've been hiding underneath a cloak. I took a deep breath before I continued, "I just keep thinking about her and wondering if maybe she found something incriminating on them. Like incriminating enough to make them want to get rid of her."

"That's one of the many Reddit theories," he said. "But it was kind of discounted by the fact that they'd be charged with murder if they were caught."

"*If* they're caught," I said. "Big if. They could've disposed of the body who knows where by now."

"Dude, the search parties were insane those first few days. You weren't here for that, but it was a madhouse. The story got global attention. There were people here from Singapore reporting on it and searching."

"They could've driven out before she was even reported missing."

"I don't know, Mae."

"Let me guess, someone on Reddit discounted that theory as well."

"It's just, these guys and girls, are rich beyond belief. I find it hard to believe they'd want to get their hands dirty."

I thought about Logan's brother, a former NHL player who was making millions, and how it appeared he got away with raping various girls. I thought about my own father, who was a known cheater, and how that affected my mother and in turn, us. I thought about my older brothers, who had followed in his footsteps from time to time, and the wives that stuck by them. Cheating wasn't murder though. It was hurtful and shattered the foundation of a relationship, but it wasn't murder. I couldn't picture any of those people committing murder or kidnapping. Well, except for Patrick Fitzgerald. I didn't know him. I knew his brother though and I would bet money that he wouldn't commit murder.

"I don't know, Max. It's all very weird," I said finally.

"I just don't think we should jump to conclusions. Besides,

we don't really know who's a member of what. Quill is the only society that lets us publish their member's names."

"Do you think that was Lana's end-game? To make sure they all let the paper publish their names and make them public?"

"She never said that, so I don't know."

I was almost at the crosswalk that led to campus, when I saw a dark figure tucked in the alley, beside a dumpster. I gripped my phone tighter and held my breath, but continued walking. As I passed, the cloaked person lifted their finger to their face in a "silence" position. I walked faster, my feet nearly taking off in a sprint as I passed it.

"Mae? Are you still there?"

"Yeah. I have to go." I hung up the phone and looked over my shoulder.

Had nobody else seen him? Had nobody thought it was freaking weird that a person covered in an all-black cloak from head to toe was standing in an alley in broad daylight? It was similar to the day the red cloaked people had been walking around, but at least that was at night and they weren't any-where near me.

On campus, there was a slew of people walking and run-ning from every direction, surely trying to get in and out of classes. In the bustle, I noticed more black figures. There were two, then three, in different directions—three o'clock, nine o'clock, and twelve, just where I was headed. Fear gripped me as I walked. Were they all here for me? I forced myself to take deep breaths and calm down. What could they possibly do to me in front of hundreds of students in broad daylight?

I set my eyes on the building I was walking toward, hoping my determination would shield me from whatever it was they were doing. Around me, I heard people whispering about the cloaked people walking around, but it didn't seem like many of them were surprised by the display.

"I'm glad I'm not the only one who finds this creepy," I said aloud.

"It's definitely creepy." The guy walking beside me chuckled. "It's not even Halloween."

"The cloaks? You'll get used to them. They only do this one week out of the year," another guy said. "Think of it as rushing for a fraternity, but they have to hand pick you."

I'd always hated the idea of sororities. It was why I never tried to join one to begin with. While I liked the fact that they seemed to stick together and help each other out, I didn't think the idea of people being excluded was cool. If I could get in, but my best friend couldn't, or vice versa, would it have been worth it? Yet, here I was, going to creepy places in the middle of the night to see what these people could offer me. I was doing it for Lincoln. And now, to find out the truth behind what happened to Lana because I was sure that if anyone knew, it was them.

I went to my first class—trigonometry, it was one I'd dropped three times and couldn't afford to drop anymore. I had two options: pass the class or not get my diploma. I couldn't get out of there fast enough when we were dismissed.

I was sitting in women's studies listening to my classmates discuss women in sports when the doors opened and Logan strolled in. Everyone stopped talking at once and stared. He was the only guy in the class. Not that women's studies should be a woman's only course, but at least today, it had been until he walked in. If it had been just a random guy, it wouldn't have been such a big deal, but not the star hockey player. Not, this godlike figure with the bad boy image and mysterious aura around him. Especially not on the day we were discussing women in sports, of all things.

He seemed utterly unfazed by the attention as he looked around the auditorium. There were more empty seats than taken, so I wasn't sure what was taking him so long. In his perusal, his gaze met mine. I froze, breath hitching. I couldn't seem to breathe as he walked up the stairs and headed right to me. He wasn't going to though, was he? Why would he sit beside me? A row of women turned their heads to follow him. The professor continued speaking as though he was just another kid in her class, which essentially, he was. It was the students who were making it feel like he was some sort of celebrity, and now that included me, because I felt like my heart was going to bounce out of my chest, as hard as it was beating.

He slumped down in the chair beside me with a heavy sigh. "Mondays, am I right?"

"Are you taking this course?"

"What—you think I just stumbled into the class you happen to be taking?" He raised an eyebrow. "You may just be more arrogant than I am."

"I'm not. And that's not what I meant." I rolled my eyes. "Besides, your arrogance is always showing. Like, say, the other night at the restaurant."

"Oh yeah." He frowned and bit his bottom lip as if trying to remember.

"Oh yeah?" I blinked. "Wow."

"What?" He put a foot against the back of the seat in front of him and splayed his other leg straight out. "These aisles are so fucking tight."

"It's an auditorium. Besides, I don't think they anticipated any boys being here."

"That's sexist."

"Yeah, I guess it is." I focused on the professor, trying to ignore the way Logan seemed to take up way more than just his seat and was spilling on mine, his arm on my armrest, his knees extremely close to mine, his scent infiltrating all of my senses. He was really too much.

"So, what did you want me to remember about the other night?" he whispered, leaning in closer to me.

"Nothing," I whispered back, refusing to look at him. "And stop talking, you're going to get us in trouble."

He reached over, ripped a piece of paper from my notebook, and chuckled at the way my jaw dropped in disbelief. He leaned back in his chair and slid the ripped out piece of paper to me.

What did you want me to remember?

I froze for a beat. Was I supposed to respond in a note? He had an impatient look on his face that made me huff out a breath and scribble: *nothing. You were even drunker than I thought.*

I passed it back and watched him write: *I remember that you looked beautiful.*

My heart skipped as he continued: *I remember wanting you to be with me and not Paper Boy.*

I met his eyes then, and not for the first time, wished I hadn't. He had a seriously alluring, penetrative gaze, and it was all just too much. I needed to stop this right now. After class, I'd continue this, but right now? Right now, I needed to stop it. I licked my lips. His expression darkened. My heart felt like it was going to explode.

"So." I cleared my throat. "When was the last time you paused to think about the fact that women in sports don't get paid as much as men do?"

He let out a surprised laugh. "Never."

"That's sexist." I raised an eyebrow. "I guess it's good that you're here then. Maybe you should join the discussion."

"Why don't you join the discussion?" He looked at me. "You're sitting isolated up here as if you want no part in any of this."

"I'm simply admiring the discussion." I shot him a look. "Besides, I'm not an athlete. I don't think it's my place to say anything. Some of the girls down there are wearing their volleyball and soccer practice stuff."

"You don't have to be an athlete to have a say in this. You're a woman. You should rally behind them. That's what I'd do. That's what men do. It's why we win."

"That's one way to look at it."

"It's the only way to look at it. There's power in numbers."

"What do you think about this, Mr. Fitzgerald?" the professor asked. "I'm sure you have a lot to say since you're obviously involved in a thrilling conversation back there with Miss Bastón."

I nearly jumped out of my seat. Every single person in the room turned around to look at us. At him. I looked as well. I figured if nothing else, this gave me the perfect excuse to get a good look at him. He had the kind of wardrobe Charles Addams would've been proud of—all black everything. Not that I could judge. It was the color I wore most these days. Logan made it look vibrant somehow though —maybe it was because his eyes were the kind of emerald green that sparked up a room. He had a perpetual five o'clock shadow and a jawline that looked as though it had been taken from a Ken Doll. Yeah, on a good-looking scale of one to ten, Logan Fitzgerald was a one hundred.

"I think women should definitely get paid equally," he said. "However, I do think it depends on the sport and the revenue it brings in. I'm not saying that because I'm a man and I know I'll get paid top dollar. According to Forbes, the revenue the NHL brings in is 1.5 billion. The international soccer club brings in 9.4 billion, so I know I can't demand Ronaldo money even if I am the Ronaldo of hockey."

"But you do believe in equal pay?" one of the students up front asked.

"Of course I do."

"What if the women's team brings in more revenue than the men's team? Do you think they should still get paid equally or more than the men?"

"If they bring in more money, they should get paid more money." His lips curved into a lazy smile. "I'm all for equal opportunity."

Everyone seemed to quiet all at once. I wondered if they were all mesmerized by the way he seemed to transform with something as simple as a smile. The professor continued talking. Logan turned to me and winked. I glanced away quickly, knowing I'd start blushing any minute.

"Aren't you supposed to take pictures of our practices?"

"Yeah. I'm going tonight. I'll be behind a camera lens and trying to be as quiet as possible, so I doubt you'll notice me."

"Impossible. I'm always aware of your presence."

I felt myself blush. The professor chose that moment to dismiss us and tell us to read the first chapter of our textbook by Thursday. Everyone got up and collected their things. I realized then that Logan had never taken anything out of his bag. I eyed him closer.

"You don't even have a book bag?"

"No."

"Where do you carry your books?"

"What books?"

"Your textbooks."

"They're at home. I only go to classes to listen to my lectures. If I wanted to stare at my books, I would sign up for online classes."

I couldn't really argue with that logic. We walked down the steps of the auditorium. As we passed the professor, she turned to us.

"Fitzgerald, are you planning on signing up for this class or should I expect you to waltz in here every week so you can hit on Miss Bastón?"

"I was just making sure the course was worth my time before I signed up."

"And?" She raised an eyebrow. "Did we meet your expectations?"

"I have to think about it, but yeah, I think you did." He flashed a prize-worthy smile. "See you Thursday."

"So you aren't in this class." I pushed him lightly.

He chuckled. "Not yet. Still thinking about it."

"So you were stalking me." I was smiling. I didn't know why I was smiling.

"Not stalking. Just . . . biding time."

"Before what? Your actual class?"

"Nah, I'm done with classes. I'm going home to take a nap before practice."

"Sounds heavenly," I sighed. I felt like I was running on seventy-two hours of no sleep and twelve gallons of caffeine.

"You want to join me?"

I eyed him sideways. "I'm not one of your—"

"Groupies. I know. I meant just to sleep."

I gnawed on my bottom lip.

"I can tell you're tired, Amelia. You look tired."

"I am."

"So, come sleep with me."

"Quiet down." I looked around. "People are going to think you mean you want to—"

"Fuck you?" His eyes danced.

"Logan."

"What? You don't want people to think we're fucking?"

"Oh my God, can you stop saying that?" I covered my face, which felt like it was one thousand degrees hotter than the rest of my body.

"I don't think I've ever met someone who doesn't want people to think I'm—"

"Stop." I got on the tips of my toes and reached up to slap my hand over his mouth.

He laughed harder, pulling my hand away from his mouth and stopping. We were now standing there, blocking the exit, so that people had to walk around us on either side, and my hands were in his as he looked down at me. His expression slowly turned serious. I just stared, heart at my throat.

"Come on."

"You said you don't let anyone in your bed," I whispered.

"You're not just anyone."

"We're not hooking up."

"We're not hooking up," he repeated.

I shrugged and started walking because what the heck. The library could wait a couple of hours.

CHAPTER EIGHTEEN

"WHAT'S YOUR MAJOR?" I ASKED AS WE WAITED FOR THE crosswalk to give us right of way.

"Business, with a minor in journalism."

"Journalism?" My brows rose. "Really?"

"I have to do something once I'm done playing professionally, don't you think?"

"I guess so." I eyed him with a new appreciation. "Why don't you work for the paper?"

"No time. Sadly. I'm a little jealous of Paper Boy's job, but I can't complain about being on the ice."

"Right, because you would be great at asking people questions. Whenever I see you, outside of people begging you to party with them and stuff, you're quiet and you look like you'd kill someone if they tried to talk to you."

"Not very forthcoming, huh?" He smiled. Sort of. I laughed.

"Not forthcoming at all." We started walking across the street.

"I wouldn't complain about my assignments if I was Paper Boy though. He gets to work with you."

I glanced away from him and looked forward, nearly freezing in the middle of the street when I caught sight of the red cloaked figure crossing in our direction. On instinct, my hand shot out to grab Logan's arm.

"What happened?" he asked.

"Those people creep me out." I stared at the red cloaked person as they walked by. I could've sworn they were looking right at us. His head turned in our direction and I could see the outline of his face, but couldn't make out what he looked like. I couldn't understand how I couldn't see their faces even in daylight. The hood of the cloak was too big. It didn't mean that anyone couldn't just walk up to them and pull it off though, but because I hadn't heard anyone else suggest that, I assumed nobody would. I wouldn't. My nails dug a little deeper in Logan's arm.

"The reds?" Logan asked. "Have they approached you?"

I shivered.

"Amelia." Logan's voice was stern, but not loud as we reached the other side of the street. "Have they approached you?"

"No. They haven't." I shook my head. It hadn't been them, per se. The ones who approached me were wearing black cloaks.

"Stay away from them. If they do try to approach you, I need you to tell me right away."

"What?" I let go of his arm and looked up at him. "Why?"

"Just trust me, okay?"

"Do you think they're up to no good?" I asked tentatively.

"I know they're not." The tone of his voice didn't leave room for question.

"Do you think they had something to do with Lana Ly?"

"The girl who disappeared?"

"Yeah."

"I don't know."

"Did you know her?"

He side-eyed me. "I didn't know her personally, but I saw her around often."

"She was really popular in high school. I wonder how she fared here."

"How'd you fare back in North Carolina?"

I shrugged a shoulder. "Fine, but I wasn't popular in high school."

"You weren't?"

"Why do you sound surprised?" I laughed. "I literally have two friends. Three if you count Max, or Paper Boy, as you like to call him. And you, so that makes a whopping total of four friends."

"Friends, huh?" Logan pulled open the door to our building.

As soon as I walked in, I shimmied and let out a burring breath.

"Cold out there, huh?" Gary asked from behind the desk.

"Freezing."

Logan laughed. "It is not freezing."

"Canadians have a higher tolerance for the cold," Gary said, laughing, "I'm from Florida. This weather is cold."

"I spent my entire childhood in Mexico City," I said. "I've never been able to get used to this weather."

We waved at Gary as we reached the elevators. Once inside, he punched in the number of our floor and I thought maybe this entire thing was a dumb idea. I could just go to my apartment and sleep there. I had a perfectly good bed. *That I hadn't gotten any sleep in in weeks*, I reminded myself. When the elevator door opened, Logan let me step out first. I did, and stood there, in front of the elevator, unsure of what to do. He started walking toward his apartment. He was halfway there when he looked over his shoulder.

"Come on, Amelia. I won't bite." He winked and turned around.

That should've been my indication to run the other way. I should have thrown in the towel and gone to my own room then, instead, I followed after him. Once inside, I shrugged off my coat.

"You thirsty?" he asked. I shook my head and watched as he took a jug beside his fridge and downed half of the contents faster than I ever could.

My eyebrows rose. "No wonder you get so drunk."

"I get drunk and then spend the next two days apologizing to my liver." He shook the jug before setting it down. I laughed. "Do you drink?"

"Occasionally."

"Not much of a party?"

"Not really."

"Because of your boyfriend?"

I laughed. "If I had a boyfriend, would I be here right now, ready to sleep beside you?"

"We already established boundaries." He shrugged. "What's the harm in just sleeping?"

"I don't know. It's weird." I frowned. "If you had a girlfriend, you would think it's okay to sleep next to another girl?"

"No, but I don't have a girlfriend."

"I've noticed," I said. He grinned. I felt myself go hot all over.

"So, it's safe to say you don't have a boyfriend?" He started walking toward his bedroom. I followed.

"I don't have a boyfriend," I repeated because obviously, he needed to hear this.

"So, if we take a selfie in bed together and you post it on Instagram, nobody is going to try to kick my ass?"

"I like that you said try to kick your ass as if he couldn't." I laughed as I kicked my shoes and socks off. "You're sure you'll win that fight?"

"Positive."

"What makes you so positive?" I pulled the sheets back and climbed into one side of the bed.

I was wearing jeans and an oversized gray cable knit sweater. Not the most comfortable thing to sleep in, but also not the most uncomfortable, and I wasn't about to take off my jeans. Logan had black sweatpants and a black t-shirt on. He kicked off his shoes and climbed into the other side of the bed.

"Your bed is so comfortable." I closed my eyes with a sigh. "Are you going to set the alarm?"

"Yes, master."

I smiled, eyes still closed. I knew I was going to fall asleep in under five minutes. As I turned over and got even more comfortable, bringing my knees up to my chest, I remembered I'd asked him a question and he'd never answered.

"Hey, Logan."

"Hm." He sounded like he was on the verge of falling asleep too.

"You never answered. What makes you so sure you'll win the fight against the boyfriend you think I have?"

"Because, Mae." He yawned. "I'd be fighting for you."

My eyes shot open. I glanced over my shoulder, but his eyes were shut and his face looked peaceful. Had he really just said that?

CHAPTER NINETEEN

WHEN I WOKE UP, LOGAN WAS ALREADY OUT OF BED. MUSIC WAS playing in the en suite bathroom, but I couldn't make it out because it was too low. As I sat up and pushed the sheets away, I stretched and yawned. I wasn't sure how long I'd slept, but I definitely felt like I'd gotten my energy back. My head whipped in the direction of the en suite bathroom door when it opened and I saw a shirtless Logan walking out. The black sweatpants he wore hung low on his hips, covering half of the V that disappeared into them. There was absolutely no denying Logan worked on his fitness. A lot. I glanced away quickly, too quickly. Too obvious.

"Did you sleep well?"

"Yes. Thank you." I continued stretching my arms, unable to look back at him. It felt weird knowing I'd slept beside that specimen and didn't do anything but. I stood. "I, um, should go. I have to do a few things before I head to the rink."

"See you later."

I smiled, grabbed my phone from the nightstand, and walked out of the room in a daze. "Thanks again," I called out.

"You don't have to thank me, Amelia," he said, picking up a shirt and pulling it over his head. "You look like you got more rest in one hour than you have since I saw you at your parent's house."

"It was dark."

"What?"

"When you saw me at their house. It was dark."

"When *you* saw me it was dark," he said. "I was there the entire time."

I stared at him for a beat. From his expression, I could tell if I asked questions, he'd answer, but I had no questions. Not about that and not for him. He'd already told me to stay away from the cloaks, which meant he wasn't one of them. Otherwise, he'd known what they did. He may have even been there. I blinked away from him and waved as I rushed down the hall to my own apartment, shivering as I thought about him being there. I couldn't fathom a situation in which he would've been there to lock me in a dark room and then gone and invited me to sleep in his bed because he knew how tired I was. I needed to stop before I continued to drive myself crazy.

I was still looking over my shoulder when I arrived at the rink. I'd pocketed the ominous little black card sent to me and the one I found that had my brother's name on it. At the very least, I'd show up and find out why they were so adamant about me going. Maybe they wanted to give me answers. I pulled open the door of the rink and walked inside, following the music that was playing. As I approached the ice, the Foo Fighters got louder, and I saw that the team had already started doing drills.

When I was little, I used to go to all of Lincoln's practices and games, mostly because we had the same nanny and Mom dropped the three of us off together. As I got older and started getting interested in dance and swimming, it was his turn to get dropped off with me. And of course, once we reached a certain age, we stopped attending each other's practices. I still went to his games though. Dad used to joke that when he was little, soccer was the only thing he knew, the only equipment you needed were legs and a ball, but his kids decided to play a sport with a stick and a ton of equipment.

The Mighty Ducks were all the rage when we were little, so of course, my brother wanted to play. Hell, I wanted to play, but no one would hear of it. They wanted me to remain unscathed and unblemished—a little porcelain doll to place on a shelf. I put my hand on the glass and looked across, scouting what angle I could take good pictures from. It wasn't like the coaches were going to let me go on the ice with them for some pictures for the school paper. I spotted an opening at the player's bench, and headed in that direction, listening to the way they shaved the ice each time they came to a stop.

Once there, I took my camera out and started snapping pictures. In my lens, I could see Logan and Nolan skating side by side. All of the players had the same rhythm, the same momentum, as if this was a synchronized dance they could do in their sleep. When the music switched up, they started different power skating drills, working on their edges and speed. The level of skills was high pace and amazing to watch. If they did this instead of play actual games, I would probably be just as entertained. The song was almost over when the coaches came out onto the ice and they all huddled around as they were talking.

I snapped pictures as they huddled together, blocked shots, and threw each other into the boards. When I felt like I had enough images, I just sat and watched them practice. I glanced at my watch, realizing that if I wanted to go to the library to look at the newspaper archives, I would need to leave soon. I couldn't make myself get up though. I was too enthralled in the music and the way they moved out there. Before I knew it, the practice was over. The music stopped, the guys and coaches got off the ice, and I was left by myself in the desolate rink. I googled to see if I could walk to campus from here, and upon finding out it would take me way too long, I decided on an Uber. I stood, grabbed my things, and started walking out.

"Did you get any good pictures of me?"

I jumped up, dropping my phone and everything else in my hands as I turned around to find Nolan standing behind me. My hand flew to my chest. "You scared the shit out of me."

"You shouldn't be staring at your phone when you're walking alone." He raised an eyebrow. He was no longer in his gear, but wearing a t-shirt and sweats. His hair was wet, with what I assumed was sweat. He kneeled down and gathered my things for me, handing them back. His eyes zoned in on the cards from the secret society that I'd tucked into the little pocket behind my cell phone, but he didn't comment as I took them from his hand. "Did you take any good pictures?"

"I think so. I hope you're not offended by this, but after a while, I couldn't tell you guys apart out there. Most of you have the long Viking hair thing going."

"Impossible." He chuckled. "I'm always the hottest."

"Well, I'm glad you're that confident in yourself."

"I don't like how unimpressed you are with me."

I laughed. He didn't. "You're serious."

"I am serious." He frowned. "Normally, girls are totally all over me by now. You like Fitz? Is that it?"

"What? No," I answered quickly, wondering if Logan had said anything to him. "Why would you think that?"

"You left the party together the other night."

"Are you spying on me?" I raised an eyebrow. "Or Logan?"

"Logan." He smiled, saying the name as if it was foreign. "I bet he likes that you don't call him Fitz like the other ones."

"You mean his harem?"

"Sure." Nolan chuckled, then winked. "Nolan and Logan sound similar, if you want to try me out instead. I won't be mad if you get our names mixed up when we're fucking, you know."

"Oh my God. Seriously?" I balked. "Is it so crazy to believe that I don't want either of you?"

"You mean after the test run?"

"I meant before the test run." I laughed at the confusion on his face. Obviously, he wasn't used to being turned down.

"Your loss then." He ran a hand through his long hair with a shrug.

It slicked back with his sweat. My nose scrunched. Some women loved sweaty athletes, but I'd guess they hadn't grown up with the stench of dirty hockey gear or dated a messy college basketball player.

"I thought you didn't like hockey." He nodded at the hat on my head. I'd worn it because my hair was a mess after my nap and I didn't want to bother trying to fix it.

"I don't, but *The Mighty Ducks* is iconic."

"Our practice was also iconic," he said. "You stayed for the entire thing. Usually, people come, snap a pic or two and leave."

"It was entertaining."

"We aim to please." He winked.

I couldn't help myself, I smiled, shaking my head. He was such a flirt. Between him and Logan, there was no way a girl stood a chance. My phone vibrated in my hand. I glanced at it.

"Shit. I have to go. My Uber's waiting. Good seeing you, Nolan."

"You too, Mae," he called out as I turned around and started walking. "We can hang out outside of bed too, you know. Unlike Fitz, I'm not opposed to having real friends that I don't hook up with."

"I'll keep that in mind," I called out.

I thought about it the entire way to the library. Logan didn't have friends that he didn't hook up with? What did that even mean?

CHAPTER TWENTY

THERE WAS A CHILL IN THE AIR AS I WALKED TO THE LIBRARY THAT had less to do with the weather than it did with my mood. I wasn't sure if it was the tower chimes, and how eerie what they were playing tonight was, or the fact that I couldn't stop thinking about whatever meeting may be going on in there at the moment. Maybe it was that I couldn't seem to stop thinking about whether or not the black cloaks were still following me. They'd left me that note saying they were watching me and I fully expected one of them to pop out in the middle of the night. The wind picked up with a hum, and I held my coat closed tighter, lowering my head to fight against it.

When I finally got into the library, I exhaled a shaky, cold, breath and walked to the back, where there were tables set up everywhere and I felt like I had my own little work space. I sent the pictures I'd taken on the camera to my phone, and emailed them straight to Ella Valentine. She'd been kind enough to let me take all of those days off and Max had been awesome and taken pictures of the football team's first home game while I'd been away. Sending these pictures was probably not a big deal to Ella, but I definitely felt good about completing another assignment.

Slinging my bag on the table, I set it down softly and opened it to pull out Lana's laptop. I'd switched it out with my

brother's after still finding nothing of interest in his. I spent fifteen minutes opening folder after folder on Lana's laptop and
not finding anything, until I saw a folder labeled: PERSONAL
SHIT and inside of that, another folder labeled: PORN. I hesitated. I didn't want to see Lana's personal videos, especially if
she was having sex in them, but it could just be regular porn.
Either way, I clicked the file. Instead of videos, what I saw were
word documents titled by date.

April 1st—

*By the time I got to the Gorges and knocked on the door, it was
12:05 am. He greeted me with a smile and told me I was late. Tardiness
was unacceptable. I told him I'd make it worth his while. I'd never
spoken to anyone that boldly before, and I definitely never imagined
speaking to him like that, but once the words left my mouth and I saw
darkness encompass his gaze, I knew I had him. He'd asked me to
bring a friend, and I couldn't. That was another thing I'd have to apologize for, or pay for, depending on how you looked at it. The next day, I
had welts on my backside and a soreness I'd never felt between my legs,
but I'd never felt more alive.*

It ended there. My jaw dropped. She'd been right to label
it porn. Who had she been with though? There were files dated
from April through May. She'd disappeared sometime in May.
I checked the date of the last file. May 23. I Googled Lana Ly
to verify when in May she'd disappeared and caught my breath
when all of the searches with her picture came up. *Missing girl:
Lana Ly. Another missing student. Kidnapping victim or runaway?*
My eyes were riveted on that word: *another.* I clicked on one article, then another, until I ended up on a Reddit message board
about the missing students. According to Reddit, which I knew
to only take with a grain of salt, girls had started going missing
on campus since 1902. One of the users said the reason it wasn't
made a bigger deal was because a lot of the girls came back,

claiming they'd just run away for a little while. Some people on the message board suspected a serial killer in the area. Others argued that was stupid because if that was the case, the cops would be vigilant and on it. The serial killer topic caused an argument between people that went on for forty pages.

I bookmarked the page and decided I would go back to it after reading legitimate articles about the students who disappeared. Most were girls, but there were a few boys too. It was odd—the last three had been from prestigious families, families you would never think would lose a child and call it quits on their search. I remembered seeing them on the news at one point or another and pausing to offer a small prayer, the only thing I could think to do in a situation like that. One of them had been gone five years and still hadn't been found. My chest squeezed as I thought about Lana in those terms.

Glancing around the library, my eyes wandered to the window. I jumped in my seat when I caught a glimpse of a cloaked figure staring back at me. I looked at the next window and saw another figure, and the next, and the next. I tore my gaze from the windows to look around the library. Everyone in here was either talking quietly to the people they were with, busy on their laptops, or leafing through pages of whatever book was in front of them. I looked back at the windows again, but they were gone. Just like that. Goosebumps pricked my skin. *Were they waiting for me outside?* From my peripheral, I saw someone walking toward me and whipped my head in that direction, fully expecting it to be one of them. It was a petite blonde, smiling at me as she approached. I felt my brows furrow slightly. *Was she in one of my classes?* She dropped a white envelope on the table in front of me.

"They told me to tell you not to be scared."

"Who?" I looked at the envelope and back at her.

"The cloaks."

"They just approached you and gave this envelope to you and asked you to give it to me?" I picked up the envelope, still looking at her.

"Pretty much."

"And you weren't scared?"

"Not really. Maybe the first day of freshman orientation, but I'm used to them. Besides, I heard they give their members $50,000 just for joining." She shrugged a shoulder. "Doesn't sound half bad."

"Right. Let's all die for $50,000." I tore open the envelope in my hand and looked back at her briefly. "Thanks."

"Sure." She stayed put. I shot her a *can you get out of here* look, but she remained.

"Did they also tell you to watch me as I read this?"

"No, but I'm curious to know if you're going to be one of them. Or are. And like, which society is it? Quill?"

I blinked. She was seriously not going to leave until she got an answer and what was I supposed to say? I didn't know their names. I didn't know whether or not I was officially one of them yet. I didn't know what they looked like. I literally knew as much as she did. I shook my head after a moment.

"Honestly? They're trying to play a prank on me. I don't know their names, who they are, what they look like, what they do, so your guess is as good as mine." I shrugged. "It's probably Quill though."

"Oh. Well, they publish their member's names in the paper, so the cloaks and secretiveness is kind of overkill." She frowned, looking at the envelope. I nodded my agreement. The cloaks were totally overkill. She hesitated, idling for another beat before shrugging and walking off.

I exhaled, though I didn't know why I was relieved that

she'd left it alone. It wasn't like I knew what was in this envelope. I stared at my name written on it. Their calligraphy was really on point. I had to give them credit where credit was due.

Amelia,

We trust you have not told anyone where you were last night. For this, you get a point. Two more and you're in.

X

I stared at the black X. It was long, scripted, and looked as if it had been added quickly to the bottom of the page. I re-read the note again. One point. That was what I'd gotten for being locked in a dungeon and not telling anyone about it, which was what a sane person would have done. I put the note back in the envelope and pushed it aside. I went back to Lana's computer, which was running out of battery, and of course, I'd left my own computer charger back home so I couldn't do anything about it.

April 25th—

He invited me to a dinner party. He's the kind of man that you just don't say no to. Sex in the car, while driving? Sure, why not? Dinner with senators and mayors who know damn well I am not his wife, but speak to me with respect, as if I'm supposed to be there? Again, yes. These are things I would have never done before discovering this little club. I mean, these are things I still hesitate doing, but every time I hear his voice now, I cave. When I see his name on my texts, I give in. Never in my wildest dreams would I have thought I'd be that girl. He's my friend's father, for God's sake. Which is another story all together. He's onto us and I don't know what to do about it. I keep denying it, but I wear my heart on my sleeve so it's hard. Maybe I'll stop.

I sat back after reading that entry and stared at the screen. *Discovering this little club.* What club? Did she mean the octopus people? Was this secret society some sort of sex club? That would be my next question to them, no doubt. If it was, I was out. I did not want to be tossed around from person to person for their enjoyment. *What would Logan think of this whole thing?* I shook the thought away quickly. He'd told me to stay away from the cloaks. Also, he was not my boyfriend. It didn't matter what he thought. I clicked on another one, skipping the rest of April and going straight to the last one she'd written in May. With the computer about to die, I needed to focus on things that may have answers.

May 25th—

The people around us were making it virtually impossible for us to see each other. I don't blame them. Each of them have their reasons for not wanting to see us together. The one that bothers me most is Ella. She acted like my friend for so long, a mentor, an amazing boss, and the minute she saw me walk into that party with him it was like a light switch went off. All of a sudden, she's in every restaurant, every event, and every bar we visit. We try to be inconspicuous when we're together. We keep a safe distance when we're out in public, but somehow she knows. She knows that behind closed doors we're more and she seems to be going to great lengths to keep us from being together. I hate that it bothers me. I didn't set out to be part of this. I wanted to expose the hidden secret societies around campus and now I'm stuck under their thumb because I fell for the one person I shouldn't have.

I met a friend though. I won't say her name here in case this gets into the wrong hands. She's helped me see that my feelings for him are valid, that I belong with him, so that makes me feel less crazy. That doesn't mean I'm an idiot. I know he's going to leave me soon. I've seen the pictures of him with past girls in my situation. I've looked them up, too. He wasn't lying when he said he could help build my career. Two of those girls have been in Forbes Magazine already. I'm trying not to think about it, but I know I'll just have to lick my wounds and move on. Who knows, maybe I was right all along. Maybe the societies wield too much power and need to be exposed. I just don't think I can do that to him. Maybe his son is right. Maybe I need to be the one to walk away from this.

I re-read the letter three times. Whoever she was having an affair with was obviously linked to Ella. My father was the first person who came to mind and I hated that. A chill rushed through me. Could he be the one? Her mentor? Could Lana have gone that far and slept with my father? *No.* Not Lana. Maybe this was someone else's notes. Maybe someone else was doing this research and sent it to her. I thought of the pictures of my brother with her. I needed to see them again. I needed to see them after reading this and really pay attention to how they looked. With that thought in mind, I gathered my things and left the library.

CHAPTER TWENTY-ONE

I WAS LOOKING OVER MY SHOULDER, THINKING ABOUT THE LETTERS I'd just read. God, was Lana having an affair with my father? Could *he* do that? I knew he wasn't a saint. My parents seemed to be on the brink of divorce every five years, and a lot of their arguments stemmed from him being unfaithful. It was something they would never discuss in front of us, but we weren't stupid. Lincoln had almost come to blows with dad last Christmas. That made me pause and stop dead in my tracks. Could it have been about Lana? She'd started writing those entries in April. It was possible that she was with whoever she was writing about in December. She disappeared in May though. This was all too much. I started walking again. Obviously, Lincoln was involved with this secret society, but was dad?

Even if I didn't manage to get the two points I needed, I'd find out. Evidentially, as secretive as they thought they were, a lot of people knew about the money. They must have dangled it in front of countless people. I wondered how many chomped. Most of us were wealthy kids from wealthy families, trust fund babies who knew under very rare circumstances they'd end up poor and wanting, yet that money called to us for some reason. Maybe because despite what was promised to us by our last names, what we really wanted was something that was wholly ours. What I wanted above anything else was a way to help

Lincoln. A way to understand what he'd been through and why he'd ended up the way he did. I needed answers because I absolutely knew he didn't try to kill himself. He'd said it himself, but even if he hadn't, I knew my brother.

"Boo."

I shrieked at the sound that came out of the darkness and braced myself for a fight. When he walked out in front of me, it wasn't a cloaked figure, but Nolan, laughing at my reaction. Laughing so hard, in fact, that he doubled over. I pushed him as hard as I could, hard enough that he fell over onto the grass and continued to laugh.

"What the hell, Nolan?" I pushed his leg with my foot.

"Holy shit. I would apologize, but that was the highlight of my week," he huffed. I kicked him in the shin, and he laughed harder. "Ouch. Okay, I'll stop. I'll stop."

I crossed my arms and waited. He laughed a few more times until he finally recovered and stood up, dusting off his joggers and grey school sweatshirt. I started walking again.

"Why are you walking all alone anyway?" He started walking beside me. "You know the rumors aren't just rumors. That girl really did disappear."

"You mean Lana?" I looked at him quickly. I was already on edge for so many reasons, and he'd gone and brought her up. "What do you know about it?"

"Not much except that she disappeared."

"Do you think she's alive?"

"I think if she was, she would've been found by now."

"So you think she's dead."

"I mean, her parents had crews of privately hired people who looked for her everywhere." He shrugged. "It is sad though. She was a great girl."

"You knew her?"

"She used to take pictures of the team. Kind of the way you do." He smiled a little. "She was always nice."

"Do you know if she got into any bad things?"

"What's your definition of bad?"

"What's yours?"

His eyes danced. "I don't know but something tells me your definition of bad is way tamer than mine."

"Probably," I said. "Do you know if she was with someone? Like in a relationship?"

"I don't know." He glanced away from me and looked forward as we walked. Something about the way he answered that question and the way he looked away, made me think he was lying. "Some people think she ran away," he added.

"Why would she run away though?"

"Dodging responsibility? I don't know."

"Would you run away to dodge responsibility?"

"No." He chuckled. "Even if I did, responsibility would hunt me down and find me."

I thought about that. Would Lana have run away? Maybe once things ended with the man she was seeing, she decided to leave? Maybe she'd left because she wanted to prove a point, to make him miss her? It didn't make sense, but anything was possible.

"Have you seen any cloaked people walking around?" I asked.

"Why? You looking for one?"

"No."

"Well, that's unfortunate." Nolan's wide grin sparkled in the moonlight. "Because we've been waiting for you to leave the damn library all night."

CHAPTER TWENTY-TWO

THE LOOK ON MY FACE MUST HAVE SAID ALL THE THINGS MY VOICE couldn't, because Nolan stopped walking and set a hand on my shoulder. Despite the sympathetic look he was giving me, my fight or flight response was kicking. Adrenaline coursed through me, the way my martial arts instructors had often described to me, but I never actually experienced until this very moment.

"Relax. We're not going to hurt you." He grinned. "Much."

"I'll scream."

"Scream." He shrugged.

"I'll fight."

"You think you can take all of us?" As he asked that, five figures appeared out of the shadows behind him, walking toward us in unison, all wearing black but not cloaked, no longer cowering beneath sheets.

In the darkness, I couldn't tell who was who. I could only tell there were also women amongst them and I could only pray that a woman wouldn't let them hurt me, not physically anyway. I met Nolan's gaze.

"What's the game? What are you going to do to me today? Lock me up in another dungeon?"

"Of sorts."

"Of sorts," I repeated the words back slowly, fighting the fear they brought with them. "What does that mean 'of sorts?'"

"If it makes you feel any better, we've all done some version of the things we expect you to do."

"It doesn't."

"Well, you won't be alone tonight. Maybe that'll make you feel better."

"It doesn't."

"Then you're shit out of luck. Let's go, Bastón." He turned around, facing the others. "You want answers, we got them, but you need to play our game."

He didn't make an attempt to grab me or carry me or anything that I expected. Instead, he walked, leaving enough room between them and me to make it clear that I was free to make the decision. With words like those, it was impossible for me to just go home right now. Following them into the dark seemed crazy, and a part of me argued that it was stupid, but another part of me, the part vibrating with adrenaline, wanted to chase after him. I hesitated for a second.

Thanks to Lincoln and his little "let's lock you in the dark closet" games when we were kids, I wasn't just afraid of the dark, I was terrified of it. I was also the kind of person who ran toward things that scared me, not because I wanted to get over my fears, but because I'd been so sheltered my entire life that I felt I had something to prove to myself by conquering small feats. It was that thought that made me take a step forward, toward the darkness, toward the row of strangers dressed like they were going to a funeral, and for all I knew, it would be mine.

Three of the five in front of Nolan walked in another direction, not bothering to turn around to say goodbye. Nolan glanced at me over his shoulder.

"You'll meet everyone when the time comes. For now, onto the first challenge. It'll be easy."

He led me through an archway between buildings that led to a park I hadn't seen, not that I'd ventured out much. There were two more people dressed in black. *Logan.* My pulse spiked when our eyes met. I wanted to punch him for telling me to stay away from the cloaks and not admitting he knew what the calling card was when he saw it that night. For all I knew, he was the one putting them on my doorstep. I glared.

They led me to a spot in the grass that had cones all around it and a big bright light—like the ones you see in outdoor arenas—shining over it. I almost laughed. Were they going to make me do drills? I wasn't sure I could do any drills right now.

"If you look closely, you'll see that the grass is covered with blades," a guy I didn't know or recognize said.

He waved me to walk forward. I moved forward and saw some sort of iron square laid out with what looked like pieces of shards glittering through, each of them placed like stakes coming out of the ground. They were placed on the iron in a way that made it impossible to do a drill around them, not a fast one anyway. You would have to meticulously step in order not to drive one of them into your foot.

"What is it that you're asking me to do?" I looked between Nolan, the guy, and Logan.

"It's a trust drill. We expect you to go from point A to point B by following your guide's instructions," Nolan explained.

I balked. "Without looking down?"

"Yep."

"Yeah, right." I started to laugh nervously, but stopped when I realized they were serious. "Is that even physically possible? At one point I'll look down. It's human nature."

"You won't be able to look down," Nolan said. "You won't be able to see anything at all."

"What?" My jaw dropped. "You're going to blindfold me?"

Nolan nodded once.

"How am I . . . who's going to . . . I don't think I can . . . "

"I'll lead you to the other side," Logan said, his voice ringing clear in the silence.

"You expect me to believe that you're going to get me to the other side unscathed? While I'm blindfolded?"

"I do."

"And why would I believe that?"

"Because I'm telling you I will."

"What if I asked you to take my place in this drill? Would you trust me to lead you while you're blindfolded?"

"Yes." He didn't hesitate, but he had to be bluffing.

"Have you done this?" I asked, and he nodded. A part of me—a really stupid part of me—didn't want to ask who he trusted enough to lead him to the other side, but I had to ask anyway. "Who got you through your drill?"

"Your brother."

I took a step back. I had *not* been expecting that.

"Are you doing it or not?" That came from one of the other guys.

They all looked so damn sure that I'd hightail out of there. It was probably the only reason I stepped forward with a nod. I was doing it. I looked at Logan. He didn't look any more impressed by my confirmation than anyone else did. He looked bored. As he walked over to me with the blindfold in his hand, his expression was all business. He put it over my head and placed it on my forehead, his eyes on mine.

"You're going to get the urge to reach up and snatch it off. Don't."

"I don't know if I can do this."

"You can. I'll be on the other side guiding you."

I looked behind him, at the trap on the ground that looked

like a serial killer's idea of a good time. When my gaze met his again, I saw concern in his. I thought he was going to talk me off the ledge, or reassure me that I would be great at this. Instead, he tapped my head and started walking away.

"She's ready."

I opened my mouth to say I wasn't, but closed it again. They explained the object of the game again: get to the other side with my partner's help. Rely solely on him, without giving in to the urge to yank the blindfold off. The area was quite small and without the blades, I could get there in four or five steps. With the blades there, it wasn't simple at all. Without relying on my own sight, it seemed impossible.

"We're going to do this in counts. Like this—" He picked up his right leg and moved it slightly without setting it down. "This is one count." He moved the same leg a little further out. "This is two counts. We'll do it like that—one count, two counts, two counts, one count," he said as he demonstrated. "You understand?"

"Do I understand that you want me to die tonight?" I nodded. "Yep. Crystal clear."

He rolled his eyes. The rest of the guys chuckled before going silent.

"Take one step forward," he said.

I did. I wasn't in the actual square yet, but my palms were already sweating and my knees were already shaking.

"Set the blindfold over your eyes," he said. I held his gaze as I shakily lifted my hands to the blindfold, holding it at my forehead for a beat. "Come on, Amelia. You can do this."

It was his deep voice that coaxed me into doing it. Once it was over my eyes, I couldn't see anything at all. I looked around, toward where I thought the light was, and I could definitely see brightness behind the blindfold, but nothing beyond that.

"Look at me," Logan said.

My head instantly snapped in his direction. "I can't see anything."

"It's okay. You can do this," he repeated. "Pick up your left foot and step forward."

My blood pumped wildly as I did as he instructed. I took a deep breath, then another one, trying as best I could to calm down.

"Listen to me, Amelia. My voice. Only my voice."

Under any other circumstance, like Spin the Bottle or Seven minutes in heaven, I would absolutely be okay with closing my eyes and having him talk to me. While standing in the middle of knives though, wearing a ridiculous helmet over my head? Not so much.

"Pick up your right foot, remember the counts? One count forward, one count to the right. Pay attention. This is important."

I whimpered, my body shaking as I lifted my foot and did as I was told. Once it was on the ground, and I didn't feel a knife on it, I let out a breath.

"Left foot, one count forward, one count left."

I did as I was told, my foot shaky as I set it down. I whimpered, my lip trembling.

"I don't think I can do this." My teeth clattered. "I don't think I can do—"

"Well, now you really are surrounded by blades, so you have to."

I shook my head quickly. "I can't."

"Listen to my voice," he said. "I vouched for you. You have to finish."

"I didn't ask you to vouch for me," I shouted, because it was the only thing I could do.

"Yet I did."

"Why?" I shook.

"Because I believe in you."

"You don't even know me." I took a deep breath. "You don't even like me."

"This isn't about me. This is about you. Do you believe in yourself? Do you like yourself?" He paused. "Matter of fact, how much do you like your toes? You're about to slice one open if you don't follow my instructions.

"Oh my God," I whispered.

"Left foot forward. One count."

My heart pounded as I did it.

"Pick up your right foot and move it two counts left. I'll count. Ready?"

"No." I bit down on my lip.

"Pick up your foot," he instructed. I did. "One count left. Good. One more. Good. Now drop it."

I bit down harder on my lip. He could've very well been telling me to drop my foot right on a blade. Maybe that had been the challenge all along—get Amelia to slice a blade through her foot.

"Drop it," he said again. "If you move in any other direction, you're fucked."

"What if you're lying?" I screamed, tears wetting my cheeks. I hadn't even realized I was crying until I tasted the salt on my lips. "What if this whole thing is designed for me to end up with no foot?"

"I'm impressed you're able to hold that position for so long," he said. "Yoga much?"

My chest shuttered with a sob. My left leg wasn't tired yet, but it would be. I could hold this position well enough on a yoga mat or a dance floor, but out here in the slick grass, it was completely different. Thunder sounded above us. It had been forecast to rain tonight. Was that why they were making this my challenge? Because they wanted me to be a sopping, crying mess? Instead of dropping my foot, I brought it up against my left leg in a tree pose.

"This is about trust, Amelia." Logan's voice rang out in the darkness. I focused on him again. "This is about trust."

"How am I supposed to trust you? You told me to stay away from the cloaks, yet you are a cloak!"

"I meant the red cloaks," he explained, as if I was being petulant.

"You drugged me the other night!"

"I did not drug you. I was against that."

"Yet you let it happen."

"I was late. I wasn't there when it happened." He paused, I thought I heard him exhale. "All that is in the past now. You have to trust that I have your back, forever, through everything."

"I can't." I was screaming and shaking and my foot was going to freaking slide off of my inner thigh any moment. "I'm scared."

The others laughed loudly. They were enjoying this display. I could hear them saying things about my brother and how he'd broken, and it took everything in me not to yank the stupid thing off, grab a blade, and throw it their way. Logan told them to shut the fuck up. They did, but snickered.

"Listen to me. I know you're scared but I'm going to get you through this." His tone was softer now. "Set your foot down. Slowly. Slide it down your leg. That's it. Like that . . . slowly . . . and set it down right beside your other foot. Wait! Stop! You weren't supposed to bring it forward. I didn't tell you to bring it forward, dammit."

I didn't know why he was yelling at me until I felt a pinch over my right ankle. I yelped.

"I got cut," I yelled.

"Because you didn't follow fucking directions," he yelled back. "I told you to trust me."

"Trust isn't something you give people when they ask for it. It's something that's earned."

"I'm trying to earn it, but you're being impossible."

"Impossible? It's about to start raining and you have me out here playing with knives!"

"Okay," he said, and I could tell his patience was wearing thin. "Let's finish this. You have a few steps to go. Pick up your right foot and move it two counts. Ready? One. Good. Two. Good. Drop it."

I did with a flinch. Then, he instructed what I should do with the left, and the right again, and left, and then, nothing. I was standing there, shaking, with my arms wrapped around myself, when I felt him walk up to me. He lifted the blindfold slowly. I blinked, trying to adjust my eyes.

"I'm done?"

"You're done."

"I . . . I . . . " I blinked faster, shook harder, held myself tighter.

"Hey, Mae," he said, his voice barely a rasp over the thunder that roared from above. My heart pounded as I craned my neck to meet his gaze. He grinned then. A slow, huge grin that I'd never seen on his face before. It felt like sunshine amidst the darkness. "You fucking did it."

I felt myself smile for half a second before I started laughing. He was watching me closely, an amused look in his eyes, despite his set jaw.

"We have more to do," he said after a beat.

I stopped laughing. "What? Right now?"

"The night isn't over," Nolan called out. "Don't get excited."

"I seriously need to do something else?" I crossed my arms. "This wasn't enough?" I lifted my leg to where I'd been feeling liquid crawl into my socks. "I'm bleeding."

"You'll live."

"Says the guy who didn't get cut."

Logan's eyebrows rose. "You wouldn't have gotten cut if you'd followed my exact directions."

"I would have followed directions if you'd . . . " I struggled to find blame to pin on him.

He cocked his head, waiting, amusement touching his lips. I turned around and walked toward the others, arms still crossed. I'd do another weird mission impossible thing, but I wasn't going to do it with him as my partner. Just as those thoughts entered my mind, the skies opened up and it started pouring down on us.

CHAPTER TWENTY-THREE

"Now what?" I yelled over the rain.

"Now, we scale the falls."

I blinked. "What?"

"There's an old research lab behind the falls. The only way to get there these days is by scaling it."

"I . . . I'm not even wearing shoes with grip."

One of the guys walked up, waving a pair of shoes.

"I've never climbed before. How high is it?"

"Look for yourself." Nolan walked in the direction where there was a trail, we all followed. I lifted a hand to shield my eyes from the rain, and squinted. It took a second for my eyes to adjust to the view in front of me. There were lights coming from below, illuminating the falls, and beside it, I could see holes on the rock wall.

"I can barely make anything out. How do you expect me to climb that?"

"We'll provide all the equipment."

"And the weather? It'll be too slippery."

"I've done it." Nolan shrugged a shoulder, his chin jutted toward Logan, beside him. "He's done it."

"Congrats, but I'm not willing to die for this." My eyes went back to the falls. There was no way in hell. "What is the alternative to this?"

"You sure you wanna know?" Nolan grinned. I wanted to punch him.

"Obviously."

"It involves stealing."

"Does it involve jail time if I get caught?"

"No."

"So, I'll do it."

"Just like that?" Nolan chuckled and looked at Logan, who looked completely unamused by this entire exchange.

"You don't want to know what you're stealing?" Logan asked, frowning. "Or from who?"

"I definitely don't want to scale that." I pointed toward the fall. "So I don't really care."

As I followed behind them to the closest building, I realized I did care. I wanted to know at least who I was going to steal from. Maybe I could conjure something bad about them in order to avoid feeling guilty about taking whatever it was I was taking. I wrapped my arms around myself, teeth clattering as we walked through the building, in the back and out the front. It had stopped raining, but we were still soaked.

"Where are we going?" I managed to ask.

"You're going to The Tower," Nolan said.

"What tower?"

"The only tower you've heard of. I can tell by the expression on your face." That was Nolan.

"The one you guys have not-so-secret meetings in?" I looked at the lot of them. None of them seemed to be cold and if they were, they weren't showing it.

"We don't have meetings in there." Nolan chuckled.

"Wrong cloaks," Logan added.

"The red ones meet there?" I picked up the pace until I caught up to them.

"Yes." That was the third guy who was there, who I hadn't been introduced to.

"If you can get in and get through without someone spotting you, there's a painting up there," Nolan explained.

"A famous painting," Logan added.

"Are you familiar with Caravaggio?" the third guy asked.

"No."

"He's from the Baroque era," the guy added.

"Okay, I'm not an art major, I'm freezing my ass off, and you're speaking a foreign language," I said. "Please get on with it and tell me what painting to look for."

The guy searched for something on his phone and showed it to me. It was a painting of people around a baby who lay on the ground. It was titled *Nativity with St. Francis and St. Lawrence*.

"What do I do once I have it?"

"Pray you survive long enough to get it to us," Logan said.

My eyes widened on his, his tone dead serious. I wiped my forehead, unsure if it was the water dripping from my hair or sweat forming.

"Just so I know what the stakes are here—who am I stealing this from and why is this painting so important?"

"The red cloaks," Nolan said. "Don't worry, they've stolen shit from us in the past. At this point, it's a game we play. Think of them as the stepchild we don't want but have to keep around."

"It's important because it was painted in sixteen hundred and after being in Sicily for that long, it suddenly vanished. Poof. They say the Sicilian Mob carried out the theft. We know for a fact it's hidden in the tower," the third guy said.

"If it's there, how has nobody noticed? They do tours in there all the time."

"How do you think we know about it?" The guy said,

raising an eyebrow. "The tour guide happens to be my girl-friend. I saw it when I was helping her clean the chimes before the tour one day."

"So she knows it's there?"

"I didn't call attention to it when I was in there. That thing has to be worth at least fifty million."

"Do I get a cut if I steal it?"

"We'd have to split it between all of us," Nolan said. "But yeah, you'll get a cut at the end of the year."

"Meaning, us right here or the entire society?" I asked. "I'm assuming there's some kind of alumni association that delegates where the money goes."

"Good question." Nolan raised an eyebrow. "And smart fucking girl."

"Obviously." My teeth were chattering. "Can we just go and get this over with? I'm going to catch a cold or worse."

We walked out the front door. They went ahead, Logan idled behind them with me.

"I can't believe walking around knives wasn't enough for you idiots."

"Believe it."

I lifted my leg up and pointed to the cut I had over my an-kle. The blood had already dried, but it still hurt.

"What's left after this?"

Nolan piped up again. "After what you just did, and what you'll do next, it'll be easy. You fall back and let Fitz catch you."

I blinked. "What are we, in church?"

"Basically."

"God, this is so stupid." I brought my hands to cover my face and dragged them down.

I probably looked like utter shit right now, wet hair and wet face. I'd just survived walking around sharp knives and the only thought running through my mind was *thank God I'm not wearing mascara*.

"Do we take turns? I catch him and he catches me and then we sing kumbaya?"

"You think you can catch me?" Logan's lips twitched. Not a smile but close to it.

"Are you willing to fall back and let me try?"

"Sure, why not?" He eyed me up and down.

"You're insane."

"So I've heard." His lips spread into a wolfish grin that set my insides ablaze. He turned his attention to the rest of the guys. "Amelia has a point. She gave us enough of her trust out there and if she's willing to risk her life stealing that painting, I don't think a fall backward is going to change that."

"So, we skip it." They all exchanged looks and shrugged. "Let's go to the tower and call it a night. We'll link up at The Lab tomorrow for the initiation."

I froze at his words. The Lab. That was what my brother told me with his Morse code. He wanted me to find these people. For what though? I looked at the three of them. They were my brother's friends, his brothers at one point, before whatever happened had ruined it, yet they all went to his mass. They all went to show respect. I pushed the thought aside for now. I had another mission to get through today, and that was exactly how I was thinking about them—as missions, like in a Mission Impossible movie or 007. The tower was right by us. Thankfully, the rain stopped completely. Not that it did anything to help with the cold. If I didn't die trying to steal this thing, I would die from hypothermia. All for $50,000 and loyalty I wasn't even sure I wanted. I did want to find out the truth about what happened to my brother though, and Lana, if they even knew that much. *What if they didn't know anything at all and this was all a ploy?* I closed my eyes briefly, *please don't let this be a ploy.*

"The lights are off, that means they're not there," Nolan said.

"Good," the other guy said.

"What's your name?" I asked.

"Marcus."

"Marcus." I nodded. "I like to know who's fault it's going to be when I die."

They laughed. I didn't.

"You'll go up the winding stairs where the organ is. You'll see a small door in front of it, it's so small, you can miss it, so pay attention and use your flashlight. In there, you'll see the painting. Roll it up and bring it out."

The adrenaline must have still been coursing through me because none of this seemed difficult and I was still one-hundred-percent game for it. I'd go in there, go up the stairs, steal the painting, and get out. I could do this. Totally.

"How will I get in? Do you have a key?"

"Let me worry about that," Logan said.

"You're coming with me?"

"Everywhere you go, I go."

I would've found it sexy, if he didn't look like he wanted to rip my head off. I ignored it because I didn't want to go in there by myself. Nolan held his finger up for us to wait and ran somewhere. When he came back, two seconds later, he threw each of us a big black T-shirt. I thanked him, put mine over my head, and slipped the wet one through one of the sleeves. Logan peeled his wet T-shirt off, tossed it at Marcus, and put the dry one over himself. The luxury of being a boy.

We made our way over to the tower, walking nonchalantly, as if we were just walking through campus.

"I can't believe you lied to me about the secret society," I said as we walked.

"I didn't lie."

"You didn't say anything when you clearly knew that the flower and card I'd received was about this."

"That doesn't mean I lied."

"Whatever. For the record, I think all of this is dumb. I'm only doing it because . . . " I hesitated, peering up at him. He was busy looking around and didn't seem like he was paying much attention to me at all.

"Because?" he asked, or rather said, in a stern tone.

"I want answers." I shrugged.

"About Lincoln."

"And Lana."

"What makes you think we have anything to do with Lana?"

"The other day, when you drugged me, you showed me pictures of them together." I raised an eyebrow.

"I didn't drug you." He scowled, then pointed at the side of the tower.

I headed there, but Logan reached for my hand and held it in his, steering me in the direction he wanted. My heart skipped.

"What are you—"

"Just play along."

"Oh. Okay," I whispered as he pulled me onto the side of the building, beside the door.

My back was against the wall as he caged me in with both arms on either side of my head. A few people walked by, talking and laughing. My eyes widened on Logan's. He was looking at me but didn't say anything. More people walked by. He rolled his eyes, exhaling.

"You're going to have to move and press yourself against the door," he said.

I was only two steps away from it, so I moved in that direction. One, two. Logan moved with me as if we were in the middle of a dance. I felt the cold surface of the metal door behind me as I looked up at him.

"Wrap your arms around my neck." He leaned forward, making it easier for me to reach. I did as I was told, ignoring the way my heart galloped as I wrapped my arms around him and he hoisted me up slightly with his knee between my legs.

His eyes were on the door as he pulled something out of his pocket. I couldn't make out what. I looked beyond him, watching the people as they walked back and forth, keeping a lookout in case anyone walked too close to us. It was too dark beneath the tower for them to see what we were doing. We probably looked like two horny college kids, not two thieves who were about to steal a painting allegedly worth millions of dollars.

"Keep your eyes on me, sweetheart. Don't worry about everyone else." His voice was gruff as he concentrated on the lock behind me.

"If I don't worry about everyone else, I'll focus on the fact that your leg is between mine and I look like I'm about to kiss you."

"Is this turning you on?" His lip turned up, his gaze flicking to mine.

"No."

"Liar." He chuckled darkly, going back to the task at hand.

"Aren't you getting tired of having my weight on you?"

"Nah. I can carry you all night long." His gaze was on mine again.

The way he said that, with that undeniably sexy undertone, made my stomach flip. I licked my lips. He kept staring, his hands working on the lock. It made me wonder what else those hands could do if given the task. I needed to stop. My overactive imagination and libido needed to simmer down. Yet, I couldn't stop looking at his lips and wondering just how soft they'd be against mine. It was the situation we were in. It was. He was mean and rude, and he didn't like me.

"Let's take a selfie by the tower!"

I tore my gaze from Logan's and looked at the group of guys walking in our direction. They were all wobbling on their feet, obviously drunk, but they were coming our way nonetheless.

"Are you almost done? They're coming this way," I whisper-shouted.

"Fuck. I swear I almost got it." The door clicked. I gasped, smiling at him. He'd unlocked it. He shoved the tools in his hands into his pocket. "Now we have to wait until they leave."

"I'm really uncomfortable in this position," I whispered.

The guys came closer. They were on the grass now, walking directly toward us. These were the things that pissed me off about humans. Why did they have to take the picture right beside us? Why not on the other side of the damn building? It's like arriving at an empty parking lot and deciding to park beside the one car there. Stupidity. Logan shifted me so that he was carrying me, his hands on my ass as he hoisted me against the wall. I gave out a soft, unexpected yelp.

"What are you?"

"Stop looking at them."

I brought my eyes to his. He was entirely too close to me, his nose touching mine, his mouth just a touch from mine. I wrapped my arms tighter around his neck, so that we were closer still, our breath mingling, and as the guys finally reached us and stood just a few feet away, Logan's mouth pressed against mine. The kiss seemed to suck the air out of my lungs.

It started as what I would call a soap opera kiss, fake, just lips moving, no emotion, but it quickly bloomed into something more.

With our wet hair and faces and adrenaline pumping through us, the kiss turned into something animalistic—needy and hot, completely overwhelming. His tongue rolled against mine with a familiarity that made me second-guess every kiss in my past. The way he devoured my mouth made me think there was no way I'd been doing it right, no way the guys who came before him had any clue what they were doing. Our surroundings vanished, the drunk guys taking pictures, the people walking, the task at hand were all second place to this. Logan broke the kiss slowly, as if it was taking every ounce of self-control to do so. His breathing was hard as he searched my eyes.

"They're gone."

"Huh?"

"The coast is clear. We can go inside now."

"Oh." I blinked, unwrapping myself from him and placing my feet on the ground slowly. "Right."

He opened the door and pulled me inside. I wasn't sure what I thought was going to transpire, but it was definitely not business as usual. That's exactly what happened as Logan took the stairs two at a time and I followed behind, heart pounding, trying to ignore the rawness of my lips. He was a player. That's what they did, they kissed girls and moved on without second thought. Who knows how many of them he'd kissed this week alone. I shook the thought away. It didn't matter. When I reached the top of the stairs, I brought out my phone and aimed my flashlight. I could see why Marcus said the door was small. Not terribly small, just smaller than people were today.

"When do you think this was built?" I asked as Logan stepped forward with his tools to break in.

"Eighteen-hundreds."

"No wonder the door is so small," I said, illuminating the lock with my flashlight. "Where'd you learn how to pick locks anyway?"

"Jail."

I stepped back. "You went to jail?"

"No." He made a noise that I wasn't sure if it was a laugh or a scoff. "You're moving the light."

"Sorry." I stepped forward.

He turned the knob and pushed the door in, standing up and letting me pass. I pointed the light inside the room. It was a tiny room, with a couple of boxes, and the painting. It wasn't in a frame—it was just on the wall, tacked on as if it were elementary school artwork in a grandmother's kitchen. I removed it carefully from the wall and rolled it up as I was told, stuffing it into my shirt for safekeeping.

"You're going to put a fifty-million-dollar art piece in your shirt like it's a five-dollar bill?"

"They had it tacked onto the wall like it was a kid's painting," I said. "Besides, it's the only way to get out of here without looking like we stole something."

I was feeling good about the whole thing as I walked down the stairs until the alarm started going off. Logan and I looked at each other for a second before we took off running at full speed. My footsteps landed on the concrete as I chased after him, holding onto my chest with one hand and swinging my other arm for momentum. The ground was wet and my sneakers sloshed as I ran faster, harder. There were police sirens approaching, the unmistakable lights of a police car illuminating the night. Logan stopped running suddenly and turned to grab my hand, ushering me toward the woods. We didn't speak, our breaths coming out in pants as we walked through the woods, and the same area we'd done the previous exercise in. We walked to the other side of the street, where there was a black four door Porsche with the lights on.

"Get in." Logan opened the back door for me. I did as he said and he climbed in right behind me.

"Did you get it?" Nolan asked, turning in the driver's seat.

I nodded, still panting.

"We got it. Cops are here though," Logan said. "They must have had a silent alarm we triggered."

"Do you think they have a tracker on the painting?" I asked, mostly because I'd seen *The Da Vinci Code* and one could never be certain.

"Shit," Marcus said.

"You better check that before we take it to The Lab," Nolan added. I slid the rolled up painting out of my shirt and handed it to him.

"Drive," Logan roared as the clear sound of sirens neared.

Nolan floored it. The car accelerated so fast, my back hit the seat. I pulled my seatbelt on as he took the first turn. Logan did the same thing beside me. We drove a couple of blocks. We were driving by Hailey's coffee shop and bar when Nolan's phone rang. He picked it up, his gaze flicking to me on the rearview as he spoke in what seemed like codes—yes, no, maybe, yes, tomorrow. When he hung up, he announced he was dropping me off at home.

"Thank you." I let out a relieved breath.

"Tomorrow night, Logan will take you to The Lab."

"And then I can ask questions?" My knee bounced.

"That's how it works," Logan said. "After we give you the rundown on things. How we started, why, all that fun stuff."

"For now, you get some rest," Marcus added. "You look like you need it."

"Thanks. I am painfully aware of the fact that I look like shit."
I stared at him. "Are you on the hockey team too? Because I can
make it a point to take pictures from your worst angles."

They all laughed. I found myself smiling a little at my joke.
Marcus looked over his shoulder at me.

"Thankfully for myself and the team, you won't find me on
the ice." He winked.

"Marcus used to play soccer, but he got injured," Logan said.

"I'm sorry."

"No biggie." He shrugged a shoulder. "I didn't have professional ambitions. I'm perfectly content being an accountant like
my dad."

"Well, everyone needs an accountant," I said.

"That's right." He smiled and turned around.

The car slowed down and came to a stop in front of my
building. Logan got out of the car first. We both said bye and
watched the car drive off for a beat before turning and walking
into the building.

"I'm surprised you didn't go with them."

"I need a shower and I'm tired. I have to be up early tomorrow."

"Oh." I waved at Gary before turning my attention back to
Logan. "To work out?"

"Yeah. I have family coming into town and want to get it
over with."

"Seeing them?" I pushed the button to the elevator.

"Yeah. Seeing them, hanging out and pretending I'm okay
with their existence. Shit like that."

"Sounds torturous." We stepped into the elevator.

"It is."

"Well, if you need moral support, I'm not doing anything
tomorrow morning and I'm willing to sacrifice myself for the
sake of saving you during that terrible time."

"Why would you subject yourself to that?" He side-eyed me as we stepped out of the elevator on our floor.

"I know what it's like to deal with a dysfunctional family in the morning." I shrugged as we idled in the hall, between both our apartments.

"Yeah, I've heard horror stories about your Thanksgiving dinners."

"From Lincoln?" I frowned. "Horror stories?"

"I was being sarcastic. The fact that you all choose to get together for any kind of dinner kind of means you're not as bad as you think."

"Dysfunctional doesn't necessarily mean bad."

"What does it mean then?"

"Not normal."

"Ah." His lip turned up slightly. "Well, my family isn't dysfunctional. It's practically non-existent."

"Is that why you joined this thing?" I frowned. "What is it called anyway?"

"You'll find out tomorrow, and yes, that's part of the reason I joined."

"Well, I better go get some rest. Marcus said I look like shit." I smiled weakly.

"Marcus is an asshole. You look fine, but you should get some rest."

"Good night then." I started walking toward my apartment.

He gave a salute and started walking toward his. He didn't invite me to tag along in the morning and I honestly hadn't expected him to. A part of me wished he would have though. It was the same part of me that wanted to get to know him better, for reasons I didn't quite understand. He left a lot to the imagination. Maybe that was it. He gave just enough to pique interest, but not enough to satisfy.

CHAPTER TWENTY-FOUR

UNKNOWN NUMBER: SHES STILL OUT THERE.

Unknown number: I KNOW WHO TRIED TO KILL YOUR BROTHER.

I blinked as I read the text messages. Normally they were at least accompanied by one from my mother letting me know what Lincoln's status was and another from either Hailey or Celia, trying to see when we could hang out. This time, it was those lone messages that greeted me first thing in the morning when I looked at my phone. I pressed my palms to my eyes and took a deep breath. What could I do? Go to the police? It was an unknown number from phones that were disconnected as soon as they were sent. I got out of bed, taking my phone with me to the bathroom.

As I brushed my teeth, I sent Hailey a text letting her know I'd be at the coffee shop in half an hour. I needed to talk to someone about this. Normally, Lincoln would be my someone, but he wasn't here right now. Not really anyway. My chest squeezed at the thought. Two weeks were almost up. Soon he'll be awake and able to tell us what happened. At least that was what I was hoping for. Mom wasn't as hopeful. When she spoke to me yesterday, her voice only held grief and regret. She said the brain was a fragile thing and we weren't sure how he'd be once he woke up. Hearing that broke my heart. I asked her who had been in the house, who had access to his room, and she called me crazy, said that he'd done this to himself, despite what I thought he said. What I thought he said. Meaning, she didn't believe he'd shaken his head to tell me he hadn't tried to kill himself.

By the time I left the apartment, I felt as gloomy as the sky above me. I kept my head down as I walked to the coffee shop. I was supposed to take pictures of football practice this afternoon and I had the initiation tonight. Not that anyone had bothered with telling me at what time or where that was. I also needed to go back to the rest of Lana's notes on her computer and at some point, do actual school work. I was just so tired. So, so tired. Last night, I'd gone to bed as soon as I got home, but not even the exhaustion in my limbs helped me with the tossing and turning. I pulled open the door to the coffee shop and let out a shaky, cold, breath. Normally, it was busy in here. This morning, it seemed as though it was just me. Becca smiled at me as I approached.

"You look exhausted. How's your brother?"

"The same."

"I'm sorry. I'll keep praying for him." Her brown eyes furrowed slightly.

"Thank you. It means a lot." I tried to smile, but as usual when discussing Lincoln, I wasn't sure my mouth moved much.

"Do you want your usual?"

"Yes, please." I took my wallet out to pay. "You know what? Just give me whole milk. Fuck it."

"You only live once." Becca laughed lightly.

"How's school going?"

"It's . . . okay. I'm applying to schools everywhere. I mean, everywhere except here." Her cheeks tinted as she leaned in and whispered, "Don't tell my sister."

"I won't." I smiled, handing her the money. "Have you always wanted out?"

"God, yes."

"Do you know what you want to do?"

"Not yet. I'm thinking maybe become a teacher. Something that helps shape kids. You know, pick up the slack for absent parents. That sort of thing."

"Ah, so daddy issues do help after all."

"I also have mommy issues. And all the issues." She laughed. "I hide them well."

"I can see that. You always look so upbeat."

"No, I mean, I am upbeat. I just work with what I have, you know?" She lowered her voice again, looking around quickly. "Unlike my sister. She just bottles things up. She's going to blow one of these days."

"She seems to be doing well enough," I said. "Is she here? I texted her and she said she would be."

"She'll be here soon. Uncle Deacon needed help with some things at his farm." Her gaze flicked over my head, to where I knew the small television was. Hailey said they'd installed it there for the world soccer games during the summer and left it because it was easier than taking it down. "Did you hear the police got an anonymous call on Lana Ly?"

"What? No." My head whipped around and zoned on the news playing. "Can you turn it up?"

She did, and we caught the tail end of the report, with the newscaster saying, *"Authorities are looking into the anonymous tip and urges anyone who may have any information about the disappearance of Lana Ly to please come forward."*

"Damn," Becca whispered. I turned to her, heart pounding. "Do you think she's alive?"

"I don't know," I whispered back, pulling out my phone to see if I could find what the anonymous tip had been.

Becca moved away and started making my latte as I stood

there, unable to move from my spot as I scrolled through the first page of my search. The door opened behind me and the bell over the door gave a light ring as it shut again. I turned around in time to see Hailey walking inside. She'd dyed her hair brown and looked completely different, more sophisticated, with her high cheekbones and brown eyes more visible. Just as I was telling her I loved that color on her, a man walked in behind her. Everything about him was massive, from his thick arms that stuck out of cut-off denim sleeves to his stature, which was well over six feet. He was probably closer to Travis's height than Logan's, but even Travis, with all his athleticism, didn't look like this. This guy had a mean look about him. He zeroed his dark eyes on mine and smiled. It wasn't kind.

"Pretty," he said.

"This is my friend, Mae," Hailey said, her voice loud and clear. "Friend."

"Pretty friend." Deacon grinned.

There was something obviously wrong with him, but I didn't know what. My automatic assumption of him and thinking he was mean was way off though. Deacon obviously had an impediment. I took Hailey's lead and spoke in a raised, clear voice, and hoped it sounded less like a shout and more teacher-like authority.

"Hi, Deacon." I smiled.

He walked over to me, boots stomping loudly, stared at me for a moment longer. It was enough to get me frazzled. His clear blue eyes were zoned in on me as if trying to uncover the thoughts inside my head. I tore my gaze away and looked at Hailey, who was on her phone, then Becca, who was busy making my coffee.

"Your latte, Mae," Becca said after a beat.

I turned and bolted in that direction, grateful for the interruption. When I looked back, Deacon was still standing in the same spot, staring at me. A shiver rolled through me as I picked up the latte, which thankfully was in a to-go cup. Normally, I got it in a ceramic mug because I sat here for hours. Today, I wanted nothing more than to get out. Deacon walked toward me, but instead of stopping, he went behind the counter. I moved away from it, toward the couch I usually sat on. Hailey walked over, gnawing her bottom lip as she approached. She looked like she had a million things on her mind today and I wasn't sure I wanted to stick around long enough for her to tell me what they were. Not with Deacon here.

"I like your hair." I set down my latte. "The brown looks good on you."

"Thanks. I did it myself." She smiled, sitting across from me. She looked over at where Deacon was. Even Becca was keeping a distance, I noticed, but it could have been my imagination.

"Is he okay?" I asked. Her attention snapped back to me.

"He had a motorcycle accident when he was seventeen. Suffered major damage to his brain, so he's in and out. Sometimes he has completely normal conversations, sometimes he doesn't speak for days, and other times he does this thing where he only says words here and there."

"God, that must be so hard," I whispered.

I instantly thought of Lincoln and felt my eyes fill with tears. What if he woke up and was like that? We'd help him, of course. We'd love him, no doubt. How would he cope though? After having such a huge personality. How could he cope like that? My eyes followed Deacon as he got something out of the glass case that held the croissants and loaves.

"You're thinking about your brother."

"How could I not? Who knows how his brain is right now and whether or not he'll react like this when he wakes up?" I wiped my face quickly.

"Maybe." She stood and walked behind the bar and started fiddling with the coffee machine. "So, what's new with you? How are classes? How's the newspaper stuff going?"

I was still stuck on the *maybe* and the nonchalant way in which she'd said it. She didn't know Lincoln, not really anyway, but she'd had a crush on him, possibly even slept with him if he was the hockey player she'd told me about.

"Classes are fine. Newspaper is fine," I said, responding to her question in hopes that it would distract me from reading into things too much.

I looked over at Deacon and Becca. He was scarfing down a croissant, while she was texting someone on her phone. The front door opened and people walked in—two police officers and one blonde pregnant lady behind them. Hailey walked back over to me and sat down in the same seat. She picked up the remote and unmuted the television, where once again, there was a picture of Lana.

"The anonymous caller claims to have seen Lana Ly, a student at Ellis University, who disappeared earlier this year. When questioned, the caller said she'd been in the woods drinking illegally with friends and didn't think anything of it until the following day," the news reporter said. They displayed a different picture of Lana, wearing a floral spring dress and smiling at the camera. *"If you have any information, please reach out to the police."*

"Pretty doll," Deacon said from behind the counter, pointing at the screen. "Pretty doll."

"She's not a doll, Deacon. She's a girl who's gone missing," Becca said, clearly irritated. She gave me an apologetic look, shaking her head.

"Hey, Becca. Hailey." One of the police officers took his hat off and greeted them. "How are the cows, Deacon?"

"They're good," he said slowly. "A lot of milk."

"That's great. So you're still using them for dairy?" the other officer asked.

"Yes, until I can't no more. They're my babies." He shrugged.

He didn't look mean or creepy when he spoke to them. I realized it was the first clear sentence he'd spoken since he'd arrived. The officers continued speaking with him and I sat down in my usual spot, clicking on one of the articles, even though I'd already seen what the anonymous caller said.

"I am so tired." Hailey yawned loudly. "Deacon called me at the crack of dawn saying his stupid sheep ran away and I had to help him go find her."

"That sucks." I cringed. "Did you find her?"

"Yes. I swear I never hit anything but I wanted to kill that thing." She took a sip of her coffee. "Are you going to the toga party tonight?"

"I don't know."

Celia had been the one to tell me about it. She'd texted saying her house was one of the ones participating. Apparently, it was a party that went on for an entire block. You paid at one house, got a wrist band, and were able to go to all of the houses participating. If I went, I'd only go to Celia's though. It wasn't like I had a ton of friends. Unless you counted Max and Logan and Nolan, and possibly Marcus. I sat back in my seat. When the hell had I become the girl who had predominantly male friends? I'd always had them growing up because of Lincoln, but it wasn't like I went out of my way to be friends with guys.

"Come on. You should go." She set down her coffee.

"Between your schedule and mine, I feel like we're never on the same page."

"Maybe I will." I shrugged, smiling, but got serious. What if the person sending the texts was watching me? What if they were waiting for me to slip up and go to a party like this? I couldn't imagine the secret society being behind the texts, not after getting them this morning. That would be stupid. It had to be someone else. Someone connected to both Lincoln and Lana. But who?

"You look worried. What's going on?"

"I've been getting weird texts." My gaze snapped to Hailey's. I pulled out my phone to show her.

"Creepy." Her eyes widened on mine as she held my phone. "Have you tried calling?"

"Of course. It's always disconnected when I do."

"It must be a burner phone."

"A burner phone? Why would they use a burner phone? They obviously don't want a response from me if that's the case."

"I don't know." She shook her head, handing it back to me. "Be careful with that though." She picked up her mug again. "I mean, why would they say that about your brother when they know you know what happened was drug abuse?"

"It wasn't drug abuse."

"Didn't he overdose on heroin? That's drug abuse, Mae." She raised an eyebrow.

"Lincoln didn't try to kill himself. He doesn't even . . . he hates drugs."

"I know it sucks to hear this, but it's what happened."

"No. It's not." I shook my head as I gathered my things. I could feel myself getting angry the longer I sat there, and worse, feeling watched. Every time I looked up, I saw Deacon standing there. "I should go. I have to get my things ready for later."

"See you later," Hailey said, smiling at me as if she hadn't just completely insulted my brother's situation. "Text me when you're on your way there."

I waved at her, waved at Becca and sort of waved at Deacon. He was talking to the police officers again but his eyes were on me. I walked back to my apartment, thinking about everything that had happened these last few days: the pictures of my brother with Lana, the short entries Lana had written in her computer describing the man she'd been with and how my first thought had been my father, which was absolutely insane. Still. The clues were there. Why would she be arguing with my brother? I couldn't dismiss the possibility that he could be the son of the man she was having the affair with. I couldn't deny it, especially after knowing Ella was somehow involved with him. I'd seen the way Ella talked about my father. I hadn't had further contact with her, aside from the thank you responses via email when I sent her pictures, but that didn't mean much.

I was still lost in my own thoughts when I reached my apartment and bumped into someone, a hard someone. I glanced up, apologizing, and found myself looking at a carbon copy of Logan. *Patrick Fitzgerald.* He grinned, and it was so beautiful that I had to remind myself what this man had done. He raped women. Well, according to the news. And Max. Max believed the women. Hell, I believed the women, but having him standing in front of me made my brain falter, like what if he hadn't done those horrible things?

"Let me hold the door for you," he said smoothly.

"Thanks." I walked through. He followed. I shot him a look. "Weren't you leaving?"

"I was, but maybe I changed my mind." He kept grinning.

There was no warmth in his eyes as he smiled. Even this reminded me of Logan, the way he had the ability to turn his warmth on and off. I heard a conversation and turned my head in that direction. Logan was sitting there with a man that had to be his father, because even though his skin tone was a few shades lighter than theirs, he looked just like them—dark hair, chiseled jaw, green eyes.

"So, you live here?"

"Yeah." I blinked back at Patrick, whose eyes were now making a slow perusal of my body. Again, I didn't feel creeped out. What was wrong with me?

"Absolutely not." The shout came from Logan, and it was more of a growl than a shout. Our attention whipped in that direction and I saw him stomping over to us, a fierce expression on his face. "Weren't you leaving? Get the hell out."

"Oh." Patrick chuckled. "You like this one?"

"Get out. Now."

"I don't think I will. I was having a conversation with, what's your name, sweetheart?" He brought his hand up, but before he could get it anywhere near my face, Logan slapped it down and got between us.

"Try to touch her again and I'll kill you," he said, his voice unnervingly low. "If you ever so much as look at her, I will fucking kill you. If you even think about her once you leave this building, I'll fucking murder you in your sleep. Is that clear enough for you?"

Patrick chuckled again. "Pops, you hear this guy?"

"Please leave, Patrick. We'll talk later," their dad said.

Not that I could see him from behind Logan, who took up my entire line of vision. I could feel the anger radiating off him and that was enough to keep me there. If he was acting like this, it was serious.

"Mr. Fitzgerald, do you need assistance?" That was Gary.

"No, Gary. Thank you. I think I've made it clear to my brother that he's not welcome here," Logan said.

"Crystal," Patrick muttered, walking away. He waited until he was by the door to say, "See you soon, little bro. I guess I'll wait until you're done with your plaything to have a go."

I wrapped my arms around Logan just as he moved to charge at the door. It didn't work. He dragged me with him. Gary ran over and Logan's dad ran over and they both managed to form a blockade in front of him. I managed to unwrap my arms from around him and step back, waiting for him to calm down. I'd never seen him like this. Ever. At hockey practice he'd come close, when he'd played against his teammates, but this was something else. If he brought this kind of energy on the ice, I would hate to be his opponent.

"You should go," his dad said. "We'll take it from here."

"Thanks. I'll wait."

"He's right. You should go." Logan turned around quickly.

He wasn't breathing as hard as he had been a moment ago, but his eyes still looked murderous. He still looked beautiful. The urge to drag him upstairs and make us both forget this shitty morning was enormous. I licked my lips, wondering if I should offer, but stopped myself. His father was standing right there. Gary was standing right there, and I didn't think he would report such a thing to my father, but you never knew. It was all it would take for him to fly over here and make me go home. My parents weren't the most involved, unless they thought there was a chance I could get pregnant. Then, they were all over my shit. Just looking at Logan made my ovaries hurt, and kissing him last night had been . . . a lot. He watched me as I watched him. The longer I stood there, the less upset he seemed. I wasn't sure if he could read my thoughts or not, but I swear I felt like he could. I felt myself blush. His mouth lifted slightly. Not a smile, but the tell of amusement.

"I left something at your door that you need to do. Someone will come pick it up shortly," he said.

"Okay." I frowned.

"And I'll pick you up at five. For the thing."

"Five. Okay. I have to take some pictures of the—"

"Football practice. I know. I'm picking you up at five, we'll go by there, and then do what we need to do."

"Cool." I smiled. "Have a good rest of your morning."

"So far, this has been the best part of my morning." He scoffed. "See you later, Mae."

"Later, Moriarty." I winked as I walked away, smiling at the elevator doors as he chuckled behind me.

I heard his father question him about me calling him by his middle name, but the elevator doors opened before I could hear the rest of that conversation. When I got to my floor, I saw a bag by my door. I opened it as I walked in. There was a tiny blood strip, a saliva swab, pee cup, and a note.

Don't worry, we won't clone you. We need to make sure you're clean.

X

Ps. We know this is really weird and promise we are not a sex club.

I looked at the contents again. Everything came with instructions. They wanted my blood, pee, and saliva. This was more extensive than hooking up with someone from an app.

CHAPTER TWENTY-FIVE

LOGAN

"**Y**OU LIKE HER."

I glared at my father. "You don't get to talk about her."

"Stop being so dramatic. I understand you not wanting your brother near her after all of the rumors, but—"

"You call him going to court and getting sued for rape by four different women rumors?"

"They all dropped the charges."

"He paid them off."

"Only to take the limelight away from him. He says he didn't do those things."

"Well, excuse me if I find it hard to believe either one of you." I shot him a look.

It wasn't like my father was the most innocent or respectful of women. He'd had two incidents with two different secretaries.

"Those were consensual."

"It doesn't matter. Forget I brought that up." I threw my hands up.

I was tired of discussing all the ways he was a worthless man only to have him argue why he wasn't. A foolish man made mistakes, but only a fool tried to justify them. My father was both, and the mistakes he made went way past cheating on my mother. His mistakes left marks and bruises, and often broken bones, at least when it came to my brother and I. So, was I happy to see him? Hell, the fuck no. Did I need to sign the papers that got me out of the contract in which I was currently listed as one of the owners? Yes.

It was something I should have never signed. Even as I did it, I knew it was a stupid mistake, but my father's lawyer had driven a hard bargain—my signature for a quarter of the profit that would come in the first two years. They needed someone to oversee things and it had to be someone with their name on the contract. Because I was the one closest to the restaurant, that person was me. My brother couldn't even have his name on it because of all of the disgusting things he'd done. I felt my blood boil again. It wasn't enough that he was just as worthless as our father. It wasn't enough that he'd gotten in trouble and almost arrested. He had to come in here and also try to hit on Amelia. This was after he started an argument with me about signing an NHL contract. He thought that because he'd played in the league, he should tell me what to do, where to go and who my agent should be once I graduated.

"This is ready." Dad put the papers in a folder and set them in his briefcase. He closed it and snapped the handles as he stood again. "I hope I see you before next year. Maybe you can bring your friend to the island for a weekend."

"No, thanks."

"You know, your mother forgave me for all of that shit. I fucked up, yes, but she forgave me, why can't you?"

I stared at him for a moment. "If you can't answer that question yourself, you're worse than I thought. I'll see you when I see you."

I turned around and headed back up to my apartment. He'd

one-hundred-percent ruined my mood. As the elevator door was closing, I caught sight of Marcus jogging my way. I held it for him.

"Shit. I'm running late today." He exhaled as we rode up to my floor. "I hope she already did all the stuff. I have to take it to the lab and run tests myself."

"You're running the tests?"

"Obviously. You know anyone else who's pre-med with access to the labs?"

I glared at him. Why were all of my friends such smart asses? Couldn't any of them be mild mannered and just nice? It was stupid, but I didn't like the idea of him handling something so personal of Amelia's. This girl had me tripping over everything. The elevator doors opened and I started walking to my apartment. I heard a door open behind me and Mae's laughter made me freeze in my tracks. I looked back and saw her talking to Marcus as she handed him the bag. She'd just met him yesterday and somehow was acting like they were old friends. Maybe it was because I'd dealt with my dad and brother this morning. Maybe it was because of the little sleep I'd gotten last night, or the fact that hockey practice had been shitty the day before yesterday. Maybe it was the kiss her and I shared, and the way I couldn't get it the fuck out of my head.

Whatever the reason was, I found myself fighting the urge to run over there, punch Marcus and take Mae inside where nobody else could look, touch, or talk to her. Yeah, I was being absolutely ridiculous. Maybe I needed to get laid. By someone who wasn't Mae, so that I'd quit thinking about her exclusively. I opened the door to my place and walked inside, making it a point not to look back at them. The last thing I needed was for him to know just how interested in her I was. As it was, I'd made an exception for tonight's initiation and I knew I'd never hear the end of it from them.

CHAPTER TWENTY-SIX

AMELIA

I GOT A TEXT AT FOUR THIRTY THAT I THOUGHT WAS GOING TO BE from Logan, until I remembered he didn't have my phone number. It was from Travis. I hesitated opening it. I hadn't spoken to him since the location incident, and even though we'd ended that conversation politely, I was afraid of what talking to him would lead to. On my end, I was one-hundred-percent done with Travis, but I knew him. He was the kind of person who was never done with you until you moved on. It had been like that with his ex-girlfriend Tasha. He'd only let her go because we'd gotten together. At the time, I'd found it hot. Now, it was not.

Travis: Hey. In town this weekend. We still hanging?

Me: I have some things to do, but maybe we can meet up at some point

Travis: You going to the toga party?

Me: Yeah, I think so, if I'm done with everything else.

Travis: It doesn't start until ten. Wanna go together?

Me: Let's meet there. Are you with the entire team?

Travis: Yes but I can ditch them

Me: Nope, it's okay.

Travis: See you later then

I sent him a thumbs up in response. I dressed in jeans, black long sleeve shirt, wool tan jacket, and black slip-on sneakers. I wasn't sure what to expect, but I definitely wanted to be warm and comfortable. He knocked on my door at four fifty-five, and I grabbed my camera, bag, and rushed over and pulled it open. Logan looked like he'd just stepped out of the shower, hair slicked back, beard trimmed perfectly, green eyes looking right into mine. He looked rough, with a dangerous air to him as he looked at me intensely.

"Do you think I should switch out my khaki jacket for a black one?" I licked my lips. His expression softened.

"You look perfect."

"You guys are always wearing black though. I can . . . it would take me a second."

"You look perfect."

"Are you sure? Because I could—" I turned slightly. He grabbed my hand to stop me from walking away. I whipped back, heart pounding.

"You couldn't look more perfect if you tried. Leave the jacket."

"Oh," I whispered. "Thank you."

He let go of my hand and I locked the door, walking beside him to the elevator.

"So, that was weird with the bag and the blood and pee and stuff," I said.

"It's necessary."

"The card said they wouldn't clone me." I felt myself smile as we rode down in the elevator. "And that it's not a sex club."

"Pity." He glanced over at me.

"Which part?"

"Both."

I laughed. "The world does not need two Amelia Bastón's."

"I beg to differ."

I thought about it some more as we walked through the lobby and decided I would hate having a clone.

"Do you normally go to football games?"

"Not really." He walked to the left. I stopped.

"Isn't it that way?"

"I'm driving."

"Oh."

"Are you going to follow me or are you expecting me to pull the car up like one of your chauffeurs?"

"I don't have chauffeurs." I blinked and started walking toward him again.

"You don't? Wow. Could've fooled me."

"I use Uber drivers, thank you very much."

"Do you always request a black car?"

"First of all, I feel judged." I paused, pursing my lips. He bit his lip to keep from laughing and I wondered what I could say to push him over the edge. "Secondly, I am not that much of a diva."

"No? What sneakers are you wearing?"

"I said diva. I didn't say I don't buy nice things." I stuck my tongue out.

He smiled, pulling out car keys and clicking the button. I stopped walking again, this time right in front of the passenger seat, which he opened for me and helped me as I got inside the cabin. I inhaled a deep breath and exhaled. It smelled like him, like his sheets, like what I'd been craving the last few days but couldn't have because I mean, what was I supposed to do? Tell him I found him insanely attractive and funny and fun to be around and that I never wanted to leave his bed again? Yeah, it didn't work like that. He climbed into the driver's side, shut the door, strapped on his seatbelt and started the truck.

"I don't know what I was expecting you to drive, but a Ford truck wasn't it."

"What were you expecting?" he glanced at me. "A Chevy?"

"Not a truck at all." I laughed. "Nolan has a Porsche and you guys are like twins, so I figured something like that."

"I'm not willing to ask my father for anything, especially not a fucking Porsche." He winked. "But if that's the kind of stuff you're impressed by and you want me to get a Porsche next year, I will."

"I'm not impressed by that." I felt myself blush as I looked away. "Besides, who's to say you'll even know me next year?"

"You don't think you will?"

"I'm not sure. You're already sort of famous. By then, you'll be off in the NHL getting paid big money. I doubt you'll want to hang out with me."

"Whose bed will you sleep in when you're tired and can't get any rest in your own?"

"I guess I'll have to find another willing participant." I focused on the way his hands seemed to tighten on the steering wheel.

It was impossible that he was jealous, right? I mean, Logan Fitzgerald jealous of a hypothetical scenario in which I shared a bed with another man? *Yeah right.* Still, from where I was sitting, it looked like he cared. We arrived at the football stadium and walked inside, through the door labeled for media, where a security guard was manning the door. I flashed my badge. Logan flashed his smile. We both got in easily.

"Do you think they always have security here?" I asked as we headed toward the field.

"Only when both teams are using the premises to practice. It's new. We have them too."

"It's so weird that they'd think two-hundred-pound of muscle guys would need protection."

"Do you feel like you need protection?" he asked. I made the mistake of whipping my head toward him too quickly before saying no and I could tell he didn't believe me. He stopped dead in his tracks. I did too because it would've been weird not to. "Why do you feel like you need protection?"

"No reason. I never even said those words."

"Your face did."

"Well, ignore my face."

"Can't." His lips twitched. "I'm looking right at it."

"Well, stop looking." I turned around and walked faster toward the field.

He chuckled as he walked after me. I didn't know why, but the way he went zero to sixty when he thought I could potentially be in trouble, rattled me. It was the same earlier today. Logan had gotten between us before I could even tell his brother to fuck off. And now this? It was nothing. I shook it off. I took the cap off the camera and walked to the sidelines, snapping pictures of the guys as they ran drills, drank Gatorade, and huddled around the coach. It was a series of snaps that lasted about fifteen minutes, but they'd do. I closed the cap on the camera and shot a text to Max, telling him I was done with this and would send over the pictures in the morning.

"You don't want to stay for the entire practice?" Logan asked as I walked back to him.

"For what? To look for my replacement sleeper for when you're gone?"

The amusement left his face. "No."

"The quarterback is cute." I glanced over my shoulder for show, not that I cared or even knew what the QB looked like underneath his helmet. "I guess he'll do."

"He has a girlfriend."

"How do you know?"

"Because I know him."

"Well, maybe this time next year he won't have a girl-friend." I shrugged.

"This time next year you won't be here. Aren't you graduating next semester?"

"Good point." I laughed. Damn it. Logan didn't laugh though. I watched him as we walked back to his car. He was so serious half the time and so flirty the other. "I think you're jealous."

"Of what?" he sounded genuinely surprised.

"Of the thought of me sharing a bed with someone else."

"I am not jealous." He scoffed. "Please."

"Okay, you're not jealous." I shrugged as I got in his truck.

He started driving toward campus, making a left at the library. I thought he was going to go into one of the houses that sat nearby, but he passed those as well, and drove down a street that went on and on, until there were no more houses in plain view and all I could see was forest. In the rearview, I could see that we were driving upward and wondered if this was where the first house I'd been to was, on top of the fall. It seemed like we were going in the right direction but I couldn't know for sure without the map and address. He took another turn, and houses finally came into view. They were far apart from each other though.

"Nolan told me he had an interesting conversation with you," he said as he slowed his speed.

"What conversation?"

"About you sleeping with him."

"Oh." I laughed. "He called that interesting? He was trying to get me to sleep with him. Or both of you. At the same time, I think."

"Are you into that?" His lips turned up on one side.

"Absolutely not."

"You sure? You're blushing again." He looked like he was trying not to smile.

"Positive." I hated that I was still blushing. I put a hand up to my temple to shield my face from him.

He chuckled louder. "There's nothing wrong with wanting to have a threesome with the two most popular guys in school."

"I don't want to have a threesome. Jesus Christ." I groaned, covering my face with both hands now. My words were muffled by my hands. "Maybe I'll use him for his bed."

"Fuck that," Logan growled. I lowered my hands and looked at him.

"You were literally just asking me if I wanted to have a threesome with you, but you don't like the idea of me sleeping beside Nolan?"

"Those are entirely different things." He was still scowling as we stopped at the very end of the block. He pushed a button on his rearview that opened up the iron gate we were in front of and we continued driving up an expansive driveway, with beautiful trees canopying on either side. "When we get there, you have to stay by my side at all times. Not behind me. Either in front of me or beside me. No exceptions."

"Why?"

"I can't help you if you're behind me."

I was too shocked by what I saw once the enormous castle finally came into view. Judging by the cars that were already there, the castle was at a distance from where we needed to park. I wanted to say something about it, but my mouth dropped and I hadn't been able to recover as I examined it. It looked like they'd gotten a sketch of Cinderella's castle from Disney World and put a Gothic flare on it. Like a creepy castle that had been dropped in the midst of the modern homes around it. There was nothing beautiful about it, except everything. I continued gaping at it as we got out of the car and walked over to it, our shoes crunching the pebbles beneath us. When we reached the long bridge that led to it, I froze. It was cobblestone and they clearly had covered up a previously existing moat. My head whipped in Logan's direction.

"We're in a castle," I said.

Logan chuckled. "Yup."

"Who owns this?"

"We do."

"But . . . how is there a castle here? Does anyone know about it?"

It was covered by a heavily wooded area on either side. Even the drive in here didn't give it away. When had it been built? What had been the purpose of it? Did someone actually need a castle in upstate New York? My heart pounded faster at all of the possibilities as we stared at the huge oval wooden door.

"No one knows about it. If they do, it's because they've heard rumors about it and they all think the land is haunted anyway so they probably wouldn't come near it," he said. "Besides, the only way to get here is through those gates, or through the backwoods. You'd have to be crazy to try either one."

"Wow," I whispered, looking around.

"I'll give you a short tour now and a longer one later," Logan promised as he took out the skeleton key that opened the front door. Even that was the coolest thing I'd ever seen.

"Can I see that?"

"You'll get your own." He chuckled as he handed it to me.

It was heavy. Engraved on it was: *LMF* and the words *The Eight* beside it.

"I guess you can't lose this key." I raised an eyebrow.

"They take the money out of your account when they have to replace it. Let's just say, most of us wear it around our necks, underneath our shirts."

He pushed the door opened and for a moment, I stood in the threshold completely shell-shocked, wondering what the hell I'd gotten myself into.

CHAPTER TWENTY-SEVEN

"THE HOUSE IS, BY DESIGN AND HISTORICALLY KNOWN, TO BE THE perfect spook house," Logan said as we stood right at the entrance. I eyed the staircase at the far corner, that seemed to only lead to a single gold door. There were sconces that held candles. It gave the castle a dim orange glow throughout.

"That's random," I noted, looking at the stairs.

We continued walking, down a corridor that seemed endless. There were busts and paintings alongside us as we walked. It was just what you'd expect in a castle and it seemed like the people of the society hadn't changed much of it.

"Truly, I've never seen a castle like this in the US," I said.

"And we have two in town." Logan smiled when he caught my disbelief. "The red cloaks own one too, not too far from here. You can see some of their land from our yard."

My eyebrows rose. "Do you guys talk to them? Do you know who they are?"

He shrugged a shoulder, non-committal. I took it as confirmation. He changed the subject, back to the castle we were in. "The woman who once owned this castle was the granddaughter of a German lord. It's said that she had her husband build her this castle to be a smaller version of theirs in Germany. Have you heard of the Eltz family?" He waited for me to shake my head.

"Well, the outside was drawn as inspiration from that. In general, this is a much smaller version. Once it was built, she poisoned her husband and kept his estate. Once she inherited his money, she remarried four more times, killing each husband in peculiar ways. Peculiar, but realistic enough that they never charged her for murder."

"So it's haunted," I said, looking around.

"Definitely haunted. If you wander through the house long enough, you'll find dead ends and weird shit all over," he said. "Like that lovely staircase that leads to nowhere."

"Who owns this place? Like really owns it?" I whispered.

"We do." He turned to me with a grin. Even that looked more scary than sexy in this setting.

"Why'd you say you couldn't help me if I walked behind you?"

"They like to snatch people as they walk down these halls."

"Snatch them?" I squeaked. "Who?"

"The members. To be funny."

"It doesn't seem funny at all." I shuddered. "Is that what happened to Lana? Was she snatched?"

"No."

His answer didn't help calm my nerves. In an attempt to distract myself from those words, I turned my attention to the doors that lined the hall. There was a door on either side of the hall, one for each step you took. If they were all rooms, over forty of them. It seemed implausible, of course, but the hall we were walking seemed endless. We took a right at the end and were led to another endless hall.

"You have got to be kidding me. Does this ever end? Is that why it's called Labyrinth?"

Logan chuckled. "Yes."

"Lab for short." That came from a voice on the other side

of me. I hadn't heard him approach at all and shrieked, jumping toward Logan. He put a protective arm around me, even though his shoulders were shaking with laughter as we both looked at Nolan.

"It's not funny." I slapped Logan's arm away from me and stood between the two of them, still looking at Nolan. "Where the hell did you come from?"

"I was eating." He grinned. "All of the doors in this particular hallway lead to the same hall. We got food, alcohol, weed, other shit."

"All of these doors lead to the same place?"

I looked at the doors on either side of me. "How?"

"Two different wings, same hall, it connects at the end."

"Is this some kind of frat house?"

"Definitely not a frat house, otherwise, you wouldn't be here. We're all sleeping here tonight though. Yourself included."

"What? Why? I didn't even bring my things." Not to mention, I didn't want to stay in an old, creepy manor.

"Because it's initiation night and that's what we do."

"But I don't even have clothes, I didn't even—"

"Logan's got you. He made sure your room was stocked with anything you might need."

"How?" I gaped at Logan.

"I grabbed some things at the store for you. It's not a big deal."

"How do you know my size?"

"I guesstimated."

"Guesstimating a woman's size is exactly the kind of thing that'll get you killed."

"Well, you'll have to allow me to be far away from you when you open the bag."

"I can't—"

"All right," Nolan said loudly, cutting into my sentence. "I'll let you lovebirds get to it. Marcus is waiting for me to spark up a joint. See you soon. Thirty minutes."

"So, what now? You're going to show me to my room that you stocked for me?" I faced Logan again.

"Yep."

"For the record, I don't think it's cool that you guesstimated my size and bought things for me."

"Noted." He started walking up the stairs and I followed closely beside him, afraid of being spooked again. We stopped at the head of yet another hallway. Unlike the walls lined with red wallpaper downstairs, this hallway had dark gray walls and a long dark red rug that seemed endless.

"You're in here." Logan walked ahead and opened the second door to our right.

I followed him inside. It looked like what I pictured a bedroom at Versailles to look like, gold and red wallpaper, portraits of women from hundreds of years ago, and a gold, ornate four-post queen-size bed in the center of the room. Above it, a glass chandelier I was sure my mother would drool over. There was a duffel bag on the floor and a garment bag on the bed. I walked toward it, unzipping the garment bag. I was expecting a dress or something. What I found was a black cloak. I glanced at Logan over my shoulder.

"I'm supposed to wear this?"

"Yes." He glanced at his watch. "You have twenty-five minutes to dress and meet me downstairs. Can you do that?"

"I mean, I'm basically throwing a shapeless black thing over myself, so yes."

"I'm right next door if you need me." He left the room and closed the door behind him.

I stared at it for a moment before kicking myself into

movement. Unzipping the duffel bag on the floor, I found underwear, the skimpy kind you buy on an anniversary to wear for your significant other. Not the kind you buy to wear under a cloak.

"Bastard." I threw the underwear down, kicking myself for not having his number to text him about this.

It wasn't like I had anyone I could send a picture of this to for conversation or advice. Celia couldn't find out about this. Hailey was out of the question. So, I kept it to myself and looked at the rest of the stuff. A pair of leggings, a pair of jeans, two T-shirts and a sundress. All my size. That gave me pause, but I didn't have much time to dwell on it now. I slipped off my coat and pulled my shirt over my head. Should I put the cloak over my jeans? I frowned for a beat. I couldn't imagine why that would be a problem. I would've gotten away with leaving my shirt on too, I supposed, but I didn't want to waste more time.

According to what he'd said, I had five minutes to meet him downstairs. I made sure everything was put away before looking at myself in the mirror. I looked like a creepy nun with this getup. A creepy nun who was wearing a lacy red bra. Turning away from the mirror, I walked over to the window. The woods were behind the house, but there was a big white shack looking thing that seemed to share land with the house right beside us. I hadn't even noticed there was a house there when we pulled in. It had been impossible to see with all the trees in the way. I craned my neck to get a better look at their yard. There were holes on the ground that looked like a cemetery. I shivered. Were we staying beside a cemetery? I made myself snap out of it and walk out of the room to meet Logan downstairs.

The hall was spookier now that I was walking it on my own. I could hear a light hum of chatter as I passed some of the doors, so I hurried past those, rushing to the stairs, which I sped down. At the bottom, I found Logan standing there in a black cloak of his own, his face uncovered. Somehow, he looked handsome even in that getup, and you couldn't even see his athletic frame or washboard abs. His face though, that jawline and those dark green eyes that seemed to be tuned into everything they looked at, made him sexy regardless of what he was wearing.

"Did you do anything naughty while you were up there?"

"Did you do anything naughty while you were fantasizing about me in all the lingerie you bought me?" I raised an eyebrow.

"Maybe." His gaze heated as he looked me up and down. "Are you wearing any of it right now?"

"Maybe."

"You're not going to tell me?"

"I might be wearing something red." I leaned in closer and whispered, "but I might not be wearing anything at all. I guess you'll never know."

We stared at each other for a beat. Logan opened his mouth, but whatever he was going to say was cut off by a door opening behind us.

"You may enter," Nolan said. His head was covered, but I knew his voice now. "Pull your hood up please."

I did as I was told. I assumed Logan did as well, but I couldn't see very well with the stupid thing on my head. With the limited sight I had, the only thing I could make out was a long dinner table with candles lit all down the middle. There were at least ten others wearing black cloaks in here. I felt a hand at my back leading me, and I walked slowly, careful not to trip over the hem of the cloak. Logan, or who I assumed was Logan, stopped me once I reached the front of the room. A black wall with an enormous gold octopus painted on it was in front of me and a stage was set up there too. An empty stage, save for a podium off to the side, and a large chair fit for a king or queen. The doors opened again, and on instinct, I turned my face toward the noise, but all I saw was a black figure moving to the stage.

"Tonight, we are welcoming you into our family. You will sign our creed, you will spill blood for us as we will for you, and you will sleep under our roof, which will soon be yours as well. Being part of our family means above all else—loyalty." It was a female voice, and she paused. "You don't want to test our loyalty by talking to others about us or what happens behind closed doors here. People who have done that in the past have been banished from The Eight."

"The creed consists of five rules, five simple rules that you must follow. Much like the Ten Commandments but even simpler and impossible to forget. You will be summoned at some point throughout the night, but until then, you can relax and unwind here. We usually set up a camping night in which you will share a tent with your partner, so I'll keep you posted on that," she said. "That's all I have for you right now. Welcome, and I can't wait to meet you all without these stupid cloaks."

A few people chuckled. My mind stayed on her words about being banished from The Eight. I wondered if that was what happened to my brother. Had he gotten kicked out for some reason? Maybe for telling Lana about the society? Had that been what pushed him over the edge?

CHAPTER TWENTY-EIGHT

"I DON'T UNDERSTAND HOW EVERYONE CAN JUST BE SO nonchalant about all of this," I whispered as I sipped on the champagne handed to me.

"I can't speak for everyone else," Logan whispered back. "My mind is still on whether or not you're wearing underwear underneath the cloak."

"You're such a guy." I laughed, shaking my head.

"Last I checked." He met my gaze as he took a sip of champagne. "Are you going to tell me?"

"No."

"Okay." He shrugged, still staring at me. "I'll pretend I know."

"Let me guess, you're going to pretend I'm naked."

"Fuck no, are you kidding? I'm going to pretend you're wearing the red lace. That way I can drag it off you with my teeth."

My nipples puckered against the cloak. "You're not supposed to say things like that. You don't even know if I want you."

"Don't I?" He cocked his head. It would've been stupid of me to deny that claim at this point in the game, but I felt the need to add something nevertheless.

"Besides, I'm not one of your groupies."

"I never said you were. If you were one of my groupies, we wouldn't be having this conversation and your panties would already be on the floor."

I tore my gaze from his, ignoring the explosion of emotions inside of my chest. There was absolutely no way I was going to get out of this ordeal unscathed. This was the guy I was assigned as a partner? How? I wouldn't survive this and it had nothing to do with vanishing and everything to do with my overactive hormones. I drank the rest of my champagne.

"Slow down on the alcohol, Amelia."

I met his gaze again. "You're not my father, Logan."

"Cheers to that." He lifted his glass. "I'm not telling you to slow down because I don't think you can handle your alcohol. I'm telling you to slow down because later on, you'll wish you had. Take it from someone who got shit-faced at this thing and regretted it."

"When are you going to tell me about my brother being here? And about Lana?"

"Can we talk about this another time?"

"No."

"Then we need to head to our rooms because I'm not having this conversation here."

"What a coincidence, you want to be alone in a room with me." I raised an eyebrow. "Is that part of your plan?"

"What plan?"

"To find out what's under the cloak."

"I just want to point out that you're the one who keeps bringing it up, not me." He set his glass down. It was still full. "Let's go."

We walked to my room in silence. When we reached my door, I stopped walking and turned to him.

"I want to see your room."

He walked to the door beside me, pulled a key out of his pocket, and unlocked it.

"Why do you keep it locked?"

"I don't want any surprises."

"Do you think someone would sneak into my room?" My eyes widened as I looked at the wall that separated our rooms.

"Only if they want me to kill them."

I stared at him for a moment, trying like hell to ignore the way I wanted to kiss the hell out of him.

"So, talk to me about Lana. What happened? You guys said you'd give me answers. I want answers."

"The first answer I'm going to give you, you're not going to like."

"Tell me anyway."

"Your brother was the last person to see her," he said. "He left her in the woods."

CHAPTER TWENTY-NINE

"THAT'S BULLSHIT," I WHISPERED, THEN A LITTLE LOUDER, "That's bullshit. You're just saying that because you don't want to get in trouble."

"In trouble for what? We had no communication with Lana. Whenever we saw her, she was either with your dad or Lincoln, and trust me, I didn't want to believe that about Lincoln either."

"That's bullshit." I glared, but my anger faltered. A part of me knew there must be some truth to this.

"We were teammates. The year before last, we were partners. Your brother is like a brother to me," he said, as if to reassure me of their bond. It didn't. I focused on something else.

"You have different partners every year?"

"We take turns. Only eight people are allowed at a time, so if two graduate, two who are still here get new partners."

"Who was your partner last year?"

"It doesn't matter."

"Was it a girl?"

"What does it matter if it was a girl, a guy, or a goat?" He was looking at me like I was crazy.

"It matters." The bed creaked as I stood up, placing my hands on my hips. "Did you buy her sexy lingerie? Did you kiss her in order to create a diversion? Did you flirt with her until she uncloaked?"

"Amelia."

"No. I want to know. Is this some sort of sick game? To bed the newbie?"

"It's not a game and having sex isn't a requirement, no."

"But you did, didn't you? You fucked last year's partner?"

"I don't understand why you're getting all hell-bent about this." He ran a hand through his hair with a sigh.

"I don't know either," I said, still glaring. "I'll see you later."

If he couldn't understand why it bothered me that he seemed to have fucked the entire campus, I wasn't going to bother to explain it to him. I didn't even know why it bothered me as much as it did, but it did. I stomped out of the room and slammed the door behind me. I opened my room and closed the door, locking it behind me next. I didn't want to care about Logan or what he did or who he did it with. I shouldn't care. My blood boiled in my veins. Yet I cared. *I definitely cared.* My hands balled into fists as I looked at the underwear on my bed. This was a game. *I* was a game. And he wanted me to believe my brother had something to do with Lana's disappearance? Fuck him. I went back to the window and looked at the cemetery. The knock on my door came before I expected it, and just as I was turning in that direction, I saw one—a red cloak. Two red cloaks. They were walking the cemetery, looking into the dug up holes. The knock came harder and I had to turn away. When I reached it, I opened it and saw Nolan on the other side. Not the person I'd expected to see.

"Let's go."

"When do I get a lock to my door?"

"When they decide to give you one."

"Hm."

I thought we would grab Logan from his room, but we passed it and continued walking down the long corridor. Nolan knocked on another door. A tall, Indian guy opened it.

"Let's go."

The guy joined us. In a sense, it made me feel better to know I wasn't the only new inductee, though my mood soured again when I thought about Logan and the underwear and last year's partner. He was no better than all the other college ass-holes out there. I don't know why I thought differently. He was a star hockey player, a ladies man, a jerk. I mean, the signs were all there.

By the time we went down two sets of stairs and entered a dark room that looked like a dungeon, I was too upset at myself over the Logan thing to be creeped out. That was, until I saw the shelves that lined the walls and the jars of octopuses aglow inside them. What the hell was this place?

"Take a seat in the first row," Nolan whispered, ushering us toward the first row of four wooden bleachers.

We all sat down quietly, facing some sort of stage in front of us. The wall was black, with a gold octopus painted on it. As I stared at it, a door opened in the center of the octopus, and a person walked out in a cloak. I assumed it was the same person as before.

"When someone enters the room, everyone in it stands," she said, and it was confirmed that it was the same person.

The guy beside me and I stood in unison, our cloaks rustling against one another.

"You may sit."

We sat back down.

"You may be wondering what this is and why there are oc-topuses everywhere," she said. "Rumor has it, the founder of *The Eight* experimented on sea creatures in a Hydraulic Lab on campus. In the 1960s, there was a flood that shut everything down, and where do you think the octopuses went? Out the window and into the falls below."

"Like I said, that's just a rumor, but as you can see, we do have some of her work." She waved a hand toward the shelves.

"The Eight take pride in being one of the only legitimately secret societies left. Our mascot, if you will, is an octopus. They camouflage, they're calculated, intelligent, and their tentacles are a representation of our members. We're everywhere. Think of your favorite actor, we know him. The politician you back? We know them. The politician you hate? We know them as well. The Eight will give you options beyond your wildest imagination. Do you want to be recruited by a certain sports team? We can make that happen. Write for a specific magazine or journal? Done. Think of it like a sorority or fraternity but better, because instead of you paying us, we pay you."

She continued speaking. "The point is that once you graduate from here, we will expect loyalty in return. We will expect you to answer when one of us calls, just as we'd answer for you. You're here either because we know you're going to get far in life, or because your parents or grandparents, or someone before you is also a part of The Eight. Either way, you're welcome here. We want you to be part of our family. We want you to make the world a better place with us."

"While we are in school, we will have different responsibilities. Here, we're still students, but we can make a difference nonetheless. Don't worry, you'll figure out what your task is soon enough. For now, we need to have one last ceremony, the induction. Your partners will come up and stand in front of you now."

Movement made me catch my breath. A figure stood in front of me. I knew it was Logan, not only because she'd said my partner, but because of his height, his scent, and the way he blocked my surroundings like a brick wall.

"Hold your hands out," she said.

I did, shakily. Logan placed his underneath mine, cradling

them lightly, as if we were carrying a bomb. I glanced up, meeting his gaze, not that I could see much, but it was enough. The others in the room started to hum in unison, just a hum, and I wondered if I was about to be initiated into a cult. My hand shook, but Logan held it steady.

"Ego fidem meam erga te. Nunc membrum sum de composuit, occasionem dedit," she said in Latin. "Repeat after me: *I pledge my loyalty to you. I am now a member of The Eight and shall make The Labyrinth my home.*"

"I pledge my loyalty to you. I am now a member of The Eight and shall make The Labyrinth my home," we all said in unison.

Before I knew what was happening, Logan took his hands away from mine, pulled out a blade, and cut himself.

"This is going to hurt," he said, and it was my only warning that he was about to slice my hand as well.

"What the fuck?" I yelped.

The person beside me grunted. The girl with him yelped lightly as well. Everyone yelled out some kind of expletive.

"You are now one with your partner," the speaker said. "You are now one with us all."

Logan turned my hand over and placed it against his as if we were holding hands. My heart pounded, not because of the hand-holding, but because it hurt like hell. He laced our fingers so they were intertwined and even through the dark veil, I could feel him looking at me.

"That's it," she said, "My name is Nora. We'll formally meet throughout the weekend and next weekend we have a little gala. No more cloaks!"

With that, she left the room, stepping back into the hole she came out of. I took the thing on my head off with my free hand. Logan did the same. I stared at our hands.

"Did you trade blood with your last assignment?" I met his gaze. "You know that none of this is sanitary. I don't even know if you're clean, and here we are swapping blood instead of spit."

"Do you want to swap spit?"

"No. That's not the point."

"All of us are clean. That was the point of the lab work earlier," he said. "Also, stop bringing up last year's partners. They have nothing to do with us."

For some reason, that did nothing to calm me down. I tried to pull my hand from his, but he held on tighter.

"Calm down. If you do that, it'll go everywhere. Let it set."

"Are you crazy?" I pulled again. "We'll be stuck together if we let it set. Do you know nothing about how blood works when it dries?"

"Trust me, I know what happens when it dries." He chuckled, his eyes lighting up. "Give it a second. It won't dry. Nolan will bring us damp towels and bandages."

As if on cue, Nolan showed up with precisely that. Logan uncurled his long fingers from mine and wiped his hand roughly before turning to me. I flinched after seeing what he'd just done, but he held my hand gently and wiped softly before setting gauze on it and wrapping it in a white bandage.

"You good?" he asked, as blood trickled from his own hand.

I nodded. "Do you want me to do yours?"

"I got it." His lips twitched.

I could tell he wasn't used to help, which made me want to help more, even if he was a huge asshole. I grabbed the towel, gauze, and bandage from his hands, pulled his bloody hand toward me, and pressed the damp towel softly, slowly, until the blood was cleaned up. It was a superficial wound, so I knew it would heal quickly. I covered it with the gauze and carefully wrapped the bandage around his hand, once, twice, three times, tucking the end in.

"There. Good as new." I smiled brightly at the job I'd done on his hand, until I met his gaze again and saw the seriousness in his eyes. I lowered his hand quickly and held on to the bloody towel and discarded wrappers from the other things. "So, can I go now?"

"You have somewhere to be?" His voice was hoarse. I chalked it up to the cool air in the room.

"A party."

"Toga party?"

"Yeah. Are you going?"

"Maybe. I have some things to do before then though."

"I need to change out of this." I tugged on my cloak.

"Let's have a drink and then you change and go."

"You told me not to drink."

"That was before this. I didn't want you bleeding excessively."

"Oh." I licked my lips. "I guess a drink wouldn't be a bad idea. Maybe it'll help with the throbbing in my hand."

He took the things in my hand, dumped it in a silver thing, and turned to me, waiting.

"You're going to leave that there?"

"They'll burn it."

We walked out of there and headed back in the direction I'd come from. Instead of going up the second flight of stairs, Logan walked around the staircase and opened a door that was beneath it. He held it open as I gaped.

"There's a bar here?"

"The best one, because it's quiet."

I stepped inside. It looked like a downtown Manhattan bar but minimized for ants. It was that small. Yet, I could see how three people could fit here comfortably. It was as wide as the large staircase and tall. Tall enough for Logan to fit standing upright. He pointed up at the ceiling, which swirled like a staircase. Not the staircase it was beneath though, since that one just went straight up.

"I told you the original owner was a nutcase."

"She must have been a huge Escher fangirl," I said.

"Or a nutcase," Logan said as he walked to the other side of the bar where the bottles were. I took a seat on the barstool across from him, yanking the cloak so it wouldn't get caught in my sandal.

"This cloak really does nothing for me."

"Really? Is it the bagginess? Is it the black? You wear black normally, so it can't be that." His eyes were dancing as he checked things off.

"You pay attention to me that much?"

"Hey, I knew your size, didn't I?"

"Yes, and that's creepy and weird. How did you know my size?"

"Guesstimated." He shrugged a shoulder as he lifted a bottle of Jameson from the shelf behind him and showed it to me. "This okay?"

"Anything you give me right now is okay. My hand hurts like a bitch. I need a distraction."

He placed two glasses between us, reached down, opened something that crunched and brought up a plastic cup with ice, and poured our drinks.

"You know, there are other ways to distract from pain." He slid a glass my way.

"Let me guess." I lifted it to my lips and took a sip, licking my lips as I lowered it. "You mean sex."

"Not everything is about sex, Amelia, but I'm down for that too." He lifted his glass. I lifted mine and tapped it against his. "Cheers. To being in this weird, yet loyal family."

"Cheers." I took another sip, relishing the burn as it went down my throat. "Here's to hoping this family isn't as dysfunctional as the one we have now."

He lifted his glass and drank.

"What about your mom? Does she suck?"

"No, I love my mom. She moved away to Colorado when I was twelve. Ran away with her co-worker. I didn't understand it then, but I sure as hell did later. My father was a bastard. An abusive, cheating, alcoholic bastard. He's gotten better, but he's still not someone I'd want my mom with. My brother is a bastard. I'm . . . well . . . I am what I am." He took a gulp of the whiskey, hissing as his throat worked to swallow it.

"You are who you want to be."

"You believe that?"

"Sometimes." I shrugged. "Other times I think I'm just the spoiled little rich girl everyone thinks I am. Living in my glass castle, you know."

He set his elbows on the bar, leaned in closer to me, and whispered, "I won't cast stones at you."

"I appreciate that," I whispered back, licking my lips again.

"You're beautiful, even in this shitty cloak," he said, his eyes scanning mine. "Even with no makeup and messy hair, you're beautiful."

"Stop." I pulled away, sitting straight on my stool, taking my glass with me. "I don't want to be the girl you seduce in a tiny bar, underneath the stairwell."

"That's fair." He sipped his drink.

We finished our drinks and walked back to our rooms, idling outside my door. I thought he was going to hit on me again, invite me in, kiss me, anything. He didn't. He just watched me with those wanton green eyes that seemed to darken to black the longer he stared, and I just watched him.

"See you later, Logan Moriarty."

He smiled softly. "See you later, Amelia Elizabeth."

I walked into the room and shut the door behind me, banging my head against it and wishing I was the kind of person who could invite him in for a hookup. Then again, something told me if Logan wanted to hookup, he would have invited himself in somehow. I changed quickly and walked to the window again. There were no cloaks out there. I needed to ask Logan about the red cloaks and the cemetery asap.

CHAPTER THIRTY

I KNOCKED ON HIS DOOR WHEN I FINISHED GETTING DRESSED AND HAD ordered my Uber. Black car service because I was obviously too extra even for my own good. He opened the door, dressed in what he was wearing earlier.

"So, when Nora said we were sleeping here . . . "

"We're sleeping here tonight." He eyed me up and down. "Where's your toga?"

"I have to go home to get it. I wasn't really expecting to leave straight from here."

"When you say you have to go home and get it . . . " He squinted, tilting his head. I would've thought he looked adorable if he wasn't making fun of me.

"I got one online," I admitted begrudgingly.

"You know you can just grab a white sheet and . . ." He mimicked wrapping a sheet around himself, totally fighting a laugh.

"I know. Shut up."

"I'll take you." He laughed that time. "Home, I mean. I have to go there anyway."

"Thanks, but I already got an Uber." I waved my phone.

"So cancel it."

"And risk them giving me a one-star?" My eyes widened.

"What's your rating now?"

"4.82."

"How'd you get points deducted?"

"Probably because I let Lincoln use my account and he was probably acting like an idiot. I cannot afford to lose more stars."

"Just cancel it. Come on. I'm going home too."

"Fine." I canceled it, biting my lip as I confirmed it. "Damn it I can't believe I did that."

Logan shook his head, smiling. "Let's go."

As we drove out of the gates, I looked over to the right side of the house, where I'd seen the red cloaks and the holes on the ground.

"What's on that side?"

"Another house."

"A house?" I frowned. "With a cemetery in the back?"

"What . . . ohhhh. Yeah." He shook his head. "The red cloaks do things a little different."

"What does that mean?"

"They're a medical society, so you have to be in that field to get in there. They used to be grave diggers back in the day, when they first started. They'd dig graves and take bodies that hadn't been buried long in order to examine them. Now they use those graves for hazing new recruits."

"Hazing them how?" I felt like I could barely breathe as I asked these questions, but my curiosity, as usual, got the best of me.

"They make them sleep there overnight."

"What?" I shouted. "And nobody reports this?"

"Are you going to report us for making you walk blind-folded over knives?"

"No, but I should." I frowned.

"Right." He grinned. "That's why nobody reports them. Once you're in, you're part of the problem."

Fuck. I hadn't even thought of it like that. I didn't know

what all of these people did, what the graduates were involved with. I looked at Logan.

"What about my dad?"

He glanced my way briefly as he took a turn. "What about him?"

"Was he involved in anything . . . questionable?"

"I don't really like to comment on whether or not I agree with the things The Lab Initiative does."

"What's that?"

"They're the board that heads The Eight. Also consists of eight people, all alumni, all former Eights. They're the reason the money is funneled into our accounts without anyone tracking it."

"So what is it they do that you don't agree with?"

"A lot of things." He sighed heavily, wiping his wrapped hand over his joggers as if to scratch it. "You'll start to learn things about them soon enough."

"I want to learn them now."

He parallel parked the truck in an empty spot across from our building and looked over at me. "What is it you want to know exactly?"

"I want to know what my father was involved in and whether or not he had something to do with . . . whether or not he was involved with Lana. Like, on more than just a mentorship kind of level."

"Yes. They were definitely sleeping together." He raised an eyebrow as if to say *are you satisfied now?* I felt crushed. He knew it, but he didn't hold back, he kept going. "Your father and a group of men formed a small group for girls, students, specifically students who want their mentorship or just need money, sign up and go on dates with them, dates with expectations. Is that what you want me to clarify for you?"

I felt my surroundings closing in on me. Suddenly the

truck felt too small, the seatbelt too tight, and my heart felt like it was going to pound out of my chest. I unclicked the seatbelt and ran out of the truck, ignoring the crows above my head and the way they seemed to be there any time I felt uneasy. I ignored the chill in the air and the darkness that was falling over me all too quickly, and crossed the street quickly.

Once in the building, I waved at Gary and rushed to the elevator, riding up and running to my apartment. Only after I slammed the door shut and locked it did I feel safe. Only then, did I manage to breathe. I shook as I undressed and headed to the shower, needing to wash away everything. Everything. Everything. My fist pounded the shower walls as I let the spray hit me. I would have to blow dry my hair and re-apply my make up, but I didn't care if standing beneath this shower meant erasing everything I'd just learned about my father.

As I dried myself, I heard pounding on the door, but I ignored it. It was probably Logan and I wasn't sure if he was here to apologize or hit me with more knowledge. Either way, it was unwelcome. I had an ex-boyfriend to deal with at a toga party I didn't exactly want to go to, but Celia and Max would be there, and I definitely wanted to see them. The elation lasted all of two seconds before I realized I couldn't talk to them about this even if I wanted to because part of signing that oath tonight also meant silencing myself.

I was already dressed when my phone buzzed. I lifted it to see a text from an unknown number and froze for a second before sliding it to read the full text.

Unknown number: I was knocking earlier.

Me: Who is this?

Unknown number: Satan.

Me: Seriously, who is this? I'm tired of the games.

Unknown number: it's Logan. What games?

Me: How'd you get my number?

Unknown number: Does it matter?

I paused. *Did it?* No. Not really anyway. I knew he wasn't the one behind the texts I was getting. That wasn't his style. His style was blunt force trauma, and I could verify that from the way he dropped the news about my father and The Lab Initiative. I saved his phone number.

Logan Fitzgerald: You heading to the party yet?

Me: Soon. Travis is meeting me there.

Logan Fitzgerald: I guess I don't want to know the answer to the burning question in my mind after all

Me: what question?

Logan Fitzgerald: I was wondering if you were going to wear something under the toga. Maybe something red. Maybe something black.

Me: that's definitely none of your business.

Logan Fitzgerald: Maybe I'll find out

Me: With how I feel about you right now, I might break your hand so you have to sit out this year if you try to find out

Logan Fitzgerald: You're funny when you're angry. Are you going to break the hand that contains your blood?

I paused, biting my lip. Why did it feel like the butterflies in my stomach took flight when I read those words?

Me: Maybe.

Me: I'll be naked under the toga

After a moment of receiving no answer from him, I tossed my phone into my bag with a laugh, grateful for the slight improvement in my mood, and headed downstairs where an Uber was waiting for me.

CHAPTER THIRTY-ONE

"**F**OR THE RECORD, TOGA PARTIES ARE JUST AN EXCUSE FOR JOCKS to show off their muscles and girls to walk around almost naked." I lifted my red cup to make that toast with Celia and missed her cup, hitting the air beside it instead.

"You know you're slurring your words."

"Am not." I blinked hard.

My eyes felt heavier than usual. I hadn't drunk like this in a long time, but tonight I'd decided to escape the madness inside my head and drown out my thoughts. Maybe I was slurring.

"You are." Celia raised an eyebrow. "Have some water. You don't want to be slurring when Travis gets here. Also, let me tie your toga again. I'm scared your boobs are going to pop out."

I looked down at myself. My boobs were not in any danger of popping out. My vagina, maybe. The slit came all the way to the tip-top of my thigh, but not my boob. I said this out loud and Celia laughed.

"Dude, your slit is really high. You know people don't normally use actual sheets for these things, right? We buy ready-made togas at costume stores."

"Um, excuse me, I did buy a ready-made toga. I just made minor improvements." I looked down at my exposed thigh. "Maybe I went a little overboard."

Celia laughed again. "You're a mess."

I took another gulp of the water. Maybe I did need it, after all. My throat felt parched.

"Do you have a mint?"

"I do." She shook a tin of cinnamon Altoids and handed it to me. "Are you planning on making out with your ex? If so, I'm gonna have to advise against it."

"No way." I laughed, popping a mint in my mouth and handing her the tin back. "That ship has sailed. Am I still slurring?"

"Yes. More water."

"I'm going to have to pee. Also, I want another shot of Fireball."

"Oh my God, Mae. Drink the water, then pee." She shot me a stern look. "Then we'll do another shot."

"Be right back." I walked toward the bathroom.

The room seemed to shift a little, so I slowed down. Maybe another shot wasn't the brightest idea. Still, I'd feel better after I peed. When I was finished in the bathroom, I stepped out and held onto the threshold for a second. The party was a sea of white sheets. The only thing missing was a Trojan horse smack in the center of the room to hide in. I must have been standing there for a long time, because by the time I reached the kitchen, where Celia was now making out with Quentin, I felt like I was completely sober. I grabbed a red solo cup and vacillated between the Fireball and Cuervo.

"Fireball. I'll do one with you." Travis's voice beside me made me gasp as I turned around to face him.

He looked as handsome as ever, one brown muscled shoulder and arm exposed in his loose-fitting toga. From the way his hairline was perfectly even and his dark hair faded on the sides, I could tell he'd just gone to the barber. His smile was wide as he looked at me for a moment before wrapping an arm around me and pulling me into him. I pressed my face to his chest and breathed in his familiar scent, Aqua Di Gio cologne, and exhaled, already feeling much better than I'd felt all day. He pulled away slightly but kept his hand splayed on my back as he turned to Celia.

"Are you the roommate that left her after a hot minute?"

Celia laughed. "Yes, but I still check up on her."

"Good." He left his hand on my back. I fought the urge to shrug it off. "It was the right move for you though. This is a nice place."

"Hell yeah it's a nice place, and you can crash anytime you want," Quentin said, smiling. "But we still gonna kick your ass in ball."

Travis laughed. "We'll see about that. We got a new center and he's looking like Shaq out there."

"That just means we'll have to foul him and see how he does from the three-point line."

"Ah, low blow." Travis laughed again.

"Okay, we gotta go say hi to people," Celia interrupted. "You guys can talk sports later."

She shot me a look that said, *damn he's hot,* as she dragged Quentin out of there. I shook my head and turned back to Travis.

"Do you have a cup?"

He reached over the counter and got one from the new stack. "I do now."

"Perfect." I placed them side by side and poured a decent amount of Fireball for a shot, the amount that would burn the hell out of our throats and probably make us question our choices tomorrow. I slid him a cup and picked up mine. "Cheers."

"Cheers." His dark brown eyes met mine as he tapped his

cup to mine. We took the shot at the same time and set the cups down on the counter. "Another one?"

"One more." I laughed, pouring us another one. We did it again, setting the cups down.

"One more?"

"No. I already had too many tonight. I'm good for now. Maybe in thirty minutes."

"If there's any left." He eyed the bottle and looked at me again. "You look great, as usual."

"So do you."

"Been putting in overtime at the gym." He flexed his bicep to show me.

"I can tell."

"I guess that's what happens when your girlfriend leaves you. You get bored and workout more often."

"Hm. I bet your coach wishes I'd left you sooner."

Travis laughed. "Probably."

"Are you ready to graduate?"

"I am. Ready to graduate, ready to start law school. I'm excited." He smiled. "I got into Princeton."

"Holy shit." I gaped, slapping him on the arm. "When did you find out?"

"A couple of weeks ago."

"You should've told me." I slapped him again. "That's crazy amazing, Trav."

"Yeah. I'm happy. Mom's happy. Dad's ecstatic. I think he reported it on the news the other day instead of the weather." He laughed.

"I'm so freaking proud of you." I threw my arms around his neck and hugged him tightly. With the movement, I could definitely feel my toga riding down in my chest area, so I lowered myself and fixed myself quickly, just in case.

I'd learned as a teenager that getting drunk at parties wasn't a brilliant idea, but if you were going to do it, you should always be mindful of your wardrobe and your surroundings. I'd learned that, of course, by wearing a tube top at a party. Thankfully, there was no recorded proof of what happened, but I never let myself live it down.

"Hey, you want to go outside?"

"Sure." I grabbed a bottle of water and started walking beside Travis, quickly grabbing onto his arm when I realized the room was indeed tilting again.

"You really did have a lot of shots earlier, huh?" He smiled down at me. "You usually only do the public affection thing when you're drunk."

"Not true." I frowned. "And I'm not being affectionate. I'm holding onto your arm so I don't fall over."

The wind blew my hair wildly. I reached up with one hand and fixed the thin gold crown on my head, pressing myself closer to his body for body warmth. We walked to the edge of the wraparound porch. I let go of his arm and leaned against the column. He stood between my legs and brought a hand up to my face.

"I miss you, Mae."

"I miss you too." I closed my eyes.

Right now, in this moment, I thought maybe I did miss him. Every other day, I hadn't really. Not that I hadn't thought about him or wondered what he was doing. He was my safety for so long, it felt weird not to have him around, but still, I couldn't truly say I missed him. Or us.

"So, let's work this out."

"No." My eyes popped open. "I miss you, but that doesn't mean I want to be with you. We don't work together, Trav. You know this."

"We can try again."

"I knew this was a bad idea." I shook my head, walking a little further down the porch, pulling far away enough that he had no choice but to drop his arms.

"Mae." He exhaled loudly and reached for me again. I took another step back. "We can be friends. Forget I said anything."

I looked at him. I knew him so well, too well, to believe he'd want to talk and just leave it at that. From the way he was looking at me, I knew he still wanted me, and the only thing I wanted was the comfort his arms brought, and the ease I felt around him, not because I was in love with him, but because I had been once. I seemed to be so far from that girl though. Too much had happened.

"Do you mind if I go inside and grab a beer?" Travis asked.

"Not at all." I sat down on the white swing. "I'll be right here."

He looked at me one last time before he disappeared inside. I sat down on the swing and leaned my head back, closing my eyes as I kicked my foot away from the porch and let myself swing.

"That looks comfy." It was Hailey.

"It is." I kept my eyes closed.

"Mind if I join you?"

I shrugged and finally opened my eyes to meet hers as she took a seat. Her toga covered a lot more than mine. I'd never seen her with her hair up in a bun like that.

"How shitty is this party?" She rested her head beside mine.

"It's not bad." I smiled.

"I haven't gone inside yet. I just got here." She tapped the porch with the front of her foot and started swinging us. "Did you know that approximately ten thousand people go missing each year here?"

"I didn't realize it was that many, no." I eyed her. She looked like she was high on something. Not that I knew Hailey to do drugs, but who knew anymore. "Where did that piece of information come from?"

"I was researching something earlier and it came up."

"What were you researching?"

"Just . . . things." She closed her eyes. "I guess there's a club for girls to hire sugar daddies."

"Oh?" My heart beat faster.

"I was using my mom's computer and saw she'd marked the tab. Probably research for a story."

"What did the website say?"

"It was catered towards students who needed money and mentorships, but everything was so . . . I don't know." Her eyes popped open. She looked at me in a haze. Maybe mine, maybe hers. My head was spinning with information and the swing. "The website looked sexy."

"Did you ask your mom about it?"

"Actually, I did. She said Lana had told her about it. I guess she wanted to write a story on it for the paper. It's weird that she'd disappear while investigating that and secret societies, isn't it?"

"I guess." My heart continued hammering.

"This is why these secret groups need to be brought to light. Secrets can be dangerous, you know?"

My palm itched. I nodded in agreement. Secrets can be dangerous.

"Remind me again why you're so obsessed with this particular society?"

"If the two things are linked, they could be human traffickers for all we know."

"Oh my God." My heart pounded. "I doubt it. Wouldn't they have been caught?"

I wanted to tell her that was ridiculous, but what the hell did I know, though? I couldn't exactly scratch that off the list of things that may be going on. Could my father be involved in something like that? I wanted to shout no way, but if he was really sleeping with Lana, his friend's daughter, his son's friend, a girl not much older than his own daughter, I couldn't be sure of anything. I felt sick.

"Not necessarily. I don't doubt it at all." She looked away from me. "Have you had any more run-ins with Fitz, the man, and his little crew?"

"Um. A couple. Why?"

"Because he's watching you like a hawk right now."

I tore my gaze from hers and looked beyond the rail of the balcony. My heart galloped when my eyes met his. Even in the dark, I knew he was looking right at me. I didn't know how Hailey knew that, though. I looked at her again.

"He could be looking at you, you know."

"Yeah, right." She scoffed. "I tried that once, nothing came of it. Even when he's drunk and comes by the bar and I think I just might get somewhere, I don't. The guy has a fort built around his feelings."

I glanced in his direction again. Not too long ago, I used to think that about him. Now I wasn't so sure. Logan was the kind of guy who was used to people making assumptions about him. Maybe that was why he was always quiet and brooding in front of people he didn't know. Maybe he was trying to figure out what version of himself we wanted him to play. I liked to think that he was himself in front of me. My heart skipped a beat at the thought. The screen door opened with a squeak beside us and shut with a thump. Hailey and I turned our heads to see Travis coming back with a beer in one hand and a red cup in another.

"Oh, you've got company." He handed me the red cup. The whiskey didn't even burn my throat as I took a sip. "I was worried I'd taken too long. I'm Travis."

"Hailey," she responded. "I haven't seen you around."

"The campus has its own zip code. You know everyone on it?"

Hailey laughed. "Nah, but I'd remember you."

"Some people are worth remembering, am I right?" Travis chuckled.

I rolled my eyes and kicked my foot to start the swing again.

"Definitely," she agreed.

He was trying to make me jealous and it wasn't going to work. Either way, I didn't feel like sitting there while he flirted with Hailey, so I stopped swinging and stood.

"Going to the bathroom. See you later, Hailey." I smiled at her as I brushed past Travis. "You're welcome to take a seat beside her and continue your conversation while I'm gone."

I didn't wait for a response, instead, I actually did head to the bathroom, closed the door behind me and dragged the shower curtain open to make sure no one was there. Once I knew I was in the clear, I sat on the edge of the tub, kicking my leg up and leaning on the tile behind me with a sigh. I lifted the red cup to my mouth and took a sip. At least I had this.

CHAPTER THIRTY-TWO

MY PHONE BUZZED IN THE WRISTLET PURSE I WAS WEARING. Closing my eyes, I banged my head against the tile. It was probably Travis, calling to see where I was, and the thing was, I didn't want to talk to him right now. Seeing him was great for all of five minutes, but I was over it now. I set the cup down inside the tub and opened my purse, taking my phone out. It wasn't a call, it was a text, and it wasn't from Travis, but from Logan.

Logan Fitzgerald: Are you ready to leave the party?

Me: Currently locked in the bathroom because I'm dying to leave the party, so yes.

I stared at the little dots as he formulated a response. When he took too long, I picked up my cup again. I was mid-sip when the pound on the door came. It made me jump so fast, I spilled whiskey on the front of my toga.

"Motherfucker." I walked over to the door. "Occupied!"

"It's me."

I groaned, but unlocked the door anyway, before heading to the sink. The door opened, closed, and locked, but I didn't bother to look up as I cupped water and splashed it on the fabric over my chest.

"You made me ruin my toga."

"What are you doing in here?"

"Getting drunk." I shut the faucet and looked at him, blinking when I finally got a good look.

He looked like he belonged in a toga, like an emperor, and the rest of us mere thespians in a school play. Logan, with his dark hair—tame yet messy—his dark green eyes, his golden skin and roped muscle, in a toga was definitely something to be admired.

"You're staring."

"I'm drunk." I closed my eyes, shaking my head.

"Yet you're still drinking, apparently." He closed the distance between us just as I opened my eyes and suddenly, he was standing within touching distance, kissing distance, and my heart couldn't seem to handle the mixture of his proximity and the alcohol swooshing in my brain.

"You know what? You should just kiss me."

"Oh yeah?" His lips twitched. "Why's that?"

"Because the last time we kissed it was pretty good." I leaned closer to him. "And you obviously wanna do it again."

"Is that so?" He chuckled as he brought his hand to my face.

"It is." I searched his eyes. He was entirely too amused and apparently too sober.

"Do you want me to kiss you?" His thumb caressed my jaw as I nodded. "Tell me."

"I want you to kiss me so bad you have no idea." My arm felt like lead as I lifted it and draped it over his naked neck. I let it slide and grabbed onto his shoulder blade. "You have a big muscle here."

Logan laughed. "Oh, Mae."

"What?" I blinked. "Are you going to kiss me or what?"

"I am." He leaned closer still. I closed my eyes upon feeling his breath on my lips, then his lips landed right at the corner of mine. My heart stopped. Suddenly, I felt like I was going to puke and it had little to do with the alcohol and more to do with the butterflies running rampant "I'm just not going to kiss you right now."

"What?" My eyes popped open. He laughed. Placing my palms on his chest, I shoved him away. "You're an asshole."

He laughed louder and reached for my hands, but I stepped away.

"No. Keep laughing. I'll find someone else to kiss at this party." I moved to brush past him, but he grabbed my hand and pulled me back. I turned to face him. "I bet you if your last partner would've asked you to kiss her, you would have," I said. "Oh, that's right, you did." I yanked my arm from his grasp.

"Amelia, you seriously need to let that go. Besides, your entire chest is showing because you splashed water on the white sheet you're wearing. The fact that you haven't noticed or care means you're drunker than you think." His gaze moved from my face and darkened when it reached my chest. "And I'm not letting you leave this bathroom like that."

"What do you expect me to do, Julius Caesar? Do you have another sheet I can use lying around? Besides, who the hell cares? Nobody will notice."

"Trust me, they'll notice."

"They won't." I rolled my eyes.

"Well, I'll notice and that's enough." He grabbed the white towel hanging on the towel bar and wrapped it around me. "Here."

"Thanks." I pulled it tightly around myself. "Now, wait a minute before you come outside. I don't want to give people the wrong impression." I shot him a look. "If you would've kissed me, I wouldn't have minded the rumors, but I'm not going to go down as one of your groupies without cause."

His loud groan was the only indication I got on his agreement as I walked out and closed the door behind me. I froze at the sight of Travis in the hall, right outside the door.

"What are you doing here?"

"You took a long ass time in the bathroom." He frowned, looking at the door. "Let's go back outside." I moved forward, grabbing his arm.

"Nah, I'm good right here."

"Trav. Come on." I tugged his arm again.

His gaze met mine. "Who were you in there with?"

"A friend. It wasn't . . . it's not . . . " I stopped talking. *Why was I explaining myself to my ex-boyfriend?* "It doesn't matter."

It was loud in here with Lizzo's "Truth Hurts" blasting from the DJ's speakers and the women shouting the lyrics, but I still heard the moment the bathroom door opened behind me. Or maybe it was Travis's eyes widening slightly that gave it away. Either way, my heart picked up a few notches.

"A friend," he said, looking at me again. "Nice try. You storm in here acting all pissed off because I'm flirting with someone and grab the first guy you see? Is that what happened?"

"First of all, I was not pissed off. Flirt all you want. I don't care," I said. "Secondly, that's none of your business."

"Who the fuck are you?" Those were Logan's words, booming from behind me.

My mind instantly went to the last party I went to, where Celia said that the minute the hockey players showed up, they caused a ruckus. I stepped back, hoping to act as a shield both ways. Logan damn well knew who Travis was and he knew he'd be here tonight. He was just trying to start trouble.

"Who the fuck are *you* is the real question." Travis pushed away from the wall, standing at his full height.

I wasn't even sure who could win this fight. If I were a betting person, I wouldn't bet on it at all. I knew Logan had a rough upbringing, with his dad and all, but Travis had grown up in a bad part of the city, the kind where people took their bikes inside their apartment and chained them anyway.

"I already told you, he's my friend." I glared at Travis.

"Friend." Logan scoffed. "We're not friends, Amelia."

In my drunken state, that hurt. It wasn't that he said we weren't friends, but the distasteful way in which he'd said it that got me. I managed to shoot him a glare over my shoulder and almost took it back when I got a good look at his clenched jaw and flexed bicep. He definitely looked like he was ready to fight.

"This is my ex-boyfriend. Travis, this is my friend, Logan."

"Stop calling me your friend." Logan's glare met mine.

"Are you kidding? You wouldn't even kiss me in there and you want me to call you what exactly, if not my friend?"

Travis snorted. Logan's gaze turned murderous. I started sweating, my feet shifting as I stood my ground between them. I was definitely sober now.

"Okay, I'm going to walk away from both of you now because you're both being ridiculous."

"I'll go with you," Travis said.

"Fuck you. She's leaving with me." Logan stepped up to my side.

In the old romance movies I'd watch with my parents, this was the scene that would always make me giddy—two men fighting over the same woman. Who wouldn't want that? Well, the answer was me. I didn't want that and the entire thing was making me feel sick. Really sick this time. My stomach made an angry sound that had me running back to the bathroom and kneeling over the toilet. I held on to the bowl with both hands and threw up again. From the corner of my eye, I could see them both standing by the door. I glanced up briefly before turning my face toward the bowl again.

"Please leave," I whispered.

I flushed the toilet but stayed on the floor. I was disgusting. I'd never vomited in my life, not from drinking, not in front of Travis, who was staring at me with a look on his face that said he might vomit soon too if he didn't get out of here. I heard shuffling and closed my eyes at the loud whispered discussion they were having that I couldn't make out on top of the EDM music that was now playing. Soon after, there was banging, and then shouting and finally, the door opened and closed again. I didn't even bother to look up.

"Please leave. I'm throwing up."

The footsteps continued toward me. This time I did look up because guys were stupid and didn't know how to aim in the first place, and I definitely didn't want a drunk one to pee on me by mistake. I was surprised to see it was Logan walking toward me with paper towels and a bottle of water.

"What are you doing?"

He crouched down in front of me and started wiping my face gently. I closed my eyes because it felt so good right now. But having my eyes closed made the room shift faster, so I opened them again.

"You look upset."

His gaze met mine. "Do me a favor and don't talk."

"I'm sorry." I closed my eyes again. "I've never been this drunk before. I mean, I have, but not this year." My brows pulled. "Not in a few years."

"So why tonight? Why did you decide to come to a toga party of all places and get drunk tonight?" He stopped wiping my face.

"Because I'm sad." My lip wobbled when I said that out loud, my eyes pooling with water. I hadn't said anything aloud. I hadn't spoken about my brother's state or my father's indiscretions. I hadn't spoken to anyone about any of the things that were burdening me, and the mixture of the alcohol and information felt excruciating tonight. "I'm so terribly, terribly sad."

"Are you going to tell me about it?" He sat beside me, our backs leaning against the wall, his head turned toward me.

I bit my lip hard, shaking my head. I couldn't. I couldn't start talking about Lincoln right now, not here, not like this. I would break more than I already was. Just thinking about my brother in a hospital bed, my brother, whom I hadn't visited since I left him because I didn't want to deal with the full reality of seeing him like that. I was a pansy. I was a pansy and I was alone and I needed my best friend to wake the fuck up so that he could help me deal with all of these things. My best friend. Why hadn't he told me about dad? About Lana? Why hadn't he said anything? I could've helped him. I wasn't sure how, but I would've tried. Anything was better than the helplessness I felt right now. Anything was better than sitting drunk on a bathroom floor with the hottest guy I knew wiping vomit off my face because I couldn't seem to keep myself in check.

"Why do you care?" I sniffed. "You're not my friend, remember?"

"I'm not your friend." He put his hand on mine and held it. "I'm your blood, remember?"

I felt a crack in my chest as the tears trickled down my cheeks, as if it had grown a little, enough to fit him in, and that scared me. I hadn't known him long enough to feel this way. I didn't know him well enough to feel this deeply for him, yet I did. In the past, I'd fallen slowly, after being friends with guys for a while. This felt different. Maybe it was the fact that instead of turning his back on me, he'd helped me when I was on the floor vomiting. Maybe it was realizing that I couldn't carry the weight of my fucked-up family and really needed someone in my corner. Maybe it was the alcohol, still coursing through my veins despite my body's attempt to get it out. Whatever the case, Logan had taken ownership of a part of me and even though I couldn't understand it entirely, I knew there was no use in questioning these emotions. The heart never asked for permission, it just felt.

"Can we get out of here?" I whispered.

"Are you going to tell me what's wrong?"

"I just miss my brother. I miss him so much." I started to cry again. Logan let go of my hand and wrapped an arm around me. There was a knock on the door, then another. Someone on the other side started yelling.

"Shut the fuck up and leave," Logan roared back. I flinched at his voice beside my ear. He held my head to his shoulder again. "Sorry."

"Maybe we should just go," I said. "I feel like brushing my teeth anyway."

"Not a bad idea."

He stood up and offered me his hand. I placed mine in it, meeting his gaze. It was the same hand he'd touched just a minute ago, the same hands we'd held during our blood oath earlier. I was really grateful to have him pulling me up and keeping me steady. He handed me the bottle of water as we walked out of the bathroom, and I took it gratefully, twisting the cap and gulping down half the contents. We beelined toward the front door, but on the way, we were stopped by numerous people—guys asking where he was going, girls pressing themselves provocatively onto him as I watched.

One of them, in particular, couldn't seem to catch a clue

and brought his hand up to her breast. If Logan was caught off guard, he didn't show it. Instead, he lowered his hand and walked away until another stopped him and grabbed at him. It was a ridiculous sight, the kind of thing you'd expect from fan-girls at a BTS concert, not from students toward an athlete. I forced myself to turn and walk away. I couldn't stomach seeing it any longer—the groping, the flailing—it was all too much for me tonight.

CHAPTER THIRTY-THREE

THE CRISP AIR HIT ME THE MOMENT I OPENED THE DOOR, REMINDING me that it was fall and I was completely underdressed for this weather. I pulled the towel tighter around myself. The screen in front of the front door shut with a squeak and a clank behind me.

"You heading out?" It was Hailey's voice, coming from the direction of the porch, where we'd been sitting earlier.

"Yeah. Tired."

"You look it." She eyed me up and down. "I don't think I've ever seen you this . . . distressed before."

"Thanks for that." I drank the rest of the water.

A small smile tugged her lips, as if she was enjoying this. It made me frown. Even the bitchiest friends I had back home wouldn't be happy to see me like this, not to my face anyway.

"I should be heading out soon too," she said. "You want a ride?"

"No, thanks." I crunched the water bottle. "Did you even go inside?"

"Of course I did. I was taking shots with Travis." Her eyes gleamed at my obvious loss of words.

Maybe Hailey was a mean drunk. No, Hailey was *definitely* a mean drunk. The door opened and shut again before I could try to form a response to that. She looked away from me, eyes wide at the sight of Logan.

"You're leaving with him?"

"How is that any of your business?" Logan asked, walking to stand beside me. "Don't you have a bar to tend to?"

"Don't you have some random woman to accost?"

"I don't accost women."

"Oh, so it's only your brother who does that and your father? You know what they say about apples and trees."

I put my hand on Logan's arm when I saw him inch forward as if he was going to step up to her.

"Hey, let's go." I squeezed his arm.

"You're just mad that I never gave you the time of day," he spat.

"You never give anyone the time of day. You use women and discard them," Hailey scoffed. "Why don't you tell Mae the little game you and your friends like to play at the bar on Thursday nights?"

"Why don't you mind your own fucking business?" Logan's bicep seemed to grow two inches beneath my grip.

"Just last Thursday you had a girl sucking your dick under the booth." Hailey tilted her head. "What was her name? Tonya?"

"Let's go." I tugged his arm once more. I needed to get him out of here. I needed to get myself out of here before I threw up all over the lawn. I wasn't sure if Hailey's words were meant to make me feel this sick, but each comment made me want to vomit more. I let go of his arm and put my hand in his, threading my fingers through his and tugging. He blinked away from her and looked at me, as if he was in a haze. "I want to go home."

"Let's go." He started walking. Finally.

"Bye, Hailey." I shot Hailey a *what the fuck* look over my shoulder.

"Don't let him take advantage of you, Mae," she called out as we walked away. "Call me tomorrow."

My hand was still holding Logan's when we reached his truck. I knew he wouldn't actually do anything to her, but the screaming match had been enough for me to know they hated each other. It was odd though, she hadn't made any negative comment about him aside from saying he was an asshole. She must be drunk right now, or on some mind-bending opioid. Probably both.

"She's drunk," I said as we got in his truck. "She never acts like this."

"She's a bitch."

I blinked. I'd never heard him say anything like that. We both clicked our seatbelts on and he started driving, his grip tight on the steering wheel.

"She really doesn't act like this ever," I said again, my mind still on Hailey.

"Let it go," Logan said. "She's just mad I turned her down. She's a jealous—"

"Bitch, yes, I get it. Please stop calling her that already. She's my friend and she's been nice to me." I frowned as I said that. She had been nice up until today.

"I'll try." He pressed the back of his head on the head-rest and exhaled loudly. "This is not how I envisioned tonight going."

"How'd you envision it going?"

"Not like this."

"I have a confession," I said after a while.

"What?" His voice was clipped.

I paused before saying, "I thought all Canadians were Casper-white."

"What?" He barked out a surprised laugh. I eyed his

knuckles on the steering wheel and noticed they were no longer white. "What are you talking about?"

"I just always assumed all Canadians were super white. I mean, Alanis Morrissett, Justin Beiber, Celine Dion, Ryan Reynolds . . ."

"Ryan Reynolds isn't Casper-white."

"Yeah, but I think he spray tans." My brows furrowed as I looked at him. "Wait, do you spray tan? Can you even spray tan and get that color?"

"I don't spray tan." He laughed, shaking his head. "My mom's black."

"Oh." My frown deepened. "And she's Canadian?"

"Astounding, isn't it?" He side-eyed me, still looking amused. "You know, Drake is Canadian and he's half black."

"I think his dad is from Texas," I said. "So it doesn't count."

"We're a true melting pot. We have all colors, races, cultures. You've never been to Canada?"

"I can't say that I have. I want to though." I smiled. "Now I want to see a picture of your mom."

"She lives in Colorado."

"I know, I remember you saying that, but I still want to go to Canada."

"I'll take you."

"Will this trip happen before or after you're a hot-shot NHL player who will forget all about me?"

His right hand let go of the steering wheel as he reached over, threading his fingers through mine. "I would never forget about you."

I didn't know what to say to that, so I didn't respond to it at all. It was probably for the best. My heart felt like it was trying to jackhammer its way out of my body through any trajectory it found—my chest, my throat, my ears, my vagina. I felt it everywhere. This felt like unchartered territory for me. I licked my lips and decided to change the subject.

"So, did you drive this truck all the way down from Canada or did you buy it here?" I asked. "Or did you ship it here?"

"Not all of us have the luxury of white-glove service, you know?" He side-eyed me. My mouth dropped. How did he know about *that*? Before I could jump in and ask, he continued, "I drove it *all* the way from Canada. You do realize it's only a four-hour drive from Toronto, right?"

I snorted. "Yeah, but we've already established that I've never been."

"And if you had been, it would've been via private jet."

"You're making me feel bad about money I don't even have."

"Because it's your parent's." His lips quirked.

"You know, you're a real asshole. I should've let you stay mad." I tried to pull my hand from his, but he laughed and tightened his grip, and I couldn't help it, I laughed along with him. I felt so . . . free. In that moment, where it was just two college kids trying to finish up their last semesters. Not two adults trying to navigate the shit the universe kept slinging at them.

"I figured you'd been to Canada," he said as we pulled into the gates of The Labyrinth. "I thought you were a world traveler. Your parents are always traveling for their charity."

"You know about that?"

"It's one of the only things I like about your father." He glanced at me, eyes twinkling and full of mischief. "And the fact that he made you."

"You're a smooth talker, Logan Moriarty Fitzgerald." I blushed. Honestly, there was no way anyone who hung out with him stood a chance.

"Glad to hear it. Normally, I don't need smooth words to get women naked and in my bed."

"Ah, this is where we're headed again?"

"This is where we've always been headed. I just decided to take the scenic route with you."

Once the car was parked, he let go of my hand. We got down and walked toward the house. In the darkness, you could barely see the house. There were no porch lights on, no lights inside that you could see with the windows covered. It was eerily quiet, the only sound was coming from the grasshoppers and the leaves shaking off the trees and onto the ground. Our shoes crunched on the gravel as we reached the door. I was exhausted from the day, the party, and the alcohol and I desperately needed a shower, but I had too many questions and knew I'd be getting little to no sleep in here.

"I don't even know what the society does," I said. "I mean, what do we do while we're here? What do they really expect from me?"

"We have fundraisers happening every month. This month, all of the money raised by our donors will benefit injured veterans. Next month, it'll fund electric and hydrogen power research."

"So, fundraising?"

"Amongst other things. That's what I'm in charge of, which is why I know what we fund."

"So, you ask people for money?"

"People want to hand me money any chance they get." Logan grinned over his shoulder as he unlocked the door. "Instead of accepting it for myself, I have them donate to these causes."

"Oh." I walked inside and watched him lock it behind us. "Why do they want to give you money?"

"You ever heard of boosters?"

"Yeah." Lincoln had spoken to me about that. As had Travis, who had a couple of people giving him money for things on the down low. "Isn't that illegal? Can't you get kicked out of school for accepting money?"

"I don't accept money. Not personally anyway."

"Do you have any favorite charities?"

"Women & Children Global Fund."

I blinked up at him. "My parent's charity."

"Yup."

"Why is it your favorite?" I whispered as we walked down the hall, standing a little closer to him.

I couldn't bear the thought of walking here by myself at night. We were illuminated by the glass sconces on the wall that held orange glowing candles. Each seemed to flicker as we passed. I held onto Logan's arm.

"I like the idea of helping single mothers around the globe. They've funded a lot of small villages in third world countries, giving them opportunities they otherwise wouldn't be afforded."

"I used to travel with Mom to a lot of those villages and help out."

"So you've seen the impact firsthand."

"I have. It's a cool organization." I smiled, thinking about it. "I can see why they'd have you take on that task since people want to throw money at you and all that, but what about me? Nobody's going to throw money at the daughter of one of the richest moguls in the world."

"Humility becomes you."

"Shut up. I wouldn't be vying for $50,000 and working with a secret organization that I know close to nothing about if ultimately, I didn't want to get out of their shadow."

"They'll probably have you writing about specific things in the paper. That's what they usually do. Did you know the university awarded the first degree in journalism?"

"I did not know that."

"Yet you came over here as an English major."

"It's a long story." I shook my head.

"We have time." He glanced over at me as he stopped walking, just as we got to the stairs. I stopped with him. "In fact, we have all night."

I gave him the quick version of the story. When I was finished, I looked up at him to see if he was even listening. I'd talked nonstop and fast, and usually, people tuned me out when I did that.

"So, you are a daddy's girl," he said.

"That's what you gathered from this entire thing?"

"Basically." He laughed. "I can see why your douchebag ex-boyfriend was so clingy."

"He's not clingy."

"Yeah, maybe clingy isn't the right word." He scowled. "Either way, I don't like him."

"I noticed."

"I'm glad you left him."

I laughed. "I don't even know what to say to that."

"I'm just pointing out that I think you dodged a bullet there," he said. "You don't have to say anything at all."

"A bullet? What makes you say that?"

"I just know what kind of guy he is. He's not worth your time."

It was something that someone else would surely say about him, and maybe it was because I was no longer with Travis, but I understood what Logan meant.

"Do you think you'll settle down?" I snuck a glance at him

as we started up the stairs. "Like if you actually found the right person right now, do you think you'd give up your groupies and all of that?"

"Without a doubt."

"Really?"

"Yes, really." He laughed. "What's that face you're making? You don't believe me?"

"It's just . . . you said it without hesitation."

"When you know, you know." He shrugged a shoulder. "Why would I jeopardize a solid relationship for a fling?"

"I don't know. Men do it all the time." I thought about my father and felt my mood sour again.

"Not all men are the same, you know."

His words made my heart beat a little quicker. The way he said them left no room for question. He was talking about me, about us. I looked up at him as we stopped in front of the bedroom that had been assigned to me. On this floor, the light was even more sparse. He was standing right in front of me, and I could barely make out his eyes. The candlelight he was blocking behind him gave him a glow around his head that made him look like a fallen angel.

"You know, I think you may be onto something."

CHAPTER THIRTY-FOUR

MY PHONE VIBRATED WITH A TEXT.

Unknown number: they're part of the problem.

My phone shook in my hands as I stared at the text. Whoever was sending these texts knew about The Eight. Maybe about The Lab and The Labyrinth Initiative. Worse, they somehow knew I was now involved with them. Instead of calling, I sent a text, hoping like hell it didn't bounce back again.

Me: who?

There was no answer. I tried calling, and sure enough, the phone had been disconnected. I set it down and laid back in bed, staring up at the ivory ceiling that had been etched with intricate designs throughout. My phone vibrated again. This time, I jumped up and picked it up quickly, ready to call right away. It wasn't unknown, but Logan.

Logan Fitzgerald: how do you feel?

Me: much better after my bath. I hate baths by the way.

Logan Fitzgerald: lol why?

Me: I don't know. I'm not a bird.

Logan Fitzgerald: you are entirely too extra for me

Me: you can't see me but I'm sticking my tongue out at you

Logan Fitzgerald: you can't feel me, but I just bit it and sucked it into my mouth

My heart ceased to beat as I took a breath and read the text over. Holy hell. How was that so hot even in a text and why did I want it to come to life so badly? My foot shook as I tried to come up with a response. *Think, think, think.* I didn't have to think of a response at all, because he sent another text before I got a chance to.

Logan Fitzgerald: I can't stop thinking about you

The butterflies in my belly took flight once more. I bit down on my lip.

Me: what are you thinking about?

Logan Fitzgerald: so many things

Me: like whether or not I'm wearing the sexy lingerie?

Logan Fitzgerald: amongst other things

Me: you don't want to find out for yourself?

I'd thrown an oversized t-shirt I wore as a pajamas over the black lingerie set he'd left on my bed—black lace bra and matching panties, so strappy and thin that I wasn't sure they could be considered underwear. I stared at the little dots, heart pounding, as I waited for his follow up text to come through. My foot started shaking in anticipation. Then there was a knock on my door. My head snapped up first, then my body followed, setting my phone down as I made my way over to the door, unlocked it and pulled it open slightly. He was standing on the other side, wearing a pair of gray sweatpants, no shirt, no shoes, no socks.

He looked beautiful in this light, like a fallen angel looking for his way back to salvation, and the way he looked at me made me feel like I was it. I stepped back. He walked inside quietly, standing right beside me as I shut the door and locked it again, keeping my back facing him as I tried to gain a semblance of modesty I wasn't sure there was any sense in keeping. I felt his warmth behind me as he stepped closer to me, felt his breath tickling the nape of my neck as he placed his lips there. My head fell forward as I leaned against him. He brought both hands to either side of my arms, tucking them into the sleeves of my t-shirt. The callouses on his hands made my skin prickle as he ran them up to my shoulders and back down. He rained kisses on either side of my sensitive neck, his lips a soft caress that nearly tickled. As I lifted my head and turned around to face him, he brought his hands down and pushed them underneath my shirt. I watched his gaze heat, his throat bob as he explored my body. I wanted to make a jest, to ask if he was planning on taking off my shirt or just keep copping a feel beneath it, but I couldn't bring myself to break the spell we were cast under.

I put my hands out to touch him. His muscles tensed under my fingertips as I glided my hands over his shoulders, his chest, along the V that disappeared into his sweatpants. It made it so tempting, like an arrow begging my movements to continue south. I hooked my fingers at the top of his sweatpants tentatively, knowing I'd find him ready. I could feel him hard against my lower belly. I looked up at him then, wondering if I should keep going or wait. A chill ran through me when our eyes locked. He was entirely too intense for me. I'd known that from day one, yet here I was, welcoming him all the way, because even in my lust filled haze I knew that this wasn't going to be just casual sex. Nothing about our relationship had ever been casual. His lips formed a small smile, as if he could read my thoughts.

"I feel like I should just say it outright," I whispered. "You scare the hell out of me. This scares the hell out of me."

"Why?"

"I don't want to share you." I glanced down, unable to say this while looking him in the eye. "I'm afraid you'll move on to someone else once you tire of me. Or worse, while you're with me, and I don't even know if that's what you want. I don't know if you're looking for a relationship or—"

"Hey, Mae." He cupped my chin and brought my gaze to

his. He moved closer, the tip of his nose brushing mine, his lips barely touching mine. "If you were mine, I'd make it so that you never have any doubts."

"You can't promise that."

"I won't promise that. I'll just show you."

His lips touched mine softly, his tongue parted my mouth gently and meeting mine slowly, as if to give us time to acclimate with each other. It wasn't a fast kiss, or a rough one, but languid and gentle. As his tongue brushed against mine, he brought his hand to my face and stepped into me, parting my legs with one of his, similar to the day we were outside of The Tower. Maybe it was the kiss, or how rough his sweatpants felt through my flimsy underwear, but I felt a wave of pleasure course through me and arched to chase another. Logan lifted me as we kissed, deeper now, harder, and walked me to the foot of the bed, setting me down there. He lifted the shirt over my head and tossed it aside, taking a step back to look at me.

"God damn." His voice was rough. "This is so much better than my fantasy."

"What else do you fantasize about, Mr. Fitzgerald?"

He groaned. "So many things and you star in every single one of them."

"You don't have to impress me, you know?" I laughed, biting my lip. "I'm already naked."

"You're not naked yet, and I'm not saying that to impress you. You're everything I have ever fantasized about, Amelia. And I'm not just saying that because you look fucking hot in this lingerie."

I stood on the tips of my toes, wrapped my arms around his neck and kissed him. We fell back onto the bed together in a heap of laughter as we continued to kiss, our tongues dancing, our lips moving, our teeth biting flesh. I relinquished control over to him as he took the reins, of the kiss, and of whatever was to come. His mouth left mine and began exploring my jaw, my neck, his teeth dragging the cups of my bra down as he sucked my nipples into his mouth gently at first, and then with fervor, hot and demanding. I arched off the bed with a moan. As his hands undressed me and then himself, I felt like I had little air left to breathe.

"I need you," I whispered against him.

"Baby, I've needed you for a long time." He chuckled against my mouth as he set a condom over himself.

His mouth continued to move lower, down my abdomen, until he was between my legs and his tongue was licking there. My chest heaved as his tempo quickened, then lessened, then quickened again. He sucked me into his mouth and held me so that I couldn't move away from him when I started to explode. I chanted his name, *Logan, Logan, Logan,* and that seemed to drive him over the edge even more. I slapped a hand on the top of his head, grabbing a fistful and bringing him up. He bit my inner thighs and kissed his way up, never taking his eyes off mine as he opened my legs even further apart and positioned himself between them.

"If you feel anything like how you taste, I'm warning you, get out now." He placed his forehead against mine. "Because I won't let you go."

I smiled against his lips, but then he thrust inside me with a low growl and the only thing I could do was gasp at the feel. It wasn't unpleasant, but he was deep, and I swore I felt him everywhere. I wrapped my legs around his waist, tugging him, begging for him to ease the tension building inside me. He filled me with more tension, an ache that made my eyes roll back and traveled to the tips of my toes. I was tingling all over as he moved, my chest expanding as I gripped his arms tight. Soon I felt an explosion of emotions go off inside me. It had never felt like that—like art—colorful and raw.

"Fuck, Amelia." He thrust again. He pressed his forehead against mine, eyes shut tight as he came to a stop. "Fuck, fuck, fuck."

"Please don't stop."

"I'm not letting you go." His eyes popped open, meeting mine as he pulled out and thrust again. "I never want to let you go."

"So don't." I grabbed his shoulders and moved to his tempo.

We held each other the entire time, looking into each other's eyes as if scared the other would disappear. I came like a firework going off in the dead of night, loudly and trembling. He followed in the same fashion, his grunts decreasing as his strokes died down. He let himself fall over me until we were chest to chest, but held himself off to the side to not burden me with his weight. Our hearts beat against one another's, having a conversation that was too deep for either of us to voice aloud right now. The only time we left the bed was to clean up and start again, as if needing to satiate the ache that had been building between us. When our bodies were tired and we finally decided on sleep, he kissed my shoulder and held me close. It was the best sleep I'd gotten in weeks.

CHAPTER THIRTY-FIVE

STRETCHED MY ARMS OVER MY HEAD WITH A LOUD YAWN AND LOOKED over at Logan, who was still sleeping. I bit my lip as I smiled. Honestly, if he hadn't stayed the night, I would have thought I dreamed it all—his mouth on me, his hands, the way he watched me as I climaxed. It was all so raw, so real, and even still it felt like a dream. I pushed myself out of bed, grabbing my phone as I headed to the bathroom. I looked at myself in the mirror, messy hair, flushed skin, wearing Logan's college t-shirt that was entirely too big on me and I was never giving back. I smiled again. I couldn't remember the last time I felt this happy.

As I started brushing my teeth, I checked my texts, expecting my mother to have texted me twice, as usual. It was always the same: *good morning, sweet pea*, followed by, *Lincoln is still resting*. Resting. I'd gotten used to it, but it wasn't something I enjoyed. The only reason I didn't argue with her or tell her to stop calling it that was because I knew a part of her was saying it for her sake, not mine. Today, there were no texts. It was eleven in the morning.

When I finished brushing, I decided to call her. Her phone was answered on the second ring, not by her, but my father. Because of all of the recent information I'd heard about him, I had cut communication with him. Normally, I was a daddy's girl through and through, always texting and sending him random

I love you's throughout the day, but how could I continue that now? After all the rumors I'd heard? And that's what I hoped they were—rumors, but I couldn't just erase them from my mind.

"Hey, sweet pea. You haven't called your dad in a long time," he said. "How have you been?"

"Okay." I took a breath. "How's Lincoln?"

"They're in the process of waking him now. We're all barely breathing over here."

"Who is we all?" I crossed an arm over myself as I paced the bathroom. I didn't want to go back into the room and risk waking up Logan.

"Your brothers, mother, grandmothers and I."

"Wow. You guys didn't even think to invite me to this? I didn't realize it was a family affair." I frowned, trying not to let it get to me, but I felt the tears form anyway as my emotions took ownership of Lincoln. "He's my brother. He's my best friend."

"You've been through a lot, Amelia. We don't want you to stress more than you already are. You're in school and we all agreed that you need to enjoy your life in college." Dad was using his soft, placating voice now.

"Yeah, well, congrats. I'm having a grand old time here at The Lab."

Dad chuckled lightly. "They initiated you."

"I'm sure you knew before it happened."

"I did."

"I heard a lot of rumors about you. None of them good."

He was quiet for a beat. "Don't believe everything you hear."

"Not even when there's proof?"

"Sometimes what people try to sell as proof is nothing more than baseless lies."

"Pictures don't lie."

"Pictures tell you what you want to believe." His voice was even more hushed now. "If you want the truth you go straight to the source. I'm assuming in this case, that's me. So ask. Ask what you want to ask and stop trying to play Sherlock with the Valentine girl and whoever else you've found to play along with you."

I stopped pacing. He knew about Hailey? How could he possibly know what we talked about? My mind raced. Ella. Ella Valentine must have told him. Maybe Hailey and her mom had the kind of relationship that consisted of telling each other everything. Or maybe those little cameras I'd seen in the coffee shop caught audio. A thought occurred to me then. Had Lana ever been to the coffee shop? It seemed like everyone on campus had been. Why would Lana be the exception? I made a mental note to ask Hailey when I saw her.

"Were you with Lana?" I asked my father, and held my breath as I waited for his response.

"Anyone at The Eight and who goes to The Lab for events can tell you that I was mentoring Lana. She was a bright student and wanted to get into media when she graduated. Yes, I helped her."

"Were you with her, dad? With her. Please don't make me say the words aloud." I shut my eyes, not bothering to wipe the tears falling down my cheeks.

"I was her mentor, Amelia," he said. "That's the beginning and the end of that."

"Okay." I breathed out. Did I believe him? No, but I wanted to. I really, really wanted to. I wiped my face and bit down on the tip of my thumb as I leaned against the counter. "What's going on with Lincoln now?"

"The doctor hasn't come back out. We'll keep you posted okay?" he said.

"Okay," I whispered.

"And, Amelia? Don't mention anything about the mentorship or The Lab or The Eight to your mother. She's already been through enough."

I nodded even though he couldn't see me, and hung up the phone without saying another word. The knock on the bathroom door had me wiping my face faster. Logan opened it slowly. He looked so sexy, with disheveled hair and a lust filled expression on his face as he took me in, wearing his t-shirt. Whatever he saw on my face made him sigh heavily. I could only imagine what a mess he saw, but I didn't care, because as he wrapped his strong arms around me the only thing I could do was breathe him in and pray that I could keep him forever.

"What happened?" He pulled away slightly, hands framing my face.

"Apparently my family decided to keep me out of the loop, but they're waking up Lincoln right now." My lip wobbled as I said the words, and wobbled more as Logan's thumbs caressed my face. "They said they didn't want me to worry more than I already have."

"Oh, Mae." He pulled me back onto his chest and held me there. "I don't have a fancy jet, but do you want me to drive you there?"

"It's four hours away."

"I don't care. We could look up flights if you want, but there's a wind warning in effect. Flights are delayed."

"How do you know?" I looked up at him.

"I check the news first thing in the morning."

"Oh."

"We have the pep rally and then camping tonight."

I pulled back completely this time. He dropped his hands. Ella had told me that I needed to show up to their pep rally to take pictures. Even Max and I had discussed it numerous times, but I didn't realize that was today.

"That's today?"

"Yep." His brows furrowed. "If you don't feel up for it—"

"No. I do. I'll just keep my phone on me at all times. If there's anything worth reporting someone will call." Even as I said it, I knew I sounded doubtful.

I couldn't believe they hadn't even thought to text me a heads up that they were all going to be there. What if Lincoln woke up and I was the only one who wasn't there? I considered telling Logan that I changed my mind about the ride and wanted one after all, but he had a pep rally. He had things he needed to be here for. I wasn't going to be responsible for him missing out. I thought of my father's words and how he claimed that was the reason they hadn't called in the first place. Maybe he hadn't been lying about that. Maybe he was right and I should stay put. Logan was moving about around me. He'd gone to his room at some point and had brought his toothbrush with him and was doing that.

I moved out of his way and walked back into the room, my eyes on the messy bed. Not that I needed an outward reminder to remind me what we'd done last night. My sore limbs were telling enough on that end. I walked toward the window and put my hand on it, feeling the cold from outside against my fingertips. My mind was still on my father. I wondered if there was ever a time in the not so distant future in which it wouldn't be on my father's sins.

The fog seemed heavier than usual. I couldn't make out the white shed or the plot next door. The sound of Logan's footsteps alerted me that he was back in the room, but I didn't move, I kept my eyes outside. He walked up behind me and wrapped an arm around my waist, his chin dropping on the top of my head.

"What are we looking at, beautiful?"

"Life," I whispered, placing my hands over his arms. "It's crazy. You grow up thinking your parents are the ultimate gods, and as you grow up you realize they're just mere mortals, just like the rest of us, but this thing with my dad? It's bad, Logan." I turned around in his arms and looked up at him, blinking tears onto my cheeks. "It's really bad. I don't even want my last name. Like, I don't want it if my dad is really involved with these girls and using his mentorship as something to dangle over their heads."

"I know." He leaned down, pressing his lips lightly against mine. "You are who you want to be. Isn't that what you told me about my shitty family?"

"Yeah." I felt myself smile a little despite my sour mood.

"You want me to keep showing you around the house? Then we'll have breakfast and go home. I can't drive you to the pep rally because I have to be there way too early, but I'll be waiting for you after."

"We spend one night together and you're already planning out my entire day?"

He grinned. "Careful. I'll plan out your entire life if you let me."

"You're bluffing."

"You think so?"

I nodded.

"I don't bluff, baby." He kissed the tip of my nose, slapped my ass and walked toward the door. "You have fifteen minutes to get ready. If I come back and you're still wearing my shirt, I'll take it as a sign that you don't want a tour and you just want me to fuck you again."

He left before I could respond, but I mean, with threats like that . . .

CHAPTER THIRTY-SIX

LOGAN WALKED ME AROUND THE CASTLE, SHOWING ME THE ROOMS that others had left unlocked before we took a stairwell. The walls were made of the same stone as the exterior of the castle. The same stone that lay the path to walk up. I touched it as we walked up, admiring the roughness of the rock beneath my hand. I looked up and focused on the arched window, the only thing providing us with enough light to see the steps we took in the winding stairwell. Standing in this spot, I could almost envision myself acting out a part in Beauty & The Beast. I let my hand fall from the wall and continued on.

"When was this built?"

"Late eighteen-hundreds."

Late eighteen-hundreds. I wondered how many things these halls had seen. Logan said the first owner had killed her husbands here. They must have seen a whole lot of damage. Logan took a large step and started walking beside me, rather than behind, as we reached the top of the stairwell. I gasped as I took it in. I may not have known much art history, but I knew Gothic architecture when I saw it, and this was goth to the max, with a long wide hall made up of ivory arches and walls covered in the same material, that mimicked the arch windows on the other side. The windows were too high up for me to look out of, but the light they provided was enough to stare at the

walls and ceilings all day. The floors weren't anything spectacular, mismatched slabs of black and gold, and even still it was
beautiful.

"This is crazy," I whispered, looking around. I focused on
the arched wooden doors up ahead. "Is that a room?"

"Nope." He was walking faster now, more animated. I followed with the same enthusiasm. When he opened it, it gave
way to a library. My jaw dropped.

"How is this place real?" I stepped inside and looked around.

It wasn't very big, but it had two walls filled with books and
a stepladder that glided across each. It was like a real-life Beauty
and The Beast library. I walked around and looked at the books.
All looked like they'd been here for over one hundred years, and
they probably had been. I didn't recognize the titles, but some
of the authors were familiar.

"Does anyone come up here?"

"To study sometimes. Or for meetings," Logan said. "All of
the public areas like this one are fair game, so if there's a party
to plan with the current board members and alumni, they pick a
few rooms and host in those."

"Interesting," I said. "What else is a public area?"

"Let's go through here." Logan grinned.

Instead of walking out the doors we just came in through,
he walked forward and pulled a lever beside one of the book-
cases. It revealed a doorknob. Taking a small part of the
bookcase with him as he pulled, he signaled for me to walk
through. I did, completely entranced.

"I told you the lady was crazy," he said.

"What does that door in the entrance lead to?"

"A similar library, but that one is off-limits. It belongs to the
current board. Only they have a key to it."

"What's Nolan's major?"

"Art history. His family deals art." Logan looked over at me. "Why?"

"I was trying to find a connection between all of us. You and I are business and journalism, so that makes sense. What's Marcus's?"

"Accounting, with a minor in art."

"Another art dealer?"

"Yeah."

"What about Nora?"

"Political science. I think she just got into grad school."

"So politician, art dealers, and journalists?" I frowned. "My dad is a media mogul, as are my two older brothers, but they all studied business."

"Business is our connection, Amelia. And the fact that we all have extremely promising futures. Some because of who their parents are and others, like me, because of my career."

"In hockey?"

"Sports in general. I play hockey, but I'm not just a hockey player," he said. "The same way Michael Jordan and Lebron James and Dwayne Wade aren't just basketball players."

"That makes sense."

"You ready now?" he nodded towards the winding staircase in front of us.

"I'm ready." I smiled, but as I walked down I thought about the secret passageway itself.

Had my father brought Lana in and out of here like this? What about the other girls she'd mentioned he'd been with? He told me he had only had a mentoring relationship with her. I needed to either believe him and back him up or not believe him and . . . and what? Lana was gone and there was nothing I could do about it. God. I wished my brother would wake up already. I needed him here. My stomach growled as we reached the end of the stairs.

"We'll get breakfast soon, I swear," Logan said, opening a door that led outside. "This is the garden."

Unlike the grandiosity of the castle, this was the smallest garden I'd ever seen. The grass had been completely covered with bricks, as if to not let anything grow. There were a few tails of weeds that seeped through, but that was it. The magnificent thing about it was that it was outside, yet somehow tucked between the castle walls and those castle walls were covered in ivy. In the middle of it was a lamppost, which was currently turned off. It was an oddly charming secret garden. I turned to Logan, who was leaning against the only spot not yet covered in ivy. He was watching me with an expression I couldn't quite understand. It wasn't lust. It wasn't amusement or curiosity. The potential of what it could be held me captive.

"I like it," I said. "There's minimal upkeep."

"Which is why we like it." He smiled. "Come on, let's go have breakfast. I'm starving."

He took my hand in his as we walked back inside the house, to one of the common areas that had long tables. There were pastries set up—donuts, bagels, croissants, and coffee boxes. Nolan was sitting in there, talking to Marcus and a pretty girl with beautiful pale skin and short, brown curly hair. She smiled as we walked in, her eyes on our held hands. I wondered if she'd been his partner last year. I didn't know how partners worked exactly, but for some reason, I was dying to know. Maybe it was the blood oath that did it for me. Maybe it was the fact that my feelings for him were so big they threatened to take over everything else. Maybe it was because last night had been magical or because everything he said to me held promises I so desperately wanted.

We both served ourselves things in the plastic plates provided. I got one donut. Logan got five stacked up. We poured coffees into to-go cups and walked over to where they were sitting.

"I'm Nora," she said as I sat down.

"Amelia." I smiled. "But you already knew that."

"I did. Not to say I'm not curious about the girl who finally made Logan take a blood oath." She grinned at whatever look Logan was giving her. "Oh, this is cute. She doesn't know?"

"Nora." It was a warning.

"He doesn't even like the word blood," Marcus said laughing.

"He's having breakfast. Leave him the fuck alone," Nolan said, scowling.

"You don't like blood?" my attention whipped in his direction. He cringed. "But . . . you're always bleeding. You play hockey, for God's sake. Not to mention, get in a lot of fistfights."

"Ironic, I know," he mumbled.

"More than ironic. It's plain weird." I laughed, taking a bite of my donut and chewing. I licked my lips, looking at Nora again. "So he'd never done an oath? How is he here?"

"He had to scale the waterfall by the old lab. Twice. They told him they'd give him until this year to participate in the oath, which is insane, if you ask me. We didn't have a choice in the matter." She rolled her eyes.

"What about his partner last year?"

Nora glanced at Logan and back at me. I could tell she was hesitant about saying anything without his permission, which was crazy since she'd dished out the blood thing with so much enthusiasm.

"His partner last year was only his partner for like a second," Nolan said. "She was recruited by the Swords before she was initiated here."

"Swords?" My eyes widened. "There's a third society?"

"There are probably about five different ones in this university," Marcus said. "But they're not very secretive. Only ours and The Swords are."

"The Swords are the red cloaks," Logan said beside me. I looked over at him. He was already on his fourth donut.

"Swords," I repeated, thinking about their red cloaks and the graves they dug. "It makes sense for a medical secret society."

"Swords and snakes. Definitely apt for them," Nora said distastefully.

"So they can do that? Recruit from here? Isn't that against the rules?"

"In The Eight's Creed, yes. Not in theirs."

"So she just left? And you just let her?" I asked.

"Well, we kind of had to. It was either that or she'd expose us. She was a little upset because Logan didn't want to settle down," Nora said.

"No, she was upset because Logan treated her like shit," Marcus added.

"She felt like he'd fucked her and discarded her," Nolan said.

I couldn't help my flinch.

"Can we stop discussing my sex life?" Logan asked. "None of you know what really happened. Savannah was crazy. We fucked once and she was already planning our wedding."

"Not unlike some people I know." My gaze snapped to his. The room filled with gasps and oo's and aa's I didn't care that I was calling him out in front of his friends. In that moment, I felt betrayed. If her night with him had been anything like ours . . . I felt sick at the mere thought of that.

"It's different." Logan kept his eyes on me, donuts forgotten. He looked as pissed as I felt. "You're different. We're different. And I'm not going to explain myself in front of a guy who can't even say the word relationship without wanting to throw up, one who breaks up with every girl he finds because she's not perfect enough, and a girl who can't make her mind up as to what team she bats for long enough to entertain the idea of settling down."

"Fuck you." Nora stood up quickly. "I bat for both teams and you're right, none of us owe each other an explanation, but if you fuck things up with Mae, I'll gladly take over."

Logan's jaw was working as he glared after her. He looked at the other two at our table. "Anyone else want to try to stake claims on my girlfriend? Maybe I'll call up Adam and ask him if I can borrow a couple of their gravesites."

Girlfriend? My hands shook as I grabbed my plate and cup and stood from the table, excusing myself quietly. I tossed the stuff in the trash and walked out of the dining hall. I found Nora a couple of feet away, typing furiously on her phone. When she heard me approach, she put it away and looked up at me. Her brown eyes were shining.

"I'm sorry," I said quietly.

"If you start apologizing for him now, you'll be doing it the rest of your life," she said. "He's an asshole. I love him to death, but he's an asshole."

"He is."

"He's never been mean to me before. He always defends me to everyone." She smiled a little. "He must really be crazy about you."

I shrugged. I knew how I felt about him and it scared the hell out of me. I didn't want to jump to conclusions on his end. Not this quickly. I looked at the painting across from us and took a step back. It was my father, wearing a tuxedo, standing behind a woman sitting in a chair. I walked over. It was Ella Valentine. Clear as day.

"I hadn't seen this before," I whispered. "Is this . . . are they part of the board? Is that why they're in the painting together?"

"How much do you know about your father?"

"Not nearly enough apparently." I turned to face Nora, heart pounding. "How much do you know about him?"

She hesitated. "Come, I'll show you around."

"Logan already did. I'm pretty sure I've walked this entire thing twice now." I looked back at the painting.

"Yet this is your first time seeing this painting," she said.

"Yeah." I looked at her again.

"Let me give you a tour of the paintings then. I don't blame Logan for not wanting you to focus on those just yet, but it's your family. You should know these things. Trust me, I learned about all of it the hard way," she said. "My mother's part of The Eight. Well, The Lab Initiative now. You'll see her on these walls as well."

"Hey, are you ready to go?" The voice was Logan's as he walked out of the hall. He walked over to us, his gaze on mine first, and then on Nora's. "I was an asshole in there."

"That's the closest I've ever gotten to an apology from you, so I'll take it." She smiled. "I want to show Mae the paintings."

"No." There was a finality in his voice.

"I want to see them." I frowned at him. "What does it matter if I see them today or five weeks from now?"

"You're already fragile, Amelia." He stepped forward, bringing a hand to my face. "Come home with me. I have to be at the rink in an hour."

"I want to stay."

"I don't want you to see them without me being here."

"I can handle it," I assured him. "Nora will be with me."

"But I won't be."

"I'll be fine."

"I won't be."

The concern in his eyes as he looked at me made me smile. I brought my hand to his face, scratching his beard, which he'd let fill out but kept meticulously manicured nonetheless. Suddenly the girlfriend comment felt right. When we were together like this, I couldn't really imagine being anything except for his. It didn't mean there wasn't a long conversation to be had about all of it though.

"I'll call you when I'm on my way home."

"I'll take her," Nora said behind me. "She'll be in good hands, and don't worry, I don't mean it in a sexual way."

Logan chuckled. He leaned in and kissed me once, twice, three times, before he finally pulled away and let go. He idled for another minute looking at me with everything he wanted to say but couldn't and I knew because I felt the same, my chest heavy with an emotion I'd never felt this potently.

"By the way, we're camping here tonight," Nora said as Logan finally started to walk away.

He turned. "Where?"

"Edge of the woods."

"Isn't it hunting season?"

"They won't come near our tents," Logan said, shooting me one last look that spoke of longing before walking out.

"Hunting season?" I asked.

"It's what we call recruitment. The Swords are still recruiting."

"How do you know so much about them?" I asked as we started walking.

"Hm. I'll have to draw it up for you. It's the only way I was able to understand it." She looked at me. "It's like a huge brotherhood, split up into a lot of parts. We didn't used to know much about the other ones before they went public. The Swords share our land though because in an interesting turn of events, when The Eight acquired this house back in the day, the woman's husband bought the lot next to it," she looked at me. "The octopus scientist married while she was in college and her husband was a Sword. Instead of hiding it from each other, they were up front about it and he bought the lot beside ours, which used to be a rundown church. He acquired it from some monks. Monks still live there, by the way. They don't dress in red cloaks though." She flashed me a smile. "Also, my twin brother, Will, is a Sword. That's probably the explanation I should've given from the beginning. We tell each other mostly everything, so I know a lot."

"That does explain a lot," I said. "I used to think Linc and I told each other everything but he didn't tell me about The Eight."

"Don't take it to heart. It's difficult to explain this to someone who's not in it. My only wish is that you'd gotten here freshman year so I didn't have to do this crash course."

"Yeah."

She stopped at the foot of the stairs right in front of the main door and took out a key ring. She had three skeleton keys on it and they were all labeled. She started up the stairs that led to that one gold room. I hesitated.

"I thought we weren't allowed in there?"

"Only the board members and key master have the key." She dangled the three keys. "Lucky for us, I'm one of those."

"What about the other building? The first one I went to when I was summoned?"

"The Sphynx." She grinned. "We acquired it a couple of years ago. It belonged to The Sphynx society originally, but they've tapered off. There are talks of some kids wanting to bring it back, but I'm not sure there's any truth to those rumors."

"When do you use it?"

"Only to summon. We don't want to bring people here unless we know for sure they're going to be initiated."

I followed her to the top of the stairs, she paused by the door and turned to face me. "For the record, you're not allowed up here, so pretend you never saw any of this."

She put the key in the hole and turned. It unlocked with a click, similar to the sound the front door made when Logan unlocked it. Nora walked inside and waited for me to take in the room—a dome ceiling that reminded me of the Sistine Chapel, with paintings of naked people sitting on clouds in a blue sky. I tried to make out the faces, but couldn't really, so I figured they must be actual saints. The room itself, covered with wall-to-wall books, was smaller than the library Logan had shown me, but somehow seemed to contain more things. There were eight white busts on top of pillars that circled the library.

"I guess The Eight really loves to read," I said, looking around.

"These are photo albums."

"What?" I walked up to one, pulling it out of the shelf.

That was when I noticed the gold numbers on the spines. This one said 1924. I opened it carefully, not wanting to leave any grease from my fingers on the pictures. They were all covered in plastic, as if to preserve them.

"There were women in the group even back then." I looked up at Nora.

"We were the only society to do that." She smiled proudly.

I shut the book and put it back in its place. I wasn't going to know anyone who attended in the twenties. My father had been the first of his family to attend college in the United States. His mother always joked that he was too much of a genius for their city, even though their city had its share of intelligent individuals, but of course, Abuela Maria would think her son was the most intelligent of all. Not to knock him, despite all of his questionable choices, my father was extremely smart and business savvy. I moved to the years he would've been here—seventies. The first page I opened, there he was, standing with seven other people— The Eight of that year. Beside him, Ella Valentine.

Maybe it was because I'd just seen a portrait of them together, looking like they were a couple, but seeing the young, college version of themselves together hit me hard. They weren't even touching, but I could just tell they were together. I reminded myself of what she'd told me—they had actually been dating before he met mom. I kept turning the pages. In some pictures, they wore cloaks, in others they were serving food to the homeless, picking up trash around the park, reading to children. I kept turning the pages. My attention stayed on the next picture. It was a couple I'd seen before, maybe at one of my parent's Christmas parties. They were laughing, looking at the camera, but it was the background that caught my eye. It was my father and Ella Valentine back there, looking like they were caught in the middle of an argument. I shut the book and opened another one, and then another one, and then moved on to the one labeled Alumni—1999. I'd been a toddler then. This photo album was thinner and showed mostly photos of various parties that occurred that year. I didn't find my father until I reached the tenth page, but there he was, holding Ella Valentine's hand.

My heart was in my throat as I looked at the picture. I shut the album with a thump and looked up at Nora.

"This is disgusting."

"My father is this one." She opened up the book and pointed at the familiar couple I'd seen in the other book. "This is not my mother, who he's still married to, by the way."

"Geez." I shook my head. "Disgusting."

"I promised I'd draw up the societies for you so that you could see how they're connected," she said, pushing the books aside and grabbing a sheet of paper. Up top, she wrote Blackwell and drew two lines underneath it—one that said Dr. Elizabeth Blackwell and the other said Dr. Henry Blackwell.

"They were a couple when they were here. They married their senior year," she explained. Beneath Elizabeth Blackwell, she wrote The Eight. "She's the octopus lady. She was a marine scientist who worked tirelessly in the original Hydro Lab, which is now falling apart. You've seen it, it's right by the waterfall behind where you did the blindfold test."

"Oh yeah." I nodded. "That was an actual building?"

"Very long time ago." Nora smiled. "Which is why it's said that's the body of water with the octopuses. She threw them out the window there."

"That's a weird thing to do."

"I think they took away her funding, but I'm not sure. Point is, she built this society and modeled it after her favorite creature—eight legs, eight members, intelligent, camouflage, etcetera."

"Dr. Henry Blackwell started The Swords. He was a mad scientist. Where his wife was a marine scientist, he experimented on people. It is said, he bought the old church not only because of the cemetery, but because once upon a time these lots were combined and that was where the crazy owner of this house killed all of her lovers. Her husbands she made seem like natural causes or accidents. The lovers didn't get that lucky."

I shivered. "This house is totally haunted."

"Both of them are."

"I barely like sleeping in the dark, so I'm going to pass on the horror stories for now," I said. "I have an overactive imagination and watch too much crime television so I feel like anything and everything is going to happen to me."

Nora laughed, pointing at the paper. She drew two arrows beneath both societies that met at the bottom and wrote The Labyrinth Initiative.

"No way." I gasped. "It's connected to both?"

"Yep. Think of it as a shell company," she said. "So T.L.I. actually files under non for profit. This part is what we all know. This . . ." She drew another line beneath that and wrote Mentorships and Sugar Babies. "Is the part we're still trying to figure out, but it's pretty obvious to those of us who have been around, and it's definitely obvious after seeing these albums."

She walked away and pulled three albums off the far-end bookshelf, placing them in front of me. Unlike the black leather-bound albums around the room, these were red and black. My hand shook slightly as I opened the first one and shut it right away.

"What the hell is this? Porn?" I looked up at Nora, wide-eyed. I didn't want to see naked pictures of my father.

"Relax, members are all clothed," she said.

"Relax," I repeated, opening the album back up. "Relax?"

I couldn't imagine anyone relaxing as they flipped through this album. One picture, in particular, made me pause and stare, a disgusted taste in my mouth. Three men in suits sitting in chairs while three naked women lay on the floor with their legs spread open, touching themselves as the men looked on. One man had reached down to seemingly help the girl, mid-picture. That man was my father. And that girl looked a lot like Lana. I slammed the book shut again.

"I can't look at this. I'll be sick." I placed a hand on my queasy stomach. "Why don't you show this to people before they go through initiation? This would be the exact kind of hazing that would scare people away."

"We need you in." She shrugged, a small smile touching her lips. "You're a Bastón, you were always meant to be in The Eight."

"I don't know if I want any part in this. If I'm expected to walk around naked for these old guys—"

"No," Nora said quickly, eyes wide. "These were things we recently discovered. You'd never be part of this." She tapped on the books, then picked one up and opened it to the very first page, which I'd completely bypassed. Written in script was: Labor Union.

"Labor Union?" I said loudly. "This is disgusting."

"It's extremely complicated even for a crash course, but technically, they have this mentorship program and within that program is another in which girls are basically . . . prostitutes." She gathered the books and walked to the shelf, sliding them in their place.

"It's like a damn never-ending matryoshka doll," I said, looking at the paper. "How did you find out about this?"

"The short story? Lana told a friend about it and that friend started showing up here, lurking in the woods out back, parking in front of the gates and looking in. It was creepy. I thought it was someone's ex-girlfriend or someone Fitz pissed off." She cringed as she said it. "Sorry. But Lana was here one day, for a gala, and saw the girl and said it was a friend of hers. She went outside and asked her to please leave. Apparently, the girl wanted to make sure she was okay."

"You don't buy that?" I asked.

"Lana worked for the paper. We all knew she wanted to tear the societies down from the inside and we all agreed she shouldn't be here."

Her words sent a chill down my spine. If she had been un-wanted . . . was that why my brother was arguing with her in those pictures? Telling her to stay away from The Eight? From The Lab? From our father?

"How involved are the guys we know in this little ring?" I asked and felt the need to hold my breath as I waited for the answer.

"If you're asking whether or not Logan fucks these girls, the answer is hell no. In case you haven't noticed, Fitz is extremely particular with who he fucks and he's never brought a regular around. Anywhere." She frowned as she spoke the words, as if just now realizing this. "Honestly, you're the only person I've ever actually seen him hang out with. I mean, we hang out, but he's like a brother. He's cordial, at best, to some of the girls around campus, but I wouldn't say he's very welcoming, if you know what I mean."

I did know what she meant and it gave me a little more confidence in what we had.

"Does anyone else?" I asked. "Marcus? Nolan?"

"No. Absolutely not." She shook her head. "My understanding is that this whole idea stemmed from The Swords. They've been known to hire girls." She waved a hand toward another bookcase. The one with a row of red spines. "You can see those books for yourself. Of course, we only have blackmail power. We can't really say for sure what goes on behind closed doors over there. Not even my brother will tell me that. The fact of the matter is, in recent years, The Lab Initiative decided to mentor some of these people—girls and boys alike, and I guess some have evolved into something more."

"So they're taking advantage of these people." My stomach turned. My father was taking advantage of these students.

"My understanding is that the people being mentored don't have to do anything, but a lot of them end up actually falling for these men." She paused. "And women."

"The whole thing is disturbing." I crossed my arms.

Now I understood why Logan wanted to be here when I learned all of this. Between the pictures of my father with Ella and then my father with those naked girls, it was all too much. I thought about my brother and what he must have thought of all of this. It wasn't that Lincoln was Mr. Perfect, but he was definitely a stickler for rules and this was not something I could picture him condoning.

He obviously knew about Lana and dad. I'd seen those pictures of them arguing. But then Lana just disappeared. I looked at Nora again, trying to wrap my head around everything she told me.

"Did The Eight have anything to do with Lana's disappearance?"

"No. Of course not." Her eyes widened. "We talked about needing her to get out of here and not welcoming her in, but we would never . . . " She paused, suddenly looking contrite. "Your brother was the last person to see her."

Logan had said this to me already, but hearing it again felt like taking a blow to the chest. Could my brother have gone that far? Could he have hurt her? I checked my phone again. Still nothing from my family. I desperately needed him to wake up.

CHAPTER THIRTY-SEVEN

THE PEP RALLY WAS A BLUR. EVEN AS I SNAPPED PHOTOS, I DIDN'T feel like I was actually there. Physically, yes. If you'd been in the stands or standing beside me, you would've been able to say that I'd been there taking pictures for the paper. A true Peter Parker, hiding my face behind an enormous camera lens. Mentally, I was elsewhere. I was with Lincoln, wondering if he had anything to do with the Lana thing. Maybe she'd been in the car with him when he got in that accident. Maybe she died and he didn't know how to cope with it so he hid it? A shiver raked through me. Would Lincoln hide something that big? I thought of my father and his relationship with Lana, which I now confirmed was true. I had too much evidence to deny it. Would Lincoln hide it for dad's sake? For The Eight? My hand itched. I reached up and grabbed the necklace around my neck. Nora had given me my own skeleton key to open the front door of The Lab, a way of officially welcoming me into The Eight. I'd been happy to accept it when she dropped me off at home, but the longer I stood there with it around my neck, the more it felt like a noose rather than a gift.

"Have you gotten any good pictures?"

"I think so." I glanced at Max, who was standing beside me. "How many do you think I need? I'm dying to get out of here."

"Too many people?"

"More like . . . not in the mood for this."

"So you're not going to the party tonight?"

"What party?"

"Just a keg party out in the main lawn."

"That sounds exactly like everything I want to avoid tonight."

"Come on, let's stand on the other side where the actual media is." Max laughed and tugged on the strap of the lanyard around my neck.

We shouldered our way through the crowd until we made it to the other side. Max let out a relieved breath.

"There are a lot more people here than last year," he said. "It's Fitz's last year, so it was bound to be crazy." He pointed to the other side of the arena, where we'd just been. I'd seen people waving something around, but I wasn't paying attention. Now that I was on the other side, all I could see were huge foam gloves that said FITZ on the bottom.

"He's not even the goalie."

"I know, but Fitz's Mitts." Max nudged me. "It's a Canadian thing, I gather. We call them gloves, they call them mitts, so yeah, Fitz's Mitts. Get it?"

"No." I frowned. Just when I thought I was getting the hang of hockey, these people threw something else my way. "I thought they were called gloves?"

"Those are his Canadian supporters," Max explained. "They call people who have good stickhandling Nifty Mitts, hence, Fitz's Mitts."

"Oh. So they're like . . . his groupies?"

"Fan base, but yeah." Max laughed.

"Hm. It's cute." I repeated it in my head: Fitz's Mitts. It actually was cute, though I wouldn't say it aloud.

"Wait until he skates onto the ice. It'll be mayhem."

"It's pretty loud already."

"This is not loud in comparison to when he comes out," Max shouted over the noise. "Do you still hate each other?"

"No." I blushed. "Water under the bridge."

"Oh. Well, that's good, because Fitz is the kind of guy who could make your time here a living hell if he wanted to."

"How would he do that?" I raised my brows. "Our school has a zip code. It's not like I have to see him."

"You take pictures of sports events for the paper." He shot me a look. "You'll see him. Besides, as big as campus is, I bet you've seen all of them around everywhere."

"True."

"And I've heard the way girls talk about him. Cry over him." He shot me another look.

My heart pounded, but I tried to keep my expression neutral. I did not want to hear anything about my boyfriend's past. I'd convinced myself to get over his partner at The Eight from last year and stop obsessing over the thought of him with anyone else before me. It was a dumb thing to think about anyway. It wasn't like I could change any of that. I put it out of my mind as the crowd got louder, cheers and screams sounding as the music was lowered and the announcer started announcing the team. First, he introduced the coaches, who walked out on the ice in a large group and waved. I snapped a picture.

"And now, the moment you've all been waiting for . . . this year's hockey team!" the announcer screamed into the microphone.

The crowd roared. The lights shut off and spotlights shone on the ice, moving back and forth as the music started up again. Players were introduced as they skated onto the ice, and I clicked photos of each of them. The crowd seemed to get louder with each one. I wondered if they'd done it on purpose, given them an order of popularity to come out in. If so, I felt bad for the first one. Nolan was introduced. *Nolan Chadwick Astor*. It was a long, important-sounding name. I wondered if his mother was waiting for him to grow out of the long hair and inappropriate comments phase and grow into his name or if she'd given up hope.

Logan was last. *"Logan 'Fitz' Fitzgerald!"* The crowd went crazy, pounding on the glass, stomping on the floor, climbing on their seats, and I had to pause taking pictures to look around because I really thought they'd bring the house down. The noise vibrated through me as I stood there, and I smiled as I lifted the camera up and snapped a picture of the crowd first, and then Logan as he skated out on the ice. It got louder when he was in full sight. Unlike his teammates, who did a wave and stood in line, Logan skated around the ice and waved. It was then that it hit me. He really was popular. He really was sort of famous. And yeah, he was arrogant, but not as arrogant as you'd expect someone with this kind of following to be. When he skated toward my section, I braced myself, pressing my face to the camera and holding it tighter, as if it would somehow fall out of my hands at the sight of a close-up. I took a breath. I needed to calm down.

This was Logan, for God's sake. When he reached us, people pounded on the glass. I stood closer to it and snapped, snapped, snapped. I didn't want to miss him if he went by really fast. Suddenly, it seemed almost quiet, as if the crowd around me was waiting in anticipation of something. When I blinked into the little window of the camera, I saw his face right in front of me, staring into the lens—into me. I licked my lips, and he grinned, a slow, sexy grin that made his green eyes sparkle with mischief. He knew I was flustered. I lowered the camera but kept my finger on the button in case he did anything film-worthy. He

nodded at me. I smiled, shaking my head. *What was he doing?*
And then he did something I would have never expected in a
million years. While holding my gaze from the other side of the
glass, he opened his hand and kissed his palm.

It happened in an instant. So quickly I was sure nobody really caught it, but I did, because it was clearly for me. I smiled
wide, resisting the urge to throw the camera down and walk
onto the ice to jump on him. He winked and skated away.

"Well, I guess you can say you definitely don't have issues
anymore," Max said. "What was that kiss thing?"

"Nothing." I shook my head, still smiling.

I stayed for another hour and from the looks of it, the other
people weren't leaving any time soon either. Logan and his
team were working on some drills with no signs of stopping.
Glancing at my watch, I saw that it was almost seven thirty and
started packing up. There was no way the paper would need
more pictures than what I took. The announcer said they were
finished with the pep rally shortly after I packed up and the guys
skated off the ice. I walked with Max to the general area of the
rink, standing off to the side as the crowd of people walked by
us waving their Fitz Mitt. Max stopped a couple of them and
interviewed them for the paper. They all gushed about their
golden boy, Fitz, and mentioned they'd driven down for this and
would drive down again for games. When they walked away,
I turned to Max, who was making sure he'd jotted down the
notes.

"That really is impressive."

"What? That they travel to see him?"

"Yeah." I nodded.

"I told you. He's a legend."

I wasn't sure how I felt about dating a legend. Old inse-
curities started to bubble as I thought about it. How would I

deal with all of the attention? Would I be able to handle all of the girls that constantly clung to him? Would he really not pay attention to them? With Travis, it was a gamble I was willing to take because even when we were "on" I didn't feel this lost in him. With Logan, I felt like I was on a completely different playing field. Yet, Logan hadn't ever given me a reason to doubt him. Not yet anyway. We'd been friends for a while now and I hadn't seen him so much as look at another girl when I was around. I needed to trust he meant it when he said he wanted to be with me. Besides, he'd called me his girlfriend.

"Why are you so smiley?" Max asked.

"I can't smile?"

"You normally don't unless I'm saying something funny, and then I think you may just look amused for my sake." He smiled. My cheeks hurt from smiling so hard. I pushed him playfully. "Uh-oh, Mae has a secret," he said.

"What secret?" The voice came from Logan. Some people swarmed him when they saw him. He was wearing a team t-shirt and jeans, his gaze on me as he smiled for his fans. "I just have to . . . "

I waved him away. "I'll be right here."

"Holy shit," Max breathed. "You could've given me a warning."

"A warning about what?"

"You and Fitz are a thing."

"Her and Fitz are dating," Logan said loud and clear. Some of the people waiting for a picture gasped and directed their camera toward me.

"Eyes on him. I suck on the ice." I blocked my face. "I'm just here for moral support."

They laughed, but obeyed my wishes and kept their attention on him.

"You think you can handle all of this?" Max whispered.

I shot him a look. Logan had the best hearing out of anyone I'd ever met. I wouldn't be surprised if he could hear him right now. I looked over at him and he was talking to a guy so I figured it was fine to talk about this to Max quietly.

"I don't know."

"It'll be hard. This is nothing." Max pointed to the small crowd. "This will get worse when he goes pro."

"I know." I looked on at Logan.

It was too soon to tell what would happen between us, but as far as his career went, I was completely content with cheering him on from the sidelines. I knew that meant seeing episodes like this, where some girls didn't seem to get a clue and touched all up on him even after he made it clear he wasn't available, but I was oddly okay with it. Maybe it was because his eyes continuously found mine and reassured me that he belonged to me and that was enough to accept the madness.

"I hope he treats you right, Mae." Max put his hand on my arm. "You deserve it."

"Paper Boy," Logan called out. "Hands off my girl please."

"The fact that all of that is going on and his attention is still on your surroundings speaks volumes." Max dropped his hand with a blush. He chuckled. "Maybe this is different after all."

His words made me smile. Max had been around Logan long enough to know what he was normally like around women. I gave him a hug as he said goodbye. Once the small crowd finally dissipated around Logan, he walked over to me. The anticipation of that walk was killer, as he ran his fingers through his hair, not taking his eyes off mine. His swagger was normally pretty high up in the charts, but his swagger tonight seemed to be on ten thousand.

"Was he trying to make a move on you?"

"No." I rolled my eyes, fighting a smile. "Unlike your harem."

"I don't have a harem." He wrapped a hand behind my neck and reached down and kissed me. "I have you."

CHAPTER THIRTY-EIGHT

LOGAN AND I WERE SITTING ON MY COUCH, WATCHING SEINFELD reruns when we got a text saying the camping trip was postponed a couple of days. It seemed like they were all walking on eggshells because The Swords were still not finished with their hazing process and nobody wanted to see what that process entailed.

"Plausible deniability," Logan said when I asked him about it. "If you don't like to get shit on your shoes, you don't step in it."

"But aren't you curious?"

"Not at all."

"Do they know about your hazing?"

"Maybe." He shrugged a shoulder. "Our hazing isn't bad though."

"Walking around knives isn't bad? Stealing shit isn't bad?" I asked. "Did they ever find out we stole that painting from them?"

"Not yet." He chuckled. "When they figure it out, they'll come knocking. Until then, they're too busy with their weird little seances."

"So you do know what goes on over there." I raised an eyebrow.

"Some, but honestly, Mae? After walking into one of their

weird meetings by mistake . . . " He shook his head. "If you think what your dad and the other guys from that class are doing is sick, you don't want to know what The Swords are up to."

His words made a shiver roll through me. They'd said they were grave diggers and experimented on cadavers. Maybe I didn't want to know what they were up to after all. I checked my phone and saw a text that hadn't been there when I'd checked it ten minutes ago.

Mom: he's awake. He's asking for you.

Me: I'll be there as soon as I can

I turned to Logan. "Lincoln's awake. I have to go home."

"I'll drive you." He sat up quickly, brushing a hand over his hair before replacing the backward red and gold Toronto Raptors cap he had on.

It would take us four and a half hours if we drove. While I walked over to my room to pack a few things, I sent a text to my dad's pilot friend in case he was in town and the private jet he normally flew for dad's other friend was in the hangar. I set my phone down to focus. Logan called out that he was going to his apartment to get an overnight bag of his own. The text message from Manuel, the pilot, came back quickly.

Manuel Ramos: I'm here. The city again?

Me: PLEASE. DAD WILL PAY YOU AND I'LL BAKE YOU COOKIES.

Manuel Ramos: I'll pass on the cookies. No offense (last ones you made were pretty bad)

Me: LOL THANKS.

Manuel Ramos: I just brought your dad over here, but he's taking another plane back, so I was going to head out in 40min. Can you be here by then?

Me: Leaving in like 10.

My dad was in town? And he hadn't called? I wondered

how often he did that. I wondered if he was here to see Ella. Still. You would think he would at least want to say hello to his daughter. I shook the thought away and finished packing, locked up, and ran to Logan's apartment. He was stepping back out as I reached it. His brows rose.

"What happened?"

"We have a flight to catch in 40min." I took a deep breath and let it out.

"You booked a flight?" He was looking at me like I'd lost my marbles. I had.

"Private flight. Long story. I'll explain on the way there. I'm sure we can jump on one coming back. This family travels every three days, I'm not even exaggerating."

"What the hell family is this?" he asked, still standing by his door. At least he was locking it.

"I'll explain in the car." I grabbed his arm and pulled him towards the elevator.

"I need to be back by Monday afternoon," he said. "I have a game at seven."

"You'll be back by then, I swear. Worse case we'll have one of the drivers bring us back."

"I'm so glad we didn't meet when we were in high school." He shook his head as we walked out of the elevator.

I was still pulling him along as we walked into the lobby. Gary laughed when he saw us. Once we were in his truck and he started driving, I let out a breath. We'd definitely make it in time. I knew Manuel would wait for us a few minutes if he needed to, but not too long. If his boss had called him to go back to the city, he'd have to drop everything and go.

"Why are you glad we didn't meet in high school?" I looked at Logan as we drove away from our neighborhood.

"Because I would've never dated you. Private jets? You are

way out of my league." He chuckled. "I wouldn't have even tried to date you."

"You?" My brows rose. "Mr. I Can Get Any Girl I Want, with the harem of girls waiting for you to drop me and pick one of them up? You think you couldn't have gotten me to date you?"

"Amelia." He shot me an amused look. "I barely got you to date me now and this has been me trying my damn hardest."

"That's so untrue." I rolled my eyes, but felt myself smile at the thought that I wasn't like his other girls. "Besides, a private jet or fancy car is not impressive. Travis was from a questionable part of town and I dated him."

"Can we not bring up that loser?"

"Fine." I reached over and threaded my fingers through his. "Thank you for coming with me."

"Anything for you, baby." He brought our joined hands up and kissed the back of mine.

"Did you have a girlfriend in high school?"

"Yeah. For like six months, then she got tired of the attention I was getting from the other girls and dumped me for some up-and-coming rapper."

"Ouch." I laughed. "So it's not like you're opposed to having a girlfriend?"

"I have one right now." He winked at me. "I'm definitely not opposed. I just don't like the idea of wasting my time with girls I know I have no future with."

"This ties in with the when you know, you know thing, doesn't it?" Butterflies swarmed my belly. This entire conversation was emotions overload yet for some reason I wanted to have it.

"When you know, you know," he stated, glancing over at me.

I felt myself blush.

By the time we reached the airport and were cleared to drive up to the parking lot beside the hangar, my nerves were shot. I was finally going to see my brother and he was finally awake and obviously aware enough to ask about me. I considered sending my older brothers a text message, but decided against it. They hadn't communicated with me all these days while they were there, so I wasn't going to communicate with them either. Still, the unknown was getting to me. Logan grabbed my hand as we walked and I squeezed it back, grateful for the reminder that I wasn't alone in this.

We small-talked with Manuel and his co-pilot and boarded the plane for our short flight. My mind was mostly elsewhere, thinking about Lincoln and my parents. I tried so hard not to think about my father because every time I did, I got flashbacks of that photo album and it made me sick. When I did take time away from my thoughts during the hour and a half flight, it was to admire the way Logan looked sitting across from me. He was reading one of the Dennis Lehane novels he borrowed from me and had rarely paused to speak. He'd mentioned that he didn't get as much downtime to read as he'd liked, so I tried not to interrupt him. Besides, a hot dude reading was my favorite kind of distraction.

We landed and had a car waiting for us, courtesy of my father. We went straight to one of my parent's properties, where they'd moved Lincoln with two around-the-clock nurses and a doctor that came by every morning. My mother spared no expenses when it came to her baby boy, her favorite boy, whether she admitted that or not.

"And here I thought the most impressive thing I'd see today was the private jet," Logan said beside me as we drove up the path to my parent's Hampton's estate. "Is this where you grew up?"

"I grew up in Mexico City. Still in a mansion, yes, but entirely different life no matter how you put it." I chewed on the tip of my thumb. "We moved here when I started high school though and my parents bought this house when I was a junior, so yeah, I sort of grew up here."

"Out of my league," he whispered.

"You're not fooling anyone, Fitzgerald. Your parents have money too."

"There's money, and then there's money," he emphasized, looking at the house.

"Money that you'll be making very soon," I reminded him. "Then you can buy your own mansion like this."

"I would never." He scoffed. "Give me a little cottage by a lake and my girl and I'll be happy as can be."

The image made me smile. I could completely picture Logan living that kind of unassuming life even after he starts making crazy money playing pro and with the athletic clothing contracts he's bound to get. I could picture myself living like that with him. We finally arrived at the front of the house, we didn't even wait for the driver to open the door. Logan grabbed our bags and we bolted out of the car, rushing to the front door. I hadn't even bothered to bring my key. I was about to knock when the door opened. Mirna stood there, smiling when she saw me. I gave her a quick hug and introduced her to Logan. Mirna had been with my family since I was a kid and was more like an aunt than a housemaid.

"Leave the bags here." I turned to Logan as we were passing the grand staircase.

He looked like he didn't even know where to look. I always forgot how fancy the house was until a new person walked in and made me stop and see it for what it was—there were paintings and sculptures and marble and gold. My mother's love of

Versailles shone through this house. Logan dropped the bags carefully, as if scared he'd scratch something. I grabbed his hand and walked quickly toward the back of the house and through the doors, and then through the corridor that led to the guest house.

"Remember that cottage I said I dreamed of?" Logan said as we approached the guest house.

I laughed. It was the perfect cottage, or guest house, with three bedrooms, three baths, and a full kitchen. Basically, it was someone's dream family home and my parents had it sitting in their yard. This was why I had a hard time with their charity sometimes. They donated a lot of money and time but it was hard to be a champion for the poor and come home to this. At least that's what I always thought. Mom didn't see it that way. Dad always reminded me that Princess Diana had been the people's princess and visited poor people yet lived in luxury.

I paused in front of the door and took a deep breath, then another, trying to calm down before I walked in there. Logan let go of my hand and set it on my shoulder, squeezing. I turned the knob and pushed the door open. Mom was sitting at the dining room table, her computer opened up and her headset on. She'd been working predominantly from home and everywhere else in the world for a year now, using a program to have video meetings with her patients when she was out of town, and sometimes even making house calls when she was in.

"She's on a call with a patient," I whispered, turning to Logan.

We waved at her. She pointed toward the room Lincoln was in. She looked like she'd aged ten years these last few weeks. My heart pounded harder as we walked up to the room. The door was slightly ajar, and as I pushed it open, it revealed Lincoln on a bed, looking pale, but not nearly as frail as I envisioned. He actually looked like he'd put on some weight, his cheeks filling out. His mouth moved into a smile when he saw me, but fell quickly when he saw Logan behind me.

"Not him." He shook his head.

My heart stopped beating. "He just wants to make sure you're okay, Linc."

"Not him."

Logan sighed heavily, touching my arm. "I'll wait for you outside."

I wanted to stop him. To tell him not to be ridiculous, that he was welcome wherever I was, but my brother wasn't in a clear state of mind and I needed to respect his wishes. As I neared the bed, the nurse also took it upon herself to leave us alone. Tears pricked my eyes as I reached for him. I placed my hand on his smooth face. My handsome brother, my best friend that I almost lost for good. It wasn't until this moment that I realized how much I truly missed him. How truly empty and sad living in a world without him would be. Sure, I'd made myself stay busy, but his absence was always there, waiting to greet me at the end of a long day.

"You shaved," I whispered. His own eyes filled with tears as he brought his hand up and closed it around mine, and that was what put me over the edge. I started to cry, really cry, all the tears I'd been holding back all of these days finally exposed. I pressed my forehead to his shoulder and cried as he held my head and cried along with me.

"I'm sorry," he said, his voice hoarse. "I'm sorry I wasn't there."

"You died, Lincoln." I pulled back, wiping my tears. "They used Narcan and still could barely bring you back and then the only thing you do is Morse code me The Lab? What the fuck?"

"Is that why you brought him?"

"No." I wiped my face again. "He's my boyfriend."

A multitude of expressions passed over his face—confusion, pain, more confusion, before he settled on laughter.

"What's so funny?"

"Fitz doesn't do girlfriends."

"I've heard." I sighed. "But as it turns out, Fitz has a girlfriend and it's me."

"You trust him?"

"Why wouldn't I? He's never given me a reason not to."

"The person who did this to me . . . the person who injected me with that shit was wearing a black cloak. It could be any one of them."

"It wasn't Logan."

"How do you know?"

"You really think Logan would try to kill you?" I scrutinized him. "You think Marcus or Nolan or Nora would?"

I hadn't formally met the other two members yet, but I couldn't imagine they'd have anything to do with it either. Why would they? They had nothing to gain and everything to lose if they did some extreme thing like kill another member.

"I don't know, Mae. I don't know what to think and all I do is think." His voice wasn't his own and it had little to do with the hoarseness and more to do with the way he was slurring his words, as if his tongue was tripping over itself as he spoke.

"I know about dad and the girls," I said, lowering my voice so mom wouldn't hear. "And Lana."

Lincoln flinched at the sound of her name.

"You tried to convince her to stop seeing him," I said, "and the rest of the members wanted her out, they didn't want her to be around or write about anything she saw."

Lincoln kept his eyes on me, a faraway look in them as I spoke, as if he was physically here, but mentally elsewhere.

"She's dead," he said after a while. "Lana. She's dead."

"What?" I placed my hand on my heart, willing it to stop beating so hard. "What do you mean?"

"She jumped the fall. There are so many rocks down there, beneath those waterfalls. She just jumped." He blinked away tears. "She just jumped and I just let her."

"You're not making any sense, Lincoln. When did this happen?"

"The night of the accident. We were arguing about dad. I was on the verge of just reporting all of them to the police, fuck the consequences, and then the accident happened and then she jumped." He paused for a long time, taking deep breaths. "I don't even remember how we got into the accident. I must have lost control."

"So she got out of the car and jumped?" It didn't make any sense. "What did she say before she jumped?"

"I can't remember. I don't remember. I just remember she jumped. The look in her eyes . . . she looked like she'd been defeated." He wiped his wet face. "I think I made her jump."

CHAPTER THIRTY-NINE

THINK I MADE HER JUMP.

What did that mean? Did he ask her to jump? He didn't remember details of what happened, but was it possible that my brother would ask another human being to commit suicide? The Lincoln I knew would have never done that, but now I wasn't sure. I remembered what Logan had told me the night of initiation and how he also blamed my brother. Had they all been willing participants in that night? Was I being kept in the dark? I couldn't picture Logan doing that either. It wasn't up to par with the man I had growing feelings for. That was yet another issue though. Love blinded people and I could have very well been blinded by my love for my brother and the way I felt about my boyfriend. I didn't want to be that person, the one who supported a man in the wrong just because I loved them, but I also couldn't fathom either one of them knowingly hurting someone like that. Logan didn't even like his brother because he'd been accused of rape and he'd chosen to believe the victims. He wouldn't be capable of murder or plotting one. He didn't even want to camp out while The Swords were hazing because of plausible deniability. That didn't sound like a man who would participate in something this sinister.

That only left my brother. He stopped talking about it, probably because I was trying to convince him of his own innocence and he was tired of hearing it. After an hour, he warmed up to the idea of letting Logan visit with him. I left the room to go get him, and paused when I saw my mother, no longer working. She was sitting across from Logan with a glass of red wine in her hand and an array of snacks on the table, from chilled shrimp and mussels to Doritos.

"You're going to get a stomach ache," I told Logan, who was slurping down a mussel. He shrugged, grinning.

"Well, I'm glad somebody told me you have a boyfriend," mom said, standing up. "Otherwise, I might have found out via a wedding invitation."

"Mom." My jaw dropped. I felt my face redden as Logan chuckled. "So embarrassing."

My mother stood with a smile on her face, wrapping her arms around me. "I missed you, and I really like this one. He's a keeper."

"Wow." I pulled away and glanced at Logan. "Good luck trying to escape now. Mom rarely gives her seal of approval."

"It must be my lucky day, eh?" He grinned, that devilish grin that made everything inside my body come to life.

"I'm assuming you'll stay the night," mom said, sitting back down.

"Yeah, but we need to leave early in the morning. Logan has practice and games all week."

"Pity." She took a sip of wine.

"My brother wants to see you," I told Logan. He wiped his hands and stood, taking a healthy gulp of the wine in front of him before walking into the room. I took the seat he vacated and poured myself wine in his glass.

"We have clean glasses, Amelia." Mom gave me a disdainful look.

"This one is perfectly fine." I took a sip and set the glass down.

"How does he look to you?" Mom whispered, leaning forward. "Did he talk? Sometimes he doesn't talk. It's maddening. The doctors said he's doing much better than anticipated. He'll need months of therapy."

"I can't believe you guys didn't call me when he woke up." I ran a finger along the rim of the glass. I wasn't one to voice my feelings often, which made my psychologist mother crazy, but this was one time I was willing to do it because as much as I tried to ignore it, I knew I wasn't going to just get over it. "That was really hurtful."

"I'm sorry. I thought we were doing the right thing. Your brothers agreed that it came off as selfish instead of selfless." She reached over and put her hand on mine. "I don't want to lose another kid, Amelia. I want you to have regular experiences in school. I know what it's like to go through trauma at that age, trust me, I don't want that for you."

"But still. I would've liked to have been there."

"It won't happen again." She squeezed my hand before taking it back to her glass. "I hope none of this happens again."

"You look tired."

"I skipped three Botox appointments."

"Mom." I shot her a look, then shook my head. If she wanted to make jokes, so be it. It was better than crying. "What does the doctor say about his memory?"

"He's had a lot of long-term memory loss, but not nearly as bad as we thought it would be. His short-term memory is foggy, but Dr. Ginsburg thinks with time he'll regain it."

"That's good." I brought the glass closer to me, thinking about what he'd said about Lana. He had months to report it and hadn't. They'd searched those woods though, including where the accident had taken place, and all of the waterfalls around, and found nothing. I thought about my father and his role in this, and then remembered what Manny said about flying him upstate. "Where's dad?"

"He went to a meeting with Dean Ellis. You know universities are only worth as much as their donors."

"Right." I set the glass aside and stood. "I'm going to check in on Lincoln and Logan."

As I walked over, I heard them talking quietly. Logan was on the other side of the bed, so I got a clear view of his face. He was smiling. My brother was too. I sighed. Thank God for small miracles. When they heard me open the door they stopped talking and looked at me.

"Are you having a super secretive conversation I'm not privy to?"

"Nah. I'm just trying to figure out how I told you that staying away from this asshole wasn't a drill and you still ended up going for him."

"I didn't go for him." I walked over to Logan. He put his arm around me.

"It's true. She made me work for it."

Lincoln smiled, then turned serious. "Did mom tell you I have therapy?"

"Yeah."

"I need help to do everything. I can't eat, can't shit, can't shower without help." He sighed, closing his eyes.

"You'll bounce back quickly." I put my hand on his. "You always do. Remember when you broke your arm in high school and played on the team with a cast?"

Lincoln smiled. He opened his eyes. "That was pretty badass."

"Maybe you can play in a wheelchair. I bet you'd still score more goals than Ryan."

Lincoln laughed, shaking the bed. "Fuck, he's still on the team?"

"Warming the bench, but hey. Kid's got a jersey."

Lincoln shook his head. I frowned.

"Is that the one that tripped at the pep rally?"

They both laughed.

We spent the rest of our stay like that, joking with my brother, until he got too tired and fell asleep. According to the nurse, he needed to keep resting as much as possible. I didn't want to leave him so quickly, but I needed to get back to class as much as Logan needed to get back for practice, so I left, begrudgingly, promising I'd be back much sooner. I thought having my brother awake would help me answer more questions, but I still had the same ones: who did this to Lincoln and what happened to Lana? If Lincoln's memory wasn't faulty, and she had jumped and died.

CHAPTER FORTY

AYBE I'D GOTTEN TOO USED TO LOGAN SKIPPING HIS OWN classes to come to mine, but I felt like every class I sat in was a bore. Half of the time, I spent working on my articles about the various community events around the city, all which of course included members of The Eight. Logan had been playing catch up in his own classes and making sure his grades were up before he left for an entire week.

"Do you think there's a secret society of only women?" A girl in the front of the auditorium asked. Some of her friends laughed.

"If there is one, I hope you get your invitation soon, Miss Camelot," the professor said. "As I was saying, The Sex Disqualification Act of 1919 made it possible for women to enter universities or get jobs they may not have been able to get prior to that."

I tried to pay attention and take notes, but I ended up falling asleep instead. I woke with a start, at the sound of someone shutting their book, and realized class was over. I grabbed my things and walked out. Thankfully the professor didn't call me out for sleeping, but she did shoot me a dirty look as I walked past her. When I stepped outside, I was surprised to see Logan. As usual, he didn't have a bookbag or books in his hand. What he did have was two girls smiling up at him. He looked bored, but they obviously didn't care. If I'd been jealous before, I didn't even know what this feeling threatening to rip me apart from the inside could be considered. I wanted to grab them by the hair and claim him as mine. As if hearing my thoughts, he looked up as I approached. Only then did he smile. Only then did he push off the wall and walk forward, brushing past the girls as if they weren't even there. When he reached me, he made a show out of kissing me, framing my face with both hands, sticking his tongue down my throat, pressing up against me. I pushed my hands under the t-shirt he wore under his jacket and scratched his back. He groaned into my mouth, deepening the kiss. When he pulled away, his eyes were hazy.

"Do you want me to fuck you in front of all these people?"

"No." I smiled up at him, feeling my cheeks burn at his words. "But you can take me home and fuck me there."

He kissed me hard one last time, the grabbed my hand and started walking, as if he didn't notice any of the people who had stopped to look at us.

"That's going to end up on a blog somewhere," he commented.

"The kiss?" I blinked up at him. "Are you serious?"

"Babe, everything I do ends up on the internet."

"In that case, I'm glad I didn't click on too many links when I Googled you."

He chuckled, squeezing my hand.

"I guess if it does end up on the internet, you won't be able to deny that you have a girlfriend." I frowned. "Not that most girls would care that you have one. If anything, that might make you more attractive to some of them."

"You know what's crazy?"

"What?"

"I don't give a fuck what they think. I'm with you, remember?"

"Yeah, but maybe—"

"No maybe. I'm yours."

"Okay." I smiled.

I felt like I hadn't stopped smiling since we got back from visiting my brother. Well, with the exception of when I stopped to think about Lana. Then, my mood soured all at once.

"Do you think Lana's dead?"

"Mae." Logan sighed. "This again?"

"I just . . . Lincoln thinks she's dead."

"Really?" He raised an eyebrow.

"What does that mean?" I let go of his hand and walked into our building. He followed. I waved at Gary. He waved back with a smile.

"What does what mean?"

"You said *really* like that and raised your eyebrow like you find it hard to believe that my brother said that."

He shrugged. I pushed the button to the elevator, crossing my arms as I looked at him. He looked at me without a care in the world, as if he hadn't just said something slightly insulting. The doors opened. We walked in. They closed. I kept my distance and kept staring.

"Why did you say it like that?"

"You're really trying to pick a fight over this?"

"I'm not trying to pick a fight. I'm asking you a question."

"And you're getting upset that I'm not answering it." He waited for me to step out of the elevator.

"Yeah, because you're implying my brother had something to do with it."

"How am I implying that?" He stood beside me as I unlocked my door.

I didn't even hold it open for him, I just walked through and let him catch it as he walked in behind me. I tossed my keys on the counter, let my messenger bag drop to the floor and faced him again.

"What do you think happened to Lana?"

"I have no fucking idea because I wasn't there."

"I asked you what you *think* happened."

"I don't know." He sighed, running a hand through his hair. "Your brother was the last person to see her and if he says she's dead then I believe him."

"You think he killed her."

He was quiet for a beat, staring at me, his eyes calculating words that he wanted to say but wasn't sure how they'd be received. I knew that look. I owned that fucking look. Damn him.

"You think he killed her," I stated before he had a chance to respond.

"It's the only logical explanation," he said, bringing a hand up to check off, "Your father was having an affair with her, your brother wanted to expose the little sex ring they have going, Lana was your brother's friend and would not listen to anything he had to say in regards to the affair, and nobody wanted her around The Lab out of fear that she'd expose it all."

"Expose what?" I shouted. "There is nothing to expose."

"There's a lot to expose." He chuckled darkly. "Starting with your father."

I staggered back. He wasn't wrong. I knew he wasn't wrong. I knew what he was saying was one hundred percent true. I also knew that it was my family he was insulting. My family that would suffer if my father's disgusting habits and secrets were exposed. My mother would be crushed. My nieces would get the brunt of it from their schoolmates. That was the way it always happened. The family always suffered more than the culprit. Logan closed his eyes and looked up at the ceiling as if summoning a higher power to help him out. There would be none. Not one that could help him out in the very near future anyway. He looked at me again.

"I'm going to go pack for my trip. If you want to talk about something else, I'm down the hall. You can come over or call me or I can come back later."

I crossed my arms. "You don't want to talk about the fact that my brother is not a murderer?"

"We don't know that, Mae. We don't know what happened. He doesn't even know what happened."

"But we know him," I insisted. When he didn't budge, I sighed heavily. "I guess I'll talk to you later then."

He walked to the door slowly, as if waiting for me to call him back. I wouldn't. He cast one last glance at me as he walked out.

"This doesn't change how I feel about you."

I nodded, hating the way tears pricked my eyes, because despite my anger, it didn't change how I felt about him either. How could it? But I needed him to be on my side here. I needed him to be on our side.

CHAPTER FORTY-ONE

I T HAD BEEN EXACTLY THREE DAYS SINCE I'D SEEN LOGAN AND I still wasn't sure who was to blame for our fight. Probably him. Maybe me. Definitely both of us. It would've been over by now if I'd called him, but after he left my apartment, I just kept getting more and more upset. I'd ranted to Nora over the phone and she listened quietly, but I got the sense that she was on Logan's side of the argument. Unlike Logan, she'd kept that to herself and just listened. In his absence, I'd met the other two members of The Eight, Annette and Beatriz. We met over Skype, because they were both away for a semester abroad in Scotland. Nora had already filled them in on Logan and my relationship, which of course, they were shocked about.

Also, in his absence, I'd been stalking Nolan's social media and overanalyzing everything in the background of his photos, but it was just the usual—Nolan grinning at the camera and Logan in the background sulking over a sweaty drink. It gave me peace to see the infinite scowl on his face. Every once in a while, in an Instagram story or snap chat video, I'd catch him checking his phone in the background and that really made me smile, and then cry softly, because I really missed him. I was getting to the library, where I told Hailey I'd meet her after she sent me a series of text messages I could only classify as absolutely manic. My phone buzzed in my hand. I'd been waiting for a call from my brother via my mother's phone. She hadn't given him his phone back because she was afraid it would be too much, so whenever we spoke it was through hers. It wasn't a call though, it was a text message, and it wasn't from my mother's phone, but from Logan's. My chest tightened before I even swiped to read the message.

Logan: I'm sorry.

I stopped walking and leaned against the nearest column, closing my eyes and letting out a shuddering exhale. He'd never apologized before, not that he'd ever done anything worth apologizing for, aside from the times he was a jerk before we actually got together. It wasn't a Logan thing to do though. I knew that from every single interaction I'd seen him have with everyone around us. His apology actually meant something. My eyes popped when a second text came through, but I stayed leaning against the rough column.

Logan: I was an asshole.

Me: I'm sorry too.

Logan: I miss you so fucking much

Me: I miss you too

My phone rang. I answered his call quickly.

"Does that mean you didn't go looking for someone to share a bed with?"

I laughed. "I hadn't gotten around to printing out the flyers with my number."

"Good. That's less people I have to kill when I get back."

"How many do you currently have to kill?"

"Just Paper Boy. He uploaded a picture of the two of you together and I've been envisioning punching him in the face since."

"Logan." I laughed. "Max is like your number one fan."

"You think that'll stop me?" he asked and I swore I could

hear the scowl coming through the phone line. "I want you to be my number one fan."

"I still know nothing about hockey. I guess I'll get there if we're going to stay together." I pushed myself off the column I'd been leaning against and kept walking.

"If?" He sounded offended. "We're staying together."

"I don't like to jump to conclusions. For all I know, I'm just a footnote in your college experience."

"Oh, Mae." He sighed into the phone. "How could you be a footnote when you're the whole damn textbook?"

My heart skipped. He said things like that all the time, little glimpses of just how serious he wanted us to be. I loved that about him. My ex-boyfriend had always been too cool to talk to me in front of his friends and God forbid he ever said anything that sounded remotely like he wanted us together forever. He'd said, I think I can fall in love with you, once. It was what made me decide to follow him to college. Like an idiot. Logan didn't say anything as if it was something he thought. He said it all with clarity, so there was no room for confusion, and he only said things he meant. I wished so badly I could tell him right now, but I was too scared. What if those three little words, that held such promise, were what would scare him away?

"Hey, Logan," I said quietly, heart pounding loudly in my ears. "You should just come back right now."

"Yeah?" He chuckled. "Did I say the right thing?"

"Yep."

"I'll be there . . . " He stopped talking. Someone in the background started shouting at him. "Coach wants me to get off the phone. I'll call you tonight."

"I'll be waiting. In my red lingerie."

"Jesus, Amelia," he groaned. Another shout came from the background. "Fuck. I gotta go."

I laughed at the sound in his voice when he hung up and continued on to the library. Hailey had said she wanted to meet with me because she'd found some things in her mother's home office pertaining to Lana. To say it had piqued my interest was an understatement. I hadn't seen her since the incident at the toga party, not for her lack of trying. A part of me had been really turned off by the way she'd screamed at Logan and me, even though I knew where she was coming from. She was jealous because I'd caught his attention when she hadn't. Every girl on campus had been watching me like I was some kind of wizard, the girl who managed to tame Fitz. What they didn't understand was that I had done nothing. I hadn't tamed Logan. He'd decided he wanted to settle down when he met me, hopefully because of me, but I hadn't pushed him to get there.

I spotted Hailey outside of the library. She was on the phone, smoking a cigarette. That gave me pause. I didn't even know she smoked. Her head snapped in my direction. She flicked the cigarette away and waved a hand at me, as if I'd miss her, even though she was blocking the entrance.

"I didn't know you smoked," I said as I closed the distance between us.

"Only when I'm nervous."

"Why are you nervous?"

She raised an eyebrow, lifting a yellow manila envelope in her hand. My heart quickened. Instead of wasting more time with questions out here, I pulled the door open and held it for her to walk through. The vacant tables basked in the sunlight coming from outside. Unlike every other day this week, which had been cold and gloomy, the sun was out today, slightly warming the crisp temperature. We sat down side by side and pivoted to face each other.

"I printed this out. It was on her desktop." Hailey's hand

shook slightly as she handed the envelope over. "I don't know what to make of it."

I opened the envelope and took out the few sheets of paper inside, my eyes scanning the words on the first one before moving on to the next. They were email exchanges between Lana and Ella Valentine. I could instantly see why Hailey had been so ominous about it over the phone. In one email, her mother basically told Lana she no longer needed her at the paper, while Lana responded that it was illegal for her to fire her just because of jealousy. Jealousy. That stood out amongst the sea of words. I glanced up at Hailey, who was now chewing on the tip of her thumb. The move startled me. It was something I often did. A habit I'd tried to break countless times to no avail. I moved on to the next page. Another email exchange, this one between Max and Lana.

"I guess my mom has access to all of the emails sent within the system," Hailey explained before I could ask.

I nodded and continued reading. Lana had apparently been sending Max all of her locations. He didn't always respond, and when he did it was a mere thumbs up or "got it". What could this mean? I thought back to when I sent Travis my location and what my mindset had been then. I'd been scared. Terrified. And he'd been the only one I trusted. According to these emails, he would have had to be the last person she emailed and it would have been a location. The last email was sent to him May 23rd. She'd been reported missing May 24th. Max had said they emailed back and forth, he just never said what about.

"Do you think Max told the police about these?" I looked up at Hailey, who was still chewing on her finger.

"I don't know. Should I tell them? I should, right?" she asked, knee bouncing, replacing one nervous twitch with another. Had she always done this or was she mimicking the things I did when I was nervous? Seeing her made my own knee start bouncing.

"I think we should take it to them."

"Do you think it'll incriminate my mom?" she whispered. "I mean, you see the emails. What if she had something to do with it?"

I thought of Ella. Of all of those pictures and paintings of her and my father that adorned the locked study of The Lab. This seemed like the exact thing that would drive a jealous woman to the brink of insanity. But then again, dad was married. He'd been married. I didn't know how long their affair had lasted, but he'd been married for the majority of it. He left her for my mother when they were in college, and at some point, they'd started hooking up again, but then they'd stopped. *Was it because of Lana? Because of the other girls that were part of the rumored sugar daddy ring?* The next page held names of girls. *Lana Ly* was the only one that stood out to me amongst the eight names on it. I knew without a doubt that this was that list. Maybe it was the mentorship list, but either way, it didn't change the reality of what went on there. It wasn't a coincidence that there were exactly eight names on here. It wasn't a coincidence that Lana's was one of them. Suddenly, I didn't know what to do. Reporting this to the police meant possibly exposing The Eight and I couldn't do that. Not when I loved everyone involved. They were my family. I'd pledged loyalty. My palm itched. I thought of Lincoln. He said he'd made her jump. At least that was the memory he'd held. I thought of what he said about the cloaked person injecting him with the drugs. Could it have been my father? No. He wouldn't. My father was a lot of things, but a murderer wasn't one. Poor Lana. I couldn't imagine what she'd gone through.

"You should take this to the police," I said finally. "Turn it in anonymously. Your mom won't know it was you."

"But *I* will." Her brown eyes widened. "Are you willing to throw your dad under the bus? This will incriminate him for sure. My mom could probably get away with saying she was accumulating proof, which could very well be what's happening, but your dad? His name would be tarnished. He may even go to jail. You'd be okay with that?"

I thought of mom and what she must have suffered in silence because of his indiscretions. I thought of Lincoln, who had a long road to recovery and in my opinion, had only gotten into this mess because he was trying his best to stop my father. He'd pledged his loyalty to The Eight, and hadn't been afraid to act out when it came to doing the right thing. I wasn't sure who had tried to kill my brother, but I couldn't deny the connection to my father. Facts couldn't be ignored, and getting rid of my brother would eliminate the possibility of people finding out about Lana and the other girls. Disgust twisted in my belly. My mind went back to the black cloak. Would he have tried to kill his own son to silence him? Hailey was still staring at me. I reminded myself that she'd asked me a question. *Was I willing to throw my father under the bus?*

"I don't know," I said quietly. "But all of this could lead to Lana. She could still be out there."

I thought of the texts I'd been getting since moving here. This was bigger than I could imagine. I felt that in my bones. Whoever was behind those texts knew truths I couldn't fathom. I wasn't sure I was willing to find out what that entailed, but I owed it to Lincoln and to Lana to turn these into the authorities. That much I knew. I'd do it anonymously. In their wildest dreams, the police couldn't possibly find The Eight. If they did a thorough investigation, these girls would be linked to The Labyrinth Initiative through the mentorship program, but even that wasn't connected to The Eight. Not on paper anyway.

So, what was the worst that could happen? The Lab Initiative would shut down. They'd start a separate corporation under a separate entity and continue to fund members of The Eight and the charities they were responsible for. Dad would lawyer up. The other members that played a part in the sugar daddy scheme would get lawyers. The rich never suffered as much as the regular folk. I stood. Hailey followed suit.

"You're really going to go to the police?" She asked, wide-eyed. "You're willing to throw your father under the bus?"

"I can't think of any other solutions." I put the papers back in the manila envelope and started walking back toward the entrance.

"Let's go this way. It's faster," she said, walking in the opposite direction, typing on her phone as I followed. "I just don't know about my mom, you know?"

"What don't you know? You saw the exchange between her and Lana."

"That doesn't mean she's guilty of anything." She glanced at me, opening the side door that led to one of the tunnels. I walked in first, and she followed behind me, our feet tapping on the stairs as we walked down at the same pace.

"So you think she's innocent?"

"I think she was probably jealous, but I can't imagine just handing this over and letting her take the fall for that."

"But it could be what saves Lana," I argued. "If she's still alive."

The halls were dark, a sign of no people walking through them, which wasn't uncommon on a Sunday afternoon. The overhead lights flickered when they sensed our approach, buzzing as they illuminated over us. Unlike in the past, when I'd been nervous about walking these halls, I felt no fear. The adrenaline overrode my sense of everything else, even direction. I was following Hailey, hoping she knew where the hell we were going as we spoke. We took a right turn at the end of the tunnel and were met with another dark set of stairs. The lights flickered on as we approached and we ran up, Hailey ahead of me. She opened the door and stepped out, holding it for me.

Once outside, two things happened simultaneously: I tried to assess where we were and realized we were nowhere near the streets and that the exit had led us to the entrance of the woods. The other thing I registered was that Deacon was there, smile on his face as he looked at me right before he whacked me on the side of the head with a shovel.

CHAPTER FORTY-TWO

I WAS FLOATING.

No.

Falling.

Moving.

Swaying.

My head felt like someone was pounding on it from the inside and out. I groaned. Or maybe someone else did. My movements weren't my own. My body rocked back and forth. Someone was carrying me. As I tried to peel my eyes open, I could see the trees above me, the sun peeking through the branches. I focused on the sounds of crunching on scattered leaves and branches beneath us. The person carrying me was wearing boots. I opened my eyes wider. Deacon. Deacon was carrying me. I tried to scream, but it came out a groan.

"Pretty doll." He looked down at me and smiled.

I shook my head, the dreadful thought of him doing something to me sending a jolt through me. I moved my body, tried to thrash in his arms so that he'd drop me, but he held on tighter. I realized, the moment I tried to lift my arms, that they were tied. My feet were tied as well. I stood no chance. Not with the massive headache and disorientation I felt. Not without knowledge of where we were going or even a voice to ask. My tongue felt like dead weight in my mouth. Where was Hailey? Where the hell was Hailey? I looked around, my eyes moving to and fro, but saw nothing. I focused on the crunching beneath us, trying to figure out if someone else was walking with us, but couldn't tell. Why would Hailey let Deacon do this to me? So that I didn't go to the cops about her mother? Jesus. She could have asked me not to say anything to them. She could've not brought this information to me in the first place. The swaying was lulling me to sleep. The swaying and the headache and the heaviness of my eyes. I shut them, my head hitting Deacon's chest with the movement. He smelled like farm animals and mechanic. It was the last thing I thought of before I completely passed out again.

CHAPTER FORTY-THREE

AWOKE TO THE SOUND OF TWO FEMALE VOICES. HAILEY. HAILEY and Ella? I tried to make out what they were saying in their hushed whispers and quick chatter. The sun was setting now. I could barely see the trees above my head. I'd been set down though, no longer in Deacon's arms.

"Hailey." My voice was scratchy and weak.

They stopped talking. I heard the sound of boots pounding into the fallen leaves and branches as someone walked up to me, then saw Hailey as she crouched beside me.

"You want to know why I'm doing this," Hailey said.

"Hailey." I wheezed.

Fuck. I hadn't needed my inhaler in a long time, but my chest felt tight and knowing I didn't have it on me made me feel eager for it.

"Why don't I give you the run-down?"

"Hailey, I don't like this." The voice came from the person she'd been talking to.

It was a soft, melodic sound that shook, and vibrated inside me when I realized it was not Ella. I fought to look at the person. Hailey acknowledged my curiosity and put a hand beneath my neck, lifting me slightly, gently. Lana came into view. *Lana.* Alive. She wasn't dirty. She wore jeans and a cashmere coat. Her hands seemed to be tied, but other than that, she looked fine.

Lana was alive. She hadn't jumped. *What the hell had my brother seen?*

"You're alive," I choked out.

"Of course she's alive."

"Hailey, I don't like this," Lana repeated, tears in her eyes.

I hadn't known Lana on a personal level, but she'd always been kind to me. The Lana standing here was a contradiction of the high school Lana, popular and bright. She was a contradiction to the naked, naughty Lana I'd seen in pictures at The Lab. This Lana was frightened, and off. Something was wrong with her, but I couldn't pick up what. Was she drugged? Maybe. A loud thump made me turn away from Lana, toward where Deacon stood. He was wiping his forehead with the sleeve of his jacket, a shovel in his hands before he started digging. My eyes widened. A strangled noise built in my throat. I coughed again and it seemed to go on forever. I felt like the dirt beneath me was weighing down on my chest. *Was Hailey planning on killing me? Burying my body? Or was that what she was doing to Lana?*

"What are you going to do?" My voice shook, a slight wheeze escaping me.

"Maybe you can use your investigative skills to put two and two together," Hailey said. I looked at her as she lowered my head. She touched my temple. "You're bleeding pretty bad."

"You're going to kill me," I whispered.

"It's all I've been thinking about since I was a little girl," she said, her brows furrowing as if she almost felt sad about admitting it.

"Hailey. Please." I shook my head. We didn't know each other when we were kids. She was losing her mind.

"Our father should have paid attention to me," she said with a tsk. "But instead, he was busy doting on you, his little princess. Little princess with the hip clothes and lavish birthday parties."

My head was spinning. It took me a moment to wrap my head around her words. *Our father.* It struck me at once. I jerked back and looked at her, really looked at her, then shook my head. She couldn't be. It was implausible. How would my father have . . . she was the same age as Lincoln. He couldn't have . . . could he? *Couldn't he?* Bile rose in my throat. I started coughing, then choking on it. I needed my inhaler.

I wheezed. "Hailey."

"Hailey. She has nothing to do with this," Lana's words were slurred. Somehow, she'd picked herself off the ground though.

"She has everything to do with this," Hailey screamed, casting a glare up at Lana. "She's part of their little secret society. I saw her there in that creepy house at the end of the woods."

She looked up. I tried to follow her gaze, but couldn't turn my head all the way. Were we close to The Lab? I screamed just in case. Screamed louder for good measure. She clamped her hand over my mouth, my eyes were wide on hers as I tried to scream again.

"Shut up. No one can hear you anyway."

"This is going too far," Lana said. She was shaking.

"So playing dead wasn't going too far?" Hailey shouted. "Causing an accident and making your friend think you committed suicide wasn't too far?"

"That was different," she whispered. "I was trying to protect—"

"My father, yes, I know." Hailey looked at me again. "Lana's been fucking our father. She wanted your brother to butt out so I helped her plan this whole scheme. I watched them go to parties at that creepy house. I watched them as they fucked outside. I watched those people for months. Stupid elitist secret society. I should be a member you know? My mom's a member."

"Is that what you want?" I coughed once, twice, three times. "Is that why you're doing this?"

"No. How silly do you think I am?" She laughed. "I already have what I wanted. My mother, on the other hand, is sad. Cries herself to sleep because dad no longer wants her. Because Lana took up all his attention."

"Ella never had him," Lana shouted. "Felipe is married. He's always been married and always will be married. Your mother should've learned by now that she wasn't going to keep him."

"It doesn't matter."

"You won't have him either. He'll never give you the Bastón last name," Lana said.

"Yes, he will." Hailey roared as she lunged at Lana.

I whimpered, helplessly trying to break free of the ties around my ankles and wrists. I didn't want to hear about women fighting over my father. I didn't want to hear about his relationship with Lana or Ella or how Hailey believed she was his daughter. The rational part of me knew she was probably telling the truth, but a bigger part of me wanted to fight it, to shield myself and my family from the wave of embarrassment and heartache this would bring. I closed my eyes as I thought of my mother. She'd always been so rational, taking her time to truly understand people's reactions and feelings, but no amount of experience as a family therapist could save her from her own husband's betrayal. My brothers would be pissed. Lincoln especially.

"Deacon, take care of this," Hailey shouted. "Your little doll is getting out of control."

"Digging grave," Deacon called out.

Digging grave. I kicked into overdrive and thrashed some more, pulling my feet apart, my ankles. Nothing worked.

"Lana please," I begged, but they were still having a face-off.

"I didn't want you to get hurt," Lana said. "I swear. I didn't want to hurt Lincoln either but he kept getting in the way. Felipe kept blaming me for Lincoln's actions and saying that he should've never gotten involved with me, so I tried to help by leaving." She cried. "I didn't know he'd lose his mind like that."

"I don't care," I shouted. "I don't fucking care. That's in the past. Help me now."

"Our father hid her away." Hailey walked over to me, pushing the sole of her boot onto my chest. I coughed again. "Can you believe that? I came up with this brilliant plan to get rid of her and his solution was to keep her hidden away until he figured everything out. Hidden away so that he could keep fucking her."

"You blackmailed him," Lana shouted. "You took pictures of us together and blackmailed him!"

"I saved your fucking life, you little shit." Hailey took her foot off my chest and glared at Lana before looking at me again. "We bonded over that though, dad and I. We bonded over this secret. How I was keeping Lana safe until he figured out what to do and how to save the rest of his little friends from going down. He trusted me not to let her leave. Not that she wanted to."

"I did want to," Lana whined. "I tried to leave."

I thought about the exhaustion on Hailey's face that day at the coffee shop when she showed up with Deacon. I thought of the scratches on her hands and how she said she'd chased a sheep that escaped. Lana was the sheep. My chest felt heavy.

"You sent the text messages," I whispered.

"I did." Hailey smiled. "God, my sister is smart."

"I wanted to leave," Lana wailed. "I wanted to leave and all you did was tie me up and drug me. I told you I wouldn't tell and you kept drugging me."

"Bullshit," Hailey roared. "Don't believe a word she says, Mae. She caused that accident and then threw herself off that cliff so that Lincoln would believe she was dead."

"I wish I would have died!"

"Bullshit," Hailey roared again. "You knew you wouldn't die because I told you where to jump. Don't act like you're innocent. Mae's not going to believe the bullshit you're spouting."

"My brother could have died." I fought against the rope again, my muscles tightening with every movement.

"Your brother has nine lives," Hailey said, disdain in her voice. "Deacon injected him with enough drugs to take down a horse and even that wasn't enough for that fucking . . . " She took a deep breath and exhaled. "It doesn't matter."

"Hailey said the accident had to happen. Lincoln had to think I was gone, dead, so that he wouldn't report your dad. If he thought . . . if he thought I was gone, he'd just let things be." Lana hiccupped.

Hailey shot me a look. "Lana wanted dad to move her to Mexico City so she could live in one of dad's lavish penthouses."

"Stop calling him dad," I screamed, wishing I could cover my ears. "Please stop. Please stop."

"He is my dad though, and now he's finally ready to act like one." Hailey grinned maliciously. "And when you're gone, he's going to need a new daughter to dote on."

Dread flooded me. I glanced around, looking for ways I could escape this. Deacon had stopped digging and was chugging down a bottle of water. How deep was the hole? Would they kill me before tossing me in there? Would they stab me and make me suffer or shoot me and get it over with?

"Lincoln didn't even go to the police to tell them I'd jumped," Lana said, her voice still shaking. "He just kept quiet."

"That's not something a good friend would do," Hailey said. "Right, Mae? You're a good friend, aren't you?"

"I won't tell anyone about this." My words were rushed, desperate. "I won't tell anyone about this if you let me go. I swear."

"You won't tell." Hailey crouched beside me again, reaching over and patting my head twice. "You won't tell because you won't be here to tell. I'm sorry it's come to this, but it's my turn now." She tilted her head. "Dad and I are thick as thieves. Who would have thought my obsession with secret societies would have led to this?"

"I have to give him credit though, he wasn't so forthcoming at first, but when he saw that I knew about the sugar daddy ring and had proof of his affair with Lana, well, he had to give in. After all, I could expose the others easily. Did you know he's visited me every week since? He's been in town so many times and he never once called you to meet up with him. How does that make you feel?"

My chest tightened. I took a few deep breaths, trying to dictate to my lungs what to do in order to ease the feeling.

"If he's really your father, you should have a relationship with him," I said finally, licking my lips and focusing on breathing.

"He is my father," she screamed. "And we do have a relationship. Better than yours."

"Hailey, she's not breathing right," Lana said, dropping to the ground beside us. "What did you do to her?"

"Do you want to go back home or not?" Hailey shouted, turning to look at Lana.

"You promised you'd let me go," Lana yelled back, tears streaming down her face. "You promised!"

"I didn't promise anything," Hailey shouted.

"You promised," Lana whimpered.

I coughed again, turning over on my side as I struggled to bring more air into my lungs. It was too much information to handle. What was Ella's role in all of this? Did she know her daughter was a psycho? As I coughed, the side of my head where I'd been hit touched the ground, and I groaned in pain.

"I don't like this," Lana said quietly. "You should just take her to Deacon's. Get Felipe's attention like that, how you did with me."

"This is a different scenario from yours, dumb ass," Hailey said. "I wanted you as bait. I want her to suffer."

Lana was silent for a beat. "She's going to get her wound infected if she keeps her head like that."

"What will it matter if she's dead?"

"You would really kill your own sister?" Lana whispered. "Think this through, Hailey."

"I have thought this through," Hailey shouted. "I almost, almost convinced myself not to do it, but then she said she was going to the police with incriminating information on our father and I knew I'd been right all along. She doesn't care about him. Dad will thank me for this. He'll understand I did the right thing. He doesn't need his own children betraying him."

"Other people know too," Lana said, her voice sounded like a plea. "You can't kill every single one of them just because you want a relationship with a man who's not willing to give himself freely."

"Pot meet kettle." Hailey snorted.

"That's why I'm saying it. If anyone knows this plan of yours is impossible, it's me."

"You know what? I don't fucking care."

"Think this through, Hailey. Are you going to be able to live with the guilt of killing your sister?"

"Shut up, Lana. Shut up." Hailey stood up and glared down at her. "If he doesn't pay attention to me once she's gone, fine, but he won't have her either."

"What about Becca?" I asked.

"Becca isn't his. Leave her out of it." Hailey glanced at me over her shoulder, then up. "Deacon, where's the special water?"

Deacon didn't respond, but Hailey got up and started rummaging a bag nearby. She walked over to Lana and handed her one of the bottles of water in her hand. The rope around Lana's wrists was definitely looser than mine, she was able to hold it between her hands perfectly.

"Drink."

"I don't want to," Lana whispered.

"Drink it or I'll have Deacon make you."

Lana's eyes widened. She twisted the cap off and drank the water. I imagined it was drugged. It was obviously how they'd kept her compliant all this time. Hailey came up to me with a water bottle.

"Open your mouth."

I clamped it shut, twisting my head in the other direction.

"Trust me, you're going to want this. It'll help with the pain and everything else. I'm trying to be a good sister."

I made a sound. I didn't want her calling herself my sister.

"Fine. Half-sister," she said, as if that made it any better.

I kept my mouth shut and my face moving away from the water bottle in her hand. I knew it wouldn't go on forever. Sooner or later, she'd force me to drink it. Tears trickled down my cheeks. This was it? This was the end for me? Surrounded by three people I meant nothing to? I thought of Logan, of the call he promised and how I'd miss it. I'd miss hearing his voice and seeing him when he got back. I'd miss his warmth and his sweet thoughts about our future. I'd miss his career and his other accomplishments. Hailey reached over and started trying to force my mouth open.

"This would be easier if you cooperate."

I kicked again. "Lana. Please help me."

"I can't." She swayed, stumbling on her feet before she hit the ground with a thump.

I gasped, feeling the last ounce of hope I had vanish. Hailey started to pour the water over my closed mouth, her other hand still working on prying it open. I wasn't sure whether or not she was successful, but I started to taste chalk in my mouth. I turned over to cough, my chest still tight. It seemed to take a while for me to pass out, I could still hear movement, hear Hailey bossing Deacon around while he freaked out over something he couldn't quite verbalize. My eyes drifted shut despite my attempt to keep them open, the world around me spinning beneath my eyelids.

Then, I only saw darkness.

CHAPTER FORTY-FOUR

LOGAN

MY KNEE BOUNCED INCESSANTLY AS I WAITED FOR THE POLICE officer to finish up his notes. She glanced up from her computer, looking at me over her reading glasses.

"This is what I have so far. You spoke to her on the phone at five o'clock on Sunday. You don't know where she was headed. You told her you'd call that night, and when you called she never answered, so you tried again, but you figured she was sleeping so you left her alone," she said, reciting what I'd just told her. "You got home Monday, this morning, at eight o'clock, went straight to her apartment, and she wasn't home. You called and she didn't answer, you went to her classes but she wasn't there, so you went to the coffee shop she frequents and asked her friend Hailey Valentine if she'd seen her, and she said no. You went to the newspaper and asked Max Stein, and he also said no. Ella Valentine told you she'd emailed with her Sunday morning about a potential story and hadn't heard back from her." Officer Wright took off her glasses and set them on her desk. "Did you try calling her parents?"

"Of course I did." Ella Valentine had the same idea and called Mr. Bastón while I was in her office. "Her dad said she wasn't home and that he hadn't seen her since Friday night when she visited her brother."

"I'm inclined to tell you to wait a few hours," Officer Wright said. "Maybe she's going through some things. Did you two fight?"

"Yeah, but we were fine already. We spoke yesterday and everything was back to normal."

"Sometimes women need a little break, Mr. Fitzgerald." Officer Wright shot me a kind smile. "I know it's hard for you to understand that, but it happens."

"Nobody has seen her." I leaned forward, gripping the edge of her desk. "Nobody has seen her or heard from her since yesterday afternoon. This isn't something Amelia does."

"I'm just—"

"What Logan means is, you don't want another Lana Ly case on your hands, officer. We're trying to prevent your department from looking like a total joke, and the only way you can do that is by starting this search right now, as soon as possible. Maybe she's taking a break, and that's great, but if that's the case, don't you want to be the ones who find her safe?" Nolan asked. He set a hand on my shoulder and squeezed so that I'd stay quiet. I breathed out, letting him have his moment because he really was doing a better job than I could right now.

"I'll have some of my officers take a look around," she said.

"Thank you." I brought my face down to my hands with an exhale.

People like Amelia Bastón didn't just disappear without a trace and I refused to believe she was doing this to take a break from us. That was bullshit and not the Amelia I knew.

CHAPTER FORTY-FIVE

AMELIA

I WOKE UP IN THE COMPLETE DARKNESS, MY EYES TRYING AND FAILING to adjust to it. My feet were still bound, but the ties around my wrists felt a little looser than before, probably from me trying to pull them apart. I kicked my legs out and hit a wall. I turned over and hit a wall. I tried to sit up, and hit the roof. Realization started to sink in slowly, and I was suddenly overcome with panic. Was I inside of a box? My chest heaved. I wiggled around as much as I could. I was inside some sort of coffin. She'd buried me alive in the hole Deacon had been digging. The thought alone was enough to have me come apart. I hated confined spaces. Hailey knew this. She fucking knew this and she stuck me in a fucking coffin.

"Hailey," I screamed. "Hailey get me out of here. Please. Please. Oh my God get me out!"

No answer. I couldn't even hear anything above me. Suddenly, I couldn't breathe, and I wasn't sure if it was the mild asthma that came with my allergies or the fact that I really couldn't breathe in here.

"Hailey!" I kept shouting her name over and over before switching to, "Lana! Deacon!"

Nothing.

I started thrashing, against the ropes I was tied to, against the walls I was confined to. I heard a clinking sound and stopped to try to feel around for what it could be. My fingers tapped against metal, round, a pipe? I grabbed onto it and tried to place it between the rope in hopes that I could pull it apart far enough to stick my hands out. It didn't work. Anger bubbled inside me and I thrashed again, as hard as I could, banging the wood above me with the pipe. Dirt seeped through when I did that, so I stopped, coughing as I tried to clear my face from it. Bringing my hands up, I felt the wood. It was definitely thin. As I felt around, I noticed a hole. It felt like one of those white pipes people used for plumbing. Some sort of PVC pipe maybe? I'd used those once for a science experiment. Tentatively, I touched around it and noticed no dirt coming out of it. I took the pipe in my hand and stuck it in there, placing my mouth against it.

"Hello?" I called out. "Hailey? Please. God. Hailey! Lana! Deacon! Help!"

Nothing.

I pressed my ear beside the pipe and found that I couldn't hear anything from it either. How long had she been planning this out? My chest raked with unshed tears. I closed my eyes. She hadn't even left water.

She didn't want me to suffer.

She wanted me to die.

CHAPTER FORTY-SIX

LOGAN

THE INVESTIGATION WAS MOVING TOO SLOW FOR MY LIKING. TODAY marked two days and God knew how many hours. Mr. Bastón had enlisted the help of people who dressed and acted like the S.W.A.T. but weren't. They'd brought search dogs with them. Search dogs. The mere thought of what that could mean sent a chill down my spine. I'd missed two days of hockey practice and was planning on missing tonight's game because I knew damn well I wouldn't be able to give it my all. I was pacing the corridor of The Lab when Nora walked in with Will and Adam at her tail. I froze. Will and Adam were Swords. We only allowed each other in our perspective house under extreme circumstances. It was funny. Will was Nora's twin and Adam was Nolan's. Nora and Will looked nothing alike, and Adam and Nolan you could barely tell apart. I always did a double-take when I saw him, even though Adam wore his hair shorter than his brother.

"They're helping," Nora said.

"How exactly are they helping if they're here?" I looked between the three of them. The only reason I was here was because I had to use the restroom and now I was trying to figure out places I hadn't yet been to try to look for Amelia.

"We're still hazing," Adam said. "We're making the guys do a search on the back end of our woods right now. We'll take over tonight."

"You look like shit, by the way," Will added.

"Fuck you." I started pacing again. "I just don't understand why we're only searching the woods. She would never have gone to the woods by herself."

"I think . . . " Nora started and paused to lower her voice. "I think they're searching in case someone kidnapped her and tossed her body."

"Don't talk like that." I cast a glare at her and then at the other two guys. "She's not dead."

"It's only been two days," Adam said. "The body is meant to survive ten days without water."

"Don't give me a fucking scientific countdown, Adam. I don't want to fucking hear it. I want to hear you tell me that my girl-friend is going to be okay. I want her to call me and tell me she needed a break and apologize for driving me out of my mind. I do not want to hear about survival."

"I'm going to go back out and search," Will said. "I have to go pick up my cloak."

"I'll go with you," Adam said. He turned to me once more. "If you need anything at all, we're here."

"Thanks."

They left out the back and the front door opened. Nolan walked inside. I did a double-take, making sure it was the right brother.

"Your brother just left," Nora said. "With mine."

"He told me they were helping." Nolan sighed heavily, running a hand through his long hair. "Are you missing tonight's game?"

"What do you think?"

"I think we have enough people searching the woods and

campus and every building surrounding the perimeter," he said. "I think you should play. You already missed two practices."

"I don't care."

"Since when do you not care about hockey?" he stared at me.

"Since my fucking girlfriend has been missing for two days," I yelled. "Are you seriously going to give me shit for missing a game?"

"No, man." He shook his head. "I just think it would help if you played. Everyone has got this covered."

"Not me. I don't have it covered. I'd never live with myself if someone found . . . " I stopped talking, feeling a knot climb up my throat. I didn't want to verbalize what I was thinking. I didn't even want to think what I was thinking but Nora's comment had sunk in and I couldn't just ignore the possibility.

"Have you gone to the coffee shop?" Nora asked.

"Twice," Nolan said.

"Have you seen Hailey in the search?" I asked.

"I think she's out there with Felipe right now."

"Out where?"

"North side across from the library."

"I have to go." I grabbed my keys. "I have to talk to campus security anyway. They promised me I could see a surveillance video."

"I'll go with you."

I spotted Mr. Bastón talking to Hailey outside of the library. Nolan was walking beside me typing furiously on his phone.

"Coach said he understands if you miss the game," he said. "But I still think you should play."

"I'll keep you in mind when I need your counsel."

Mr. Bastón stopped talking to Hailey and looked up when he saw us approach. I hated the man, but I had to respect everything he was doing to find his daughter. I couldn't stand Hailey either, but she looked like she'd been crying. I wondered if this was another one of his many conquests. She didn't fit the bill. She wasn't exotic enough for him, but he was a sick man. Perverts didn't have a type.

"I'm headed to campus security," I told him.

"Campus security for what?" Hailey asked. I cast a glare at her and hoped she would shut the fuck up. "Security doesn't patrol the woods."

"I have a really hard time believing Amelia would run off into the woods by herself," I said, reminding myself to breathe with each word.

"Thank you, Logan. Please keep me posted on what they say," Mr. Bastón said.

"I'm not doing this for you, so don't thank me." I walked off with Nolan.

"Dude, that's your girlfriend's dad."

"Fuck him."

Nolan laughed, exhaling with the shake of his head. We both turned around when we heard someone running toward us and saw Hailey trying to catch up.

"What are you going to ask them?" she asked. "Why don't you ask the guy at the front desk in her building for information."

"We did that," Nolan said, stopping. "When was the last time you saw her?"

"Sunday morning."

"At the coffee shop?" I walked back to them. "Around what time?"

"Eleven? Twelve?"

"Did she say where she was going after she left?"

"No. She was talking about an assignment she needed to get done for the newspaper but that's it."

I stared at her. She glanced away after a moment. So she'd been at the coffee shop that morning and then . . . headed where?

"Maybe she's with her ex," Hailey suggested, looking at me again. "Did you try calling him?"

My stomach coiled. I felt my fists close. Nolan stepped forward and grabbed my arm.

"We'll keep you posted," he said, pulling me away. "Dude you need to calm down."

"I wasn't going to hit her." I felt anger radiating through me.

"Sure didn't look like it." He paused. "Call Lincoln, get that guy's number, and play the fucking game tonight. You need to do something with this pent-up anger."

He had a point. I called Lincoln as we approached the security office. His mother answered the phone.

"Hey, Mrs. Bastón, this is Logan. Have you spoken to Travis by any chance?" I grit my teeth. "Maybe Amelia decided to visit him?"

"Travis?" she asked. "Travis took the first flight over there. He's in the woods looking for her with some teammates."

"Okay. Just checking. Thank you."

"I'll see you later," she said. "Lincoln wants me to take him. He won't be able to do much, but he wants to be close by anyway."

"Let me know when you're here." I hung up the phone and gripped it when I looked at Nolan. "Travis is fucking here with some teammates."

"Dude. We need all the help we can get."

"Fuck everything."

I was seething by the time we went inside the security office. We asked for Jeff, who was a big hockey fan and nice guy around campus. He ushered us into his office quietly, as if he was plotting something.

"I want to let you know that the police are on their way so that I can hand over this video. It's grainy, but I think I see her in it." He let us stand behind his desk and stood with us, clicking the mouse. He fast-forwarded ten seconds and then slowed it down. My pulse quickened. It was her. She was wearing jeans, a trench coat, and sneakers. Even in black and white she looked beautiful. Her hair was in a long braid, covering her face partially as she typed on her phone. She stopped right underneath the camera to type, leaning against a column and then answered the phone with a huge smile on her face. She was laughing. I could practically hear the laughter in my ears as I watched her. My chest felt heavy. I knew it was me she was talking to. She pushed off the column and hung up, still smiling, as she continued walking.

"Wait wait wait." I tapped the screen. "Where does she go now?"

"She has to be going into the library," Jeff said, clicking the video to a stop.

"Is there another angle?"

"I tried it but you can only see her feet." He clicked another button and a second video started playing. I could see her legs and someone else's in the shot, but no faces.

"Where are their faces?" I asked. "We need it to be higher."

"It doesn't go higher. That camera has been pointing in the wrong direction for months. Every time I fix it, it falls again."

"Fuck. Fuck. Fuck." I punched the desk with each curse, then bit my knuckles to stop myself. "Jeff, we need more, man."

"Is there a video from when she leaves the library?" Nolan asked.

"Nope. She never leaves."

"What do you mean she never leaves?" Nolan asked.

"It seems impossible, I know. There's only one entrance, but she never left."

Nolan and I looked at each other. There wasn't only one entrance. Both of us ran to the door at the same time.

"Thanks, Jeff," I called out as we ran.

We pushed the doors to the library hard, nearly knocking out Paper Boy Max, who was walking out.

"I just asked them, they don't remember seeing her," he called out as we ran. "I'll keep checking."

"Where the hell is the door?" Nolan ran a hand through his hair. "Fuck. The one tunnel we never fucking use."

I lifted my phone and dialed Marcus. He was a nerd. He would know.

"It's . . . shit. I never use that tunnel. I did once and it left me way further from where I was trying to go," Marcus said. "I think it's behind the classics."

"Got it." I hung up and looked at Nolan. "Behind the classics."

We stood in the middle of the library, taking in the magnitude of it. In a building filled with old books, who was to say what was considered a classic? Nolan called Marcus this time.

"Dude, what the hell is a classic?" he asked, his gaze wandering. He looked at me. "He says it's around Harry Potter."

"Harry Potter's a classic?" I frowned, walking in the direction of the information desk. The girl behind the desk looked up from her book. "Hey, where can I find Harry Potter books?"

She pointed toward the back of the library. I thanked her and headed in that direction.

"No running," she called out.

I lifted my hand to stick my middle finger out, but just

held it flat and slowed down. I didn't know that poor girl and she'd just helped me out. Nolan caught up to me.

"Can you believe Harry Potter is a classic?" he asked.

I shot him a look. "Look for the door."

We walked to the end of the row. There was an emergency exit door, but that was it. I exhaled, putting my hands over my head. Where the hell could this door be? It had to be here. Marcus had taken it. We'd heard about it. Amelia had never come back out of the library. She had to have gone through a tunnel. Maybe she'd gotten lost and had no cell phone reception. Maybe her phone died, like every other iPhone user in the world. Those thoughts eased my mind slightly.

"Look," Nolan said, pushing a door behind us open.

I could've kissed him. I slapped him on the shoulder instead and started running down the stairs, the lights flicking on as we went. I looked up and down the tunnel. It was as big as they all were. This one didn't even have funny street names up top like the rest of them, it was just white walls and endless gray floors. We searched it anyway. There were three exits. We went to all three, looked around and ended up right back where we started. Square one.

"There aren't even cameras on each exit," I said. "That's just plain stupid."

Nolan brought his phone out. He glanced at me. "I'm calling Adam."

We walked out through one of the exits, the one closest to the apartments, and walked in that direction. I felt like the weight of the world was on my chest. Where could she have gone? What could have happened?

Against my better judgment, I played the game. I shouldn't have. I didn't remember anything that had transpired. I remembered the feeling—the anger as I skated the ice, the adrenaline as my legs pushed me forward. My first actual recollection was sitting next to Nolan in the box.

"What the fuck happened?" I asked.

He looked over at me. "What the fuck happened was that you sent someone to the hospital."

"What?"

"Uh, yeah." He chuckled. "That'll teach him not to fuck with the Smash Brothers."

I blinked, looking around. There was no one on the ice. I did see the blood though. Fuck. I turned to Nolan. "Is the game over?"

"Did you not hear me?"

"Yeah, but is it over?" It wasn't like this hadn't happened before. What was hockey without a little blood anyway? I'd already replaced five of my teeth and I hadn't even started playing pro yet. None of this was surprising.

"Yeah, it's over. I don't think they wanted to feel your wrath after that last one."

"Is he okay?" I frowned.

"Yeah, they called. Concussion, broken nose, split lip." He shrugged. "He's fine."

That was a new record for me. I'd never sent someone to the hospital with all of the above at the same time. My thoughts drifted back to Amelia. She would've probably been horrified at whatever I did out there. I found that unlike insistences in the past, this one had left me feeling empty, not any better than I did when I walked out there today. It was the worst kind of feeling, the emptiness.

Rage, I could handle.

Sadness, I could handle.

Emptiness was something I didn't do well with.

CHAPTER FORTY-SEVEN

AMELIA

IT FELT LIKE SOMEONE WAS SQUEEZING MY HEAD TOGETHER. THE pressure was immeasurable. It wasn't a migraine, not quite, because I felt it everywhere, in my skull, in my temple. Opening my eyes made it worse, but something had made me open them. I'd run out of oxygen soon. I could feel it in the way my breathing had turned shallow and my pulse was slowing. I'd die here in these woods, in this dark box. I'd gotten accustomed to being surrounded by people and I was going to die alone. It served me right for being a brat, for not appreciating what I had when I did. I heard something above me. A person?

"Hailey?" I tried to call out, but couldn't.

I no longer had a voice. That had been the first thing to go. I was about to close my eyes again, but then I heard it again. A loud sound. I tried to move, but my body was sore, aching all over from kicking and screaming, from trying to fight the wood above me. I'd used the pipe to push with and it had done nothing but fill me with dirt. More dirt fell now, tiny granules, almost like sand seeping between fingertips. I tried to move again. Tried to scream, to no avail. The sounds got louder. Voices? There were voices. My heart seemed to accelerate at that. Maybe Hailey changed her mind. Maybe Lana made her. Maybe Deacon? Voices. Louder. Male.

"You're going to stay in this one," one of them said. "Don't worry, it's only overnight."

The wood was pried open slowly, dusting more dirt onto me as they lifted it. It was evening, but my eyes still squinted as I looked up. Red cloaks.

"What the fuck?" one of them said loudly. "Will, is this her?"

"Who?" another guy asked, coming into sight. Another red cloak. "Holy fuck it's her."

"I'm gonna be sick," a third guy said.

"Shut the fuck up. Go get me that towel," the first guy shouted. "Oh my God, dude."

"What the fuck is she doing in here?" the other one said.

They sounded panicked.

"What do we do with her?"

I felt my chest rake. I had no tears left. I had nothing. One of them came over with a bottle of water and opened it quickly. He yanked the red cloak from his head, took it off and tossed it aside.

"Dude," another one said. "She's going to know what you look like."

"Shut the fuck up. She's one of us," he said, his blue eyes familiar, so familiar. Mine widened. Nolan. He looked exactly like Nolan. "Call my brother," he said. "If we call Logan, he'll total his car on the way over here." He leaned closer with the water, but the sight of the clear bottle made me shudder. I shook my head. I couldn't. I didn't want to be drugged again. "Hey, it's just water," he coaxed. "It's just water."

My mouth opened, my lips breaking as they parted. I could taste the blood in my mouth as the water trickled down, slowly at first, and then faster, pouring down the sides of my cheeks. I licked my lips. Nolan's lookalike was staring at me like he was afraid to move me.

"We're going to help you get out of there, okay?"

I nodded, emotion clogging my throat. They were helping me. They were lifting me out of the darkness.

"Spoke to Nolan," the other guy said. "They're stitching Logan up and then heading over."

"Oh, that's right, they had a game."

"Something you would think you'd know about your brother," the third guy said.

Nolan's lookalike glared over his shoulder before looking back at me. "How the fuck are we going to lift her without breaking any of her bones?"

"How long has she been missing?"

"Five days."

The two guys looked at each other with a shocked expression on their faces. I closed my eyes. I was so tired. So tired. I coughed, then wheezed, then coughed. My chest sounded like a beat up old car.

"Get the nebulizer and Albuterol. Now." Nolan lookalike pointed. He looked at the other guy. "Recruit, make yourself useful and help me lift her. Carefully. If you hurt her, you're going to have to deal with her boyfriend."

I only felt pain. Every touch, every movement, just pain. They lifted me carefully, slowly, and one of them carried me. The Nolan lookalike. I held onto him, grabbing his shirt so there was no way he could toss me into another hole, no way he could leave me out here in the woods. We walked forever. My eyes wanted to shut but I wouldn't let them. I wasn't losing sight of where we were going, even if I couldn't see anything.

"Hey, fuckface, hold the flashlight right. If we fall into a ditch you're not getting in," the guy carrying me shouted.

I couldn't tell where they were taking me, but I knew we were close because I could see more lights now. I squinted.

"Oh my God." The voice was Nora's. I knew it was. "Oh my God. Where was she?"

"One of our plots."

"What?" Nora screamed. "She fell in?" He didn't say anything. Nora didn't seem to notice. She put her hand on my cheek, on my forehead. "Oh my God. We've been going crazy, Mae."

"I think she's in shock," Nolan lookalike said.

"She's been missing for five fucking days. Of course, she's in shock. Did you call Logan? I'm calling Logan."

"He's on his way."

I was still swaying in the guy's arms. He set me down on something soft, a couch? A bed?

"I got the albuterol," the other guy said.

"Did you bring Atrovent? Get some and mix it," Nolan lookalike said.

"Adam, you better know what you're doing. Logan will kill you for not calling an ambulance," Nora said. "Fuck. We need to get her to a hospital."

Adam, Nolan's lookalike, put a mask on my face and turned on a machine. I froze. He must have sensed it, because he set a hand on my shoulder to keep me from panicking.

"Relax. This will help you."

Hailey's words replayed in my head. The water that was drugged and supposed to help me. My entire body started to shake.

CHAPTER FORTY-EIGHT

THERE WAS SOMETHING ABOUT HOSPITALS THAT GAVE AWAY WHERE you were even before you knew you were actually in one. Maybe it was the smell. Maybe it was the beds, thin and uncomfortable. Maybe it was the air of predetermined life and death. Whatever the case, I knew before I opened my eyes fully that I was in a hospital. Someone was holding my hand. I tried to tug it away. I didn't want anyone touching me. When my eyes opened fully, I saw that it was Logan sitting by my side. He looked disheveled—his hair, his wrinkled t-shirt, his untended beard, and somehow seeing him still brought me some semblance of peace.

"Oh my God," he said, his voice hoarse. He looked up at the ceiling. "Thank you. Thank you."

Tears formed in my eyes, and then more formed when I realized I had tears left after all. Logan threw his arms around me and I started to sob against his shoulder. His own body shook with mine.

"Oh my God." The voice was my mother's, her shrill making Logan and I pull apart slightly. She ran up to me and threw her arms around me. I cringed.

"Mrs. Bastón," Logan said, and I could hear the warning in his tone even though he tried to keep it neutral. "She's in pain."

"I'm sorry." Mom wiped her face. "The doctors are coming. The nurses." She looked around wildly. "Where's your father?

Where's Lincoln?" She looked around again. "Where's the police officer. There's a police officer here who has questions."

"Mrs. Bastón." Logan's voice was no longer neutral. Mom's eyes widened. "Please. She just woke up."

"I'm going to get her father." She walked back out of the room with the same frenzy as she'd walked in.

Logan sat on the bed beside me, taking my hand in his again. "I was so worried."

I tried to smile a little, but wasn't sure if I was successful.

"Do you need anything? Do you want to sit up more? Lay down?"

I shook my head.

"Mae." He sighed heavily. "What happened?"

My eyes widened. He didn't know?

The doors opened again and my mother walked in with my father in tow. The minute I saw him, I started kicking. I was trying to tell him to get out, but the noise coming out of my mouth sounded more like a feral cat in heat, sharp cries, no words. Logan held my hand tighter as he turned around.

"Can you please leave the room?" he asked in a kind voice. "Leave the room. Get Lincoln."

"What happened?" My mom asked, eyes wide.

Dad moved from behind her, trying to come up to me. I started kicking again, making that sound. Kicking harder, pinching Logan.

"You need to get the fuck out." Logan stood.

"She's my daughter. Last I checked you were here out of the kindness of my heart. That can change very quickly." Dad raised an eyebrow. "You're not family."

"Keep talking like that, old man, and I'll make sure when I put a ring on her finger and change her last name she never sees you again." Logan paused. "She probably won't want to anyway."

"I'll get security." Dad's eyebrows furrowed as he walked out.

I shook my head, shook my legs. The nurses walked inside, tending to me quickly.

"You need to calm down," one of them said. "She can't be like this."

"What's happening?" the other asked.

"She got like this when she saw her father," Mom said quietly. "They must have had a fight."

I shook my head. The door opened again. Lincoln walked into the room using a walker to lean on as he pushed forward. He paused by the door, his eyes meeting mine. He exhaled and kept walking over to me.

"Jesus, Mae." He sat on the other side of my bed. "You scared the hell out of us." I raised my eyebrows. He chuckled. "Yeah, I know. Payback is a bitch, huh?"

I started crying again, my chest heaving dry sobs.

"You can have ice chips, but you need to go slow," the nurse said, bringing over a white foam cup. She handed it to Logan. "And please keep her calm."

"You don't want to see dad?" Lincoln asked. "You finally came around to realizing he's the devil?"

I nodded, tears welling in my eyes. My chest heaved again.

"Oh my God," Mom gasped, looking up at the television, which was muted on the news. Lana's picture was on there. Mom grabbed the control attached to my bed and turned up the volume.

"Lana Ly's body has been found after months of searching," the news reporter said in her best sympathetic voice. *"The police chief is expected to hold a press conference on the matter later today. Our thoughts are with the Le family."*

Lincoln buried his face in his hands. I grabbed his wrist and squeezed, then squeezed again, and again until he looked at me. His eyes were shining. I shook my head, licking my lips.

"She was alive," I said. My voice sounded foreign and scratchy, barely audible. "I saw her alive."

"That's impossible, Mae." The words came from Logan. I looked at him and nodded.

"Hailey," I said, but as soon as I said her name, I started sobbing uncontrollably. I looked up at Mom, who'd aged a hundred years in one and was about to age one hundred more and I couldn't bring myself to say anything other than, "Hailey."

"Your friend from the coffee shop?" Mom asked.

I tried to shake my head, but my entire body shook, the bed creaking with it. Not even Lincoln's weight on it could hold it steady. She was not my friend. She was not my friend.

"Baby, calm down." Logan got closer to me, setting a hand on my shoulder. "Calm down."

I stopped shaking the bed and nodded, tears streaming down my face. Through the haze, I could make out the marks on my wrists. I imagined my ankles looked similar. I felt sore all over, but especially on my wrists and ankles. I cried again. I tried to close my eyes to spare them from my sadness, but when I did, it was dark and I couldn't bear to deal with that either. Hailey hadn't killed me, but she'd managed to break me, and sometimes being broken felt like a heavier burden than the idea of not being here at all. The nurses walked back into the room, one checking my vitals while the other placed a mask over my face and switched on the nebulizer. I breathed in and out. The door opened and my father walked back inside, this time with a security guard. My eyes widened. He'd said he'd kick Logan out.

"Get out." Lincoln stood, his legs shaky as he leaned on his walker.

"He needs to get out." Dad pointed at Logan.

"You're going to have to make me. I'm not leaving her side." Logan's entire body seemed to flex, from his neck to his forearms.

"Felipe. You need to get out." That was Lincoln.

"Felipe?" Dad raised an eyebrow.

He also looked like shit, like he hadn't slept in days and days. I thought of Lana on the news and how they said they'd found her body. Her body. Not alive. Tears sprung in my eyes. She didn't deserve that. Had he killed her? Had Hailey? Had Deacon? Had she done it to herself? Did it matter? She was gone, for good this time. I took the mask off.

"Get the fuck out of my room."

The six of them—mom, dad, Lincoln, Logan, the security guard, and the straggling nurse—whipped their heads in my direction.

"You killed Lana," I said.

"What?" Dad's eyes widened. He staggered back.

"You were having an affair with her. I saw her. She was alive before they . . . ." my lip trembled. "Before they put me in that hole."

The security guard left the room and walked back inside with a police officer. They must have been standing right outside my door, waiting. I kept talking. I didn't fucking care anymore. Let them arrest my father. Let him pay for his own sins. I was tired of the rest of us taking the fall for him.

"She was alive. Hailey kept her in a house. A farm. Deacon's." I could barely form words, but I continued saying the flashes of what I remembered from that dreadful night. "Hailey is our sister." I looked at Lincoln when I said that, new tears spilling out of my eyes. He sat down on the edge of my bed, jaw hanging open.

"We asked Hailey," Logan said. "She was helping search for you." He stopped talking, brows pulled in. He cast a glare at my father just before he lunged at him, fist closed, aiming for his face. "You mother fucker."

Logan took dad down easily. The police officer and security scrambled to get him off. There was screaming. The door opened again, more people walked inside—another officer, then another. I couldn't see what was happening on the floor, but between mom's screams and cries, the grunting, the clear sound of bones breaking, and the police officers yelling as they tried to pull Logan off of my father, I knew enough. Two officers held Logan up and pinned him against the wall. The third one and the security guard helped dad up. His eyes were wild. Logan's were wilder.

"I will end you for this." Dad wiped blood off his mouth with the back of his hand. He looked like he was struggling to stand upright, his other hand pressing up on his side.

"Not if I end you first," Logan said, smiling. He looked terrifying.

"Tell the officers what you said," the security guard said, breathing heavily.

"Lana Ly was having an affair with my father." My entire arm shook as I raised it to point at him, so that there wouldn't be any room for confusion. It dropped onto my lap with a light thump. I had no strength. "She was alive. She was there when they buried me in that hole. She . . . she was alive."

"Who buried you?"

"Hailey Valentine." My lower lip wobbled again.

Logan pushed the police officers off him and walked to the side of my bed, lifting my hand in his. His knuckles were bloody. I squeezed his hand nevertheless because I needed it. I needed someone to carry this burden with me and I knew if anyone could, it was him.

"Take your time, baby." He leaned in and wiped the tears that wouldn't stop cascading down my face.

"Hailey Valentine is m . . . m . . . my half-sister." I took a deep breath. "She tried to kill me because of him." I glared at my father.

"Oh, God." Mom wailed, pressing a hand to her mouth and another to her stomach. "Oh, God. What have you done, Felipe? What have you done?"

"We're going to need you to come down to the station with us," the officer closest to dad said.

The other two stepped forward, in case he put up a fight. He didn't. They all walked out of the room. Mom continued to cry. Lincoln stood shakily and went over to her, his walker and her sobs the only sound in the room as he reached her and wrapped an arm around her. I felt like shit. If there was anyone I could have spared it was her. When the doors opened again, I nearly screamed. I wanted everyone to leave me alone. My brothers George and Edward walked in, dressed in suits, looking desperate and confused.

"Dad got arrested?" George asked.

"What the fuck is happening?" Ed followed. He got a good look at me and walked over. "Jesus, Mae."

"Dad's daughter tried to kill me," I said, my voice hoarse.

The truth liberated me. The more I said it aloud, the lighter I felt. I was coming to terms with my father's actions. Not to say I'd forgive him, because right now, I couldn't imagine doing that.

George looked at mom and Lincoln. "What the hell is she talking about?"

"Your father had a daughter with Elle Valentine," Logan said.

George paused, seemingly just noticing Logan. "What's your role in all this?"

"I'm her boyfriend."

George's brows furrowed. He looked just like dad when he did that. My stomach coiled.

"Jesus," Ed breathed. "Fuck."

My older brothers shared a look. It was something Lincoln and I could do, and they could do, but the four of us really couldn't do together.

"Go down to the station and find out what's happening," Mom said after a long time.

She'd stopped crying, though she didn't look any less disturbed. Ed and George walked up to me, both saying goodbye to me and shooting warning looks to Logan. He didn't even flinch. The minute they left, Lincoln exhaled loudly.

"Wow." He glanced up at me. "She was really alive?"

I nodded slowly. I didn't want to think about it anymore. I didn't want to talk about it or recall the way things played out, but for my brother, I would. For his peace, I'd give up my own. Mom and Lincoln left shortly after, promising they'd be back soon. Mom said she needed a shower. Lincoln agreed that she needed a break from things. I felt awful and when she hugged me goodbye, I held her as tight as my weak arms would allow and apologized into her perfectly brushed back hair. She wiped her tears as she left the room and thanked Logan before closing the door behind her.

"You can take a break too if you want." I glanced at Logan, who was now sitting in the chair beside my bed.

"I'm fine."

"Do you have a game?"

"No."

I watched him. "You do, don't you?"

"I'm not going, so what does it matter?"

"You can—"

"Amelia. Stop talking. I'm not moving from this chair unless I need to pee and even then I may just call the nurse and have her bring the pan." He stared at me. "I'm not leaving your side."

"Okay," I whispered. Who was I to argue with him? I didn't want him to leave my side anyway.

"You should probably get some rest."

"I can't." My voice was a broken whisper. "Every time I close my eyes, I'm back in that coffin."

"I'm sorry." His eyes glazed over as he caressed my hand. "I'm so sorry I wasn't here."

"It wouldn't have mattered." I shook my head. I'd thought about that a lot.

Hailey had planned this meticulously. I wasn't sure where she was now, but I was grateful for the police officers guarding my door because at least I knew I was safe in here, with Logan. She would've found a way to hurt me anyway though.

"She could have killed you."

I stayed quiet. A part of me felt like she had. Maybe I would feel better once she was caught. Maybe I would feel like I could close my eyes once I knew she was no longer around the corner from me. As I lay there, I thought about all of it—from my first day here to today. She'd probably purposely planted that flyer of the coffee shop right in my apartment door, knowing that I'd take the bait and go seek it out. I thought of her mother and wondered if she was complicit in all of this? Had her jealousy led to her daughter's obsession? Had she known? I shivered again. I wanted to graduate and get my degree from Ellis, but I wasn't sure I'd be able to stick around long enough.

CHAPTER FORTY-NINE

I T HAD BEEN TWO MONTHS SINCE I WAS BURIED IN THE GROUND AND left for dead. Two months since Hailey and Deacon's arrest. One month since their conviction. Two months since dad and Ella Valentine were also arrested and both let go without so much as a slap on the wrist. Maybe Ella hadn't been guilty after all. Who knew? I saw her once after the whole thing. She broke down in tears when she saw me and apologized for her daughter. She seemed like she meant it, but honestly, I didn't care. It seemed like not much moved me these days. I didn't cry. I barely ate. I barely participated in anything at all. Some days I hung around Logan and my apartment. I'd moved out of mine and taken all of my things to his. Some days, I hung out at The Lab, wandering the haunted halls, almost wishing something would jump out and scare me. Some days, I just sat in a dark room to test my bravery and see if I could handle it. The Eight thought I was crazy, though they didn't say it and I knew they wouldn't blame me if I was. I wasn't. I was just trying to find myself again. Sometimes on the road to finding oneself, one must do crazy things.

Adam and Will, the guys who found me, came around often to check on me. I found it hard to believe that The Swords were as sinister as The Eight made them out to be, but then I remembered the coffins. Logan didn't like when they came around without him being there. Logan didn't like it when anyone tried to hang out with me without him being there. He was more paranoid than I was. He dragged me to all of his games and I was okay with that. Sometimes I took Max. Other times I took Celia and Max. Sometimes Nora went with me. I was never alone unless I was in my room in The Lab or our apartment when he was in practice. I didn't like to be alone anymore. My brother was still recovering. He was getting stronger though and stayed at The Lab whenever he was in town.

Some days, like today, I sat outside in the little garden between the walls of The Lab, staring at the ivy, wondering when it would take over everything around it. I glanced at the door when it opened and watched as Logan walked out and over to me. He sat down in the chair beside me. On days like today, when my depression felt suffocating, I wish he'd just let me go, but like the ivy, he stayed. He grabbed my hand in his and kissed it, staying quiet as he sat there.

"You don't have to stay," I said, my voice hoarse. As much as I wanted to push him away, to keep him free of this darkness, I wanted him to stay. I needed to give him the option though. It felt selfish not to.

"Stay where?" he asked after a long moment.

"With me." I met his gaze, his green eyes rivaled the ivy behind him.

"Where would I go?"

I shrugged a shoulder. "Somewhere happy."

"Somewhere happy." The side of his mouth pulled up. "You are my happy."

"I can't . . . I can't just expect you to put up with this," I whispered. "You can find another girl. One with less . . . baggage."

"Oh, Mae." He sighed heavily. "When I'm not with you, you're all I think about, to the point that I just want to leave whatever I'm doing to come right back to you. I wouldn't go find someone else. There is no one else."

"But I'm sad." I blinked. My eyes filled with tears again. "All the time. All the time I'm just . . . sad."

"Yet you're still my happy."

I shook my head. The tears began trickling down my cheeks.

"I'm never leaving," he said.

"You should."

He turned his body toward me, grabbing both hands in his. I turned mine toward his, squeezing my legs between his.

"You're my family. You're my blood." He brought up my right hand and kissed the palm, where my scar was already fading, but the pledge would forever stay. "I love you."

I started to cry then, gasping sobs pushing out of my chest. I loved him so much. Logan wrapped his arms around me and pressed me to him. I tucked my face into his neck and sobbed harder, big fat tears falling down my face. It felt like I'd finally opened myself up to the possibility of letting go of the sadness I'd been carrying. I wasn't stupid though, I knew sadness came in waves, and just as it was leaving me now, it would be back.

"I want you forever, Amelia," he said against my hair. "And forevermore after that."

EPILOGUE

LOGAN

I T HAD BEEN SIX MONTHS. TWO OF AMELIA DWELLING IN HER SADNESS and four of her taking action and refusing to succumb to it. She'd been seeing a therapist. We'd all seen the damn therapist. She was against going in the beginning, so I signed up with her. And then Nolan signed up. And then Nora did. And then Marcus. And Lincoln. And Annette and Beatriz all the way in Scotland said they would as well if we thought it would help. So, we were all going to therapy once a week. I went for her, but stayed for myself. I hadn't even realized how much I needed it. Old trauma has a way of living in the cracks and waiting for the least expected time to show up.

Felipe Bastón hadn't come around. Nor had Ella Valentine. They were both absent in the yearly holiday gala and even though the whispers around the room had been about them, their presence hadn't been missed. I tried to put a petition in to have them removed from the board, but it was knocked down before it could even reach any of the other board member's desk. It didn't surprise me. There was money, and then there was *money*. As long as they weren't hurting innocent people, the current Eight was okay with it, and from what we could tell, the only ones who had been hurt throughout all of this were the ones with ties to Felipe Bastón directly—Lana, Lincoln, and Amelia.

Felipe didn't have much left, aside from his billions, but what good was that if you had nobody who loved you to share it with? His wife filed for divorce. His sons were at odds with him. Lincoln wouldn't even speak to him. Soon enough, Amelia wouldn't even share his last name. I was just waiting for the right time to put a ring on her finger. I wanted to do it in the hospital, but figured I should wait until she was herself again. These days, she was. She was back to taunting and flirting and was fully focused on writing for the paper until she graduated in four months. She'd already received two job offers, and even though she hadn't said it, I could tell she was waiting for me to pick a city. I'd graduated after fall semester and was now waiting to see what teams were offering me. My agent had already gotten me an athletic clothing deal, and from that money alone, I could technically retire without having played one professional game. My agent said teams would have offered me a lot more, had I not chosen to attend Ellis and get my four-year degree. I didn't care. I just needed enough money to afford me that cottage on a lake with my girl. Everything else was just the cherry on top.

ClaireContrerasbooks.com

Twitter: @ClariCon

Insta: ClaireContreras

Facebook: www.facebook.com/groups/ClaireContrerasBooks

OTHER BOOKS